Holidating

Holidating

SARINA BOWEN

Tuxbury Publishing LLC

BOYFRIEND

A NOVEL

The hottest player on the Moo U hockey team hangs a flyer on the bulletin board, and I am spellbound:

Rent a boyfriend for the holiday. For \$25, I will be your Thanksgiving date. I will talk hockey with your dad. I will bring your mother flowers. I will be polite, and wear a nicely ironed shirt...

Now everyone knows it's a bad idea to introduce your long-time crush to your messed-up family. But I really do need a date for Thanksgiving, even if I'm not willing to say why. So I tear his phone number off of that flyer... and accidentally entangle our star defenseman in a ruse that neither of us can easily unwind.

Because Weston's family is even nuttier than mine. He needs a date, too, for the most uncomfortable holiday engagement party ever thrown.

There will be hors d'oeuvre. There will be faked PDA. And there will be varsity level awkwardness...

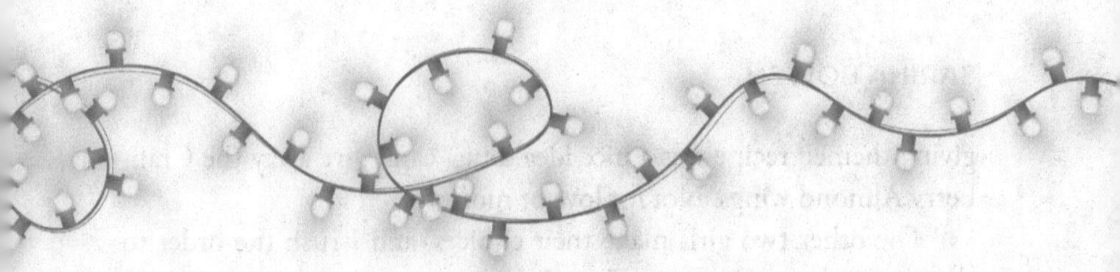

CHAPTER 1
STICK WITH THE USUAL FAVORITES

ABBI

Thursday nights are always busy at Moo U's favorite bar and grill. By nine o'clock, I've been hustling burgers and wings for eight hours. But my apron pocket is full of tip money, so I can't really complain.

I have one party that just sat down, though—three women about my age wearing matching hockey jackets. "Welcome to The Biscuit in the Basket." I pull out my order pad. "The special salad tonight has spinach greens, apple slices, and a warm bacon vinaigrette. The special wings are Cranberry Almond."

"Did you say Cranberry Almond?" one of the girls asks, lifting one eyebrow as if she doesn't believe me.

"You heard correctly." I lean a little closer and whisper. "Nobody likes them. Stick with the usual favorites."

"Got it," she says with a smile. "I'd like a half dozen of the Honey Garlic wings, in a basket with fries."

"Wait—what are the flavors again?" one girl asks.

I could rattle them off in my sleep. "We've got Honey Mustard, Honey Garlic, Tikka, Thai spiced, General Tso's, Chili Bacon, Chicken Parm, and—of course—Buffalo style in mild, hot, or wild."

And that's just the regular menu. The chef does a special flavor every week. Whiskey Maple is always a winner. Teriyaki is pretty good. But this week's special has been a disaster. Making a Thanksgiving-themed recipe was a nice idea, but I can't give away the Cranberry Almond wings. Not for love or money.

The other two girls make their choices, and I rush the order to the kitchen before it closes. Then I take up a position leaning against the nearly empty bar with my friend Carly, who's also on shift. She worked the bar tonight, while my section was in the dining room.

"We survived another one," she says, passing me one of the mints she keeps in her pocket. "What was your best tip of the night?"

"Depends how you look at it," I tell her. "A six-top tipped me fifty bucks. But my history professor tipped me fifteen bucks, and warned me to look over the Articles of Confederation before tomorrow's quiz."

"He gave you a *clue?*" Carly looks scandalized. "And a fat tip? I think he wants your body."

"Think again." I give her a smile. "He was here with his husband and their baby. I think he just felt bad that I was serving his dinner while the rest of my classmates are studying at the library."

And the man has a point. I work a lot of hours, and I go to school full time. There's no time for anything else. But that's just the way it is.

"Fine, fine. So he's not going to be your new boyfriend." Carly drops her voice. "Besides, I know you only have eyes for that crew over there."

My glance jumps involuntarily to table number seventeen. She's not wrong. Who wouldn't be interested in an entire table full of sizzling-hot hockey players? "I have no idea what you're talking about."

"Uh-huh," Carly says, eyeing them. Then she lets out a little sigh of yearning. "More for me then."

"You wish," I tease.

"You bet I do, Stoddard. Let's face it, table seventeen is the best thing about working here."

Once again, Carly is right. Neither of us can quit until springtime anyway. The owner pays a $1500 bonus to wait staff who work for him for an entire year. I need that money. So I'm going to smell faintly of chicken wings for the next several months, no matter what.

At least I can ogle the hockey players. Table seventeen is a long, high table surrounded by a dozen bar stools. And it's usually open by the time they wander in at eight o'clock, after practice. They're always starving for wings and fries.

For Carly and me, it's like a delicious buffet. The hockey team has as many flavors of hotness as The Biscuit in the Basket has flavors of wings. First you've got Tate Adler, who's six feet tall, at least. His flavor is what we'd call Brown-Haired Defenseman Hot. Next to him sits Lex, who's Pretty Boy Freshman Hot. And then Jonah—the Grumpy Hot Giant.

And we can't forget the Twins of Hotness—Paxton and Patrick Graham. I can't actually tell them apart unless I take their order. Paxton likes the Chicken Parm wings, while his brother goes for Buffalo style with extra blue cheese.

My favorite player of all, though, is Weston Griggs. He's a defenseman, sporting thick brown hair in a tidy cut. He has a winning smile and inquisitive blue eyes. But he's also got tattoos that poke out from the sleeves of his T-shirts.

I've had a thing for him ever since he scored Moo U's first goal at the start of last season. And then my thing became a full-blown crush when he came into The Biscuit in the Basket that night and flashed me a huge smile, called me by name—or at least the name that's printed on my nametag—and then ordered a dozen wings and a side of coleslaw.

If I were a braver girl, I would have jotted my number onto his bill. But that's not how I roll. I'm the kind of girl who says nothing but then thinks about him all the time instead.

Weston often shows up in my daydreams. *Hey girl, I can't help noticing how sexy you look tonight. I have a weakness for women wearing T-shirts with hockey-playing chickens on them, shooting a Southern-style biscuit into a net. And even though I can have my pick of the campus women, I like mine wearing a polyester apron just like yours.*

I might as well fantasize, right? It's not like I have a real social life. I spend all my free time here.

Table seventeen has a big game tomorrow. So it's a little quiet over there. They're much rowdier on actual game nights. After a win, they drink beer by the pitcher. And after a loss, they also order shots.

But there are more wins than losses. Moo U is a hockey school, and our guys have brought home more league pennants than any other team in the Hockey East conference. And this year could be big. The team looks great. They could go all the way to the Frozen Four.

They're decent tippers, too. Especially for college boys.

"Tell you what," Carly says. "All my other tables are gone. And since you can't stop watching the hockey players, how about you tip me forty bucks and you can close 'em out in my place? You know you want to."

"Forty bucks?" I yelp. "They're not drinking tonight. I'll be lucky to break even on that deal."

"But I'm giving you my eye candy! Duh. And besides—they just ordered two pitchers of beer. It's someone's birthday." Carly chirps. "Weston's I think."

"Weston's birthday," I say stupidly.

"Yup!" She holds out her hand. "Now pass me forty bucks, and bring the tattooed hottie his birthday beer. You know you want to," she repeats.

My glance travels, unbidden, to the strapping defenseman at the head of the table. The one whose smile makes my heart go pitter-patter. And now I know when his birthday falls. That will come in handy when we're married.

"Earth to Abbi! Are you going to let me go off shift, or what?"

"Fine," I say, digging two twenties out of my apron and passing them to her. "Go already."

"Give Weston my love," she says with a smirk. "Along with the big moony eyes you always give him."

"I don't give anyone moony eyes."

"Just keep telling yourself that." She winks, tosses her ponytail, and leaves for the night.

Weston must be turning twenty-one, or maybe twenty-two, if he played junior hockey before college. I'm surprised he's celebrating his birthday so quietly with his teammates. It's not unusual for Weston to show up here with a girl on his arm. Or on his knee. Or anywhere on his person, really.

It's a different girl every time. He's a player in every sense of the word. The women always seem happy to be his girl of the hour, though. There's always a lot of giggling at table seventeen when Weston has female company.

He likes them giggly. That's his type, I guess.

I really have no chance at all.

The bartender wakes me from this daydream by setting two pitchers on the bar, then knocking his knuckles against the wood. Twice. "Carly around?" he calls to me.

"I've got it," I say, darting over to load the beer onto a tray. I carry the pitchers and a stack of glasses to table seventeen.

There are two freshmen at the table who probably aren't twenty-one yet. But Kippy, the lazy manager, left a half hour ago, and these guys all walk home. I'm not in the mood to play cop, so everyone gets a glass.

"Evening boys," I say, setting the pitchers down in front of Weston one at a time. "This one is the IPA, and this one is the IPL. Enjoy. Does anyone need anything else?"

"Yeah we do!" one of the freshmen shouts. "You know it's Weston's birthday? Maybe you should do a striptease for us."

Oh lovely. I don't know this jerk's name, but I make a mental note to remember his face, so I can stay well clear of his hands. There's enough trouble in my life already.

"*Rookie!*" Weston barks. "Our server doesn't need a side of sexual harassment with her job description tonight. Don't be that kind of asshole. And only an idiot would be rude to the woman who serves your food at least three nights a week."

I let out a startled laugh, and fall a little more deeply in love with Weston. "What an *excellent* point."

But he isn't done. "Now put ten bucks in the kitty." He pats the table and waits.

The freshman blinks. But then he reaches for his wallet. The team kitty is a stash of money that builds all season long. The captain and assistant captains are in charge of deciding which infractions require a contribution. And in the spring—after the last game is played—they choose a charity and make a gift.

Weston puts the younger man's ten into an envelope in his backpack. "Now apologize to Gail," he demands. "Or I'm not pouring you one of my birthday beers."

The younger guy scowls. "Sorry, Gail," he says gruffly. "My bad."

Weston turns his handsome face toward mine and meets my gaze. His is warm and cautiously amused. "How would you grade that apology?"

"Um...?" I've gotten a little lost in his blue eyes. "Sorry?"

"I think the kid deserves no better than a B-. But I'll leave it up to you. Should we let him pass?"

"Sure," I say, not wanting to make a fuss. "I've heard far worse, to be honest." And I wish I could say it was rare.

"That is unfortunate," he says softly. "But not tonight, okay? It's my job to train up the rookies—for the good of Moo U, and for the good of hockey. It's my sacred, noble mission."

"Sure it is." His buddy Tate elbows him. "Last night you said that convincing me to order the Thai wings was your sacred, noble mission."

Weston shrugs. "A guy can have two sacred, noble missions."

"Especially on his birthday," I add. "Cheers, boys. Drink up, because it's last call." We close at ten on weeknights.

Then I leave them to it. I need to do some side work so I can leave as soon as they're through.

By the time I deliver the sorority girls' food, the candles on the tables are burning low in their votive cups. This is my favorite time of night at The Biscuit in the Basket. It's peaceful, as the murmur of quiet conversation replaces the dull roar we hear throughout the dinner rush.

The Biscuit has a cozy, old-time feel, like it's been here forever. The walls are paneled in dark brown wood, but most of the space has been given over to group photos of Moo U sports teams from every consecutive year since the turn of the last century.

I love to stop for a glance at the oldest photos, with the baseball players in their baggy, pinstriped knickers. And the hockey players with their 1960s haircuts. The women's team photos start up a bit later, in the eighties. There's basketball and cross country too.

One thing you won't find on these walls, though, is a photo of a football team. Moo U doesn't have one. We're a D1 hockey school, and we do well in lacrosse and baseball, as well as winter sports like skiing and ski jumping. But football just isn't very Vermonty. So we don't bother.

To finish up the night's work, I take a seat at an empty table and roll silverware for tomorrow's shift. And I just happen to pick a table that's within earshot of table seventeen. Eavesdropping is good service, right? I'm easy to find if they need anything.

Plus, it's entertaining. The hockey players are making celebratory toasts. "To winning the league this year!" one of the twins says.

"The *league*?" Weston yelps. "Why not the national championship? Aim high, Patrick."

"To Professor Reynolds for postponing the Rocks for Jocks test!"

"Wait, really? It was postponed?"

"To cold beer and warm women!"

That was the obnoxious freshman again. Weston ignores him this time.

"To Weston!" Tate cheers. "Another trip around the sun!"

"Aw, shucks, guys. You're all buying me dinner, right?" He sets down his beer. "Speaking of dinner, I almost forgot about my flyers." He pulls his backpack off the floor and unzips it. He pulls out a folder from the copy shop and flips it open. "It's time to hang up my sign."

Tate looks over his shoulder and laughs. "No *way*. You're doing that again? Why?"

"Because I love Thanksgiving. It's my favorite holiday."

"You could come out to our farm, you know," Tate argues. "You have a standing invitation."

"That is a tempting offer, especially because your grandma makes that apple pecan tart with the crinkly edges." Weston makes a motion with his fingers, as if crinkling imaginary dough. "And the crumble topping is spectacular."

It's so cute I find myself smiling into the silverware bin.

"So what's the problem, then?" Tate demands. "And if you pick on my grandma's cooking, I will hurt you."

"Your grandmother's cooking is awesome. My problem is with

your father's football picks. I can't root for the Patriots, man. Besides, this way I'm providing a public service."

"What service?" Someone snatches a flyer out of the folder and reads it aloud. *"Rent a boyfriend for the holiday. For $25, I will be your Thanksgiving date. I will talk hockey with your dad. I will bring your mother flowers. I will be polite, and wear a nicely ironed shirt. Note: I don't cook, so I am not able to bring a dish. I'm from out of town, and have no plans for the holiday. But I love Thanksgiving, and would be happy to celebrate with you. Especially if your mother is a good cook. Or your father. I'm not sexist."*

There's a smattering of laughter and sarcastic applause.

"You're charging money?" one of the freshmen squeaks.

"It's a nominal fee," Weston says with a shrug.

"But it makes you sound desperate," the youngster says.

"Nah, it makes me sound like I value my own time and company. And I always get multiple offers. The fee keeps the nutters away. Only women who really need my help will apply."

Someone asks: "What if it's a dude who calls?" And the whole table snickers.

I'm surprised when Weston just shrugs. "That would be fine I guess. Fake love is fake love."

Twelve hockey players howl with laughter.

And I am captivated. There's nothing on Netflix that's half as interesting as Weston Griggs hiring himself out on Thanksgiving. *Boyfriend for Rent.*

I wonder if there's a rent-to-own option?

"Weston, is this even legal?" one of the twins asks. "Coach will be pretty pissed if you're busted for solicitation."

"Does the team have a bail fund?" his brother asks. And then they high-five each other.

"Don't twist my good deed into something tawdry." Weston lifts his perfect, masculine jaw and gives the twins a glare. "My intentions are pure. Last Thanksgiving I had a lovely meal with a sophomore nursing student in Winooski. She'd recently broken up with her high school boyfriend, and her parents were upset about the breakup. God knows why. So I went along and they didn't mention him once the whole day."

"Huh," Tate says. "So I guess she got her twenty-five bucks' worth in peace of mind."

"Exactly. And I enjoyed a lovely turkey—cooked sous vide style, so it was extra moist and juicy. Then her mother rubbed the skin with butter and crisped it up under the broiler. And there was a sausage stuffing with water chestnuts so good I almost cried."

"Water chestnuts?" Tate shudders. "That's just wrong."

"No, it's glorious." Weston puts down his beer glass. "And now I'm hungry again. We've got to stop talking about Thanksgiving. It's a whole week away."

"You started it," Tate says with a chuckle. "And the Pats are totally going to win this year."

"Bullshit," Weston mutters. "Maybe I should come over just so I can watch your dad cry."

"Bet you a four-pack of Goldenpour they win," Tate challenges.

"Deal. We'll settle up after the holiday."

Then Weston gets up and hangs his flyer on the bulletin board right by the door.

———

They depart forty minutes later, leaving behind a tip of fifty-five bucks. Totally worth it! I yawn my way through the rest of my side work until it's time to race home to burn the midnight oil for my test.

But before I leave the Biscuit for the night, I stop in front of the bulletin board. If I hadn't overheard that conversation tonight, I wouldn't have looked twice at this sign. Weston didn't put his name on it. There's nothing there to advertise the fact that whoever hires Weston on Thanksgiving is getting a date with the hunkiest man on the hockey team.

I reach out and tear one of the phone numbers off the bottom corner. And then I tuck it into my pocket on my way out the door.

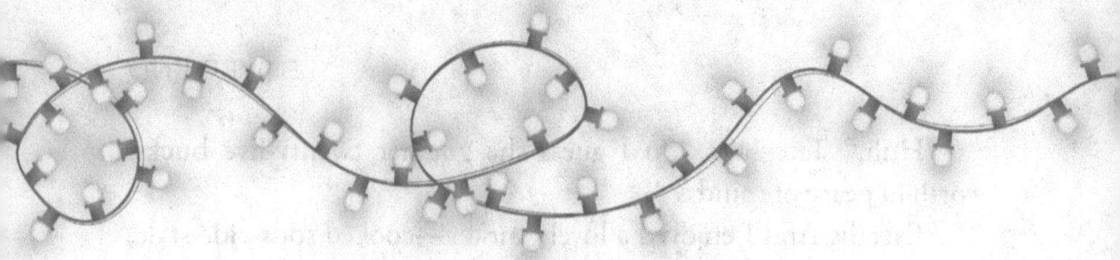

CHAPTER 2
PEOPLE GET RESTLESS

WESTON

My phone rings when I'm on the way into my econ class. This class bores me, so I stop outside the lecture hall and answer my brother's call. "What's shakin', Stevie?"

"You're coming home for Thanksgiving, right?"

Uh-oh. Cue the awkward silence. "Nah, I'm sorry. My practice schedule is awfully tight."

"Bullshit!" he says immediately. "You're a lying liar who lies!"

"Aw, come on now. It doesn't make sense for me to rent a car and drive across the state for a meal, Stevie. I'm a busy guy, and it will be a—"

"Shit show," he grumbles. "That's why you should feel obligated to come home and suffer with me. It's not like we live in Texas, asshole. Get a Zipcar. Drive a hundred miles. A hockey game is longer than your drive home."

"I can't, man. I have a date." This is strictly true, seeing as I have at least three offers already this morning.

"A date," he says, his voice betraying flat disbelief. "On Thanksgiving."

"Yup."

"That's what you said last year, too."

"It was true last year as well." He doesn't need to know that I've hired myself out. In truth, I feel bad that Stevie has to suffer through Thanksgiving at one of our parents' homes. He's a year behind me at Dartmouth, which is just a few miles away from our mom's house in Norwich and a few more miles from our dad's place in Fairlee. He can't blame the hockey schedule, either, because he hasn't played since high school.

He's trapped. But that is not my fault. "You'll have Lauren's company though, right?" Our sister lives in town with her fiancé.

Stevie makes a disgusted sound. "You know what she's like right now. All she can talk about is the wedding. Flowers and colors and the rest of that bullshit."

We both shudder. As the owner of a dick, weddings were never interesting to me. But since our parents' spectacular divorce a couple of years ago, just the *idea* of marriage makes me feel a little squicky.

At some point in the near future, I'm going to have to put on a tux and watch my sister marry her boyfriend of three years. I'm going to have to clap and smile and try not to suffocate in my bow tie, while I watch my sister make the biggest mistake of her life.

Nothing against her guy, either. He seems nice enough for now. That's the problem, though. Once the glow wears off, people get restless. And then they do stupid, crazy things to each other. And they make their kids watch.

Fun times.

"Look." I level with my brother. "I'm not coming home for Thanksgiving. You don't have to either, you know. You don't owe it to them."

"Dad, though. He'll be all alone."

"That's true," I murmur. And I feel for the guy. "But our father is an adult, you know? The destruction of his marriage is about to celebrate its third anniversary. He can either stew about it, or he can find a way to move on."

"Good luck telling him that."

"Oh I've tried." I was gentle, of course. I'm not a monster. The problem is that my father prefers rage to action. He'll spend the whole holiday muttering about "that bitch," which is how he refers to our mother.

Or, if Stevie went to Mom's house instead, Dad would be mad at him for days. You really can't win with him anymore.

He doesn't see how much this upsets us either. Sure, we were all pretty astonished when Mom left Dad. It was brutal. But she's still our Mom, and she still loves us. Three years later, and our father still expects us to take sides. It's fucking exhausting.

I shove a hand into my pocket and absently rub the smooth piece of obsidian stone that's resting there. Our assistant coach is really into crystals. He said obsidian would help me get rid of "emotional blockage" and give me strength, clarity, and compassion.

But what if I'm not the one who needs it? How much obsidian can I sneak into my father's house without him noticing?

My parents' divorce is why I no longer go home for Thanksgiving. And also why I will never *ever* fall in love. It turns you into a bitter freak when it ends.

"Dude, you *have* to come home for Christmas," my brother says. "If you tell me you have a date, I'm going to drive up there and haul you back here myself."

"Yeah, okay." There's no way I can pretend to be busy on Christmas Day. "I'll come home. We'll stay with Dad, yeah?"

"Yeah. And bring some nice clothes."

"Why?" I demand. "For church?" My parents still insist on attending the same church. Neither one of them is willing to be the one who leaves. As far as I can tell, they sit on opposite sides of the room shooting daggers at each other while the priest stands up front preaching about love and forgiveness.

"Worse," Stevie grumbles. "Mom is throwing an engagement party for Lauren on the day before Christmas Eve."

"Oh shit," I whisper. Then I let out a groan.

"Yeah." My brother sighs. We both know what that means— Mom and Dad at the same party for the first time in three years. With alcohol, too. It could be bad bad *bad*. "You'll be there, right? If you try to blow this off, I'll tell Dad it was you who scratched his Mercedes by having sex up against it."

"*Rude*," I grunt. "You know that was a freak accident." I'd set my date up on the hood and we'd had a fine time. Who could have guessed that her short little skirt had metal grommets on the back? What kind of fashion designer thought that was a good idea?

"Still your fault, though." He snickers. "Don't make me do it. If I have to go to this thing, then so do you."

"Yeah, okay," I grumble. It's not my sister's fault that our family has become just like a daytime TV show. If she's crazy enough to get engaged, I'll make sure there's someone at her party who isn't going to make a scene.

Even if it hurts me. And I expect it to hurt plenty.

"Who's this date with, anyway?" my brother asks.

"Hmm?"

"Your date. On Thanksgiving."

"Oh, uh, a new girl." I haven't chosen one yet, of course.

"They're all new girls with you."

"You say that like it's a bad thing."

He snorts. "Yeah. But we're not all hockey stars. The talent pool works harder for you than it does for us mere mortals, bro."

"It's good work if you can get it." Just because I'm never marrying a woman doesn't mean that I don't enjoy them.

"Later, Weston."

"Later, punk."

I slip into the back of the lecture hall and nab an empty seat. I'm just settling in to the lecture when my phone buzzes with a text. I don't look right away, because I assume it's Stevie busting on me again. He probably thinks he can guilt me into coming home for Thanksgiving.

But as the professor drones on about monetary policy, I decide to check. I don't want to be a dick, but it's a big lecture hall and I've perfected the art of texting while pretending to pay attention.

The number is unfamiliar. It must be another inquiry for Thanksgiving. I've gotten three already this morning.

Hi there, the new one begins. *My name is Abbi. I saw your sign at the Biscuit, and I wonder if I could take you up on your Boyfriend Rental offer. I'm a junior here at Moo U, and my family's place is just fifteen miles away in Shelburne.*

Hmm. Two of the other inquiries are from girls who live further afield. So I already like Abbi. I'm just about to respond when an additional message appears.

She adds: *You should also know that my step-stepmother is*

the sort of cook who goes to a lot of trouble. There will be a dozen homemade dishes on the table. Like butternut squash soup with shredded bacon and croutons on top. Roasted turkey, of course. But also steamed Chinese dumplings filled with turkey and scallions. Plus an army of side dishes, and three kinds of pie. She's a superstar cook.

Well, damn. My mouth is watering already. And before I think better of it, I ask a follow-up question. *Is there a dipping sauce with the dumplings? Wait, was that a rude opener? Let me try again. Hi Abbi! I'm Weston. I really like Thanksgiving, and your dumplings intrigue me.*

Abbi: *Your curiosity is justified. You can't go home with just anyone for Thanksgiving, right? What if the mashed potatoes were out of a box?*

Weston: *Bite your tongue! Only a monster would make boxed mashed on Thanksgiving.*

Abbi: *I'm just pointing out that you have to be careful going home with strangers. And, for the record, last year there were two different dipping sauces for the dumplings. There was soy ginger and also cranberry.*

That does sound promising. I think Abbi's Thanksgiving spread sounds like a winner. I decide to just accept it on the spot, and let the other women down gently.

Weston: *Okay Abbi, you're on. Please text the details when you're ready. I'm happy to meet you anywhere on campus. I don't have a car though.*

Abbi: *I can drive. And I really appreciate this. Holidays can be tense.*

Weston: *True Story. Send me the deets and I'll see you on Thursday.*

———

When Thanksgiving Day arrives, I am careful to arrive—showered and shaven—at Abbi's front door right on time. I might even be a minute or two early. I'm wearing a crisp Dad-pleasing shirt and my best Mom-pleasing tie, because I make it a point to always know my audience.

I get teased for it, too. The guys at the hockey house call me Mr. Smooth.

"You're referring to my skating, right?" I'd said the first time I heard it.

"Nah, man. Everything about you is smooth. The hair. The whole polite-guy thing. The ladies really go for it. I bet even your ass is smooth, but I don't need any proof, thanks." That had gotten a lot of laughs.

So sue me. Life is easier when you take control of every situation. If my skills with hair products and parents earn me the occasional ribbing, I'm perfectly okay with that.

Abbi's address turns out to be an old Victorian mansion that's been chopped up into smaller apartments. In the wallpapered vestibule, I push the buzzer for apartment 2, and a female voice calls, "Just a second!" on the other side of the door.

I wonder what Abbi is like. It doesn't matter very much, of course. I haven't agreed to marry her. It's just one day of my life. And people fascinate me, so even if Abbi's family is irritating as fuck, I probably won't take it personally.

But I have a good feeling about Abbi herself. She's local, which is interesting. Vermonters are pretty cool. They have a rugged mentality, and they rarely complain. And they're usually hockey fans. What's not to like about that?

The door opens, and I immediately lose my train of thought. I'm blinking at a pretty blond woman with shoulder-length hair. My first reaction is all *hell yes and thank you, Jesus*.

Then I realize this is not just any woman. It's the hot waitress from The Biscuit in the Basket. The one who remembers every order without writing it down. The one who always seems to know when we need something more, or when it's time to drop the check.

The one with the kissable ivory neck and gray eyes that always make me a little stupid. I've never asked her out, because it's rude to hit on a girl who's just trying to get through her shift at work. But man, I'd like to.

"Hi," she says, frowning at me. "Wow. You're wearing a tie."

"Too much?" I ask, my hand flying to the knot of silk at my throat. "I could lose the tie." And, heck, why stop there? If she asked me to lose my trousers, I'd do it. *Anything for you, honey.*

"No, you look very respectful. Thank you for doing this."

I blink slowly. I can't believe my luck. She's my date? "You work at The Biscuit in the Basket," I say stupidly. "But your name tag says *Gail*."

She smiles. "That's right. The lazy manager put the wrong name on it, and then wouldn't redo it for me. But I'm glad you can recognize me without the uniform."

"Well, sure. You look nice. Your hair is different. Fluffier. Wait. Is fluffy a good thing?" I babble.

She laughs suddenly. "Fluffy is fine. At work they make us wear those visor caps. Like we're all golf caddies."

I smile back at her and get a little lost for another moment. And her laugh is terrific. A little husky. I dig it.

"So, uh, are you ready to go?"

That's when I realize I'm blocking her way out of her own door. "Yup, sorry," I stammer, leaping to the side like a frisky goat.

Oh, man. Nobody would call me Mr. Smooth right now, that's for damn sure. I'm glad my teammates aren't here to witness this. I'd never live it down.

Abbi locks her door. "Where are you from, Weston? Is it too far to go home for Thanksgiving?"

"I'm from the eastern edge of Vermont. But I don't have a car, and we have practice tomorrow anyway. Hey—does your family drink? I brought a bottle of wine." I hold it up, along with a bouquet of flowers, too.

"That's lovely of you," she says. "I have a bottle in my car too. I find that where alcohol and my so-called family are concerned, more is more. Although I'm driving tonight, so I can't drink."

"Your so-called family?"

"Well, it's complicated without being terribly interesting. But we're going to my stepfather's house. I mean, he used to be my stepfather and now he's married to someone else."

"Your step-stepmother," I say, recalling her text message.

"Right." She leads me off the porch and down the walkway. "My car is just around the back. It won't take us long to get there. You'll be eating turkey dumplings in no time."

"Sounds good. My body is, like, fifty percent wings and fries at this point. I'm sure you know that. I'm at your restaurant all the time."

"Table number seventeen," she says cheerfully. "The hockey table. Do you know that we prep a different portion of wings depending on whether you guys win or lose?"

"No, really? Why?"

"Because you eat more and get drunker on the nights you lose than on the nights you win."

"Huh. That's very scientific of you."

She unlocks an elderly Honda Civic and opens the driver's side door. "Last chance to back out."

I wouldn't dream of it. I have to remember how to be Mr. Smooth, though, and flirt properly with Abbi. Who knows? After a great meal, we could make this a night to remember. "I'm at your *service*," I say, hoping it sounds a little sexy and not creepy. "Let's get our turkey on."

Huh. Mr. Smooth seems to be on vacation today.

I give myself a fifty-fifty shot at success. But I've faced worse odds. Game on.

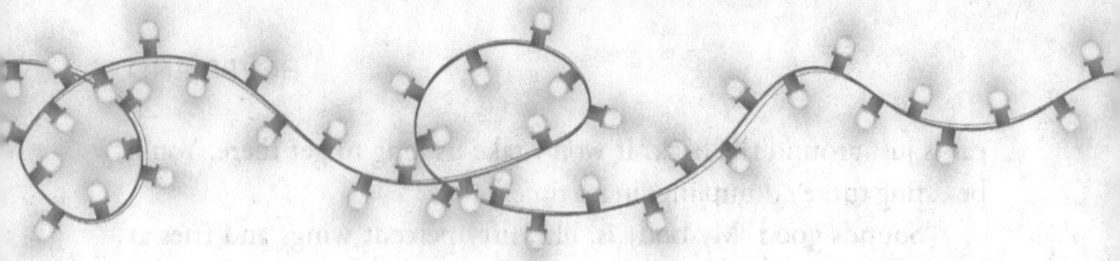

CHAPTER 3
ARE WE REALLY DOING THIS?

ABBI

"So, set the scene for me," Weston says as I drive toward Shelburne. "How much of an acting job do you need? I can be the new love of your life. Or I could be just one in a string of casual boyfriends. Or even just a friend from far away that you brought home to dinner out of pity. However you want to play this is fine with me. I just need to know ahead of time."

"Right, okay." I have to think fast, because I hadn't actually planned this through. I honestly assumed he wouldn't show up. "Nobody keeps very good tabs on me," I say slowly. "So if I say that we've been dating about a month, it wouldn't raise any eyebrows. And that seems plausible without being a big deal, either."

"A month it is!" he says easily.

This isn't nearly as awkward as it could be, thanks to Weston. He's good company, which I already know since I've listened to a thousand hours of hockey smack talk. He has a fun outlook on life.

"Names, please," he demands. "Who am I meeting?"

"Dr. Dalton Ritter is my stepfather. You can call him Dalton. The new Mrs. Ritter is Lila."

"Lila and Dalton Ritter, MD," he repeats. "I'm premed, so he and I could have plenty to talk about. One more question—can I ask why you felt the need for a date tonight? And are there any topics

I'm supposed to avoid? Any conversations I'm supposed to interrupt?"

"Well..." I do have my reasons. But Weston doesn't really need to know what they are. "We should avoid the obvious tricky subjects—like politics. But there's no specific issue between Dalton and me."

"Gotcha," he says. "So I'm just here as a buffer? Is it a big gathering?"

"Nope, which is why I need a buffer. It will just be them and her son."

"Your step-stepbrother?" Weston guesses.

"Yeah, and he's a tool. You'll see."

"No problemo," he says easily. "So you might as well tell me about you too."

"Me? I'm just a student like you. I grew up here in Vermont. And I'm trying to finish my degree in three years plus the summer terms I've done."

"Whoa! Major?" he asks.

"Business, with concentrations in finance and marketing."

"Ooh, finance? That sounds hard. I'm currently suffering through Modern Global Markets."

"Huh, I loved that class," I admit. "Plus, the business degree is practical. I'll be on my own after graduation. That's why I accelerated my degree. But it's been *so* stressful. And all my extra time is spent delivering wings to drunk hockey players, so there isn't much else to tell about me."

"Oh, sure there is," he says. "If we're dating, I would know more about you than the basic facts. What's your favorite song? What's your favorite food? What's your favorite color? Give me something to work with."

"Let's see." I chuckle. "Food? Lately just anything that didn't come out of the fryer at The Biscuit in the Basket. My favorite color is orange. My current favorite song is "Ain't No Man" by the Avett Brothers."

"Ooh, good one!" Weston says. "Put it on. Do you want to take the chorus or the verses?"

"Uh, what?" I reach for my phone and unlock it. Then I hand it to him, because Vermont has a law against holding a device while driving. "Go ahead and play it."

"Okay, but you're singing with me. We'll do the chorus together."

A few seconds later the guitar intro starts up. Weston starts clapping his hands with the syncopated beat. "Ready?" he says. And then he launches in.

And it's rude not to join him, right? So I sing along. And we sing *loud*, the same way I would if I were alone.

Weston doesn't embarrass easily, I guess. He sings every word of every verse, and I belt it out too. Three minutes later we've done the whole thing.

"Whew!" he says, leaning back against the headrest. "That was fun. I always sing loudly before tests too."

"Is today stressful for you?" I ask. "This *was* your idea."

He laughs. "Not at all. I'm fine, but you look ready to barf."

Huh. He's probably right. A trip to Dalton's always stresses me out. Although the words *you look ready to barf* were not part of my fantasy date with Weston.

"Don't worry," I tell him. "I won't barf. They're not really worth it. I just have to show my face on the holiday, make nice, eat some gourmet turkey and then it's over until Christmas."

"Fair enough. Where's the rest of your family? Out of state?"

"Well..." Oh man. I was hoping he wouldn't ask. I swallow carefully before speaking my truth. "This is actually all my family."

"Oh," he says quietly. "I'm sorry. What a stupid question. Way to put my foot in it."

"No, it's okay. I never met my dad. And my mother passed away three years ago." I can say it smoothly now. For a while there I couldn't really talk about losing my mom. I don't remember the last part of my senior year in high school. I spent it curled into a ball, in shock that my mother had taken my dog to the vet one morning, and then died in a car crash an hour later.

It's not supposed to happen to a forty-year-old woman. But it did.

I clear my throat. "So tell me about you. I bet you come from a huge family."

"Uh..." He chuckles nervously. "It's kind of true. I have a million cousins. And an older sister and a younger brother. Thanksgiving can get rowdy."

"That must be fun. No wonder you like the holiday—it must be a huge party. How big is your table?"

"Big," he says. "And my Aunt Mercedes practically has to drive an eighteen-wheeler to shop for Thanksgiving."

"I can't even picture it," I say. Although I've always wanted to be part of a big family. My mom didn't marry Dalton until I was twelve. So for years it was just the two of us, living in various run-down apartments around the greater Burlington area.

My mother had been Dalton's receptionist. He married her about eighteen months after his first wife left him. They were married for six years. So now he's on wife number three.

I moved out about ten minutes after his recent wedding.

Dalton isn't a monster. But I am not his child, and neither of us ever did a good job of pretending differently. He owed me literally nothing after my mother died. She had no assets to speak of. She cut back her working hours after she married him, because he wanted her to have time to take care of his home, and to cook and to entertain.

My mother *loved* this arrangement. She learned to play tennis. She went out to lunch with friends.

What she didn't do was buy a life insurance policy. Or put any savings in my name. And since my mother entered her marriage with no assets, save for a beat-up car and a nice collection of 90s music on CD, there was nothing for me to inherit.

I get a lot of financial aid from the university because my mother passed away. But Dalton pays a few thousand dollars every year toward my books and fees. He didn't want to pay for me to rent an apartment, though. "Seems silly when you could live in your old room," he'd said.

That was a generous offer, but it didn't feel like a real option for me. So I work a lot of hours at the Biscuit, and I'm going to graduate a year early.

"What was Thanksgiving like?" Weston asks me. "Before? With your mom?"

"Oh!" I say stupidly. But it's been so long since I thought about this. "When I was a little girl, it was just the two of us. We'd get up and watch the Macy's parade from start to finish. And then mom got KFC chicken, mashed potatoes, and corn. She made the pumpkin pie, though. From scratch. My mother was an impractical person. Back then, she didn't cook all that often, but she would bake the most exquisite things. I didn't mind. And I really loved the ritual of Thanksgiving."

"I bet," he says. "The ritual is half the fun. Maybe more than half."

We both go quiet for a few minutes after that. I'm picturing one of our small apartments, with its ugly green carpet and the sagging sofa. The truth is that I would give anything to go back there one more time. My whole childhood, I never had any cause to doubt my mother's love. Even when she married Dalton, I still knew I was her number one.

"Sorry," Weston says quietly. "Didn't mean to bring you down. Do we need another song?"

"Too late!" I pull into Dalton's grand driveway. "We're here already." I park behind Lila's shiny BMW and put the car in park.

"Hey." Weston turns to me in his seat, and makes no move to get out. "It's never too late for a song. I sing loudly and badly whenever the mood strikes."

Wow, is my only lucid thought. Those blue eyes are quite debilitating at close range. Weston Griggs is in my car. For the next couple of hours, he's my Thanksgiving date.

"Once more for luck," he says, hitting the play button again. The Avett Brothers launch into the intro again.

"Are we really doing this?" I laugh.

"We really are."

Then we both open our mouths and launch into the song. This time I'm not driving, so we can watch each other. I'm sure I'd feel self-conscious if Weston weren't hamming it up like a drunk karaoke singer.

He's even dancing a little in his seat. It's so ridiculously cute that I can't help but giggle my way through the song.

Oh God, I'm *giggling*. Just like the girls who are always perched on his knee after hockey games. I get it now. Giggling makes more sense when Weston Griggs is smiling at you.

We're both red faced and laughing as the song ends. Reluctantly, I climb out of my car. Weston grabs the flowers and the wine, and then wraps an arm around my shoulders as we approach the house.

It feels—*wow*—really nice. He's naturally talented when it comes to this fake boyfriend thing. He even gives my shoulder a little squeeze just before the front door opens onto my step-stepmother.

"Abbi! Happy Thanksgiving!" she gushes. "And you must be Abbi's young man. I've heard so much about you."

"Really?" he asks with a chuckle. "What did she say?"

Oh no! When I'd called Lila to tell her I was bringing someone, she'd asked polite questions about my "new man." And since I already admired Weston, it was easy enough to provide some details. *Terrific at hockey. Fun person. Lovely manners.*

Praising him came easily to me. But if she repeats any of it, I'm going to sound like a creepy stalker.

But I'm in luck. She gives him a generic smile instead, probably because she wasn't listening to me anyway. "It's good to meet you. Come right in."

"These are for you," Weston says, offering the flowers. "And I brought a bottle of sauvignon blanc."

"How lovely," she says. "Hang up your coats, and meet me in the kitchen. I'll pour you a drink." She leaves us alone in the entry hall of this house, which I've always thought of as Dalton's. Never mine. Not even when I lived here.

"Oh jeez," I say under my breath, realizing I've left something in the car.

"Problem?"

"The wine I brought is still outside."

Weston glances toward the door. "If you want, I'll step outside right now and grab it for you. But I have a better idea. You could think it over."

"What's that?"

"Leave it out there for now. And you and I can drink it *later*," he says, his voice richening to a suggestive pitch. "If you're into that."

Wait. Now hold on a second. Did Weston just proposition me? For *real*? I might do a happy dance right here on Lila's fussy new rug.

"Hello, sir," Weston says in the next breath. "You must be Dr. Ritter."

And sure enough, my stepfather is right here with us, reaching out a hand to shake Weston's. "Call me Dalton," he says.

They introduce themselves to each other while I stand here feeling befuddled. A second ago—when Weston suggested we save the wine for later—it felt so *real*. My mind offered up a few naughty ideas on command.

But now I realize that Weston probably saw Dalton approaching and whispered to me because it made us look like a convincing couple. Just a hot hockey player having a private moment with his girlfriend, right?

That has to be it. Weston is just doing his best to nail this acting job.

And it's too damn bad. Because white wine and a hookup with Weston Griggs would be the most fun I've had since...ever.

"Abbi?" Dalton's voice breaks through my reverie. "Are you coming?"

"Yes," I say quickly.

Weston takes my hand in his and gives it a friendly squeeze. And that feels nice, too.

It's all pretend, Abbi, I coach myself. *Don't you forget it.*

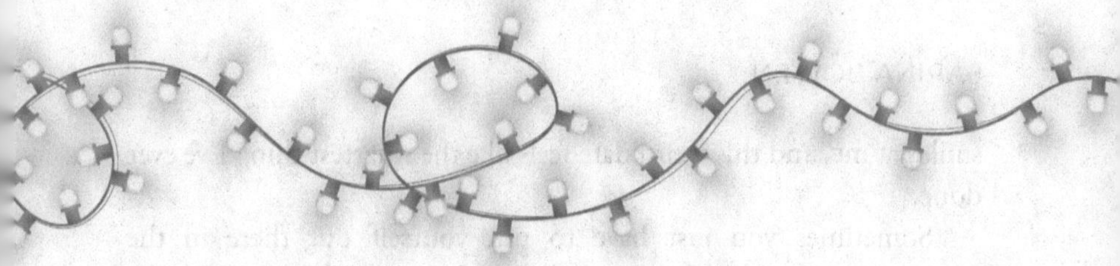

CHAPTER 4
MR. SMOOTH HAS FLED THE BUILDING

WESTON

Mr. Smooth must be losing his touch. I nearly propositioned Abbi under her stepfather's nose. Awkward much?

Now Abbi is looking at me like she doesn't quite know what to think. And who could blame her? I should have been more patient before breaking out my *hey baby, let's drink wine and dance the naked tango* speech.

This girl, though. She makes me a little stupid. I've got to pull myself together.

After hanging up our coats, I follow Abbi and her stepfather through a fancy-ass house to a gleaming kitchen. "It smells amazing in here," I say, because it does. "Is there anything I can do to help?"

"Not a thing," Lila crows, the corkscrew in her hands. "Would you like a glass of wine? I also have beer."

"I'll have a glass at the table," I say. "I don't drink much during the hockey season."

"Unless you lose a game," Abbi points out. "Then it's like the whole team is on fire and beer is the only thing that will extinguish it."

I let out a bark of laughter because she's right. "Good thing we don't lose very often."

"Good thing," she says with a little toss of her head. Then she smiles at me, and this weird date feels like the smartest thing I've ever done.

Sometimes you just have to put yourself out there in the universe, you know? Hang up a flyer and see what happens. Maybe the cutest girl at Moo U will call your name.

We make some small talk in the kitchen for a while, until Lila announces that dinner will be served momentarily. Abbi and I help to ferry several dishes through to a dining room with a large round table containing five chairs, five gleaming china plates, and enough silver and crystal to stock a palace.

I pull out Abbi's chair for her, and she gives me a glance of unguarded appreciation.

Yeah, Mr. Smooth is back. And he's going to close the deal later.

I sit down beside her. And that's when an unfamiliar guy sort of slumps into the room. Midtwenties. Dark, shapeless hair. Beefy face and body. He wears the half-alert expression of someone who's just awoken from a nap.

"Who are you?" this creature demands.

I glance at Abbi, and for the first time today, her expression shutters. Interesting.

"My name is Weston Griggs," I say, pushing back my chair and standing again so that I can shake his hand.

He scowls, then leans over the table to shake my hand limply.

"And you are?" I ask, trying to keep my tone polite. At least one of us should be.

"This is Price, my son," Lila says quickly. "And I see you've met Abbi's young man. Price, would you fetch me a glass of ice water and whatever you want to drink?"

He doesn't acknowledge the request. He just narrows his eyes toward our side of the table. "Abbi doesn't have a boyfriend. She never brings anyone home."

Abbi glances down at her plate.

"Price, sweetie, the drinks?" his mother says in a melodic voice. I wonder if she's just saving face, or if she really can't hear how obnoxious he is.

Whatever. I settle back in my chair. That's the glory of visiting with strangers on Thanksgiving. None of the family drama is *your* family drama.

A few minutes later we're all seated, and Dr. Ritter clears his throat. "Weston, do you mind if we join hands for a quick prayer before we dig in?"

"Not at all," I say, offering my hand to his wife on my right. I slip my left hand into Abbi's, and her smooth palm lands easily against mine. I give her hand a quick squeeze. It feels surprisingly natural in mine.

"Heavenly Father, we thank you for this bounty..." He launches into his prayer at a brisk pace, like a man who wants to do the right thing, but also wants to eat his turkey while it's still hot.

I lower my eyes respectfully. But a moment later I feel Abbi stiffen beside me. And then—if I'm not mistaken—there's a bit of violence under the table. As if a feral cat has wandered into the plush family dining room to bite Abbi's ankles.

But I'm pretty sure there's no cat. And when I shift my eyes to the side, Abbi's face has reddened in anger. And she's biting her lip so hard it might bleed.

"Amen," says Dalton.

Not a second goes by before Abbi yanks her hand free of Price's. She sits back in her chair, spine straight, chin held high.

But she is *pissed*. I barely know her and I can tell.

Our hands are still joined, so I give hers one more squeeze before letting go.

"Weston, why don't you start the platter of turkey around?" Lila says cheerily.

"Of course." I pick up the serving fork and turn to Abbi. "Can I serve you some?"

"Yes. Thank you." She still looks angry. So I choose a juicy-looking slice of turkey and deliver it to her plate before serving myself. Then I pass it across to her step-stepbrother, who's grinning evilly.

"So where did you two meet?" Dalton asks, passing a plate of dumplings in my direction.

"At work," Abbi says smoothly. "Weston's team comes into the Biscuit several times a week."

"We love the Biscuit. I'm half chicken wing at this point, as Abbi knows. She keeps me from starving."

"That's a nice story," Lila says sweetly.

"Abbi works so hard," Dalton says. "I'm glad that job brought her something good. She works so many hours just to afford that cramped little apartment."

"I like my place," Abbi says quickly. "So convenient for school. Besides, I have to put up with that job for a little longer. In a few months I'll pass the one-year mark. Everyone who makes it a year gets a fat bonus."

"Nice," Lila says. "I guess I'd stick with it, too."

"I will," Abbi agrees. "But you know what's crazy? The weekend bouncers get a bonus at the three-month mark." She rolls her eyes. "There's a lot of turnover in that job. But it doesn't seem fair."

"Pretty easy job, too," I point out. "They just have to stand at the door and look tough."

"They don't even have to stand," Abbi scoffs. "They have a stool to sit on, and free soda or coffee. They check IDs and walk the waitresses to their cars at the end of the night. If I could bench two hundred pounds, I'd switch jobs."

"Sorry, babe," I say, drizzling sauce all over my dumplings. "You aren't scary enough to be a bouncer. Maybe if we gave you a Mohawk and some tats."

Abbi puts a hand in front of her face and laughs. "I swear, it would almost be worth it."

We exchange an amused glance, and I give myself a mental high five for getting her to smile.

———

"I may never eat again," I declare an hour later as I dry off the crystal goblets that Abbi hands me. "That was magnificent, Mrs. Ritter." It's not a lie. This was my best fake Thanksgiving date yet. "That pumpkin chai pie was exquisite."

She beams. "There's a pie shop in New York City that I admire —Posy's Pie Shop—and I recreated the recipe."

"My compliments to whoever Posy is," I say. "I'm so full I may burst."

"Too full to play some pool?" Dalton asks. "I like to shoot pool while I digest. There's a TV in the game room, too, if you need to keep track of the football score."

I glance at Abbi. "What do you think? Want to play on my team?"

"Sure," she says. "I'm terrible, though."

"Me too," I promise her. "Let's be terrible together."

And we are. Abbi's stepfather knows how to set up complicated shots that quickly leave us in the dust. "It's a good thing I'm on a hockey scholarship and not a pool scholarship," I say as I scratch on the eight ball.

"Good thing," Abbi chirps, and we smile at each other like a couple of conspirators.

I don't mind losing at pool, because I'm winning at life. Every time we step back from the table, there's a new opportunity for me to talk to Abbi. I've woken up Mr. Smooth from his food coma, and put him to work.

I'm putting out all the signals, and she's waving me in. I hope so, anyway.

Life is good, in spite of Abbi's creepy-ass stepbrother smirking at us from a sofa across the room. Every time I miss a shot, he chuckles.

Whatever, punk. Meet me on the ice sometime, and I'll show you how it's done. The guy looks like he's never been to the gym in his life.

As the sky begins to darken outside the windows of the well-appointed game room, I see Abbi sneak a look at her watch. And I remember that there's a bottle of white wine chilling outside in the car, and a quiet holiday night ahead of us, when nobody is expected to work or go to hockey practice.

Maybe Abbi will invite me in when we get back to her place.

After we lose another game, and Abbi checks her watch a second time, I slip an arm around my fake girlfriend. Even this simple gesture is a shock to my system, because she feels so good leaning against me.

And it's not just me, either. I catch Abbi's sideways glance, and it's full of heat.

"Should we head back soon?" I ask, my voice weirdly husky. Mr. Smooth has already deserted me. "Uh, I was hoping to put in an hour or two on that...anatomy paper I told you about."

"Oh, sure." She licks her kissable lips. "No problem."

"What's the paper about?" Dr. Ritter asks. "I used to teach anatomy to the first-year med students at Moo U. Are you premed?"

Well, fuck me. Why did I have to invent an assignment? And why did I pick *anatomy?* I don't have a paper due. My subconscious is obviously hung up on exploring Abbi's anatomy. *Thanks, brain.*

"I am premed. And my topic is, uh, the spinal cord," I say quickly. "And which parts affect which, uh, motor skills."

Abbi's smile widens. She knows I'm talking out of my ass right now. I can only hope that she finds idiots attractive.

"Step into my office," he says. "I have a skeleton that's really great for understanding vertebrae in 3D."

"Wow, thanks," I say as Abbi hides a smile behind her hand. At least we can laugh about this later.

"I'll grab our coats," she says.

"Abbi, honey?" Lila says as we leave the game room. "Could you come with me a moment? There's a stack of your mother's cookbooks I want to ask you about. Maybe there's something here you'd like to keep."

Abbi's face falls. "Sure. No problem."

Lord, I can't even imagine what this must be like for her. A new woman in her mother's former space. Regretfully, I allow myself to be pulled into Dalton's office for a lengthy description of the regions of the spinal cord.

It's a shame I'm not writing a paper on this. It would be a snap now. The man drones on and on while I nod politely.

"Well, thanks," I say at the first moment that it won't seem rude. "I'd better get Abbi home so I can get some work done."

He claps me on the back. "So great of you to be here today. Abbi works too hard and has too few friends. I worry about her."

"It was all my pleasure," I say, feeling like a chump, because I can't really reassure him. Although I'm glad the man cares about his stepdaughter. He seems like a genuinely nice guy, if a little bland and clueless.

Luckily the phone on his desk rings just then, and I can drop my boyfriend act. I excuse myself and go searching for Abbi. She's not in the foyer. So I venture through the living room and toward the dimly lit kitchen, where I think I hear voices.

"Come on. Move." I hear Abbi say. "Weston is probably looking for me."

"Not until you admit it," a male voice says.

I turn around in confusion. I'm alone in the kitchen. Where are they?

"It's none of your damn *business*," Abbi says, the pitch of her voice rising.

"Did you give it up for him right away? Or did you make him work for it. I bet you just spread your legs for him. Is that it? Are you one of those hockey sluts? Do you let the whole team do you?"

"Get *away* from me!"

All my blood curdles. I spin around again and finally notice a door that blends right into the kitchen cabinetry. Like a walk-in pantry, maybe. I cross the kitchen in two steps and yank the door open.

Price's back is to me, but he's got Abbi caged in against a tall built-in bookshelf, his hands on either side of the narrow space.

His reaction time is slow, so he's just turning his head when I grab him by the waistband of his khaki pants and yank him backward.

"Hey! Fuck!" is all he manages to say before I haul him out of the pantry.

"Shut up," I snarl, shoving him roughly against the refrigerator. I am made of adrenaline right now. I can actually feel blood pulsing against my eardrums, and my right hand is already wrapped into a fist.

"Take it easy," he hisses. "I don't want any trouble."

"Too fucking *late*," I sputter. "You don't *ever* put your hands on her."

"I didn't. We were just having a friendly chat."

Somehow I manage not to punch him in the mouth. I don't even know how. My hand is itching to feel the bite of his teeth against my knuckles.

But some kind of protective impulse makes me glance toward Abbi first. She's watching with wide eyes. And she gives her head a little shake, like she can read my mind.

I grab his shirt instead, my hand close to his throat. "No more friendly chats. You don't look at her. You don't talk to her. Or I will punch you so hard that you'll be coughing up your teeth for days. Even if I break my goddamn hand, it'll still be worth it."

His eyes narrow. "Get your hands off me, fucktard. This is my fucking house," he hisses. "She's the little stuck-up bitch who keeps showing up here so that Dalton will keep writing checks. It will not look good for Abbi if I tell 'em you're a violent piece of shit."

That's when I hear the *tap tap tap* of Mrs. Ritter's heels approaching the kitchen. And I take a quick step backward.

Abbi grabs me by the elbow and turns me toward the kitchen door just as her step-stepmother walks through it. "Oh there you are!" she says gaily. "Abbi, did you decide which books you want to keep?" she asks.

"All of them," Abbi says quickly. "She made notes in them."

Lila frowns, as if that answer isn't to her liking. "I could box them up and put them in the basement, I suppose."

"Thank you," Abbi says tightly.

"Thanks for everything," I say, finding my voice. "We've really got to run, though." *Before I maim your shitbag of a son.* I can hear him behind me, where he's opened the fridge. I hear the pull tab of a beer can as he goes about his shitbag day.

"Of course!" she says brightly. "It was so lovely to meet you. Come back anytime!"

I manage to make the right polite noises as we get the hell out of there. And two minutes later I'm standing outside Abbi's car as she bleeps the locks open with a shaking hand.

"Hey. Can I drive?" I ask.

"Uh, sure. If you want."

I take the keys out of her hand, and walk around to the street side of the car. It takes me a minute to move her seat back far enough that I can fit my body into the vehicle. Then I buckle up, start the car and locate the headlights. I pull away from the curb and navigate toward the main road.

Driving calms me down. It isn't until I reach the intersection that I turn and glance at Abbi. She's sitting ramrod straight in the passenger seat, eyes glassy, expression grim. Like a person in shock.

Right there at the intersection, I put the car in park. It's dead quiet anyway. There's nobody behind me. "Are you okay?" I ask softly.

"Yes," she whispers. "I'm fine."

She doesn't look fine. And it's just dawning on me that I failed her. "If I'd known why you needed a date today, I wouldn't have let you out of my sight."

Abbi glances quickly in my direction, and then away again. But not before I see tears in her eyes. "It's embarrassing. I didn't want to explain."

I put the car back into gear and proceed onto the little highway that will take us back into Burlington. "That sucks, Abbi. And I don't mean to pry. But is there any reason we didn't march his stupid ass in front of your stepparents and tell them that he harasses you?"

She lets out a long breath. "I tried. Before he moved in, I told Dalton that he was always making inappropriate comments to me. And Dalton said that Price was just intimidated by me. That I was so much smarter and more successful, that he was just trying to get my attention."

"That's bullshit."

"Yeah, it is. But he's newly married. He doesn't want to hear me say anything bad about Lila or her thug of a kid. I'm not his daughter, Weston. I need him to help me with one more term at school. And I need to finish sorting through my mother's things, before Lila throws all her stuff away. One year from now I'll be free. Then I'll never have to set foot inside that house again."

"Oh. Shit." That's so depressing. But I can't say I'd make a different choice if I were her. "Is Price the reason you moved out?"

"Yeah." She wipes her eyes. "I'm pretty good at avoiding him. Dalton and I go out to lunch sometimes. That's how I stay friendly with him and avoid Price. But Thanksgiving is hard."

"What about Christmas?" I ask, worrying.

She shrugs. "I'll think of something. A weekend away at a friend's house, maybe. Or—worst case scenario—a pretend last-minute ski trip opportunity."

That's just grim. But I'll be across the state, and in no position to help. "I'm sorry," I say again. But it sounds useless.

"It's really okay," she says. "You put the fear of God into him anyway. Seriously. That was your best bit of acting, by the way."

"Because it wasn't," I snort. "I was ready to rip his face off. A guy like that can't get a woman to talk to him unless he backs her into a corner. And apparently that's okay with him."

"He'll probably leave me alone now," she says, just to sound upbeat. "Thank you."

"You're welcome. Anytime."

And to think that I had a tryst planned for the two of us. That's not happening now. You can't put the moves on someone who only needs you around so that she can keep a slimy asshole's mitts off of her.

Abbi doesn't need another guy trying to get her clothes off. She needs a pay raise and a night off and a new family. And none of those things is something I can help her with.

"But how was the play, Mrs. Lincoln?" I joke. "Those dumplings really were excellent. Just saying."

Abbi laughs and then shakes her head.

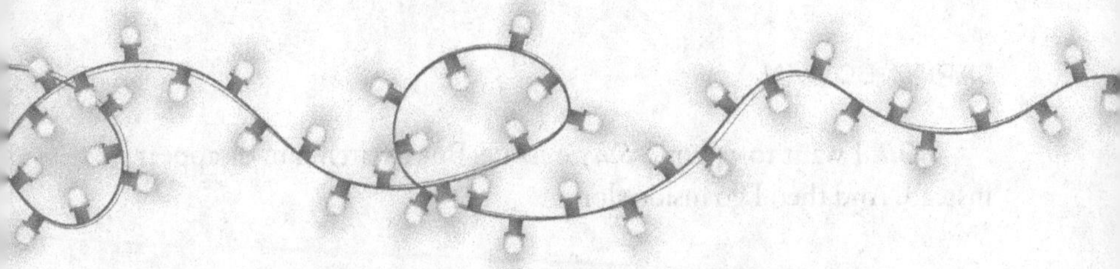

CHAPTER 5
TINY EGGROLLS, PIGS IN BLANKETS

ABBI

After Weston parks my car, he walks me all the way to the front door and waits patiently while I open it. He's the perfect gentleman.

I already knew Weston was a good guy. My mistake was in thinking that I could pretend—even for a few hours—that my life was the fun kind, with a handsome date and no worries.

"Thank you," I say in a low voice. "I appreciate all that you did today." I still have the shakes, too. I should have known that I couldn't be alone long enough to page through a couple of my mom's baking books without that creep harassing me.

I found a handwritten recipe in one of the books. And it's in my pocket right now. That's the silver lining of this shit show. Every memory I have of my mother is precious.

"It was nothing," Weston says gruffly. "My pleasure. You take care of yourself now."

We stare at each other for a beat longer. Earlier tonight I could have sworn that Weston looked at me the way a guy looks at a girl. With possibility. But all I see now is pity.

He reaches out and gives my shoulder a friendly squeeze. "Goodnight, Abbi. Sleep well." Then he gives me a Westonesque happy smile and turns to go.

Wait, I want to call out. *Stay a while*. But I watch him disappear instead. And then I go inside alone.

———

When I wake up the next morning, the humiliation hasn't completely worn off. I can still smell Price's hot breath as he loomed over me in the pantry. And I can still see the disgust in Weston's eyes as he flung Price against the refrigerator.

That last bit would have been very enjoyable under different circumstances. I'm not a violent girl, but Price had it coming. And then, as I roll over and sit up in bed, I have a brand-new, awful realization. I forgot to give Weston the twenty-five bucks that I'd tucked into my purse.

He spent the day with strangers and fought off Price. And then I stiffed him.

I let out a little shriek of horror. And then I reach for my phone and start texting.

Abbi*: OMG, I just realized I never gave you the 25 bucks! I'm an idiot. Seriously. A waitress should really know better! I'm so embarrassed.*

To my surprise, he starts to tap out an answer immediately.

Weston*: Hey! I wasn't actually going to accept it. I only put that in to keep the nutters away. Seriously. Well, also because it amuses me to charge for my acting skills.*

Abbi*: Your acting skills are on point, though.*

Weston*: Thank you. If this hockey thing doesn't work out, I'm considering Hollywood. There are roles for dumb jocks, right?*

He's so much more than a dumb jock. But I can't say that without revealing how deep my crush on him runs.

Abbi*: I smell an Academy Award for last night's performance. And I am very grateful. How about I treat you to your next platter of Thai spiced wings?*

Weston*: Well, Abbi, I would be happy to accept this as a token of your appreciation for my fake boyfriend performance. An actor has to eat, right?*

Abbi: *Right. See you soon.*

True to my word, the next time Weston comes into the Biscuit, I bring him a double portion of wings and a basket of fries. He gives me a big smile and a high five. But after that, I avoid him. Because every time I see his smile, I feel sheepish about treating him to a front row view of the horror show that is my life. I just want to forget it ever happened.

———

Between school and work, I'm busy enough to forget almost anything. November lunges into December. Exams loom. Two waiters quit, which means Kippy keeps scheduling me for extra shifts.

But hockey season is in full swing, so at least I have that. Just because I'm avoiding Weston doesn't mean I've stopped following the team. They've had a great start.

Their biggest matchup in December is against Boston University. And I'm on shift that night, checking the score on my phone every few minutes as I wait tables in the bar.

It's a tense game. It's tied 2-2 with only seven minutes left to play. But then Jonah Daniels feeds a wrister to Lex Vonne, and Moo U gets the lead back. When the buzzer rings, we've won 3-2.

For a long moment I feel pure jubilation. But then it occurs to me that The Biscuit in the Basket is about to be flooded with happy hockey players and the fans who love them. And table seventeen is in my section.

"Hey, Carly?" I tag my friend on the elbow as she passes me. "Switch sections with me? You can have the bar. I'll take your dining room tables. Forty bucks for the trade."

"Wait, what? Are you crazy?" she demands. "Who would give up table seventeen on the night they beat BU? You're throwing away extra money *and* extra hotness?"

"I'm just a little tired," I say. It isn't even a lie, because I'm always tired. "You handle the boys. I'm not in the mood to celebrate. I just want to go home and put my feet up."

"I'm worried about you," Carly says. "You need a vacation, and a one-night stand with a hockey player."

"Well *that's* not likely to happen." And I'm really not in the mood to watch if Weston spends the evening with a giggling woman on his arm—and then leaves with her. I haven't seen anyone hanging on him lately. But a win against BU should do the trick, right? "Go serve beer and shots," I say, nudging her toward the bar. "I'll bring out the last few dinners and go home early."

"Fine." Carly pushes two twenty-dollar bills into my hand. "But we're going to have a talk about this later."

———

The next time we're on shift together, Carly reports that Weston asked for me. "*Where's Abbi tonight?* He knew your real name, too. Did something happen between you and Weston?"

"Absolutely not," I tell her. "We're just friendly, that's all. And that's all we'll ever be."

"*Okayyy,*" she says, her tone full of disbelief. "But he looked really disappointed that you weren't around."

"I highly doubt that."

A week later, though, I'm sitting in an empty booth one night before closing, rolling some silverware, when somebody plops down on the seat across from me. When I look up, it's Weston.

My tummy flutters immediately at the sight of his clear eyes taking me in. "Hey, Abbi," he says.

"Hey, Weston," I echo. "How have you been?"

"Down in the dumps, if you want to know the truth. I got dumped by my fake girlfriend." He grins.

Um...what? "You can't get dumped by a fake girlfriend. That's kind of the point."

He laughs. "Don't I know it. But you *are* avoiding me."

"Am I?" I ask lightly. "Maybe I'm just busy rolling all this silverware into napkins."

Weston studies me for a second. Then he takes a napkin off the pile and positions it on the table in front of him. He takes a knife and a fork out of their respective bins and lines them up in the center. "Like this?"

"Sure," I say, amused. "It's not brain surgery."

"I'm premed," he says. "So someday I'll get to say that unironically."

"Dr. Weston Griggs has a nice ring to it. What specialty?"

"Pediatrics," he says. "You get to talk to kids for a living." He shrugs, like this is obvious. And, yup, Weston just gets hotter by the minute. "Am I doing this right?" He rolls the silverware up tidily inside the napkin. Then he wraps one of the green tapes around it.

"Looks good to me. But, if I may ask, why are you rolling silverware with me instead of drinking with your friends?"

"Oh, I'm done for the night. My party shift is over. But I had a favor I needed to ask you. Remember how I told you I had this big, fun family, and Thanksgiving was always a blast?"

"Yes." I roll another napkin and wait to hear where this is going.

"Well, it used to be true. But my parents got this really ugly divorce a couple of years ago. And now the holidays are murder."

"I'm sorry," I say quickly. "There's nothing like a little tension during the holidays."

"Yeah." He laughs awkwardly. "I know you understand. But here's the thing—if you told your stepfamily you were going out of town for Christmas with me, then you wouldn't have to see them, right? Free pass?"

"Well, sure. I was thinking about telling them that exact thing." After the words leave my mouth, I regret them. Do I sound like I'm pretending he's really my boyfriend?

He sets down another finished silverware roll, and looks me right in the eye. "What if it were true, though? It's me who could use a buffer this time. My sister is having an engagement party on the twenty-third, which means that my mom and dad have to be in the same room together. You could, uh, come with me." He swallows uncomfortably.

"Really? How would that help?"

"They, uh, like to yell at each other. But if I bring home a new girlfriend, my father will be on his best holiday behavior all weekend."

I think about this for a second. "Their own daughter's engagement party isn't reason enough to behave?"

"Well…" He bites his lip.

Before now, I'd imagined Weston Griggs to be the kind of guy who was always comfortable in his skin. But maybe nobody on earth is ever so lucky. I guess he's just human like the rest of us, because he looks plenty uncomfortable right now.

"Look, Christmas is going to be super awkward. My mom is throwing this party with her new man. That's never happened before. So my father knows he has to show up and be civil, even though he can't stand it."

"Ouch."

"Yeah, it's been three years, but sometimes it's like his anger is all that keeps him warm, you know? I'm making him sound like a dick right now, but he really isn't. He is a super nice guy whose wife left him in the worst possible way. And if you spend the weekend with us, he won't complain to my brother and me the whole time. He'll have to smile and make waffles and small talk. It would be a nice break."

"Oh." I think this over for a moment. "Well, I don't really have plans for Christmas."

Weston beams. "And this would put you out of Price's reach, right? You could just skip the whole sorry holiday."

"I could. But, Weston…" I don't quite know how to ask this question without sounding like a self-centered freak. "This isn't just a ploy so you don't have to worry about me, right? I'm a big girl. I can handle myself."

He takes another napkin and smooths it onto the table. "Abbi, I promise you that I'm truly a guy in need of a date. You should know that there are Swedish meatballs in it for you. My sister made me listen to the entire party menu. I can also promise tiny eggrolls, pigs in blankets, and fancy cocktails. Oh, and hopefully waffles on the morning of Christmas Eve."

That does sound promising. "Is the maple syrup real?" I ask sweetly.

"That's my girl!" He cackles. "It's real, I promise. They throw you out of Vermont if you serve the fake shit on Christmas Eve."

"Well okay, Weston." His smile makes me feel fluttery inside.

Spending a weekend with Weston isn't the smartest idea. My crush will only grow stronger. But even so, I hear myself say, "You've got yourself a date."

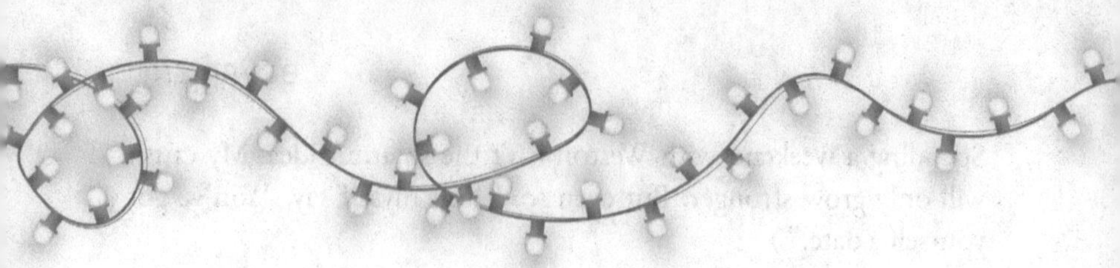

CHAPTER 6
CAN YOU DRIVE A STICK?

WESTON

On Christmas Eve-Eve, I meet Abbi at noon outside the Vermont Tartan Flannel Factory. She comes bouncing out of the building right at noon, and stops short when she sees me leaning against the driver's side of her car. Her eyes widen.

"Hey, sister. Something the matter?"

She blinks. "Nope. Not at all. Thank you for meeting me here. You look nice."

"Thanks. You too." In fact, I'm glad I put on nice slacks and a V-neck cashmere sweater. Because my fake girlfriend is wearing a dark red velour dress that my sister would describe as artsy. It looks soft and fluid, like red wine in a fabric form. There's just a hint of cleavage at the top. Just enough of a peek that I'd like to put my face right there and kiss the skin above the neckline of that dress.

She looks delectable.

Abbi opens the hatchback and tosses in a duffel bag and her winter coat. I snap out of it and follow her back there to do the same thing. "You mind if I drive?" I ask. "Since I know where we're going?"

"Sure thing." She holds up the keys. "But it's a manual transmission. Can you drive a stick?"

I snort. "That's like asking a man if his dick works."

"Well, does it?"

I grab the keys out of her hand. "I'll show you," I growl.

She snickers. But the truth is I'd like to show her more than my driving capabilities.

Down, boy. I unlock the car and get behind the wheel, scooting the seat back about eight inches so I can get my legs into the car. In fact, I drove this car once before. But Abbi was so rattled, she doesn't remember.

She's not rattled now, though. She slides into the passenger seat, humming to herself. "I'm so happy to have a couple of days away from school and work. I will go anywhere with you this weekend, so long as it does not involve serving fried food to drunk people."

"You won't have to serve any food," I say as her old engine roars to life. "And hopefully there won't be many drunk people." Honestly, drunk people are fine. Unless we're talking about my father.

In this situation, that could be problematic.

I pull out of the parking spot at the flannel factory. It's in an old brick building on the Winooski River. "What do you do at this place, anyway? How many jobs do you have?"

"This was my fun job," she insists. "My internship here is just ending, and I got course credit instead of pay."

"Cool. Which kind of business major are you?" I head for the highway. Abbi's car is a little sluggish. I wonder if she's gotten it serviced lately.

"I'm doing two concentrations—finance and marketing. I want to work on product development, but when I look at job openings for next year, most of them are in marketing."

"Marketing might be fun?" I say hopefully.

"Possibly," she hedges. "This internship was in marketing, and I spent a lot of time trying to take good pictures of flannel with my phone. But I guess everyone starts somewhere."

"True." Stepping on the gas, I accelerate onto southbound 89. But the needle doesn't budge. "Um, Abbi? I don't think your speedometer is working."

"Oh, it's not. You have to just watch the other traffic and blend in."

"Okay." I chuckle as I ease back into the right lane. "Any other quirks I should know about?" She insisted it would be a waste of money to use a rental for the weekend when she had a "perfectly good" car that just sits around most of the time.

Her idea of "perfectly good" and mine are apparently different.

"Well, the gas gauge is also broken. But you don't have to worry about that, because I keep track of my mileage on the trip odometer."

"Ah, okay?" I glance nervously at the gas tank indicator. "So we don't really have three-quarters of a tank?"

"The tank is full, Weston," she says gently. "You're not going to run out of gas. Not today, anyway."

"Good to know." And it's not like I need any extra things to worry about. I'm drumming my fingers on the steering wheel, wondering whether this whole trip was a colossally bad idea.

Abbi reaches over and momentarily places a hand over my twitching one. "Do we need to sing it out? I could cue up a nice loud song."

"Oh, definitely," I admit. "At some point. Why don't you find us something seasonal to listen to?" I like holiday music. Or at least I used to, in the Before Times.

"Good idea," she says, grabbing her phone to scroll through the available tunes. "I'll find something."

I glance briefly toward the passenger seat, where the sun illuminates her silky hair. We're cruising down 89 South toward my corner of Vermont. It's the day before Christmas Eve, and the highway is empty, even for Vermont. There's crisp white snow blanketing the landscape.

There's beautiful scenery everywhere, especially on the passenger side of the car. I'd just like to take a gulp of her.

But I won't, of course. "Hey, Abbi? We'll probably have to share a room. But you can trust me to be a gentleman."

"I know that," she says easily.

"One of the rooms has two sets of bunk beds in it, and that's probably the one we'll get anyway. You can have first dibs." I can count on my brother to claim the other room with the double bed in it.

"Thanks," she says, still scrolling. "Tell me where we're going, anyway. I never drive around Eastern Vermont."

"It's nice there," I promise. It's the one good thing I can say about this weekend—the accommodations are a good time. "My dad's place is right on Lake Morey. It's a cool old lodge that has been in his family for generations. They used it as a summer lake house."

"And he lives there year-round, now?"

"Yeah. He did a big renovation and winterized the place. But we left the bunk room the way it was, because he likes it when we bring friends home." Although I usually do that in the summertime, when Dad's place feels less claustrophobic.

Abbi turns on a playlist. It's a cappella Christmas music by *Straight No Chaser*. But the volume is low, so I guess we're not singing off my tension yet.

"Now, let's take a moment to discuss our story," she says cheerfully. "Who are the major players, here? What do I need to know in order to play my role effectively?"

"Let me guess—it's a lot more fun to be on the other side of this question."

"Why, yes it is!" She smooths her dress over her knees. "You were right—someone else's family drama is much easier to handle. So what do I need to know?"

I guess I can't put it off any longer. "Well, first I'd like to say that I understand why you didn't fill me in on the whole Price situation ahead of time."

"Because it's weird and embarrassing?"

"Yeah. My situation is pretty bonkers. But there's no way that you're not going to notice. So I'll just come out and tell you that my mother left my father for..." I take a deep breath.

"A woman!" Abbi guesses.

"No way." I snort. "That would have been so much better, seeing as my dad doesn't have any sisters."

Abbi is silent for a second, and I can practically hear the cogs turning in her brain. "Wait," she gasps a moment later. Her voice is hushed, like she's afraid to voice this suspicion aloud. "She left your father for his..."

"*Brother*," I say heavily. "My uncle Jerry is now my stepfather."

Abbi clutches her chest. "Holy crap. That's some serious drama.

How did it happen? Wait—never mind. I don't really need to know. But was this recently?"

"Four years ago my uncle got into a serious snowmobiling accident. He was always the wild man of the family. My dad is a nerdy architect, a studious kind of guy, right? And Uncle Jerry is a mixologist, a ski bum, and gave me my first hit off a bong."

"I hope you weren't five years old," Abbi grumbles.

"Nah." I laugh. "I was in high school. But anyway—he gets into this accident—which was his fault, by the way—and he had all these broken bones and three surgeries. My mom is a physical therapist, and he needed a lot of help. So she took him on as a pro bono patient. His rehab took months."

"Oh." Abbi sits with that for a moment. "And they spent a lot of time together."

"Yup. They didn't just jump into the sack. Apparently they tried to be very civilized about the whole thing. One night my mother just turns to my father in bed and says, *Mickey, I need a divorce. I've fallen out of love with you and in love with someone else.*"

Just saying this out loud makes me want to shudder for my poor dad. "He had a whole life with my Mom, and she just torched it because Jerry was—quote—*more fun and life-affirming.*"

"Ouch," Abbi whispers.

"Ouch," I agree.

"I can't even imagine what that did to your family. Did your dad and his brother get along before that?"

"Not really. My dad was the serious one and Jerry was the screwup. They're five years apart in age, too, so Mom left him for a younger man. Now Jerry and my mom live in the house where I grew up. Jerry basically just moved into my dad's bedroom."

Abbi groans. "No wonder your dad is a wreck."

"Yeah." Not that he's dealing with it very well. He moved out more than two years ago, and he's still boiling with anger. When my sister suggested he go to therapy, he flat-out refused.

"Will they both be at this party tonight? Your, um, uncle and your mom?"

"You bet. Jerry would never miss a party. He probably invited half the upper valley. There will almost certainly be a special cocktail for the occasion, and he'll give a long speech about how the drink is perfect for my sister's personality, or some shit. He likes the spotlight."

"Okay," she says gamely. "We'll smile through it and make a point to drink something else."

That was pretty much my plan too, and I shoot a grateful look toward the passenger seat.

"You're very special, Weston. I never met a guy before who was his own cousin."

I snort. "My family tree is twisted, that's for sure."

"Do you have grandparents?"

"Strangely enough—or not, depending on your viewpoint—my grandpa on my father's side has gone a lot deafer since this whole thing went down. His way of dealing with the chaos is not to hear a lot of it. And never to wear his hearing aid. Can't say I blame him."

"Oh, that poor man," Abbi says. "What a mess. No wonder you don't like the holidays anymore."

She's right—I used to *love* Christmas. But the holidays are just a chore now. On the stereo, the a cappella group is singing "Jingle Bells," and I'm just not feeling it. "It's like I'm numb to Christmas," I mumble. "But Lauren would shoot me if I skipped this party. And so would Stevie—that's my little brother. He's eager to meet you."

"What did you tell him about me?"

"Nothing, I swear. But I never bring girls home for stuff like this. Neither does he. I mean—would you?"

"I tried on Thanksgiving, remember? It didn't go so well."

"Exactly."

"We need a plan," she says. "How close are we supposed to be? Am I just some girl you brought home, or are we dating? How thick should I lay it on?"

I chuckle, because I'd really enjoy watching Abbi turn up the girlfriend vibes. I wouldn't say no to a fake kiss or two. Although that's not really fair to her. "Look, you don't have to do anything that isn't comfortable for you. They won't believe it, anyway."

"What do you mean?" She gasps in mock outrage. "Am I not girlfriend material? I wore tights and a dress for you."

"No, you goof. You are more lovely and convincing than any other girl I've brought home in three years because—"

"Because you haven't brought *anyone* home in three years."

"Now she gets it. Nothing against that dress, though." I'd still like to touch it—or peel it off her. Although I'm not about to say so.

She clicks her tongue. "Weston, I think you doubt my acting skills."

"It's not that," I promise.

"Still, it's only fair that I get a chance to snow your family as well as you snowed mine."

"Okay." I laugh.

"Let's go with the same story we told my family—we've been dating about a month."

"Fine."

"And what do I win if I can make them believe me?" she asks sweetly.

A kiss. "Um... a dinner that didn't come out of the deep fryer at the Biscuit?"

"Yes! And that bottle of wine we never drank together."

"You're on. This will be fun. I mean—I totally snowed your stepdad. It's only fair to let you compete."

"Exactly."

"But it won't be easy, Abbi. My brother and I have spent the last two years insisting that relationships are for suckers. You can't really live in my dad's house and believe otherwise."

She shrugs. "I like a challenge. Besides, it will make the party more fun, don't you think? People will be gossiping about us instead of your stepfuncle."

"My—?"

"Stepfather-slash-uncle. Your stepfuncle. Besides—I already have a pet name for you picked out. It would be a shame not to use it."

I snicker nervously. "I'm terrified now. But fine. Two can play at this game. I'm going to call you..." I hesitate. What's a slightly silly but ultimately believable pet name for Abbi?

Honey is too generic.

Kitten?

Sugar pop?

Hmm.

"It's not so easy, right?" She sounds a little smug. "The name has to fit, or people will see through us."

"Eh. I made your stepdad into a believer. And I did it without a pet name."

"Pfft. Price was suspicious of you," she points out.

"Was not," I argue just because it's fun to goof around with Abbi. If she were my only company for the next three days, I'd actually be looking forward to Christmas.

"He was too," she chirps. "Do you want to argue some more? Or are we going to sing something at the top of our lungs? I just found the Avett Brothers singing '*If We Make It Through December.*'"

"That sounds more than appropriate," I admit. "Blast it, baby."

And she does.

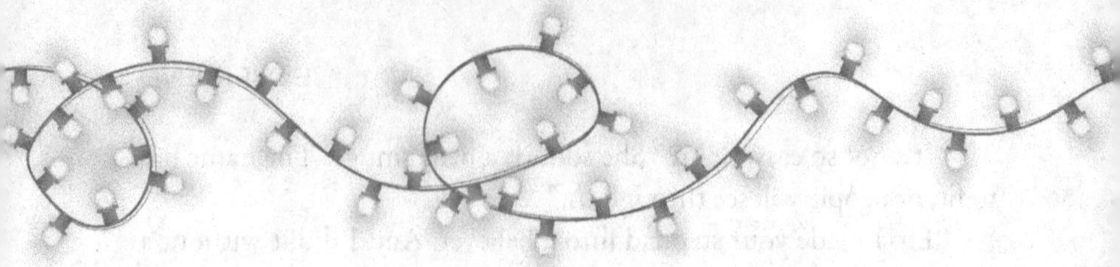

CHAPTER 7
A LITTLE OVERHEATED

ABBI

After getting off the highway, Weston begins to wind my little car down narrow country roads, while snow falls gently past my window. It's cozy here in the car with him. I almost wish the trip would never end.

I know Weston doesn't really need me here. But it's obvious he's dreading this party, and that he feels truly grateful for my company. And that's given me a useful, optimistic feeling that Christmas hasn't brought me in years.

Let's face it, if not for Weston, I'd be holed up alone in my apartment right now, thinking sad thoughts about decorating past Christmas trees with my mom. This is so much better than that.

Eventually Weston turns down a driveway between two towering pines. And as we roll toward the house, it's clear he's totally undersold the cool factor of this place. There's a stunning two-story clapboard house in front of us, with a slate roof and a wraparound porch. The doors are painted a cranberry red that's set off against the snowdrifts.

"Wow," I breathe. "It's like parking in front of a Christmas postcard."

"Didn't I mention that my dad is an architect?" Weston asks, hopping out of my car.

"I get it now."

When I climb out, he offers me the keys. "Here. In case you feel the need to make your escape from this looney bin."

"Way to sell it, Griggs." I pocket the keys.

His smile is tight. "Thank you for coming with me, Abbi. I really appreciate it."

"Hey. It's *really* no trouble. I don't mind getting out of town for a couple of days. It's nice to have a change of scenery." That goes for both gorgeous property and Weston's handsome face in front of me. "Look, Christmas is a real drag for me these past couple of years. I get stuck inside my head. It's too much alone time. It makes me sad."

"We have that in common, then," he whispers.

Out of the corner of my eye, I see the window curtain twitch. And maybe that's why I suddenly stand on tiptoes and give Weston a kiss on the jaw.

Whoa. He smells of woodsy aftershave. I have to force myself to rock back onto my heels, instead of leaning in for even more.

He grins. "Is someone looking out the window?"

"Yup!" I give him a big smile. "I'm going to win this thing, Griggs. Now introduce me to your bonkers family. I'm ready."

"Yeah, okay." We share a private smile. "But you've been warned."

As he turns toward the house, he reaches for my hand. As his roughened fingers envelop mine, this feels strangely real. I know it's a game, but his palm feels so solid against mine.

He pushes open the door and leads me inside. There's a shoe rack, so I lean down and unzip my snowy boots. He sets our bags down on the floor and toes off his hiking boots. "Dad? Stevie? We're here."

I follow him into a soaring great room with a huge stone fireplace that takes up one entire end of the room. Some ingenious person has installed a beautiful wood stove insert into it, so the fire inside casts off heat and light, but no smoke.

In front of the fire is a big plush wool rug and a lot of comfortable furniture. There's a coffee table the size of a small country there too, and I'd bet any amount of money that the Griggs men spend most of their family time right there in that spot.

The view is killer. Outside the long row of windows, the lake is visible at the end of what must be a rolling lawn in the summertime. But right now it's covered with snow. Someone has cleared a strip of the ice on the lake, and I see three people whip by on ice skates.

"Whoa. Can you skate right outside your front door?" I ask.

"Yup," Weston says, using tongs to toss another log onto the fire. "Want to try it tomorrow?"

"Maybe," I hedge. "There's no way I could skate as well as you, though."

"That's a good thing, Abbi," he says dryly. "Otherwise the hockey team recruited the wrong person." He gives me a coy smile, and my belly does a little flip.

I don't know how this happened. Suddenly I'm friends with Weston Griggs. And I'm spending Christmas with him in this winter paradise. Not that we'll be making out in front of that roaring fire.

But a girl can dream.

"Hey, Dad!" Weston calls. "You here?"

"Sorry!" comes a shout from the back of the house. And then a big, strong man appears in one of several doorways leading into the room. "I was just finishing up a call. This must be Abbi. Welcome."

My first thought is *wow*. Mr. Griggs is a silver fox. He's a handsome older version of my fake boyfriend. I can see where Weston gets his thick, wavy hair and those intelligent eyes. He steps forward, holding out a hand to shake mine.

"It's nice to meet you, Mr. Griggs," I say.

"Oh, please call me Mickey. The pleasure is all mine," he says with a chuckle. His grip is firm as he gives my hand a polite clasp. "So happy to have you join us for Christmas." Then he steps up to his son and gives Weston a playful cuff on the biceps. "That's for not coming home to see your father ever. But I guess you've been busy."

"It's hockey season, Dad. You know you can come to a game anytime. Where's Stevie?"

"Right here." Another strapping Griggs man steps into the room. Stevie's hair is lighter than Weston's, and he's a little shorter, maybe. But the gene pool has been good to this family. "So you're the mysterious girlfriend." His eyes narrow. "I'm fascinated."

Weston makes a grumpy noise, and his hand finds mine and squeezes. "Be nice, Stevie. Is that any way to greet a guest?"

His brother looks pointedly at our joined hands. "Nice to meet you, Abbi," he says politely enough. "I cleared out of the double room for you two."

"You don't have to do that," Weston says quickly. "You're staying longer."

"Oh I insist," he says with a smirk. "Let me help you carry your bags upstairs."

"We got it," Weston grumbles. "I'll grab our stuff out of Abbi's car."

"Thanks, Westie," I say in a soft, sweet voice.

His brother snorts. Loudly. "Westie?"

"Shut it," Weston says to his brother. "Be nice and offer Abbi some lunch. I'll be right back."

———

Lunch turns out to be both casual and delicious. We all sit around that giant coffee table in front of the fire eating crusty bread and a meat and cheese board that Stevie has thrown together. There are three French cheeses, two different salamis, several types of little olives, and cornichons.

I'm in charcuterie heaven.

It's also a good vantage point for surveilling the family dynamic.

Weston's dad is a good conversationalist. He tells us all about his newest commission—a teardown in Norwich, where the home-owners scrapped a 1960s raised ranch to build a contemporary mansion. "They're nice enough people, but they have a Frank Lloyd Wright fetish," he says with a smirk. "They keep asking for wood-paneled ceilings everywhere. And I keep trying to talk them out of it, or it will be like living inside a cigar box."

Meanwhile, Stevie keeps sneaking looks at me and Weston. His curiosity isn't very well disguised. So I decide to have a little fun with it. I slide my hand onto Weston's knee, oh so casually.

Weston responds by lifting my hand just as casually into his. We make a great fake couple, if I do say so myself.

But then he casually runs his thumb across the back of my hand, and shivers dance across my skin. For a second, I allow myself to consider what it would be like to be Weston's *real* girlfriend. The minute we were alone, I'd climb onto his lap and kiss him senseless.

He'd probably respond by pushing me down onto this oversized couch, where we'd make out for hours...

"Abbi?" Weston says, squeezing my hand.

"Sorry?" I say, suddenly aware that I've been asked a question.

"Would you like coffee?" Mr. Griggs ask, while Stevie smirks. "I'm thinking of making a pot."

"Yes. Thank you," I say quickly. "Clearly I'm a little dreamy today. Maybe I'll just splash some water on my face." I feel a little overheated too. Maybe it's the fire.

Or maybe it's sexy thoughts about Weston.

"There's a bathroom just down the hall," Mr. Griggs says, picking up the empty charcuterie board. "But why don't you take Abbi upstairs while I make the coffee?" he asks his son. "And find a towel for her."

"Great idea," Weston says.

"I'll just help you carry your stuff upstairs," Stevie says, popping out of his chair.

"No need, punk," Weston says, shutting him down. "What if you minded your own business for once?"

"What would the fun be in that?"

Weston wasn't kidding. Stevie is suspicious.

I can sell this thing. If I'm successful, Weston has to take me out to dinner and split a bottle of wine.

Winning is imperative. I just have to figure out how.

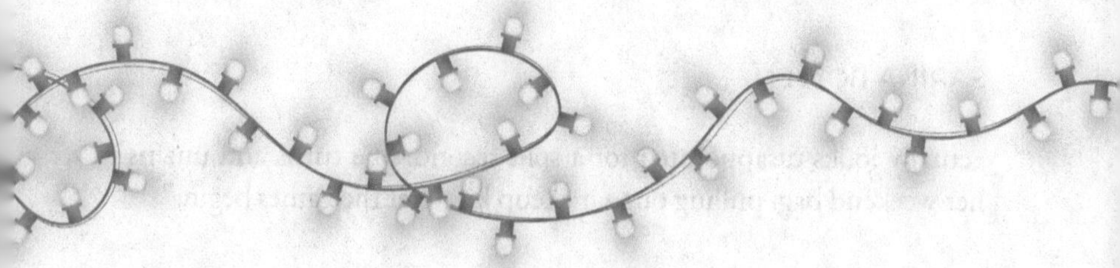

CHAPTER 8
WORLD WAR GRIGGS

WESTON

God, my brother is acting like a tool. And my dad seems tense. We just have to get through the party tonight, and then everyone can relax.

"Come with me," I say softly to Abbi. She's the only one in this scenario I can count on to behave. I already feel guilty for subjecting her to the madness of a Griggs family get-together.

She follows me to the staircase, where I step aside to let her go first. And I force myself not to ogle her legs in that dress. "It's the room on the left," I say when she reaches the top. I already put our bags in there.

But when I follow her into the room it looks smaller than ever. She eyes the double bed and then her eyes jump to mine.

"I'll get Stevie to switch with us," I whisper. "I'll tell him..." I pause. "Okay, I have no idea what I'll tell him. I'll think of something."

"No, it's fine," she whispers back. "I'm winning this thing, even if you snore like a freight train."

I bark out a laugh. "I don't."

"How do you know?" she counters, smiling fiercely.

"I guess you'll tell me, then. And I promise to be a gentleman."

"Right," she says crisply. And maybe I'm imagining it, but she actually looks disappointed for a split second. She turns and unzips her weekend bag, pulling out a makeup kit. "Let the games begin."

————

A couple hours later, after a movie in front of the fire with my fake girlfriend, it's time to leave for the party. So my brother and I flip a coin to decide who's the designated driver tonight.

And I lose. Of course I do.

"You're not even legal to drink," I whine.

"At my own sister's party? Please. Who's going to card me? Not Uncle Jerry. He gave me a beer for my twelfth birthday."

"I can be the driver," Abbi volunteers. "I don't mind."

"No," I say quickly. "You spend enough nights watching other people have fun."

"How's that?" Stevie asks.

"I'm a waitress at the hockey bar," Abbi explains. Then she slips her arm around my waist. "That's where we met. I memorized his order."

"That's so romantic," Stevie says with a smirk and an eye roll. He's not buying what Abbi has to sell. But it's not Abbi's fault. She has no idea how down on love we've all been these past couple of years.

In fact, last Christmas, after my parents had a shouting match on the steps of the church *during* the holiday service, my brother and I literally sat around asking each other questions like: *Would you rather get married or have all of your fingers chewed off by a rabid dingo?*

And we both picked the dingo.

"All right, guys," my father says, entering the mud room. "Let's get this shit show over with."

"Dad," I say, stopping him as he grabs his jacket. "Can I talk to you for a second?"

Abbi slips out the door then, and Stevie does the same.

"What?" my dad bellows. "We'll be late."

I let out a sigh. "What if you didn't go? You clearly don't want to. Lauren isn't throwing a 'shit show' on purpose, you know."

"She's not throwing this thing at all," he grumbles. "It was your mother's dumb idea."

"So you think Lauren should just cancel her party? Or, wait, cancel her whole wedding so that you don't have to feel uncomfortable?"

"Did I *say* that?" he carps. "Don't put words in my mouth."

Now he's glaring at me. All I wanted him to do was check his attitude.

Shit.

"Okay, let's go," I say as lightly as I can. Then I hustle outside because Abbi is in the cold waiting for us. And she deserves better.

———

The party is held at the Norwich Inn, which is a turn-of-the-prior-century farmhouse-style hotel on the main drag of a classy town across the river from Hanover, New Hampshire. When we arrive, I watch Abbi take in the crackling fire and the two dozen people milling about eating party food and sipping cocktails while Christmas music plays over the sound system.

It's objectively a nice party. And I thaw a little when my sister flounces over with a happy smile and offers her hand to Abbi. "So you're Weston's date for Christmas! I've been dying to meet the woman who would voluntarily put up with him over the holidays."

"I'm getting that a lot," Abbi says cheerfully. "Congratulations on your engagement."

"Thank you!" My sister's eyes dance. "Let's get you both a drink. There's, um, a special one named after me. But we also have beer, wine, and soda. And lots of food."

"Don't worry about us," I tell my sister, folding her into a hug. "Just enjoy your party while it's going smoothly."

"Don't jinx me." She sneaks a nervous look toward my father, who has planted himself at the precise opposite end of the room as his brother. Dad is standing there, hands jammed in his pockets, looking vexed. "I was kind of hoping he'd sit this out if it made him so uncomfortable."

"He's stubborn," I whisper.

"I noticed."

"Don't worry about him," I say, squeezing my sister's arm. "Abbi and I will corner him and tell him bad jokes until he gets bored enough to leave."

"I knew I could count on you." Lauren sneaks another look toward Dad. "I just wish I didn't have to."

———

Abbi and I get some food, and I bring a plate to Dad. I also bring him a beer.

Then I forget about him for a few minutes and introduce Abbi to my extended family. First there's my mom. "Weston! Hello, lovely boy! And you brought a date to meet your family! This is like a Christmas *miracle*."

Abbi gives me a helpless look before she's swept up into a hug by my mother.

Yikes. I'm going to owe Abbi after this, no matter who wins our bet. My fake girlfriend is gracious about all this weird attention, though. She chats politely with my mom and takes it all in stride.

Then I introduce her to Aunt Mercedes and a bunch of my cousins. They're all like Switzerland, somehow staying neutral in World War Griggs.

The last person I introduce Abbi to is Uncle Jerry. He's set up his mixology table at one end of the room, with a signboard propped onto the table announcing the night's special cocktail: The Lauren.

"What's in The Lauren?" Abbi asks gamely.

"I'm so glad you asked," Jerry says, dropping ice into his pretentious crystal shaker with the titanium lid. "Kentucky bourbon, fresh Meyer lemon juice, simple syrup, and a float of red wine."

"Isn't all bourbon from Kentucky?" Abbi asks. And I have to hold back my snicker.

"Smart girl," Jerry says with a cheesy smile. "Not everybody knows that. This is a special bourbon, too—Knob Creek Reserve. Very round-flavored, with notes of plum and caramel."

Abbi indulges him, watching as he squeezes the lemons and shakes up the juice with syrup and bourbon.

Meanwhile, my dad glowers at us from across the room. He can't stand it that I'm standing this close to my stepfuncle.

Jerry pours the mixture over ice. "And now for the grand finale," he says, lifting a bottle of wine with a flourish. "Watch this." He holds a spoon inverted over Abbi's glass and pours an ounce or two of the red liquid into the golden cocktail. "The wine is suspended there, like a cloud," he says.

"Cool," Abbi says convincingly. "So I shouldn't stir it?"

"No! It's meant to look just like this—with the red floating on top. It's my signature technique."

"Ah, it's beautiful!" Abbi says while I try not to roll my eyes. She takes a careful sip and pronounces it delicious.

I can almost hear my father grinding his teeth from twenty feet away. And when I next glance at him, he's pouring himself a glass of bourbon straight from a bottle. Neat. And not a small amount.

I've got a bad feeling about where this night is headed. And it's only eight o'clock.

For the next hour I try to humor my dad. I really try. And so do my aunt, my sister, and Abbi, who's a champ.

But not only has he been steadily getting drunker, he's practically brandishing that bottle of expensive bourbon he stole from Jerry's bar table, taunting his brother with that sucker.

It's like waving a red flag at a bull. I can practically hear my dad's wheels turning. You do not fuck with a dedicated mixologist's ingredients. Will Uncle Jerry run out of his pretentious unmixed drinks without it? Will he make a scene?

My dad is gunning for it, I think. He gets louder with each passing minute. I've been watching that bottle of bourbon this whole time, too, hoping to snatch it away from him. But Dad holds it in one fist like a cudgel.

"Maybe we should hit the road soon," I suggest. "I've got presents to wrap at home."

"Let me find the ladies' room first," Abbi says.

"Oh, I'll show you where it is," Lauren offers. She detaches from Nigel, her fiancé. "Right back, sweetie."

He gives my sister a soft look as the two women walk away. For a guy named Nigel, he seems pretty decent.

I sneak another look at my watch. We've been here long enough. We've spoken to every cousin and family friend who was brave enough to come over to the chilly side of the room and humor Dad.

So I clear my throat. "Dad, you want anything more to eat? Seems like the party will be winding down soon. We should go."

But my timing kind of sucks, because when I glance at the nearby food table, Uncle Jerry is *right* there.

Dad makes a snarly face. "I'm good," he says. "Lost my appetite. Bourbon?" He holds up the bottle like it's the Statue of Liberty's torch.

"No, I'm the driver. But why don't you let me put that back on the bar?"

"Think I won't," he snorts. "This is top shelf bourbon. Only an asshole would mix it with lemon juice."

I sigh.

"Is that supposed to hurt my feelings?" Uncle Jerry says to the meatball platter.

"Impossible," my father slurs. "Wasn't aware you had any."

"Dad," I warn.

"What? It's true."

Shit. I'm glad my sister has gone to the ladies' room with Abbi, so she doesn't have to hear this.

Jerry turns around, and I brace. "Let him say whatever he wants." My uncle shoves a meatball into his mouth. "He's only making himself sound like a dick. You go ahead and rant, Mickey. Or steal that bottle of bourbon. Whatever floats your boat."

"At least I didn't steal someone's family. Does that make your dick feel bigger, I bet?"

"*Dad*," Lauren gasps from the doorway.

"What?" my dad bellows. "You want to take his side? You always do."

"Mickey," my mother hisses. "Don't wreck your only daughter's party."

"I didn't wreck anything! You two did!" As he shouts, he swings the bourbon bottle wildly.

And it crashes into the brick fireplace and shatters.

"Shit!" he howls. Then, as everyone stares lasers at him, he walks right past me and leaves the room.

My fingers knot into fists, and my first urge is to chase him down and tackle him into the snow. But I get a look at my sister's face, and I don't do it. I count to thirty and breathe.

And then I bend down and start picking up shards of glass off the rug. Because the people who work here do not deserve this.

Nobody does.

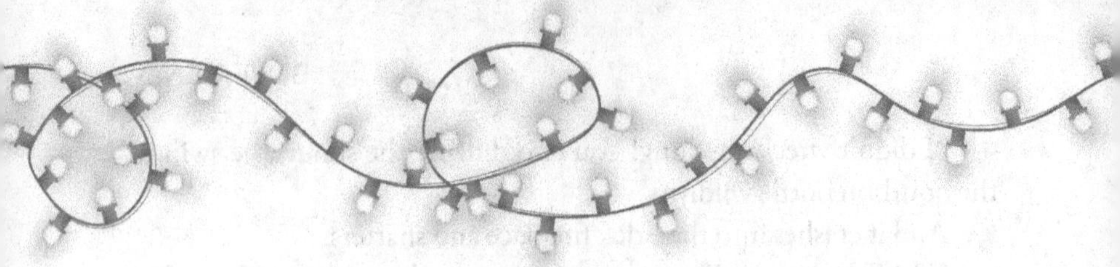

CHAPTER 9
SMELLS LIKE WOODSY GOODNESS

ABBI

I'm standing outside the building when the shouting starts. I'd been about to answer a phone call from my stepfather. He probably wants to wish me a Merry Christmas.

But I silence my phone instead, and listen as the awful sound of glass breaking pierces the silence.

Uh-oh. Poor Lauren. Poor Weston, too. This is exactly what he'd been hoping to avoid. I don't move from my spot on the inn's back porch, because the Griggs family doesn't need one more person gawking at them right now.

But a moment later, Weston's father emerges out of the back door, too.

I'm so stunned that for a beat I just stare at him, open-mouthed. "How could you?" I whisper.

Oops. I shouldn't get involved. I know this. But I'm just so mortified for his family. I turn away because I can't stand to give him any more of the attention he craves.

It's not like I don't understand that he's hurting. It's just that I know how to suffer in silence, like a grown-up. A skill he obviously never learned.

We ignore each other for a couple of very long seconds. I finger my phone in my pocket, and wonder what I could do to help Weston right now.

Meanwhile, the person who should have been helping Weston is pulling a pack of cigarettes out of his pocket and lighting up.

I hate cigarettes. Just like I hate overgrown man-babies.

"Welcome to the family," Mickey grunts. "Things are pretty hairy with the Griggs clan these days."

Oh really? You don't say. But that's all on him. It must be hard work to maintain this level of animosity for—what did Weston say? —three years?

I should just keep my thoughts to myself, I tell myself.

But Weston is hurting because of this man. The whole family is hurting.

Maybe I can't let it go. Some people just need a shake.

"It's hairy because *you* make it that way," I point out before I can think better of it. "This whole situation sucks for you. I get that. But you'd better get a grip on yourself already."

He pulls a cigarette from the pack. "You're young, honey. Talk to me in thirty years."

My blood pressure leaps up. *God*, how I hate men who talk down to women. "First of all, I'm *not* your honey. And there are worse things in life than divorce."

"Sure." He flicks a lighter. "You probably know all about heart-break and disappointment at the tender age of twenty."

"Hey!" Now my anger is driving this bus. "I only *look* young. Three years ago my only parent was driving my dog to the vet, when they both died in a car crash."

Mr. Griggs jerks backward, like he's been slapped. "Jesus Christ. That's terrible."

"Yeah, I know. But don't feel sorry for me. I don't need your pity. But for the love of God, stop giving your kids so much drama. You're not *dead*." I grab the cigarette out of his hand and throw it into the snow. "Not yet, anyway. So stop throwing yourself a damn funeral."

He drops his head. "Shit."

"Just stop," I repeat, because I'm on a roll, and some people can't take a clue until you shove it in their faces. "Get a goddamn hobby.

Get a dog. Join Tinder and find some action. But stop wallowing in self-pity. It's *not* a good look on you."

That's when the slow clap starts. I whirl around and find Weston standing in the snow beyond the circle of light from the porch. His brother is with him, too, and Stevie also starts to clap.

Oh boy. I really didn't mean to lose my temper like that. My face heats like a flame as the Griggs boys finish their ironic applause.

"I'm sorry," I blurt out. "It's none of my business."

"He did welcome you to the family," Stevie says darkly. "That would freak out any girl."

Weston laughs, and the sound is joyous instead of bitter. "It would, right?"

He and his brother look at each other and then laugh so hard that Stevie doubles over.

I edge away from my host—the man I've just insulted. And I step off the porch.

Weston reaches for my hand, and squeezes it. "Well done, Abbi girl. It needed to be said."

Mr. Griggs wouldn't agree, I bet. He stomps past us and heads for the parking lot.

———

Weston drives us home, his father stewing in the passenger seat.

I'm such an idiot. Weston invited me home with him because he wanted his dad to lighten up for Christmas. But I wrecked it. Now the man will probably avoid me, which means he'll avoid his sons too.

Nice going, Abbi. Great work.

It's deathly quiet in the car until Weston turns on the radio. Naturally there's nothing but Christmas music playing. Weston turns it up, as if he could drown out his father's bad humor with a pop star's rendition of "White Christmas."

"I like you," Stevie says suddenly. He uses a low voice, and I don't think anyone can hear him but me.

"Thanks," I grunt, wondering whether Stevie is going to be creepy. I don't get that vibe from him. Still, it's an odd thing to say.

"I like you for him," he clarifies quietly. "He needs a feisty one. Not all those easy women he takes to bed."

This comment I ignore. I don't want to hear about the women Weston takes to bed. I'm jealous, to be honest.

"If only you were real," he says.

That gets my attention. "What is that supposed to mean?"

"Please," Stevie whispers. "You're not really his girlfriend. I'm not stupid. But it's a shame."

"Careful," I say. "Or you'll get one of my speeches, too."

Stevie snickers. "See? I'm a big fan."

"Dude," Weston says from up front. "Are you seriously giving Abbi a hard time?"

"Nope," Stevie says, shaking his head. "Just telling her how it is."

He's right of course. It's hard to fault him for speaking the truth.

I do anyway.

————

An hour later, the awkward moment finally arrives—the lights are off. Weston and I are lying side by side in a double bed. Not a queen size. Not a king. Nope. Just me and the hottest man on campus in a double. Lying on our backs. Staring at the ceiling.

I thought this would be awkward because our charade has trapped us here within smooching distance of each other. I never anticipated it would be awkward for an entirely different reason— that I just told his father off in front of God and everyone.

"Look," I say. "I just want to apologize for making tonight more uncomfortable for you. I failed at my job."

"What? No," Weston insists. "You did fine. Better than fine. You told my dad what he needed to hear. We've all tried. But maybe he needed to hear it from an outsider."

"But my job was to lighten him up for Christmas Eve and Christmas."

"Nah, my idea was dumb. I thought I could turn back time. My dad used to love Christmas. He used to make waffles on Christmas Eve morning, with all the toppings. He used to get a Bûche de Noël from the bakery, and hide little presents on the tree. This year there's not even a Christmas tree in this house. It's like he's given up."

"I'm sorry," I say softly.

"Don't be. You weren't wrong about him. You told him how it is."

"I sure did. Loudly."

We both chuckle.

Beneath the covers, Weston uses his toe to nudge my toe. "Just so you know, I got my fake girlfriend a Christmas present. It's kind of a joke, though."

My heart skips a beat. "Just so you know, I got my fake boyfriend a present, too. Also a bit of a joke."

"What did you get me?" he asks immediately.

"You think I'd just *tell* my fake boyfriend his gift before Christmas? Think again."

We laugh, and suddenly this isn't so awkward. Because something unexpected has happened between us—we really became friends. That's how it goes when two people allow each other to see all the dark shadows of their lives. They bond.

And I like it. I need friends. Who doesn't need friends?

"Goodnight, Abbi," he says with a yawn.

I relax against the pillow as the awkwardness between us seeps away for good. It's comfortable here in bed with Weston. He's warm and cozy and he smells like woodsy goodness. "Goodnight, Westie."

There's a soft snort from his side of the bed. And then peace.

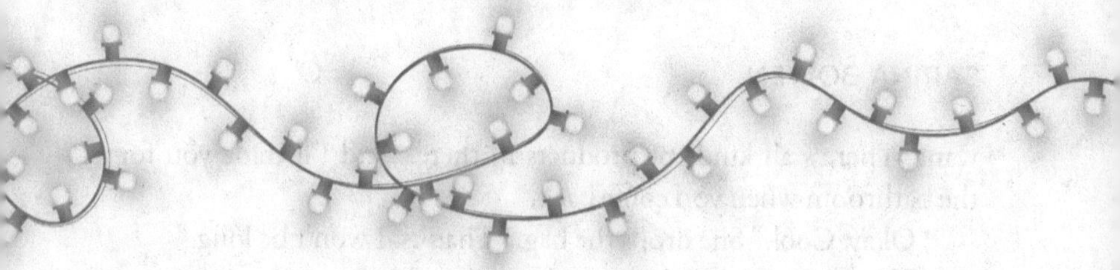

CHAPTER 10
A WHOLE LOT MESSIER

WESTON

Somehow, I don't open my eyes for almost twelve hours. When I finally wake up, it's only because I hear the bed creak as Abbi slides out of it.

My eyes fly open, and there's an awful lot of daylight in the room. "Holy God. What time is it?"

"Eleven!" Abbi gasps. "Can you believe it?"

"Wow. I guess we needed that." I roll over onto my belly and squint at her. She's wearing a cute plaid bathrobe over her PJs, and she has pillow creases on her sweet face.

But as I examine her, she grabs for her crazy hair and yelps. "Don't look. I'm a disaster."

I chuckle against the pillow. "Careful, Abbi. Don't let Stevie hear you say that. If you were mine, I'd have seen you a *whole* lot messier."

Her face goes instantly pink, and I realize that statement sounded all hot and bothered. Which is how I feel, suddenly. It's hard not to wonder what she'd look like in my bed after sex. Especially when I'm lying in this bed, my morning wood against the mattress. Oops.

"Mind if I take a shower?" she asks, grabbing her duffel bag off the floor.

"You go ahead," I say quickly. "I put a clean towel on the shower bar for you. The pink one. And you can leave your bag here if you want. There's all kinds of products in there. And I'll trade you for the bathroom when you come back."

"Okay. Cool." She drops the bag. "Thanks. I won't be long."

"Take your time. Make yourself comfortable."

She leaves the room and I sink back into the pillow. I can't believe I slept a whole night in this bed with hot Abbi. I'm lucky my subconscious didn't give me some kind of freaky sex dream, where I'd wake up humping her leg like a randy Golden Retriever.

For that, I think I deserve some coffee.

———

When Abbi returns in her bathrobe with a towel on her head, I hustle to shower and shave. She actually waits for me to take my turn, instead of going downstairs. I think she's nervous about facing my father alone.

But I know my dad. Nobody will be more embarrassed than he will over that shit he pulled last night. He'll be nothing but polite to her today.

The minute we hit the kitchen, I know I'm right. Dad puts down his newspaper and springs off his stool. "Coffee? Did everyone sleep well?"

"So well," Abbi says politely as I pull out a counter stool for her. "I haven't slept so late in ages. Maybe ever."

"Abbi works two jobs and goes to school full time," I point out. I know I'm laying it on awfully thick. But I'm proud of her, which is weird, because we haven't known each other very long. My fake girl-friend is fierce. Her life isn't easy, and I admire her in so many ways.

"Well, you're on vacation now," my father says smoothly. He pours two cups of coffee and slides them onto the counter, along with a jug of milk.

And then? He opens up the waffle iron and tips a ladle of batter in. "We've got bacon and sausage in the warming drawer," he says. "And sliced strawberries, maple syrup, and whipped cream."

"Wow," I say slowly. That's what he used to make on Christmas Eve. Back in the Before Times. "Thanks, Dad."

"No problem." He flashes me a quick smile, but it's gone in an instant. "In case you're curious, I already called your sister to apologize. She's still mad, though."

When he turns his back, Abbi and I exchange a surreptitious glance. Of course Lauren is still mad.

"I told her it was probably a good time to ask for a wedding gift. So she did, although it wasn't what I was expecting."

"Okay, I'll bite. What did she ask for?"

His chuckle is dry. "She wants me to go to counseling."

Oh wow. "And?"

"I told her I'd go. To make her, uh, feel better."

"And maybe you as well?" I suggest.

He shrugs. "I guess we'll find out. I'm buying them some of their dishes too. Just as a backup plan."

Abbi giggles into her coffee mug. She drinks it black, I notice, and file that information away for later. A guy should know how his woman takes her coffee.

"Anyway," my dad continues. "I'm headed to the office for a couple hours." He pops a slice of strawberry into his mouth before setting the serving dish onto the counter in front of Abbi and me.

"Wait, you're working on Christmas *Eve*?" I ask.

"Westie," Abbi says gently. She lays a hand on top of mine, and her smooth fingers feel sweet against my skin. A prickle of awareness settles over me. I like her touching me. I like it a lot. "That's what a man says when he isn't quite done with his Christmas shopping."

My dad chuckles. "She's a quick one, Weston. Nothing gets by Abbi. Remember that."

"Oh, I will," I say, playing along. I lift my hand from under hers, and then wrap my arm around her instead, because I'm Mr. Smooth.

She leans against me, also playing along. And doesn't *that* feel nice.

Uh-oh. It feels a little too nice. My dick is confused now. Little Mr. Smooth doesn't know that this is just a charade. He did not get the memo.

Mayday. I've got another day and night to be this close to Abbi. She smells like flowers and coffee and good times. By bedtime, I'll probably have to ice down my dick if this keeps up.

Luckily, the waffle iron beeps, and I let go of Abbi to fetch some plates and silverware.

"That smells amazing," Abbi says as my dad opens the waffle iron. "Mmm!"

If she moans while she eats, I'm a dead man. Quick—I need to find us an activity for the day. Something that won't involve us cuddled up on a couch watching a movie together. I need more separation than that.

I need to cool the fuck down.

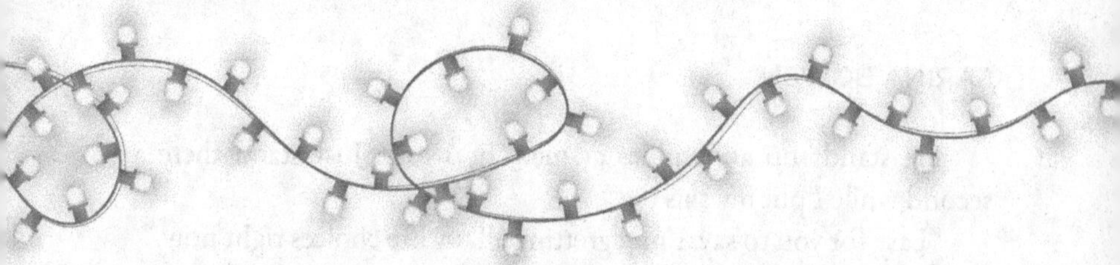

CHAPTER 11
MERRY CHRISTMAS, ABBI

ABBI

"Okay, Abbi. Now we're going to put these boots into the bindings."

We're standing outside in the snow together. It's a crisp, sunny day, and I'm decked out in borrowed cross-country ski gear. Weston had asked me if I wanted to try it. In a moment of foolish bravery, I said yes.

This could go poorly. But what does it matter, right? There's nobody around to see me fall.

Except for the hottest guy at Moo U.

He kneels down in the snow. We're wearing matching LL Bean snow pants from the Griggs family stash. "Put your toe right here." Weston lifts one of my boots in gentle hands and guides it onto a cross-country ski.

But naturally, I begin to wobble. And my choices are to either grab Weston's head or fall over in the snow.

I choose Weston's head. He chuckles as I put him in some kind of new wrestling hold in order to remain vertical. But he carries on, setting my other foot into the other ski, while I cling to him like a doofus.

"You said this was easy," I accuse, finally letting go of his head. I can't help but notice how soft his hair is. I want to sift my fingers through it.

He stands up and smiles at me. "It *is* easy. Just stand there a second while I put my skis on."

"Easy for you to say. I'm regretting all my life choices right now."

Weston had asked me whether I wanted to ice skate—which I can do, but not as well as he can—or try cross country. Foolishly, I picked this. And now there are slidey boards stuck to the bottom of my feet.

"Almost there," he says, stepping effortlessly into his own skis. Then he hands me a set of poles with straps on them. "Put your whole wrist through that loop—upward—and then grab the pole."

"Got it. Thanks. If I fall down and break something, we can use these to drag my body back to the house."

Weston cracks up. "C'mon, Abbi. You got this. We're just going to shuffle forward. The track is just over there." He points with a pole toward the trees. "Follow me." Then he scoots off in that direction.

I try to mimic his stride, with each pole alternating sides with my skis. And it's...doable, I guess. I'm shuffling along behind him with tiny little strides, taking care not to fall down.

When we reach the tree line, I see the track. It's a flattened path in the snow. And off to the side there's a set of two grooves through the snow, side by side. "Is that where we put our skis?"

"Yup," he says. "You don't even have to steer. Let the track do the work. Go on. Try it."

Gingerly, I slide in, one awkward ski at a time. When Weston leads me forward again, though, it's definitely easier. I scoot each ski forward in a rhythm, poling with my hands to propel me along.

"Yessss!" he shouts. "That's it!"

I move forward on the perfect white snow, pine trees on either side of me. There's a brilliant blue sky overhead. "Okay, this is almost fun."

"Almost?" he snickers.

"Well, I'm slow," I admit. "I could probably walk faster than I'm skiing right now."

"With all of five minutes' experience, I really would have expected better from you."

"I know, right?"

He leaves the track and glides up next to me on the path. "Do me a favor and try to ski like a gorilla."

Still striding, I throw him a quick glance. "Why? So you can blackmail me with the pictures later?"

"Thanks for that brilliant idea, but all I was trying to do was lengthen your stride."

"Show me," I demand, stopping midstride.

"Sure thing. Look. I'm bending my knees a little bit, reaching my arms out, my upper body tilted forward. And..." He starts to move. "Hoo hoo hoo hee hee," he says, pursing his lips like a gorilla.

I can't help it. I giggle just like his female fan club at the Biscuit after a game.

"Hoo hoo hoo," he says, striding forward. And—fine—I can see how the posture assists his skiing. He circles back, the gorilla noises growing louder. He doesn't even stop when a man skis by him with a tiny kid in a pack on his back.

Yup. I'm a little more in love with him than I was already. Any hot guy who will voluntarily humiliate himself to teach you to ski has got to be a keeper.

"Your turn." He stands up straight and smiles at me.

"All right," I agree. "But only because you're a really good sport."

"Nah," he says. "That title goes to you this weekend. Now let's see it. Show me some gorilla, Abbi."

I skip the noises. But I lean forward and start skiing again.

"Yeah! There you go." He glides forward and ignores the track in favor of skiing next to me. We press on as the path turns around the lake. I can see skaters out in the center, and steam rising from the little metal chimneys on several of the ice fishing huts.

"You do any fishing?"

"Nope," he says. "Too boring. Ice fishing is for old guys with beer guts. They just sit in there and drink all day."

We ski side by side, and I start to get the hang of it. But it's work. I'm puffing along now, and a light breeze sends snow glittering from the pine boughs down onto the path. "How long is this trail, anyway?"

"Oh, not long. About ten miles."

"Omigod," I squeak, and he laughs.

"It's two miles, tops, Abbster. I'm just teasing you. And we can turn around anytime you want."

"Good to know."

"Of course, then we'll go skating," he says.

"Uh-oh."

"You'll love it. I'll bring hot chocolate."

"Oooh. Okay!"

He laughs.

———

It's a really good day.

No, it's a *great* day. We ski, we skate, and we hang out in the sunshine drinking cocoa. I feel like I'm on a vacation from my real life. There are no shifts at the bar, and there's no homework.

There's no grabby step-stepbrother.

That night's dinner is another charcuterie fest in front of the fire, this one featuring—alongside the cheese—slices of ham and vegetables and dip.

"This is really decadent," I gush, swirling a little glass of red wine that Weston has poured for me. I help myself to another French olive. I feel fat and happy staring into the fire.

"Save room for dessert," Weston's dad says. "I got a Bûche de Noël. But here's a question—do you want to do presents tonight, or tomorrow morning? I'm happy to adhere to tradition, but you all seem to enjoy sleeping in."

"We're all here now, right?" Stevie says. "Let's do it."

"Sure, Dad," Weston agrees, patting his stomach. "I need a spacer before dessert, anyway." He pushes up, off the couch. "Let me get my stash of gifts."

I get up too, retrieving a shopping bag that I'd hidden in the mud room.

Weston returns a couple of minutes later with three gifts: one for his dad, one for his brother, and a big squishy one with a gift tag in the shape of a polar bear. It says *Abbi* on it in red marker, with a smiley face.

And I know my reaction is dumb, because presents don't really matter. I'd give up presents forever if I could spend one more day with my mom. But just seeing my name in Weston's cheerful scrawl does something to me anyway. It gives me an unexpected zap of optimism. It reminds me that life can still deliver surprises when you least expect them.

Weston sits beside me and drapes an arm around my shoulders. "Merry Christmas, Abbster," he murmurs. "Such as it is."

It *is* merry, though. I could be sitting alone in my apartment right now, shivering under the comforter because my landlady won't turn up the heat. But I'm here in front of this crackling fire with a cute guy who likes polar bear gift tags.

Life really could be worse.

Mr. Griggs has given each of his sons a pair of very pricey headphones for Christmas, and they are well-received. And both Weston and Stevie produce thoughtful presents for their dad, too, of the manly variety. Weston gives Mickey a leather fireproof glove for tending that wood stove we're sitting in front of. "So you can stop singeing off your arm hair," my fake boyfriend explains.

And Steve gives him a set of drafting pens from Japan. "It's what all the new kids are using," he says. "You might like them, old man."

Mickey smiles indulgently and gives his son a one-armed man hug.

Then the big moment arrives. I place my carefully wrapped gift in Weston's lap. "This is for you, Westie. I hope you like them."

"I'm sure I will, baby. You know me so well."

Across from us, Stevie actually rolls his eyes.

Damn Stevie. I've only got a few hours left of this holiday visit to convince him.

Meanwhile, Weston tears the paper off his gift like, well, an overgrown kid on Christmas Eve. And when he lifts the lid, he chuckles. "Cute, honey." He lifts a pair of super soft black flannel sleep pants from the box. They're printed with an adorable white dog in profile, who's wearing a cheery red collar.

"Those are supposed to be West Highland Terriers," I explain. "But most people call them—"

"Westies," he says with a laugh. "Aren't you clever?"

Smiling, he drops the flannel in his lap. And then our eyes meet, and we both seem to hesitate at the same time, because couples don't just shake hands when they're exchanging gifts. There's often a thank-you kiss.

And now there's a frozen look in Weston's eyes. Then he seems to shake off his hesitation. He moves, opening his arms.

Now, in my defense, I'm trying to be a better fake girlfriend today than I managed to be yesterday. So I open my arms, too, rotating toward him...

But I'm a beat late, and Weston is already in motion. The result is much more like a collision than a hug and kiss. My lips hit his throat as his face sideswipes my forehead. And I elbow his chest and he sort of crunches me against his collarbone.

At least my yelp of pain is buried in his clavicle. That's the only saving grace to The World's Most Awkward Hug Ever.

"Sorry," we both murmur in unison, pulling back, matching sheepish expressions on both our faces.

I hear a painful snort and turn to see Stevie, who's *dying* of laughter. His face is red and his body is shaking.

Weston, also red faced, puts my gift in my lap. "Open this. I've been dying to know what you'll think." He winks at me, like we're sharing a joke. "It could really go either way."

"Okay!" I say, grateful for the distraction. I remove the polar bear and set it beside me. I don't even know why I like it so much. Then I rip the paper off what turns out to be a hunter green Moo U hockey zip-up sweatshirt with a *wonderful* piled fleece interior. "Ooh! Cozy," I say. I've seen these before but they're spendy, so I don't own one.

"Don't miss the back," Weston says with a sly grin.

I flip over the shirt. And there it says GRIGGS in block letters right over his jersey number.

I laugh. Loudly. "So I'm supposed to parade around campus with your name on the back of my shirt?"

"Wouldn't that be an honor?" Stevie asks, his voice a challenge. "I mean—rumor has it that you've taken the most eligible bachelor in Burlington off the market. Unless I'm wrong about that?"

"Oh, you're right," I say quickly. "But this isn't 1965. These days a girl likes to stake her claim with a tattoo. I mean, it doesn't really say *love* unless you bleed for it, am I right?"

Weston and his dad both crack up. Mr. Griggs gets up, pulls on his new fireproof glove, and feeds a log to the fire.

And that reminds me. "I have something for you, Mickey."

"You do?" He straightens up, a look of surprise on his face.

"Absolutely. It's right here." I pull out my other wrapped gift. "My mother was big on hostess gifts. She never stopped by anyone's house without a complete set of dishtowels, or a handmade candle." I'm babbling now, because I can't seem to shut up when I'm talking to Mr. Griggs. "So I wanted to bring you a thank-you gift, and the company where I did my internship makes nice stuff." I hand over a wrapped present. "It's just a little thing."

Mickey gives me a funny smile and rips off the paper to find a pair of wool flannel slippers inside. "Thank you, Abbi. These are great."

He's not wrong. They're charcoal gray with blue stitching, because Vermont Tartan makes snazzy things, especially for the forty and older set. "I'm glad you like them. It's a nice local company, and I hope they're around forever."

"Well..." He sets the slippers down on the floor and slips his feet right into them. "As it happens, I have a little gift for you, too."

"Oh, you didn't have to do that." I feel my face heat, because I never meant to put him in this position. And now I'm bracing myself for whatever emergency thing he's just thought of to hand me.

"I know," he says. "But this is for you, because I bet you could use it." From beside his chair he pulls a shiny gift bag, with tissue paper sticking up from the top. He stands and hands it to me.

To my surprise, there's a gift card tied to the handle reading *Abbi*.

"Oh," I say stupidly. "Wow."

"Go on," he says quietly. "Open it."

Nervously, I pluck the tissue paper off the top. And when I reach inside, my hand collides with buttery leather. I pull out a gorgeous new satchel, large enough for a laptop computer. It's cut in a curvy, feminine style, in cognac leather.

I don't know if I've ever held such a gorgeous bag. And when I flip open the top, there's even a padded laptop pocket inside. "This is...wow." I babble. "So *fancy*. It even has that new bag smell."

He gives a startled chuckle.

"Way to upstage me, Dad," Weston jokes.

"Well, Abbi," his father says. "I gave one of these to my daughter the year she graduated from college. She needed an upgrade from her book bag, to look more professional. And I thought you could use one, too. Especially..." He clears his throat. "If you don't have a parent handy who can give you one."

"Oh," I say, looking up suddenly. And he's watching me with a father's compassion in his eyes. "Thank you," I say, but I choke on the words. It's such a generous thing to do, and for such a lovely reason. And—oh shit. Tears have sprung into my eyes.

I look back down at this gorgeous piece of craftsmanship and try to hold it together. But my next breath comes out as a sob. Because it's Christmas. And I'm graduating this spring. And my mom won't be there to congratulate me at all.

"Oh nooo!" Weston croons. He drops an arm around my shoulders, and this time he manages to pull me into a hug without violence. "You broke my girlfriend on *Christmas*. Quick! Someone put on a funny movie."

I laugh and cry at the same time, and Weston pats my back.

"Th-thank you," I stammer at Mr. Griggs when I'm able. "It's just gorgeous."

"You're welcome," he says, looking a little uncomfortable at the mess he's created of me. He gets up to find a box of tissues, which I need, badly.

And then Stevie puts on *Home Alone 2*, and we all watch it.

Somehow, I end the evening smiling.

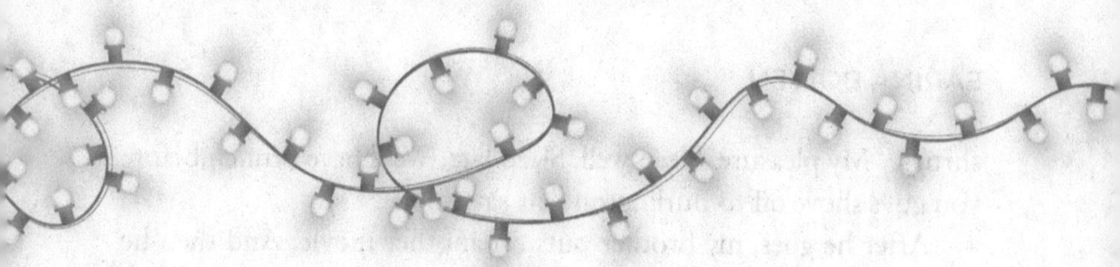

CHAPTER 12
DID SHE JUST MOAN MY NAME?

WESTON

I look around the living room as the movie winds down. We've all had cake, and we're half-dozing in front of the TV.

It's hard to believe, but Dad saved Christmas just before the buzzer. It's not that I really needed the Christmas Eve waffles or the cake shaped like a log. I'm a big boy. But it's nice to see him trying to find joy again.

Abbi gets the assist, too. She kicked Dad's ass last night and it made all the difference. He's a new man today. A very contrite one.

My fake girlfriend is quiet now, tucked up beside me on the couch, near enough that I can smell her shampoo. She's smiling, too. Whenever Macaulay Culkin pulls off another feat, she laughs.

I already knew Abbi was resilient. I knew she was alone in the world. But I didn't really understand how that must feel until I watched her lose it over a gift from my dad.

It's humbling to think about how easy I've really had it. Sure, my parents had an ugly divorce. But even that drama will be old news eventually.

My gaze wanders over to my father, who's yawning as the credits roll. "I'm going to bed, boys. And Abbi. Happy Christmas."

"Happy Christmas, Dad. Thanks for everything tonight."

My brother and Abbi chime in with the same, and Dad just

shrugs. "My pleasure. Sleep well. Sleep late. We'll have brunch before you guys shove off to Burlington," he says to me.

After he goes, my brother puts on another movie. And then he nods off.

I poke Abbi's knee gently to get her attention. And then I point at Steve, who looks particularly stupid with his mouth hanging open.

Abbi squints at him. And then she leans in so close to me that I feel her silky hair tickle my ear. "He's faking," she barely whispers.

What? I glance toward Stevie again, but I can't really tell.

"Why?" I mouth.

"To spy on us," she whispers.

I chuckle, because that is definitely something Stevie would do. Well, I'm not going to give him the satisfaction. "Stevie," I bark.

His eyes open with exaggerated stubbornness. "Whoops, I guess I nodded off."

Yeah, he was totally faking it. "We're going up to bed," I say with a sleazy wink. "Don't hurry to follow us."

Stevie reaches for the remote control and clicks off the TV. "Actually, I should head to bed too. It's important to get enough sleep."

Abbi gives me a pointed look that asks, *Can you believe this bullshit?*

We all get up. Abbi carries our glasses to the kitchen, and Stevie checks the fireplace to be sure it's sealed up tightly. I turn out the lights. Then we all walk upstairs in a line. "Sleep tight," Stevie says outside of the bunk room. Then he gives me a grin and goes inside.

Okay, so now this is back to being awkward as fuck. Abbi and I find ourselves in close quarters a moment later, whispering to each other. And we both know Steve is right on the other side of the wall.

"He's so smug!" she whispers. "I don't like to lose a bet."

"Easy, killer." I put my hands on her shoulders and chuckle. "It was never a fair fight. This doesn't reflect badly on your girlfriend skills. It's all on me."

"Pfft," she says. "*It's not you, it's me.* Girls love hearing that."

I crack up, because Abbi is hilarious. And while I'm distracted, she darts away to claim the bathroom before either Stevie or I can get to it.

When I go out into the hall, he's standing outside the bathroom door, arms crossed, waiting. "Your so-called girlfriend is hogging the bathroom."

"My *girlfriend*," I say with exaggeration, and no small amount of loyalty, "can take her time."

Stevie just smiles. "She's the best, Weston. I can see why you're actually tempted."

I open my mouth and then close it again. Because I *am* tempted. But I can't discuss this with my brother, because I have a ruse to maintain.

So I leave him there and head downstairs to use my dad's bathroom instead.

Fifteen minutes later, I'm wearing my brand new Westie pajama pants, and lying carefully on my side of the bed, as Abbi slides in beside me. The bed wiggles a little as she arranges herself at as polite a distance as she can manage in this small space.

I'm wide awake, and overly conscious of how close we are together. What would Abbi do if I rolled over and kissed her?

She'd kiss me back, that's what. I know this on a gut level. But I'm still not going to do it. I invited her here as friends. And I promised her that I would be a gentleman. And it's not fair to change the rules just because I'm attracted to her.

The silence seems really loud. I can tell Abbi is lying there, much like I am, too aware of the confined space to be restful.

"Thank you for the kickass pants," I say. "They're pretty awesome." *And so are you*, I want to add.

"Thank you for the fuzzy, yet slightly egotistical sweatshirt," she whispers.

I chuckle into the darkness. "They all have player numbers on the back, you realize. I didn't invent that."

"Of course you chose your own number, though," she says in a teasing whisper.

"Well, sure," I argue. "If you're going to have some guy's name on your back, why not mine?"

"I'm surprised it wasn't sold out already," she says with a giggle.

"They went fast," I insist. "That's what I'm telling myself anyway."

"Uh-huh. I'm going to wear it tomorrow in front of Stevie. This isn't over. I don't accept defeat easily."

"Yeah, I'm getting that." I'm realizing that it only took a couple of minutes for the awkwardness to blow over. Abbi *is* the best. She makes everything fun.

"He's right on the other side of this wall, right?" she whispers.

"Yup."

"I have an idea. Did you see *When Harry Met Sally?*"

"Yeah, why?"

"The diner scene."

I'm just processing this as Abbi wiggles a little. The bed responds with a creak. Then she *moans*. "Ohhh. Oh, *Weston*."

Holy... All my nerves stand at attention. Did she just *moan my name?*

She shifts again, and the bed begins to creak in a slow, rhythmic way. She must have braced a toe on the floor. "Mmmmm..." She sighs. Loudly.

And, wow, it's very convincing. I'm convinced. My dick is also convinced. Suddenly he's up and at 'em, wondering when the party starts.

"Oh *Weston*," Abbi croons. Then she elbows me.

"*What?*" I hiss as the bed continues its erotic rhythm.

"A little help, here," she hisses back.

Oh I'd LOVE to help! my dick screams.

What is happening? My brain and my body are on opposite tracks. On the one hand, I'm mildly amused that Abbi is trying to fake out Stevie with sex noises. It'll never work.

But on the other hand, my body is on board this train. As the bed rocks gently I have no trouble at all imaging myself as the conductor.

I swallow roughly. "You realize you have to keep this up for a really long time, right? This is only a believable scenario if I last half the night."

"Oh, *yes* baby." Abbi moans, before suddenly clamping a hand over her mouth to stifle a laugh. She's amused. She finds this whole thing funny.

I'm just turned on. This is torture.

And then she moves a little closer to me, and my senses all go haywire. But it turns out she's just trying to say something privately. "Jeez, Weston. Even you must be capable of a Christmas quickie. Just play along." Then she increases the tempo of the bed's movements. "Yessss...." she cries out. "Faster."

Then she elbows me again.

Shit.

It's risky to play this game. If I say anything, she'll be able to hear how turned on I really am. I clear my throat. And then I clench my teeth and think about hockey drills. "Okay, yes!" I say woodenly.

"Is that the best you can do?" She hisses. "Really? You sound like you're watching a game on TV. I suddenly feel sorry for all those women at the Biscuit."

Wait, what? Is she questioning my *skills?* "Oh *hell*," I grunt. "You did not just say that."

"Yes, *yes*," she moans in answer. "Let me hear it, baby."

And now it's me who's stifling a laugh. Abbi is fearless, as well as hot. She pushes all my buttons.

"*Weston*," she moans, and then covers her mouth. I can feel her shaking with laughter.

Time to step up, I guess. "What, baby?" I pant. "You need more? I got more."

"*Harder*," she manages to yell, but she's clearly laughing over there.

I roll over and brace a foot on the floor. "Oh *yeah*," I call, nudging the rocking bed into a gallop. "Like that?"

"Yes! Yes!" she moans. "Just. Like. *That...*"

Oh God. My dick is trapped against the mattress. There's some friction from the motion of the bed, and Abbi's breathy moans in my ear. I'm dying, here. "Hurry, baby," I groan.

And I'm not kidding. This torture has to stop. I move the bed even more, until the headboard smacks the wall on every stroke.

"*Westonnnn!*" she shouts.

And it's so, so easy to picture the real thing—Abbi flushed and climaxing beneath me as I strain against her soft, supple body... "Uhnnngh," I moan, because I'm so worked up. And then I flop down onto the mattress one last time and go absolutely still, which is a necessity. If I move any more I'm going to blow just from listening to Abbi fake it.

I force air into my lungs as the room goes still.

There's no more sound from the other side of the bed, either. I'm expecting a joke, or maybe a compliment on my expert acting skills.

But all I can hear is Abbi's rapid breathing.

And then I push my face into the pillow and smile. Because I think Abbi got a little more than she'd bargained for, too. I hope it keeps her awake. It's only fair.

It's going to be hours before this crowbar in my new pajama pants goes away. She might as well suffer, too.

Happy Christmas indeed.

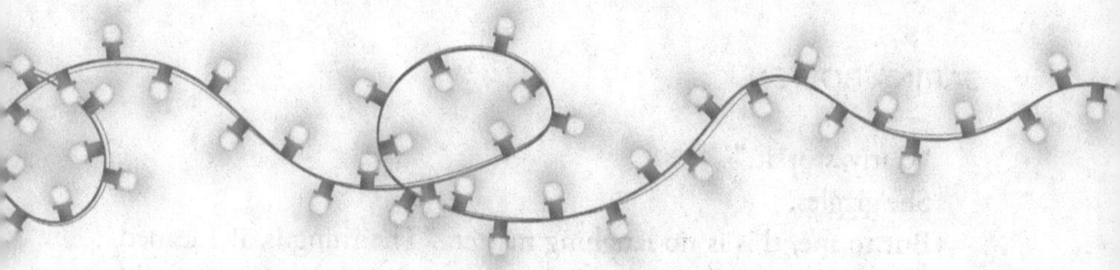

CHAPTER 13
FOUR TIMES MORE AWKWARD

ABBI

"And then what happened?" Carly demands.

"Then his brother believed us," I say, rolling another fork and knife into a napkin. "At least I think he did. How could he not?"

"No—forget the brother." Carly tosses a silverware roll into the bin and blinks at me. "Please tell me this story has a *very* happy ending. Tell me you both turned to one another and started ripping each other's clothes off."

"Nope. We went to sleep." Eventually. The truth is that I faked sleep for a good long time. After hearing Weston moan from close range, I was too stirred up to sleep.

"Abbi!" she shrieks. "Why the hell didn't you have *actual* sex?"

I shrug. "He didn't touch me. He was a perfect gentleman. I don't think he likes me that way."

She blinks. "I do not *believe* this. First of all, does it *really* matter? Anyone who simulates sex for five minutes loudly, with great enthusiasm, is going to be into it. He's a horny college guy."

"But—"

"If you'd just leaned over and kissed him, you could have spent the next twelve hours in pound town. You whiffed it! Someone lobbed you a nice easy pitch, and you let it fly right by. I'm *so* disappointed!"

"Carly, stop it."

She giggles.

But to me, this is no laughing matter. "The thing is, if I leaned over and kissed him, and he really *really* wasn't into it, then I would have made a super awkward evening four times more awkward than it already was."

"Details." She rolls her eyes. "I'm just sad for you and your vagina."

"I'll admit that part of my body isn't really speaking to me right now."

She cracks up.

"But I still don't really have any regrets. Because we're *friends*. Good friends. And that's important."

"I guess." She lets out a dramatic sigh. "But, lordy. One of us should ride that bull before we graduate. We're due for some good times, don't you think?"

"Not sure it works that way," I mumble. Good times are nice, but they don't pay the rent. I have to keep my head down and focus on what's important. Like graduating and finding a real job.

Weston got me through another holiday season without my mom, and I'll always be grateful. But Weston is not boyfriend material. And there's no other guy around here that's half as interesting to me. So I don't see the point of being sad about it.

Although—and I'm not about to confess this to Carly—I've worn my snuggly team sweatshirt, with his jersey number on the back, two mornings in a row. If anyone asked me why I like it so much, I'd point out that the sweatshirt is warm, and my apartment is cold.

But my crush on Weston is stronger than ever now. Becoming friends only made him more attractive to me. He's a good man. I'm lucky to know him. Even if I'd prefer to know him naked.

"Ladies, I have a job for you." Carly and I both look up to find Kippy—the lazy manager—standing over us with a stack of fliers.

"We're doing our job right now," Carly points out. She says this in a cheerful voice, but I can hear the underlying snark that's often there when Carly speaks to Kippy. He's such a tool.

"Yeah, but I need you two to pin these up all over campus," he says. "New Year's Eve is only a few days away. I'll need you both to work late that night, obviously. And these need to be up all over campus by tomorrow morning. You can do it together after your shift."

"After our shift," she repeats. "At eleven?"

"Sure," he says, dropping the flyers onto the table. "Thanks."

Our eyes meet after he walks away. "That lazy motherf—" She bites back the rest. "He knows we're not going to complain."

"It's too close," I point out. Both Carly and I are coming up on our anniversary bonus. "That's why he asked us."

She nods, her eyes flashing. "He could probably ask me for a damn blow job at this point, and I'd do it."

"Carly!" I squeak. "Ew."

She giggles. "You should see your expression. Hilarious."

"I'm repulsed."

"I know! I wouldn't *really* do it," she says, grinning. "But getting this bonus is like a crusade for me, now. It's more than just fifteen hundred bucks. It's an investment of a year. I've earned it. I want it. And no weasel-faced manager is going to get in my way."

"Have you started counting down the days?"

"I'm going to. Tonight. Right after we hang flyers all over the campus. In the December cold. At midnight." She rolls her eyes. "At least the event looks fun." She grabs a flyer and holds it up so I can see.

The Biscuit's Raucous New Year's Eve: Featuring Live Music from The Hardwick Boys
Midnight countdown. Two-for-one wings 6p-9p. Join the party!

"Well, the tips will be great," I point out. "If people are drinking their faces off from nine until midnight."

"Yeah," she says with a sigh. "Wouldn't it be nice to go out on New Year's like a normal person, though?"

I shrug, because I don't even know who I'd go out with.

"Maybe Weston will come," Carly says, her eyes brightening.

"Maybe. The hockey team is on campus already. They don't get a long Christmas break."

"That's right," she hoots. "Your new boyfriend probably told you their schedule."

I roll my eyes. "Don't make me regret telling you that story."

"So table seventeen might be hopping on New Year's." Her smile is brilliant. "Has he called you since you guys got back?"

"No, but why would he?" I shrug.

Her smile goes dreamy. "Because he probably misses you. I bet he woke up the day after Christmas and thought about you. He probably wants to reenact your fake sex scene for real. I bet he's still thinking about it."

"That's not how my life works," I mutter.

"It should be," Carly says, tossing the last silverware roll into the bin.

"How fast do you think we can hang up twenty fliers after work?" I ask.

"Let's hang up ten and recycle the rest," she whispers.

"But if New Year's is a flop, we won't get good tips," I point out.

"Fine," she says, standing up to tie on her apron. "But it won't be a flop. I just know it."

Four nights later, I find out she's right.

There's a sweet spot to waitressing. When the place is dead, I get bored and make too little in tips. But when the place is slammed, the customers get crabby and I get stressed out. In the middle zone is where this job is really pretty great. When the stars align, you can have happy customers and fat tips as the hours fly by.

And then there's New Year's Eve. I've never seen the Biscuit so crowded. Every table is taken, and it's standing room only at the bar. Every available staff member is on shift, and I heard they started a new bouncer tonight just to double up on security.

The clientele is in a good mood, though, and The Hardwick Boys sound terrific. It's tricky to hear the patrons shout their orders over the music, but I don't even mind. The lively atmosphere and the holiday tips make it all worthwhile.

And—even better—table seventeen is chock-full of hockey players, including my favorite one. Every time I drop off a beer or even pass by, Weston gives me a warm smile.

I'm trying not to pay too much attention. I'm a busy girl. But I haven't been able to stop thinking about him all week. Spending time together as friends has only made him more appealing.

And sometimes? I think he's attracted to me, too. Am I crazy, or does he keep glancing at me? Or did I dream that?

I did. I dreamt it. Weston isn't shy. If he wanted me, he'd just say so.

"He keeps looking this way!" Carly shouts as we stand in front of the bar, waiting for various drinks to be made. "That boy wants you!"

"What boy?" I shout back.

Carly rolls her eyes. "You don't fool me. I'm not stupid. But I think you might be. Don't look, but he's watching you even as we speak."

I don't look, because I don't want to encourage her. I'm deep in the friend zone with Weston, and that's just the way it is. "He's just waiting for his beer!"

"Yeah? Well he looks especially *thirsty* tonight," Carly yells back. "Get on that." She winks as the bartender plunks her drinks down onto the bar. With a cheeky smile, she loads them onto her tray and goes.

"Hey," the bartender says, rapping his knuckles on the bar like he always does. "Abbi, I'm gonna need another minute on your order. But the new bouncer is asking for you."

"What? Table zero is not in my section." It's always somebody's job to keep the bouncer in free coffee and soda.

He shrugs. "He just came on shift, and asked for you by name. You're very popular tonight. Go take him this?" He sets a glass of Coke on the bar. "Tell him I couldn't add rum. House rules."

Oh good grief. Like I don't have enough to do already. But it would take longer to argue than to deliver the man's soda. I take the drink and head for the vestibule.

On my way, I notice that table fifteen's beers are empty. Better make this quick. I hurry toward the front door, where the bite of winter air chills my skin. "Here's your—"

The sentence dies in my throat when I see who the new bouncer is.

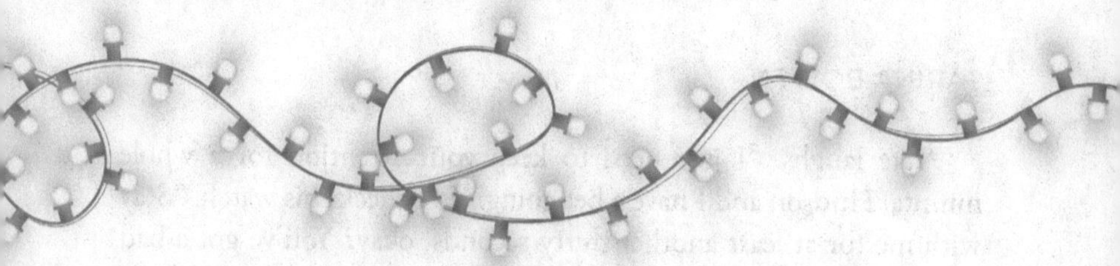

CHAPTER 14
NOT GETTING KICKED OUT
OF THE BISCUIT

WESTON

"And then Patrick wakes up in the bed with a shiner. And he's like, *Guys, guys? Who hit me?*" Tate laughs at his own storytelling. And then he punches me in the arm. "Weston. *Bro.* You dragged me out here tonight, but you're not a very attentive date. I'm starting to get offended. Did you even hear what I said?"

"Yup," I say, turning to face him. "Patrick. Black eye. Got it. Now we can tell him apart from Paxton."

Tate just shakes his head at me. "Well, at least your hearing still works. But eyes up here, big guy. If you keep staring at the hot waitress, she might decide the hockey team is creepy. The entire wait staff will start bringing us cold chicken and warm beer."

"Oh, save it." I sip from my excellent beer and fight the urge to look at Abbi again. I'm so busted.

"I don't think you realize how serious this problem could be," Tate insists. "If Abbi thinks you're a creeper, we'd have to find a new hangout. The pizza place, probably. All those carbs, man. We'll get fat and slow."

Vonne snickers. "I like pizza, Weston. I'll make the switch for you if it comes to that."

"What are you *talking* about?" I grumble. "We're not getting kicked out of the Biscuit."

Tate laughs. "I just need to keep your attention for a whole minute. Hudson and I have a bet going." He checks his watch. "Stay with me for at least another thirty seconds, okay? You've got a bad case of ADD. In your case, that stands for Abbi Deficit Disorder."

Everyone at the table laughs, while I roll my eyes. He's right, though. I'm sitting in this bar tonight just hoping to get a smile from Abbi. This crush I have on her just won't be silenced. It's actually worse now, in spite of the fact that she knows all my family's ugly secrets.

We could be so good together. And I think there's still a chance for us. We're not fake dating anymore, right? So if I put Mr. Smooth to work on Abbi, she won't feel cornered. She could just turn me down if she's not feeling it.

But she won't turn me down. I bet she'll invite me back to her place for New Year's Eve with Mr. Smooth. I've got big plans for us.

Sure, it's a little risky, because I want us to stay friends. And she already knows that Mr. Smooth is also Mr. Keep it Casual. But maybe that's just fine with her. Abbi is a busy girl who's juggling a lot in her life. She's going to graduate and move to another city.

But before she does, we could have some fun. Maybe I'm flattering myself, but I think she'd be open to this idea. I'm pretty good at reading people, which is why Mr. Smooth rarely hears the word *no*. One of my talents is knowing when a girl wants me to hit her upvote button.

There was a moment there over Christmas when we were on the same page. Several moments. And now it's eleven thirty on New Year's Eve. It's customary to get a kiss at midnight, right?

All I have to do is get a moment with an overworked waitress in a crowded room. No problemo.

Even as I have this thought, I look up to see Abbi streak by. She stops at a nearby table, clears away the empty beer glasses, nodding vigorously as she takes another order. But there's a new furrow between her eyebrows that's not usually there.

She looks worried.

Huh.

I watch her trot off to the bar. And then I watch her do a hundred other things in the space of ten minutes. She looks frantic.

And I know it's not because of the packed tables or the drink orders. Abbi doesn't get overwhelmed at work.

She keeps looking at the door to the bar, though. As if she expects Dracula himself to come through it. And I wish I knew why.

Finally, there's just a few minutes left until midnight. I'm rehearsing my speech in my head. *Listen, Abbi, there's something I need to ask you. And if you say no, I'll never bring it up again.*

This setup does, I realize, come perilously close to my personal rule of never hitting on people who are just trying to make it through a shift at work. But Abbi and I are friends. And I wouldn't go there if I didn't think she was into me.

I slide off my bar stool. "Well guys, wish me luck."

"Oh shit," Hudson says, his eyes big. "Don't crash and burn, man. We'll have to find another hangout. Hell—even if you knock her on her ass with your sex appeal, we're still in trouble."

"How do you figure?" I ask. I'm not really worried, but Hudson is entertaining.

"Dude, you're a heartbreaker," he says. "When you're done with her, she won't bring us beer."

"You know, I don't think that will happen this time."

"Oh God!" Tate moans. "I hope you all like pizza."

"And you guys call yourselves my friends? Here goes nothing."

The music has stopped, and all the bar TVs are tuned in to Times Square. The countdown is just a minute or so away. I dodge between tables, heading for the back, where I last saw Abbi.

Sure enough, she's standing in the shadows near the kitchen door, whispering with the other waitress, Carly. Their heads are bent together in conversation, and then Abbi gestures toward the door.

I hate to interrupt, but I'm a man on a mission. "Hey, ladies."

They both straighten quickly, as if caught out. "Do you need something, Weston?" Abbi asks.

"Oh yeah, he does," Carly snickers. Then she steps around me and makes herself scarce.

"Well, in a manner speaking," I say with a Mr. Smooth chuckle. "You got a minute?"

"For you, of course. But—and this is so embarrassing—I have to ask you a small favor. Another platter of wings kind of favor."

"No problem. Hit me up." I lean against the paneled wall and give her a smile. And then I let my gaze drift to Abbi's pretty mouth. I'd like to own it with mine.

But maybe I'm slipping, because it doesn't erase the crease of worry in Abbi's forehead. "Price is outside. My idiot step-stepbrother." She crosses her arms over her chest. "Remember him?"

"Unfortunately." This is not where I'd hoped to take the conversation. Behind me, the New Year's revelers begin counting down.

"He seems to have landed a job as a bouncer here. I should never have said that it's an easy job, or that the pay rate was so great." She lets out a heavy breath. "And now he's the guy who's supposed to walk me home? He just told me he was looking forward to it."

"Oh, shit," I breathe.

"Yeah." She crosses her arms. "If you're still here when I get off shift, could you, uh, reprise your award-winning role as my boyfriend? Just this once, as a little reminder."

"Of course," I say immediately. "Anytime, Abbi. Seriously. We're super good at this now, right? It's like rolling off a log."

She gives me a smile that's both sad and grateful. "I can't believe I have to deal with him *here*. The only reason I work here at all was to get away from him."

"I know. Shit. That's terrible."

"FIVE...FOUR...THREE...TWO...ONE...HAPPY NEW YEAR!" screams the entire bar.

Abbi gives her head a shake. "I'm sorry. There's probably somewhere else you'd rather be right now."

Not true. "Hey, Happy New Year. Fuck that guy."

"Fuck him," she says with conviction. "Fuck him sideways."

It's so cute that I can't help but laugh. And then I grab her into a quick, comforting hug.

It's not the New Year's moment that I'd hoped for. But it's pretty good nonetheless.

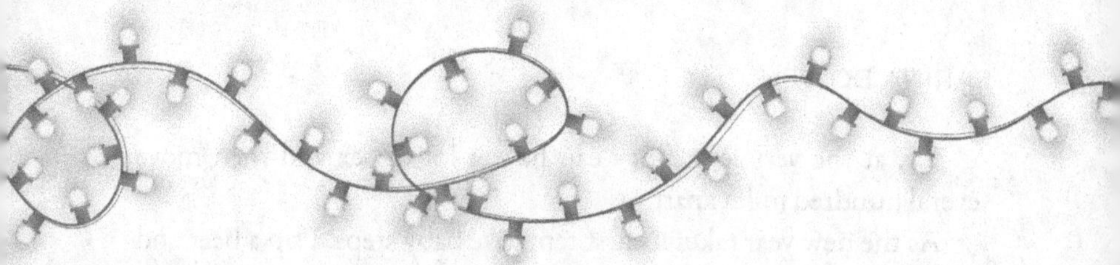

CHAPTER 15
SOMETHING CAME UP

WESTON

The boys all look at me expectantly when I get back to the table. "Well?" Tate demands. "How'd it go?"

"Something came up," I say.

"Was it your dick?" Hudson asks with a snicker, and I throw a napkin at him. "Stop, asshole. Abbi needs me to walk her home after her shift. There's a guy who's been bothering her."

"Ah," Tate says. "Could it be a ruse, maybe? Like—walk me home and take off my clothes?"

Sadly, I shake my head. "I've met this troublemaker already. Unfortunately, he's real."

"Bummer," Vonne says.

"But it's probably for the best," Tate points out. "We won't lose our table at the Biscuit."

"You have such little faith in me," I grumble. "I wasn't going to break Abbi's heart."

"That's what you always say, though," Cooper points out. "It's all sunshine until it's not."

I take a sip of my beer and ignore him. I wasn't planning on asking Abbi to marry me, for fuck's sake. I know better than to go down the path of forever. But two college students can have a fling without turning it into an epic story of love and betrayal.

Or, at the very least, they can have a lot of sex and then move several hundred miles apart.

As the new year takes its first tentative baby steps, I sip a beer and wait for Abbi's shift to end. One by one my teammates depart. Tate is the first to go. Then Lex, his phone pressed to his ear, a grin on his face.

The men of the Moo U hockey team don't share my caution around falling in love. Well, maybe Patrick does. But he doesn't leave the bar alone, either. He's found a hookup for the night, as he often does.

Eventually, I'm the last man at table seventeen. Abbi shoots me apologetic looks as she hustles around, finishing her shift. But I'm not going anywhere. Not if Abbi needs me.

"Sorry," she says, appearing without her apron around two a.m. "That took forever."

"Hey, it's okay," I insist. "Let's go." I pull on my jacket, because it's going to be a chilly walk up the hill toward her apartment.

We head outside, and I put on my game face. Protection isn't the point of this exercise, I realize. Abbi could surely figure out how to avoid being alone with Price tonight. Rather, *intimidation* is the purpose of my involvement right now. When we walk outside together, I put a protective arm around her. Luckily Price is standing right outside.

"Hey, remember me?" I ask him, stopping to make my point.

"Nah," the oaf says, scowling.

"Yeah, I bet you'd rather forget." I give him a Mr. Smooth smile. "My offer still stands, though. Bother her, and you're signing your-self up for a dental bill much higher than whatever they're paying you to stand here and watch the door. It's your call."

Then I walk her home, leaving her on her front porch, where Abbi thanks me profusely. "It's ridiculous that you had to do that. But Price and subtlety don't mix."

"I got that impression."

When I leave her on her doorstep again, we share an awkward goodbye, wishing each other Happy New Year, before I turn and go.

The truth is that I never meant to be Abbi's fake boyfriend for longer than it takes to eat a turkey dinner. But now Price is working regular weekends at the Biscuit. And so—as January rolls on—I consider it my sacred duty to keep up the charade.

And I have to say—it's not a bad life. Over the next couple weeks, Abbi and I have lots of late-night talks as I walk her home. She brings me free wings on the regular. And then there are our lengthy text conversations about hockey, wing flavors, and school.

Honestly, if we could just have sex, all my needs would be met. She's basically perfect.

Abbi keeps telling me that I shouldn't bother to walk her home anymore. That Price isn't threatening enough to warrant all this extra attention. But I don't trust Price, so I keep up the vigil. Some nights I arrive late, have a single beer, and do some homework at the bar while Abbi finishes up her shift.

I like it here. The music is good. And even though my teammates have already gone home for the night, I'm pleasantly tipsy, nursing my last beer and reading a short story for my English class on my phone.

"You really don't have to do this," Abbi says as she swings by to grab Tate's abandoned beer glass off table seventeen. She says it a lot, actually. "I can leave with Carly, or sneak out the back while he's escorting someone else to her car."

"Hey, I know," I say with a shrug. "But I like the Biscuit, and it's easier to read when there aren't hockey players calling me to watch a game on TV. This is like the library for me. But with excellent beer."

And, fine, I'm hung up on Abbi. I'm man enough to admit it. So where else would I rather be?

She gives me a sweet smile and a confused shake of her adorable head. And then she runs off to wipe down another table.

This is my life right now, and I've accepted it. Away games are a problem, though. Two weekends a month I'm on a bus with the team, playing U Mass or Maine.

Luckily, I have friends on the women's hockey team. Women love me almost as much as I love women. So it's really no problem to ask my friend Chrissy to have a drink at the bar until Abbi gets off shift the next weekend, and then walk out with her.

You really didn't have to send a friend to babysit me! comes Abbi's text the next morning. *I'm a big girl. I can look after myself.*

I know that, I quickly reply. *But a good fake boyfriend looks after his fake girlfriend even when he's busy making U Conn cry.*

Nice win, by the way. Your fake girlfriend was super proud. That assist in the third period was extra sexy.

Thank you, baby!

See? We have the best relationship on campus. We have great chemistry. We're mutually supportive of one another.

Except I haven't been this horny since ninth grade, when Joey Birnbaum showed me how to find porn on my phone. And, sure, I could have hooked up on my road trip. The female hockey fans in Maine appreciate Mr. Smooth almost as much as the ones in Vermont.

But it just wouldn't feel right, you know? Maybe I really should consider a career in Hollywood. I'm better at this acting thing than I'd thought. I've gone and convinced myself that Abbi and I are sexual soulmates. I can't cheat on my soulmate.

So I haven't hooked up at all. In fact, I haven't gotten any action since before Thanksgiving—since the night I'd hoped to hook up with Abbi and then realized why we couldn't.

After that, she was sort of under my skin, I guess. Now I'm looking at the longest dry spell in my adult life. It's hard. I mean that literally. Some nights I can't even concentrate because I'm so pent up. The guys are getting used to the way I space out in the middle of conversations.

Yesterday after practice I was sitting on the bench thinking lustful thoughts about Abbi when I spaced out in the middle of an argument between Pax and Patrick about a new defensive play we're working on.

Coach Garfunkle tried to get my opinion, but I had no idea what they'd been saying. "You okay, son? You look a little unsteady."

"He's just horny," Tate had cracked. "He's got it bad for a girl he can't have. Wait—is there a crystal for that?"

The whole team laughed, but Coach Garfunkle pulled a stone

out of his pocket. It was—wait for it—oblong and pointy at the end. Like a rose quartz dick. "This is what you need."

Two dozen hockey players roared their approval. "Really?" Lex Vonne had gasped. "Quartz can make you less horny?"

"Well…" Coach Garfunkle shrugged. "At least it will remind him that there's something in the world harder than his junk."

Yup, I'm the laughingstock of the team now. But at least there's a good reason for it, and that reason is Abbi. I'm waiting for her at the bar again until she's finally ready to leave the Biscuit.

She eventually arrives at my elbow, her apron and visor missing. She's touched up her lipstick, and now I'm staring at her mouth again, the way a puppy eyes the burger on your plate. Hungrily.

"All right," she says, one hand on her hip. "Let's get on with this charade. Although I'm sure he's got the message by now."

"What charade?" a gruff voice barks at close range.

Fuck. I look up to see Price standing right behind her. "Nobody's talking to you, are they?"

"Asshole," Price growls. "You and this stuck-up bitch can have each other. I wouldn't want your sloppy seconds anyway. She and her mom were just trailer trash."

At the mention of her mom, pain flashes in Abbi's eyes.

"Hey, fucknuts," I growl, my blood suddenly pounding in my ears. "Now you've really done it. Take this outside?"

"No," Abbi gasps, her hand shooting out to grasp my wrist. "Don't get into trouble over *him*. He's not worth it."

Price makes a low chuckle. "Please. Make my day."

I really want to. I could flatten him in seconds. I'm sure of it. But Abbi is begging me with her eyes not to.

Shit. It would feel great to deck him. But I know his type. He'll call the cops and press charges for assault. Coach will lose his mind. I can hear the shouting already.

None of that matters, though. Only the look on Abbi's face right now. It's pleading with me for patience. If I hit Price, I'll make her life more difficult in other ways.

"Okay," I say softly. "Okay, honey."

Now, the trouble with being a great actor is that sometimes you lose yourself in your work. That must be why I lean forward and give

Abbi a very gentle kiss on the lips. It's a kiss that says: *your big strong boyfriend listens to you.*

At least it was supposed to say that. But the moment our lips touch, something snaps. I'm not the fake boyfriend anymore. I'm not even Mr. Smooth. I've gone past that and straight on to Mr. Sexy Beast.

And Mr. Sexy Beast is famished. His kiss is firm and full of questions. *Isn't this nice? Can I have a taste? Why haven't we done this before?*

At first, Abbi goes still with surprise. But she gets over her shock in a heartbeat. Two hands quickly grip my jacket. Then she stands up on tiptoes to improve our connection.

I tilt my head and tease the seam of her lips with my tongue. Everything is bliss as Abbi lets out a little moan of longing.

But the sound seems to wake her up. Her eyes fly open again, and she takes a quick step backward. "Wow, I..." She takes a deep breath.

And then we both say "Sorry," at the same time.

Yup. It's awkward.

I look around and see a scowling Price on the far side of the room. He's offering another waitress a walk to her car. And she's turning him down.

Price is an honest-to-god predator. And I can't forget that Abbi only asked for protection from him. She didn't ask for my tongue in her mouth.

Right. Okay. I grab my backpack off the back of the bar stool and gesture for Abbi to precede me out of the Biscuit.

I have got to get a hold of myself. Abbi is a friend who asked for my help. The least I could do is not maul her like Price.

We walk away from the restaurant and head up the hill toward Abbi's place in silence. I hope I haven't totally fucked things up between us. But I'm not sure how to ask. And we arrive at the creaky front steps of her Victorian building before I work it out.

"So..." She clears her throat as we climb the steps. I always walk her all the way to the door.

"So." I sigh. "Back there, that was..."

"Really great," she says quickly. "Just putting that out there."

Dude, Mr. Smooth whispers into my ear. *You got this.*

"It was, wasn't it?" I smile at her. "And you know what?"

"What?" she squeaks, looking up at me with hope in her eyes.

"The truth is that I'm not a very good actor. Never have been. I'm only convincing when I'm really excited about the role."

"Is that so?"

I don't even answer the question. I take Abbi in my arms instead. And I stare down into her gray eyes as I take her mouth in a firm kiss. She melts against me. *Finally*. This kiss is 100% real. It's the one we've needed since Thanksgiving. Since forever.

Mr. Smooth is nowhere to be found. I don't feel smooth when Abbi's around. There's only the bumbling idiot who needs her so badly. And the Sexy Beast who'll take over when he gets the chance.

And now is his chance. I wrap an arm around Abbi's waist and pull her tightly to my body. Her bag goes *thunk* onto the porch, and her hands grip my jacket.

"Abbi," I say between kisses. "Come home with me."

"No," she says, and I almost weep with disappointment. But then she says, "My place is closer."

Yaaaaaas!

And then we're in motion. I reach down and grab her bag, while she whips a hand inside, fishing for her keys, hurrying to open the outer door then unlock the door to her unit. The moment we step inside her apartment, I lean down and sweep her up into my arms again.

She lets out a little gasp of shock as her feet leave the floor.

"Is this okay?" I ask.

"Hell yes. I was just surprised."

"Good." I kick the door shut and then brace her against it. "Let's get a few things straight before I carry you to bed."

"O-kay," she stammers, wrapping her legs around me.

She can probably feel my cock pressing against her core now. "Look, I've needed to kiss you for a long time. And I don't want to wait any longer." Just to prove my point, I skim my lips along her jaw, and then down her neck. "Is that okay with you?"

"Yes," she says with a shiver and a little groan.

"Good. There's a few more things I need, if it's okay."

"Like what?" she whispers.

"No more acting, honey. I'm handing over my Academy Award. This time I want it to be real." I glance into the shadows of her little one-room apartment. "Is that headboard sturdy?"

"*Y-yes...*"

Abbi rolls her hips against me, and now it's me who groans. "Aw, yeah. I'm going to need you to moan my name again. But this time, I want to be inside you when you do it."

She swallows roughly. "That can be arranged."

"Good." I sink into another kiss, and her mouth is hot and welcoming.

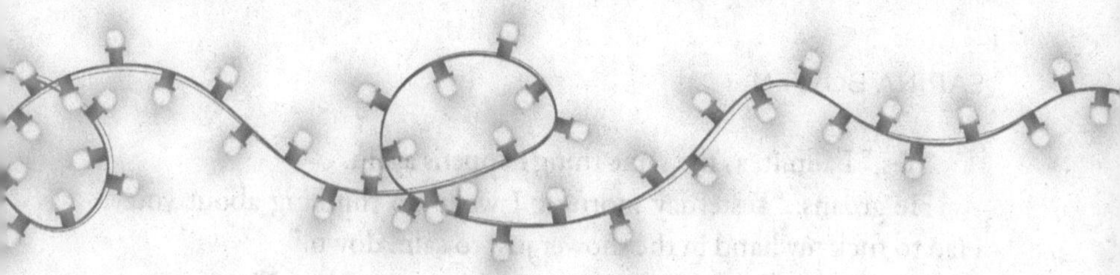

CHAPTER 16
THE SHAPE OF YOU

ABBI

Braced in Weston's strong arms, his taste on my tongue, I'm flooded with several conflicting sensations at once. His chest is warm and solid against mine. His kiss is bossy and loving. Lord knows that nobody ever holds me. I haven't felt so *protected* in a very long time.

God, I'm such a girl. But this man just *threatened* Price for me. If that's not sexy, I don't know what is.

Making a hungry noise, Weston changes the angle of his kiss and then plunders my mouth again. And wow—I didn't know you could feel utterly safe and still super excited at the same time. But here we are. I have no idea what he'll do next, but I already know I'll like it.

"Abbi," he whispers against my mouth. "Did you feel it? On Christmas Eve? I was so hard for you I couldn't sleep. I wanted to roll over and pull you underneath me."

"Oh," is all I can think to say. But that sounds wonderful. Threading my hands into his hair, I kiss him again to show that I agree.

"I need to know," he growls. "Was it just me that night?"

"No," I whisper, licking into his mouth again. I can't believe I'm making out against my door with Weston. *Finally.*

"Did you get hot for me?" His deep voice rumbles in my ear. "Did you get wet?"

"Yes," I admit, as the same thing happens again.

He groans. "Yesterday morning I woke up thinking about you. Had to fuck my hand in the shower just to calm down."

Whew. Is it hot in here? "W-why did we wait so long?"

"Because our lives are complicated. But Abbi—now I'm taking you to *bed*. So if that's not what you want, you gotta speak up right now."

"Yes. Fine. Good."

I sound like a dingus, but Weston doesn't care. He lets out a horny groan and then lifts me off the wall to do exactly what he'd said he would do—he carries me across my small apartment and deposits me on the bed. "I'm going to need you naked."

"Yessir."

Peeling off his jacket, he grunts. "Feel free to say that often. Did you happen to notice that your apartment is cold?"

"Is it?" I toss my jacket aside and kick off my shoes. I don't want to talk about my stupid apartment. I want to get back to the part where he's murmuring dirty words in my ear.

He unbuttons his shirt. And holy Toledo, I get my first full view of the vines tattooed across his chest. They're beautiful. *He's* beautiful. No wonder there's a line of women around table seventeen every time the hockey team racks up a win.

"You're staring," he says with a chuckle.

"Sorry." I avert my eyes.

"No—look all you want. But can you take off your clothes while you're doing it?" He steps closer to me, grips my Biscuit uniform shirt and lifts it over my head. "Now we're talking."

Could he *be* any sexier? From his rippling abs to his chatty, nononsense approach to sex, Weston is making me crazy. I find myself staring up at his bare chest again, at those abs that are now prickled with goose bumps. "You're cold," I say softly.

"Abbi, it's like the Polar Vortex in here. Get under the covers with me. I'll keep us both warm."

Now that's an excellent plan. I hop off the bed and turn down the covers, including the down comforter I had to buy when I realized that the landlady was never going to turn up the heat.

Weston doesn't waste any more time, either. I hear the sound of a zipper's metal teeth as he sheds his jeans. I turn away to undo the hook on my skirt, so I miss the view of Weston's naked body sliding into my bed. By the time I step out of my skirt, he's already covered himself.

Still—here's a sight I never thought I'd see—Weston Griggs in my bed, his hands folded behind his head, biceps flexing on my pillow.

Pinch me.

His eyes are smiling up at me. "Get in here before you freeze. Right here, baby." He lifts one side of the covers. Still wearing my bra and panties, I slip into the bed beside him.

Weston turns and rolls until he's spread out above me, his warm body pressing me against the mattress. And—hello—there's a very hefty erection pressed against my thigh.

Holy heck. This just got real.

"Now *this* is where I wanted you on Christmas Eve, Abbi. And on Thanksgiving, and New Year's. And every night in between." He strokes a thumb across my cheekbone. "We are going to have *all* the sex."

I giggle nervously. It's been a while for me. My life is too chaotic for fun and hookups.

And Weston is a player. Even though I haven't seen him pick up anyone in the bar in a while, I know how much he likes women. I hope he isn't expecting me to be a sex goddess or something. I hope I don't smell like chicken wings and beer. And—wait—did I shave my legs today? At least these sheets are clean.

"Hey. Abbi," he whispers, kissing the bridge of my nose. "Where did you go just now?"

"I'm here!" I say breathlessly. "We were just about to have all the sex—" I actually bite my tongue in an effort to stop rambling. Ow. "Sorry. Just a brief moment of performance anxiety."

"Do we have to sing it out?" His pretty eyes smile down at me. "Should I cue up a song on my phone?"

"What?" I snort in an unsexy way. "No! Oh my God."

"Hang on. Maybe I'm on to something." He grins. "Which song would be most appropriate for this? How about 'Shape of You' by

Ed Sheeran? It's about a bar hookup. I don't know if I can sing that high, though."

"Weston!" I clap a hand over my mouth to keep from laughing in his face.

"There's always the classic—'Let's Get it On.'" Weston props himself up on an elbow and looks thoughtful. "Or Bruce singing 'I'm on Fire.' But I think I prefer The Kinks. 'You Really Got Me' speaks the truth. Because I can't sleep at night, either."

I blink up into his handsome face, and wonder if he's even serious. Then he puts those sexy lips together and slowly hums the Kinks' guitar riff. And I forget that he's making a joke as that sexy mouth descends to the swell of my breast, tracing my curves very slowly, his hum vibrating across my skin.

Whoa. Now I've got goose bumps, and not because of the cold. As he teases my breast, I forget to be nervous. I even forget to breathe. The tickle and scrape. The heat of his mouth...

Wow.

My bra is in the way, though. Reaching back, I unhook that sucker.

"Good girl," Weston breathes. He grabs the bra and tosses it away. "Fuck, Abbi." He brings one roughened hand to my breast and gives me a gentle squeeze. "So pretty." Then he lowers his mouth to my nipple, glancing up at me as he extends his tongue to lap at my peak.

And I let out a hot gasp of excitement. Playful, dirty Weston does not disappoint. He closes his lips around my nipple and sucks. Then he pops off to torture the other breast. And all the while he watches me with those bright, curious eyes.

Is this real life? I feel *worshipped.* My hands find his muscular shoulders, and I slide my fingers all over his beautiful skin, tracing the vines of those tattoos.

But then he disappears from view, under the covers. "Weston," I cry, my hands seeking him under the sheet. "Where did you—?"

Two hands tug my underwear off. Then his broad hands land on my thighs, and lips begin to trace and kiss the curve of my hip bone.

Oh boy. I lift the edge of the comforter and peek, because this is too incredible to miss.

As I illuminate Weston, a muffled "*whoa*" comes from under the covers. He lifts his head. "Who's a bad girl, Abbi? Do you have a tattoo of a black lab on your thigh?"

"That's Friendly."

"Oh, I can be very friendly," he says with a grin. "But who's the dog?"

"No, I mean the dog was *named* Friendly. She was my first pet."

He laughs. "Kidding, honey. I got it the first time." He presses a palm down over my tattoo. "Don't watch, doggo. I'm about to go down on your master."

I moan. "The things that come out of your mouth."

"Yeah, I don't think you mind 'em too much." Weston gives me a sexy wink—an actual wink—and then he lowers his mouth to my—

Oh God. "Oh GOD." That tongue. He's shameless. It's a struggle to relax against the bed as he licks and kisses me. My toes curl, and my hips roll. It's so good. Nobody has ever lavished so much attention on me.

Never. Ever.

I just hope I'm not too sad when it's over.

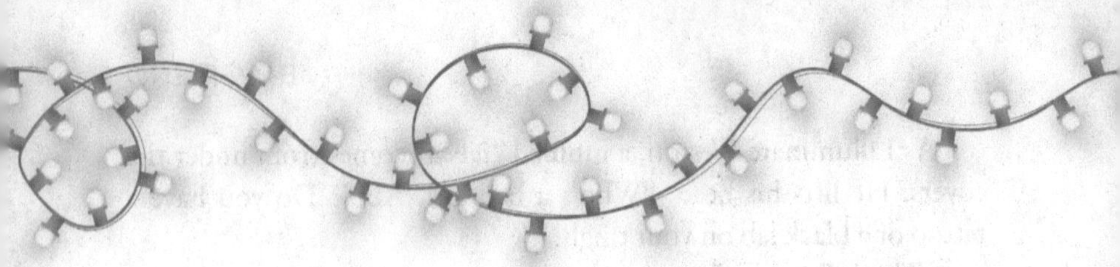

CHAPTER 17
I FEEL LIKE A SUPERHERO

WESTON

Mr. Smooth has fled the building again. And the way I feel right now, I don't even remember the sound of his voice. All that's left is this babbling, crazy guy who can't calm down.

Who could blame me? There's a goddess spread out in front of me, every curve ripe for touching and teasing. I'm driving her wild, and I feel like a superhero. If the superhero were a super horny college guy who's fallen deeply in like with his fake girlfriend.

I tease my thumb in a slow circle around her clit and try not to hump the bed. I feel loose and wild tonight. Part of it is pent-up sexual desire. I've been waiting a long time for this moment to arrive.

But I'm weirdly nervous, too. I want to please her so badly.

"Omigod *Weston!*" Abbi pants, clutching my hair.

"Is there something you want?" I tease, sliding a finger inside.

She moans.

Jesus Christ, I'm so revved up. Who knew that a bit of a dry spell could ruin a man's restraint?

Crawling back up her body, I grab for the condom I'd retrieved from my jacket as I got undressed. I roll it on while she watches with big, hungry eyes.

I'm a good lover. A confident, generous lay. *Usually*. Right now I feel like a nervous teenager on prom night. This is momentous. It's big. And I'm not referring to Little Mr. Smooth, although he's harder than ever.

It's because Abbi and I are such close friends, right? That must be why my heart is thumping like a kick drum right now. I care about her happiness, because I'm a good friend.

These are the thoughts bouncing around in my stunned head as I melt back down onto Abbi's supple body. I drop kisses on her shoulders. On her neck. Wherever I want. And that's a lot of places, apparently. I can't believe that I'm finally allowed to drag my lips across her flat belly, and then suck lightly on the tips of her dusky nipples.

God, I'm so hungry for her. And it must be mutual, because Abbi spreads her legs in invitation. "Please," she whispers. "You know you want to."

I let out a helpless groan, because she isn't wrong. Then I grab the base of my cock and squeeze tightly, trying to calm myself down. Usually the tight grip of the condom does the trick, but tonight all bets are off.

Come on, Mr. Smooth! Why has he deserted me at this crucial hour?

I give Abbi a confident smile nonetheless. Then I slide right into her tight heat. It feels so good that I close my eyes momentarily, just to appreciate the sensation of our joining.

"Oh yessss," she breathes. Her silky hands find my chest, and she wraps her legs possessively around my ass.

My eyes flip open to find hers watching me. She looks breathless and a little stunned, which is just how I feel too. "Wow," I say stupidly. It's pretty much the only thought in my brain at this point.

"This is definitely the best idea I've ever had," she whispers.

"Oh, so it was your idea?" I ask, rolling my hips provocatively. "News flash, my dick thinks about this all the time."

She grips my shoulders and moves against me. "He should have made his wishes known. You were going to leave me on the front porch tonight."

"Fair," I say, giving her a slow thrust. "He's learned his lesson."

She smiles, and I lean down and kiss her deeply. I'm so turned on that I have to proceed with caution. It's time to think about hockey practice. Drills. Conditioning. Boring sessions on the treadmill...

Abbi purrs beneath me. She runs her foot up and down the back of my leg. I kiss her as deeply as I dare while we slowly move together in the age-old dance. I wasn't kidding when I'd said I dreamed of pulling her underneath me. The way she gazes up at me with soft eyes is just perfect.

Too perfect, actually. After a while I roll over, pulling her on top of me. This small break in the action calms me down. And the view is *wow*. Abbi blinks down at me with mussed hair and luscious, swaying breasts. "You are so fucking hot," I whisper. "And I am really fucking close. Ride me."

"Okay," she breathes.

"Put your hands on the headboard."

"Like this?" She leans forward and grips the bed above me.

"Exactly like that." I reach back and slap her ass. "Go on."

She lets out a deep, sexy breath and begins to move. And I'm in paradise as she slowly picks up the pace. I'm watching for that perfect moment when she finds the rhythm that makes her body sing. And when it happens, it's beautiful. Her head drops as she sounds out a little breathy moan on every stroke.

"There, baby," I say through a clenched jaw. "Give it to me." I cup both of her tits, which bounce in my hands, and she moans more loudly. Then I skim my fingertips down her belly and right to the place of our joining.

"*Fuck*, Weston," she groans happily. "*Yes yessssss*."

Then I can't hold back anymore. My balls get impossibly tight and I groan from the effort of staving it off. But it's no use. I jack my hips off the bed and bounce her on my cock. The headboard begins to bang rhythmically into the wall, and I gasp as my climax hits me full force.

God almighty it's a doozy. Grabbing her by the hips, I let out a growl of sheer relief. And then a shout of joy. I catch Abbi in my arms as she lets go of the headboard and drops onto my body with a deep, satisfied moan. And I feel her body pulse deliciously around mine.

We end up as a pile of limbs and heavy breathing. And I have never been so satisfied in my life.

———

That blissed-out feeling doesn't go away, either. Usually, after a hookup, I wait around a little while and then head home. That's my MO. It sends a friendly message but promises nothing.

Tonight is different. I don't want to leave this bed, and Abbi's warm body. I don't want to leave, period. We just had amazing sex. Like, Division One championship sex. I think it broke my brain. All I want to do is hold her and nuzzle her neck.

"Okay if I stay?" I ask eventually. "It's kinda late and kinda cold outside."

"You can stay," she whispers, palming my heart.

"Thanks, Abbi." We blink at each other, but nobody moves for another moment. She's so easy to be around. If I were looking for a real girlfriend, I'd look for one exactly like her.

She's the one who breaks our staring contest. "One sec. Let me find you a toothbrush."

We take turns in Abbi's frigid bathroom. Then we slide into her bed together one more time and pull up the comforter that we'd kicked off the bed during our sexcapades.

"Night, hot stuff," I say from my side of the bed.

"Night, Westie," she yawns.

And then I fall deeply asleep, before I can decide whether I actually like that silly name or not.

———

In the morning, I wake up to the sound of her alarm.

"What time is it?" I croak, my hand somehow curled against her hip. My nose at the back of her neck. This is so unusual for me. I haven't woken up pressed against a woman in a really long time.

It's nicer than I remember.

"Eight," she whispers, her fingers trailing over my hand.

"You have somewhere you need to be?"

"No."

"Good," I grunt. Then I roll her, pulling her warm body onto my chest.

Ooh, a naked woman, Mr. Smooth says.

But for once I ignore him, and we sleep a while longer.

The next time I wake up, we're cuddled together like we've been sharing a bed for years. I can tell she's awake, so I run a hand down her arm. "Your skin is cold," I whisper. "Is it always this cold in here?"

"Yes," she says. "Although I didn't notice it much last night."

I chuckle and then kiss her shoulder. "Last night was epic."

"Yes it was," she agrees softly.

"Do you, uh..." I realize too late that I haven't planned what I was going to say. And I'm in uncharted territory here. "Do you think we'll end up doing it again sometime?" *Right now works for me*, I almost add.

"That sounds glorious," she says carefully. "But I just assumed you didn't do repeats."

Well, ouch. Hearing my own behavior reflected back at me shuts me up for a second. She's right, but I didn't know it was so obvious.

"I didn't mean it as a criticism," she says into the silence. "I promise."

"No—I know you didn't. But you and I are friends, right? And we'll stay that way?"

"Of course." She gives me a tentative glance.

I curl an arm around her, and tuck her cheek onto my bare shoulder. "You already know why I don't do relationships."

"You mean because your family is an advertisement for love gone wrong? Or because it's more fun to party your way through the female hockey fans of Vermont?"

I snort, although it's hard to argue with this assessment. "I meant the first thing. But I'm not ashamed of the second."

She reaches an arm up and ruffles the hair above my ear. "You shouldn't be ashamed. I'm just envious of your fun."

"We had a lot of fun last night, right?"

"We set the *standard* for fun," she agrees. "In the dictionary now there's a picture of our clothes on the floor."

"Agreed," I say, "And only because Merriam-Webster would never print a photo of the best parts of last night." I run a hand down her bare ass and squeeze. "But that's why I think—since we're both reasonable adults who enjoy our fun—we could just keep the party going. What do you say to that? It would be our special arrangement for fun."

"Like friends with benefits?" she asks.

"Exactly like that. This would be casual. You're graduating in the spring, anyway. So our fun already has a sell-by date."

"You're right," she murmurs. "It totally does."

"And there's a bonus—your idiot step-stepbrother will see me waiting for you to get off work." My voice drops in pitch as I stroke her smooth belly with my happy fingers. "I won't even be acting."

She laughs. "Okay, sure. But he got the message already, I think."

"He'd better have." God, how I still want to punch that guy.

Abbi finally rolls over to study me with her clear gray eyes. "Just because I don't think I need your help anymore with the Price thing doesn't mean I don't appreciate it. Thank you for standing up for me. It's been really nice of you."

"Anytime," I say, my voice husky. And that's when my phone alarm finally goes off. "Oh, hell. I guess it's nine thirty already."

"I should get up, too," Abbi says, sitting up.

Our perfect night is ending, and I'm just not ready. "Should we shower together? And then I can take you out for bagels and a vat of hot coffee. Just to take off the chill in your room. How do you even get out of bed in the morning?"

She smiles down at me. "That sounds nice, and I won't turn you down. But I do have a system for this. That robe"—she points at a flannel bathrobe over a nearby chair—"is strategically positioned so that I can reach it from the bed." She leans toward the chair, yanking the robe onto her bed. "Extra layers are the only way to get out of this bed when it's so cold in here."

I put a hand on the soft flannel. "This is nice. Is it from that place where you have your internship?"

"Yes. My employee discount is super handy."

"Will we both fit inside this robe?"

"No." She giggles. "But I'll turn on the water and call you when it's warm."

"Good plan."

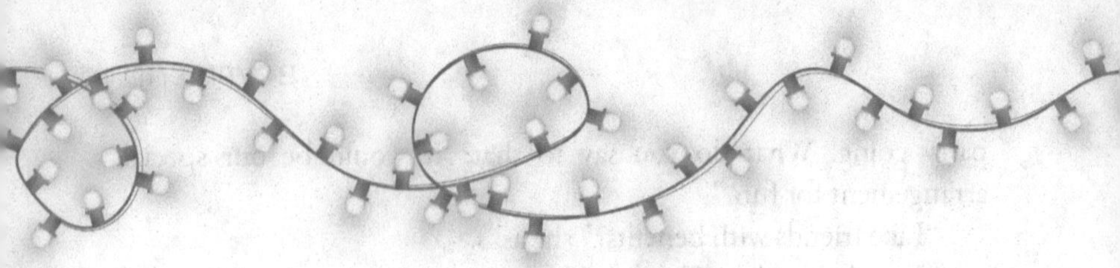

CHAPTER 18
PINCH ME

ABBI

Weston Griggs is naked in my shower.

Naked. In *my* shower.

Pinch me!

Getting clean has never been so much fun. We don't fool around, except for a few kisses. But Weston makes a point of soaping up my back—and my ass. And when I wash his hair he makes appreciative noises and then kisses my neck.

It's the most fun I've ever had on a school day. And I'm sad to leave the warm embrace behind—both Weston's and the hot water. But we both have things to do. So I pass him a clean towel.

It ought to feel super strange moving around my tiny apartment with a ripped, naked Weston. But the boy is so comfortable with himself and so goofy that it just doesn't feel awkward.

I'm starting to think that some of his good-natured cheer is a coping mechanism, though. He probably isn't the world's happiest human. He's just learned to find the light-hearted, funny thing in every situation and cling tightly to it.

There are worse traits in a human. I admire him for trying.

"Okay, who can you call to turn up the heat in your apartment?" he asks as we dry off and dress. "Not that I mind the view. It's very nipply in here," he says, eyeing my breasts through the bra I'm trying to straighten. "Maybe that's your landlord's play."

"Doubt it. The landlady is a super-cheap octogenarian. She lives on this floor, in a unit at the back of the building. Twice I've slipped notes under her door asking for her to turn up the temperature. When that didn't work, I mailed her a formal request. She never answered. I'm afraid to piss her off too badly. And I only need to live here until May, right?"

"Yeah, but I hate to let the old bat refrigerate you," Weston presses. "Isn't there a thermostat you could fiddle with?"

"The controls must be in her apartment. In my apartment, there's only this metal thing that looks somewhat important. But there's no way to control it." I point toward the kitchen, where a dull gray metal rectangle is surrounded by a small metal cage high on the wall.

Weston walks over and stares up at it. "That's got to be *some* part of the heat and hot water system," he agrees. "And you'd never put a valve that far off the ground."

"Okay..." I don't know why he's so interested. "Do you have a plumbing kink I should know about?"

"Baby, *plumbing* is very sexy." He gives me a cheesy Weston wink. "But I'm an architect's kid. I've heard a lot of dinner table discussion about heating. And that might be a thermostat."

"There aren't any controls on it. I climbed up on the counter once and checked."

"Let's just try something. Do you have a spare dish towel or a washcloth?"

"Sure." I go back into the bathroom and find him a washcloth. "What for?"

He takes it from me and wets it in the kitchen sink. Then he wrings it out. "This will cause evaporation," he explains, "which will trick the thermostat into thinking that your apartment is even colder than it actually is." As I watch, he tosses the wet cloth up until it lands on the cage.

And then it promptly slides off again, hitting my floor with a wet slap.

"Huh. Do you have a chair I could stand on?"

"I got it," I say, walking over to my tiny counter and putting the loaf of bread on top of the drying rack to make a space. Give me a hand?"

Weston makes a sling out of his hands, and I step onto it. A minute later I'm standing on the counter. Weston hands me the cloth and I spread it out over the cage. "What are the chances this will make a difference?"

"Pretty high," he says. "I think you'll come home to a warm apartment. You'll just have to reset the wet towel when you're cold. Now let's go eat bagels. I'm starved."

———

Weston is magic. And I don't mean the sex. When I return to my apartment after my morning classes, the place is *toasty*. It's mind blowing. I don't have to freeze anymore, and for a couple of days, the change is a little hard to get used to.

So is Weston, if I'm honest. I'm not accustomed to receiving sexy texts from him in the middle of my day. Or a voice message asking me if I'm okay to walk home after work the next night.

Price only works on the weekends, I remind him. ***I'm good***.

Yes you are, Weston replies, and I blush at my phone. ***And I should really stay in and study for this test in statistics. But I'd rather walk you home again***. He follows that up with a wink emoji.

Pinch me. This can't be my real life.

I have a lot of studying to do too, I admit. ***And I'm working the next four nights***.

Nooooooo, he types back. ***I have back-to-back games out of town this weekend***. He follows that up with a pouting emoji. ***Is there any chance you're free Sunday night?***

I am totally free on Sunday night, I reply quickly.

Phew. Let's have dinner together after I get back to town. I owe you from our bet.

I blink down at this lovely invitation and try not to dance around like a lunatic. ***I'd love to***, I reply instead.

"What is that look on your face?"

I jump at the sound of Carly's voice, and I shove my phone into my back pocket. "Just texting with, um, Weston."

Carly lets out a shriek. "Omigod! I knew it! He's in lovvvve with you!"

"Shhh!" I hiss. "You're wrong. We're just having..." I struggle for words, because this thing with Weston is as hard to explain as it is to believe. "A thing."

"A thing..." Carly repeats slowly as she shoves a soda glass against the dispenser and fills it with Coke. "Like a *relationship?*" There are hearts in her eyes already.

"God no. A fling. A tryst. A convenient arrangement."

"So you're not 'just friends' anymore."

"Yes we are," I insist. We're just friends who—" I don't finish the sentence, because Kippy is somewhere nearby and I don't want to be overheard.

"Oh my *God*, this is the most exciting thing I've heard in a *long* time. And speaking of long things...is his thing long?" She giggles.

"Stop it," I hiss. "That's an inappropriate question."

She lets out a dreamy sigh. "Fine. But what about his stamina. I'll bet an athlete like that can go all night."

I snort. "There will be no details given out."

"Whyyyy?" she whines. "It's not like I'll ever find out for myself. Weston is going to fall for that cute, sassy thing you've got going on. You just took him off the market. And they said it couldn't be done."

"It's just temporary," I insist. "This is just a physical thing until we both move on. I'll be leaving Vermont before June, you know."

"Still," Carly says. "A girl could have a lot of terrific sex in four months. Come on! Just give me one detail."

I bite my lip, gather up four ketchup bottles and carry them away. I will not gossip about Weston to Carly. Even though I am impressed. And I can say with certainty that hockey players do possess an awful lot of stamina.

"You have a dreamy look on your face," Carly says with a snicker. "Are you seeing him again tonight?"

"No," I say. "We're going out to dinner on Sunday. So nobody had better ask me to work a shift."

"If he's taking you out, that sounds like a relationship!"

"We're settling up a bet," I insist. "Stop using that word, Carly. Weston doesn't do relationships."

"He hasn't *yet*," she argues. "You could be his first."

"It's never happening," I tell the both of us. Because I'm not dumb enough to fall in love with him.

Thank goodness for that.

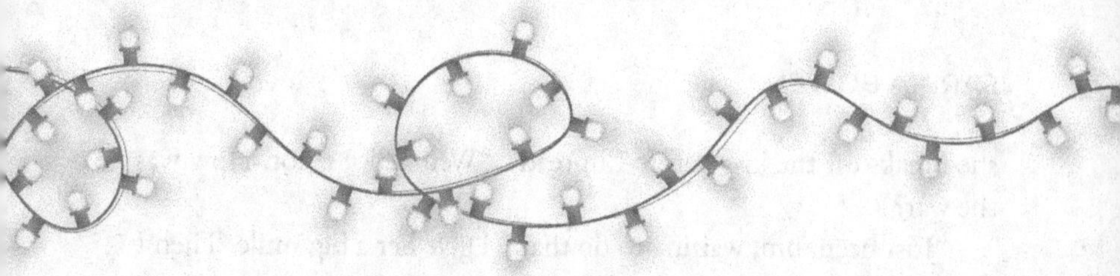

CHAPTER 19
MAKE IT A GOOD ONE

WESTON

I'm waiting outside of El Cortijo—a kickass little restaurant downtown on Bank Street—and practically tapping my toe with impatience.

Abbi isn't late. But after a long week, I'm just really looking forward to seeing her again, and having excellent Mexican food.

And, fine, excellent sex. I've been buzzing ever since our night together, and I need a repeat. Now, preferably.

I've spent the last couple of days thinking about Abbi. Actually, that's the polite way of putting it. It would be more accurate to say that I spent most of my waking hours remembering how good it was to finally spread her out and love her up like I'd been wanting to for months now.

And now I'm hooked. I can't stop thinking about it, or planning our next naked adventure. Here stands a desperate man, hungry for both tacos and sweet, sweet satisfaction.

"Weston!" I swing around to see her trotting down the sidewalk toward me, a hat perched on her head, her cheeks pink from the cold. "Were you waiting long?"

"Nope," I say, lunging for her. I pull her in and kiss her hello. *Very* firmly.

She wraps her arms around me and gives it right back. But then she breaks off the kiss before I'm ready. "Well hello, sailor. How was the war?"

"Just been, um, waiting to do that." I give her a big smile. Then I grab the door handle and usher her inside. "Have you been here before?"

"No." She shakes her head. "It's so cute."

It is, I guess. The restaurant is in one of those old metal diner cars from the fifties. There's counter seating on the right, and a single row of booths stretching the length of the left side.

Luckily, there's a spot open in the middle, and a waitress shows us to the table and puts down two paper placemats. "Can I start you off with some drinks? Beer? Sangria? Margarita?"

Abbi's eyes light up. "I'd love a margarita. On the rocks, no salt. Thanks!"

I order a beer, and then watch as Abbi scans the menu. "God, this looks great."

"It is." I chose this place because it's casual. The food is amazing here, but it isn't date-night fancy. I didn't want to make a big statement, you know?

Just a casual dinner between friends.

Friends who are definitely getting lucky later. If I have anything to say about it.

"What's your usual order?" Abbi wants to know.

"The lengua tacos. Oh, and we have to get some guacamole. This is my treat, by the way. Because you won our bet."

"Yum. This *is* a treat. Although I'm not convinced I won this bet, Westie."

The nickname makes me smirk. "You absolutely did. Besides, I was in the mood for Mexican." I am also in the mood for Abbi, who's happily perusing the specials on a card taped to the napkin dispenser.

When the waitress comes back a few minutes later, Abbi actually giggles as the frosty margarita lands in front of her. "Someone else bringing me a drink! This is awesome."

Well, hell. Now I want to bring her all the drinks. "So how's the job search going?" I ask after the waitress takes our order.

"It's...going," she says, propping her cheek in her hand. "I have two interviews coming up in New York, one at a big clothing brand, and one at a bank. But one of the jobs is in social media."

"That's not good?"

She fingers her silverware. "It *could* be good. I realize that everyone starts somewhere. But some of these brands are so big that they have a stable of young women who *only* do social media. It's a game of likes and clicks. But there's no way to advance. And when you can't stand it anymore, you quit and they just find another fresh-faced grad."

"So you'll keep looking," I say.

"I'm going to try. I have a lead on a job at a mortgage bank, too. That's the opposite situation—it's all interest rates and credit checks and building the loan portfolio."

"That sounds..."

"Dry," she prompts. "It's okay, you can say it. Maybe I have to pay my dues somewhere boring. I still need a paycheck and a foot in the door somewhere. And if I pick something in a major city, at least I'll be locating myself in a decent job market."

"You'll get there." I sound like a damn cheerleader. But I mean it. Who wouldn't want Abbi on their team? "Someone will appreciate you for more than chicken wings and beer."

"God, I hope so."

"You'll probably get a good recommendation from the flannel people, right?"

"Oh, definitely. In fact, they've asked me to come in for a few hours tomorrow."

"Weren't you done with that internship?"

"I was. But now they want to pay me fifteen bucks an hour to straighten out the *new* intern. It sounds like she's super clueless. She keeps posting rectangular images in the company Instagram feed."

"Oh the horror."

Abbi grins. "The flannel people are so confused. They don't know what to do with a millennial who can't handle social media. It's like a duck who refuses to quack."

I crack up. "Any chance the flannel people will offer you a job?"

Her eyes meet mine as she shakes her head. "It's a family business. They could be so much more if they tried, you know? The quality is there. But they've been making the same product line for fifty years. Besides—guess what they wanted from me as an intern?"

"Social media?"

She makes her fingers into a gun and shoots me. "You got it. And only social media. They see me coming with my marketing degree—and barely old enough to legally drink a margarita—and they're like, *here is our TikTok account. Please do whatever it is that TikTok is for.*"

I snort. "And did you light up TikTok for them?"

"You know it. I dressed up the owner's dog in flannel and got three million views."

"*Three million?*" I yelp.

"It's a really cute dog," she says from over the rim of her margarita glass. "And it's really nice flannel."

"But no wonder companies want you to do social media, babe. You're good at it."

The compliment makes her blush. "I probably just got lucky. But enough about dogs in PJs. What's up with you?"

"First, a big test in organic chemistry. That's going to take some work. And then back-to-back games against Notre Dame."

"You fly there, right?"

"Thank God. It's too far for a bus ride. And we always play both the season's games on the same weekend."

"Are road trips fun?" she asks me.

"Totally fun. But Sunday night is always a doozy for me. It's hard to catch up."

She tilts her head and studies me. "It's Sunday night right now. Should you be studying?"

"No," I insist. "I've been looking forward to seeing you all week." Things like that don't usually fall out of my mouth. I don't like to give anyone the wrong idea.

It is, however, true.

I see another stain of pink hit her cheeks. But she doesn't engage the topic any further. "I'll bet not many hockey players are premed. They don't work as hard at the academics as you."

"Some don't," I admit. "Next year when I'm trying to write med school applications during hockey, it's going to be hell."

"Where do you want to go to grad school?"

"Here, actually. Burlington's program is pretty good. I'm close to my crazy family, but not *too* close. And there's the possibility that I could use my fifth year of NCAA eligibility. I was injured my sophomore year and didn't play."

"Oh! So you could play hockey in grad school?"

"Yeah, or maybe do some coaching if I can't make the schedule work. Coach has been building this team so well the last couple of years. Great things are coming, and I want to see it play out."

"That's fun, Westie." She gives me a bright smile. "Table seventeen wouldn't be the same without your leadership."

I nudge her feet under the table. "You're trolling me."

"Just a little. Someone else will have to serve the beer, though. I'll be too busy running the world."

"Or at least the world's TikTok account," I point out.

"Exactly," she says with a grin.

———

After dinner, I hold her hand as we walk back toward campus. The night is frigid, and we have January air blasting in our faces. "I guess I didn't think this through."

"We're from Vermont, Westie." She squeezes my hand. "We can take it."

"If you need warming up, though, I'm volunteering."

She snickers. "Maybe you *did* think this through."

"Not to brag, but I don't usually have to freeze a woman to get her into bed."

Abbi gives me a sly glance. "Is that where the night is headed?"

"It is if I get to choose. Can I come over?" *Please say yes*. I've got it so bad.

"Yes," she says softly.

"If tonight isn't good timing, I'd understand. I know it's your only night off."

"No, it's nice," she says sounding a little shy. "I'd like to spend my night off with you."

Something warm and delicious curls through my belly when I hear this. "My place? Or yours."

"Mine," she says. "It's closer. And more, uh, private."

"That's certainly true. Your place it is." I hitch my gym bag up on my shoulder and lengthen my stride toward her little apartment.

"See?" she says when we finally arrive inside. "It's warm! And I only have you to thank."

"Holy cow," I crow as the heat hits my cold face. "It's actually hot in here. I've created a monster."

"Well, your system of tricking the thermostat is awesome, but it isn't easy to fine tune." She hangs up her coat on the back of the door before crossing the room to pick up a broom. She uses the stick to knock the washcloth off the thermostat.

"I'm glad you're not freezing anymore." I take off my coat and hang it up with Abbi's. "Plus, this is going to make it a lot easier to get you naked. Am I right?" I give her a sleazy wink.

"You might be," she says shyly. "Want a soda?" She taps her fingers against the countertop in her tiny kitchen.

"Only if you do." She looks a little shy all of a sudden. I hope that doesn't mean she's having second thoughts about us.

I *really* hope not.

Then I glance around her apartment and notice something. "You did some redecorating?"

She gives a shrug. "A little. It was cluttered before."

"But now it's *pristine*." The desk is tidy. The bookshelf is straightened. The kitchen is spotless. And the bed is made up crisply, with the pillows perfectly aligned side by side. "Do you clean a lot? Does it help you clear your head?"

"Sometimes," she mumbles, her gaze on her shoes.

"Or, and maybe I'm out of line, here..." I stalk across the room and cup her chin until she looks up at me with guilty eyes. "You cleaned because you thought I might come over tonight?"

"There might be some truth to that." She bites her lip.

"Were you hoping so?" I ask in a low voice.

"Yes."

"Then why are you shy now?" I whisper, my thumb tracing a slow arc across her smooth cheek. "Because I don't feel shy at all right now. I feel like peeling you out of these clothes and reminding you how much fun we had the other night."

She puts a hand in the center of my chest, "Because you're so..."

"So...?" I wait.

Abbi blushes. "So fun. So *extra*. And I usually fall asleep on my textbooks, smelling like chicken wings."

"Well, I do love chicken wings," I tease, moving in closer. "We should be fine."

She gives me a wan smile. "Maybe I just forgot how this works."

"Just kiss me already," I whisper. "And I'll remind you. I promise."

Her gray eyes blink up at me, and that blush grows deeper.

"I'm waiting, Abbi. Make it a good one. Set the tone. You'd be surprised what a good kiss can—"

She shuts me up with soft lips that firm up against mine.

Fuck yes. I catch her in both arms and pull her against my hungry body. She makes a soft little whimper, and that sound slices through me like lightning across a summer sky.

This is just what I've been craving. More of Abbi's kisses. More of her silken hair between my fingers. More more *more*.

I slide my hands down over her sweet ass and then lift her onto that counter. There. Now I can own her mouth without bending down. Now I can sink into her kiss with abandon. And never stop.

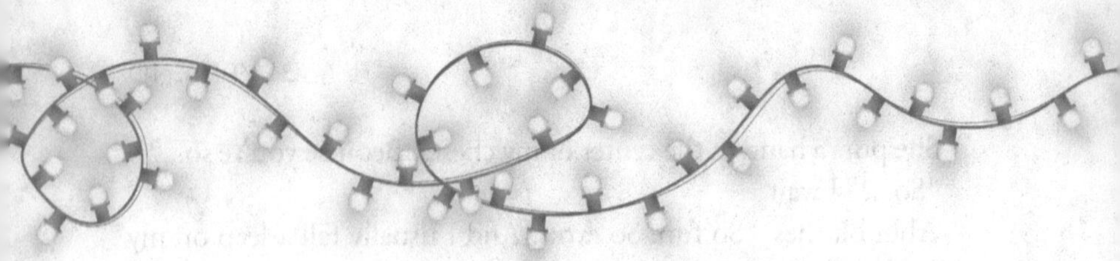

CHAPTER 20
MAYBE I DON'T NEED
TO KNOW

ABBI

"Wow." It's the first coherent thing I've said in an hour.

I lay panting on my bed, Weston's body—naked and spent—sprawled out diagonally across mine. He's trying to catch his breath.

My mind is blown. So this is what it means to have fantastic sex. It means Weston and me making out on the kitchen counter until I thought I would burst from desire. It means letting him strip off my clothes and spread me out on the bed.

It means yanking down his briefs and taking him into my mouth, while he curses and praises me, sometimes in the same breath. It means watching him suit up in a condom before prowling back to me on hands and knees, a determined look in his eye, while his shoulder muscles pop and flex.

And—this is the part that's so confusing to me—it means undulating beneath him while he stares into my eyes as he kisses me more deeply with every stroke.

Weston's skills are unparalleled. But that's not even the shocking part. The *intimacy* is. I don't know what to do with all that eye contact. And the broken sounds he makes when he comes.

My poor little lonely heart can't handle all that loving attention. It's like standing too close to a bonfire. You already know how cold you'll feel when you finally step away.

"Abbi," Weston rasps. "Can I stay over?"

"Of course," I say just a little too quickly. "I might even have an extra toothbrush."

"I brought mine," he says with a grin.

"Look who planned ahead," I tease, although my heart is still fluttering over the idea that Weston wants to sleep in my bed tonight.

"I didn't *expect* you to invite me in," he says. "But I sure hoped you would. It's a fine line."

"We could watch a movie or something," I suggest.

"Or something," he whispers.

And I smile up at my ceiling.

———

Following our Sunday night (and Monday morning!) sexfest, both Weston and I have very busy weeks.

I glimpse him once, on Wednesday night at the Biscuit, but table seventeen is not in my section.

Then, when I'm waiting for an order in the kitchen, I feel my phone buzz with a text. When I pull it out of my pocket, I see the text is from Weston. *I know you're busy. But won't you come over here and give me a kiss?*

Me: *In front of the bitchy manager who will soon owe me a $1500 bonus? Think again.*

Weston: *Bummer. You look hot and I miss you.*

Me: *Never knew you had an apron kink.*

Weston: *I have an Abbi kink. And tomorrow I'm going to South Bend, Indiana. Before we leave, I need to write a paper. So I can't even invite myself over tonight.*

Me: *That is a bummer.*

Weston: *We get back Sunday night. Come over?*

"Ooooh!" Carly shrieks.

I whirl around, and find her reading over my shoulder. "You just about gave me a heart attack."

"I'd have a heart attack too if Weston Griggs invited me over."

"Girls," Kippy says from the doorway. "What's going on?"

I shove my phone into my pocket and grab two plates of wings off the counter. "Not a thing. Excuse me." I lift my chin and march toward the dining room.

"Don't chase after the boys at table seventeen," he says with a sniff. "Be a shame if I had to fire you before your year was out."

Carly lets out an angry gasp, but I don't even break my stride. I carry the wings out and then run a new order to the bar.

And I don't touch my phone for the rest of the night. I can't afford to screw up, no matter how good a kisser Weston is. He's a great guy. I've got only good things to say about him.

He's fun, and he's sexy. But he's a distraction I can't really afford. And that's just the way it is.

———

On Thursday I dress in the best clothes I own and get on a JetBlue flight to New York City. I'm giving up a shift at work, three classes, and three hundred of my hard-earned dollars to do a few job interviews.

The investment bank where I'm interviewing for a spot in the training program paid for the plane ticket, but in order to stretch my time in the city, I'm springing for a one-night stay in a hotel.

If I get any of these jobs, it will all be worth it.

Or not. Because the investment bank interviewing process is a stressful whirlwind. I'm herded around the building with at least a dozen other candidates—mostly men. It's completely intimidating. Their crisp navy suits and silk ties make me feel like a country bunny in my sky-blue blazer.

The jacket had belonged to my mother. The tag says Lilly Pulitzer, which is a fancy brand, right? I'd saved it because she'd really liked the color. But I can see now that it's all wrong for this shimmering glass building, where everyone is wearing black, navy, or gray.

There's also a timed math test, which I take in a conference room, hurrying to finish amid the frantic scribbling of other candidates. The guy next to me is a mouth-breather. It's throwing me off my game. I don't get to answer the last question before the proctor says, "Pencils down."

The test is followed by a round of "flash interviews." It's like speed dating, with higher stakes and in uncomfortable shoes.

I paste on a grin and greet the next interviewer. He introduces himself with: "So, Abbi Stoddard, tell me why you deserve to beat out hundreds of other candidates for this job."

Hundreds?

The beat of silence that falls between us for a moment probably tells him more than my eventual answer ever will.

———

Eight hours later, I've survived both the investment bank and the mortgage bank interview gauntlets. I've also walked forty blocks in heels I borrowed from Carly, rolling my suitcase behind me, just so I could save cab money, and found a decently cheap restaurant in the process.

Now, finally approaching the hotel that I'd booked, I'm full of Chinese food but low on energy. I turn to the left and check for traffic before stepping off the curb.

But then a blur in my peripheral vision has me leaping back just in time to avoid a bicycle coming from the opposite direction.

The guy swerves and brakes. "Hey! Watch it!" he yells over his shoulder before riding away.

Okay, that was *really* close. Too close.

My heart is pounding in my chest, and the *Walk* sign turns back to *Don't Walk* before I'm brave enough to try again.

Now I realize that Seventh Avenue is a one-way street. I should have looked to the right, not the left. But that biker ran a red light! If we'd collided, it would have been his fault.

Not that it matters. If I end up dead, I won't even be able to explain that to the police. And when the light cycles back to me, I look both ways very carefully before scurrying across the avenue like a frightened squirrel.

I've only been in New York for eight hours or so. But it isn't going that well. I'm tired. My feet are killing me.

Worst of all, I feel no closer to getting a job than I did when I boarded the flight in Burlington this morning.

My hotel room beckons. I'm staying at a low-budget chain, but this one is new enough that it gets decent reviews on TripAdvisor. I push open the smudged glass door and roll my little suitcase across the hard floor toward the check-in desk. If they gave my room away, I just might break down and cry.

They didn't give it away. So that's something.

But after the bored-looking check-in guy hands me a key and sends me to the fourth floor, I discover the smallest hotel room I've ever seen. There is literally no room for anything besides the bed. It's like a prison cell, and the only window looks out onto a shaft-like space so narrow that I can only see other hotel curtains.

At least I can finally take off these shoes. I put them on the floor of the tiny closet. Then I remove my mother's old Sunday coat, and her blue jacket, hanging everything up in the closet. I take a shower and carefully dry my hair so it won't do anything crazy overnight.

But then there's nothing left to do. So I pull back the unfamiliar bedclothes and get into the bed with my phone. I set the alarm to wake me up on time tomorrow.

But I don't know how well I can sleep in this odd little gray box. There are voices in the hallway, bickering in another language. I should find it new and fascinating. But instead I just feel lost.

I *want* to love New York. I had this vision of moving to the big city and starting my life over from scratch. People do that all the time, right?

But I don't feel so fierce and brave right now. I feel untethered. As if this tiny Lego brick of a room could tumble off the tower and take me with it forever. In fact, if I disappeared tonight, nobody would even know where to look for me. Except my credit card company, nobody even knows that I came to this hotel.

My phone chimes with a text, and I feel an answering zap of relief. I need someone to talk to right now before I tip over the steep precipice of my unplanned life.

I grab the phone. The text is from the airline, reminding me to check in for my flight back to Burlington tomorrow.

Well, crap. I feel a wave of loneliness so powerful it threatens to sweep me under. So I tap Carly's name and shoot her a quick message. ***Your shoes are cute but they hate me now. I can't wait to give them back.***

Then I realize Carly is at work right now, slinging wings and beer without me. And I have a really unhealthy shimmy of longing for the Biscuit, of all places.

Get a grip, Abbi. There's no need to get sentimental for my crappy job. Besides, it's not like I'd see Weston tonight. Table seventeen won't be there. They're on their way to Indiana.

This lonely, needy girl shouldn't text him, right? Weston is not my emotional support animal. I'm a friend with benefits. My role is to be a good time. A *fun* time.

But it's fun to wish someone a good game, right? Right. *Whee! Fun!*

Yup, I'm losing my mind. But I text him anyway. **Hi Westie! Have a great weekend. Make Notre Dame cry!** Then I add a GIF of a West Highland terrier barking.

He answers me a minute later. **Thanks, Abbster! How'd it go today?**

Okay. Maybe. We'll see. Then my thumbs just tap out another text. I can't help myself. **Can I call you?**

Give me an hour, he replies. **I'll call you.**

It's a very long hour. When I get up to turn on the hotel TV, I discover that the thing doesn't work. When I hit the power button, it lights up before immediately fading back to black.

I suppose I could complain. They might move me to a different room. But that's a lot of hassle. The thing is bolted to the wall, because there's no room for a piece of furniture to support it.

Once when I was a little kid, our TV started flickering right as Mom and I set ourselves up to watch a movie together. "Oh no, Mama!" I'd panicked, thinking movie night was off.

"*Hell* no," my mom had said, getting up off the couch, crossing to that TV and delivering a sharp smack to its hulking rear.

And I swear the picture snapped right into view. Like it was terrified to disobey her. Then we'd cheered like crazy people.

I miss her so much. It doesn't help to think about that right now, though, when I'm already throwing myself a pity party in a soulless hotel between job interviews. I can't succumb to that kind of magical thinking. *If I could hug her just* one *more time...*

My phone lights up with an incoming video chat from Weston,

and I grab it like the lifeline that it is. I accept the call, and his handsome face comes into view. He's grinning at me. "Abbi! What's shakin'?"

"Nothing much." I drink in his smile and his eyes that crinkle in the corners when he's joking around. And the tightness inside my chest begins to lift. "What's it like flying with the hockey team?"

"Noisy," he says. "And when somebody says something asinine, you're embarrassed because he's wearing the same damn jacket you are."

"That's irritating," I agree. "All the asinine things people blamed me for today were things I said myself."

He winces. "Interviews went that well, huh?"

"It's just hard to stand out in a crowd. Apparently the investment bank takes a tenth of the people who apply. I thought if they were flying me here, that meant I had a chance."

"You do have a chance," he points out.

"I guess." But I realize now that I was unprepared. I thought terrific grades and a willingness to work hard were all that I needed to show. But I'd overheard some interviewees throwing around opinions about the GDP and the yield curve and equity derivatives. I know what all those things are, but I don't have opinions about them.

I just didn't understand how it all worked. And now I am blue.

"How about that other bank?" he asks.

"Oh, it was... interesting." I picture the round-faced man who'd sat across from me at that other interview. "The guy kept staring at my chest, and it threw me off."

Weston groans. "I'm sorry."

"It's fine," I mumble. Because I hadn't done that well otherwise. The man had asked me why I wanted to work in mortgage origination. You'd think I would have seen that one coming. But I'd gone blank for a second, as his eyes took another trip to the open button on my blouse.

The truth is that I don't have strong feelings about mortgage origination, either. *Everyone needs a home to live in,* I'd said eventually. *It seems like a compassionate kind of banking.*

"Let's just say I'm hoping that tomorrow's interviews go better.

But enough about me." I squint at the screen. Behind a shirtless Weston is a white tile wall. His tattoos stand out in the bright light. "Where are you right now? It almost looks like you're in—"

"The bathtub!" he says gleefully. "I'm giving my roommate some privacy."

"Why?" I blurb. "Wait, never mind. Maybe I don't need to know."

He chuckles. "He's just talking to his girl on the phone. Or at least that's all they were doing when I left. Now that I think about it, I should probably be afraid to leave this bathtub."

"I thought you guys would be partying in the lobby."

"No way," he says. "Coach is very firm with his curfew on game night. Once a year somebody sneaks out and does something stupid. And then they usually get caught. It ain't pretty. But some people have to learn lessons the hard way."

I smile at the tiny screen, and feel lighter. Weston is like sunshine on a cloudy day. "Tell me one dumb thing that somebody did."

"Well, one time—during spring playoffs—there was a Dutch women's field hockey team staying in the same hotel..."

I start smiling again before he's even finished the sentence.

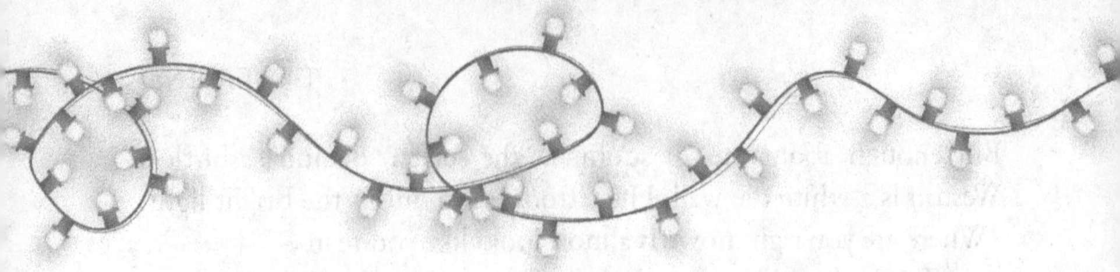

CHAPTER 21
IS THAT A EUPHEMISM?

WESTON

I tell Abbi a funny story involving a four-way room rearrangement that once became necessary just to give two couples some privacy. "There were more bed swaps that night than in a British sexual farce."

Abbi giggles. She's lying on a bed, wearing flannel PJs with little bunnies all over them. And I just wish I were there.

"Speaking of hotel beds..." I say, sounding about as subtle as a freight train. "This is a travesty. We're both in hotels. If it were the *same* hotel, we could be having hotel sex right now."

"That would definitely improve my day," she admits, propping her cheek in her hand. "If anyone is going to stare at my chest, I choose you."

"*See?* That's why all the lust-filled thoughts I have about you are okay. I'm on the VIP list. You just *invited* me to stare at your tits."

"It's a very short VIP list," she says with a smile. "With just one name on it."

"Yeah, I like it that way." Even as the words leave my mouth, I realize how true they are. Abbi and I are supposed to be just a casual thing. But I feel a little possessive of her, which really isn't fair. I have nothing to give her for the long term.

And yet, if she met someone new tomorrow—some guy at her

new job, who wanted to go the distance—I wouldn't like it one bit. This school year still has three months left, and I plan to take advantage of every one of them.

"What are you thinking about so hard?" Abbi asks suddenly. And I realize I've been lost in thought for no good reason.

"Your tits, of course." It's not strictly true. But seeing as I think about them with some frequency, it might as well be.

Abbi unbuttons just one button on her PJs, and suddenly I can see the soft swells of her cleavage. "There. Now you and the mortgage banker have the same view."

My body tightens deliciously. The bathwater has me feeling warm and loose already. "You're killing me right now. When am I going to see you next—for real?"

"Hard to say," she says. "I work a double on Sunday."

"When do you get off?" I ask. By which I mean, *when can I get you off?* Making Abbi whimper and sigh is my new favorite hobby.

"Eight," she says. "A double shift on Sunday means you don't have to close."

"Come over? We'll be hanging out at the hockey house, drinking some beers and unwinding."

"Maybe I can," she says. "What's the vibe at the hockey house, anyway? What's it like?"

"Not as skeevy as you're probably thinking," I say and she laughs. "I mean—we have some killer parties. But on a quieter night it's comfortable. Our alumni landlords make sure the place has a weekly cleaning service and every TV channel under the sun. The kitchen is actually pretty sweet. We've got a giant blender that we use all the time, and a big mixer that we never use, but it looks *very* sophisticated."

Abbi laughs again. "The things I could do with that mixer."

"My mixer is your mixer, baby. What do you want to mix?"

"I found a recipe in my mother's cookbook for this weird cake she used to make for me. I haven't had it in years..." Her smile fades, and she looks a little wistful.

"Seriously, if you want to putter in my kitchen, you can do that anytime. But come over Sunday either way, okay?" *Because I miss you.* I don't say that part out loud. "We'll be watching tonight's

Bruins game," I say instead. "We made a pact on the plane to save it until after we get back."

She blinks. "So I shouldn't tell you they're losing four to zip?"

"Wait, really?" I gasp. "*Four* to nothing?"

Her smile blooms naughtily. "You're so *gullible*, Westie. I really have no idea if the Bruins are playing tonight or not."

"Abbi!" I laugh, and try not to drop my phone in the tub. "You're so mean. Maybe you should show me some more tit as a punishment. Two minutes for unsportsmanlike conduct."

"You want penalty tits?" she asks with a giggle.

"Oh, definitely."

She reaches up... and buttons the PJs closed instead.

I let out a little moan of frustration.

"Let's wait," she says. "Until you can see them in real life. I'm not comfortable flashing you over hotel Wi-Fi."

"Ah, fine. Fine." I suppose she's being smart about that, even if I'm crushed. "Just so you know, I'm not as smart as you are. And I'm not shy. So..." I lift the phone and change the angle. First I reveal my abs, which I'm tightening for the occasion. The six-pack is looking pretty buff onscreen, if I do say so myself.

Abbi makes a small sound of pleasure.

So I keep going. I angle the phone even further, until she can see my erect cock poking mostly out of the bathwater. "Look who says hello."

"Well, *hi* there," she breathes, her lips parted. "Now I really *do* wish we were at the same hotel."

"Yeah, well." I reach down and give myself a slow stroke, and Abbi makes another noise of approval. "You like that? Or am I just being creepy right now?"

She smiles. "You're *not* creepy, Weston. Everything you do is sexy. Every. Thing."

A warmth hits me that has nothing to do with bathwater. "You know I think the same thing about you, right? Everything you do is sexy."

"No need to exaggerate."

"Oh, I'm not." I give myself another slow stroke, because it feels so good. "If you were here, you'd be in this tub with me. I'd insist."

"Mmm," she sighs. "If only."

My voice goes low and rough just thinking about it. "We'll put that on our bucket list. Things to do together before we run out of time together."

"I'm in," she whispers. "Keep, uh, going. If you want to."

"You want me to?" My voice is pure gravel. "Put on a show for you?"

"Yes. Does that make me a hypocrite?"

"No," I insist. "We all have our comfort levels. Mine is set on *slutty*."

She laughs. On the screen, she seems to sink a little further back into the pillows. Then she licks her lips. "I admire that. Mine is stuck on *cautious*."

"You've had to be," I remind her. But my mind is only half present in this conversation. "Hang on. I need to make a few adjustments."

It's just your ordinary Thursday night right here at the Marriott, with me setting up to tug one out in the bathtub on a video call with my fuck buddy. Luckily, the hotel bathtub has a shelf that stretches across it—for your glass of wine, I guess—with a groove across it for your e-reader or whatever. I prop up my phone on the shelf, which frees up my hands.

Then I grab the little body wash bottle and squirt some into my palm. Now my hand is all slicked up, and I run it casually over my chest and my neck, while Abbi lets out a breathy gasp. "If I were there, I'd do that for you," she whispers.

I feel her gaze like a caress. Enough teasing. I drop my hand to my stiff cock and take myself in a firm, slick grip. I tease the underside with my thumb, and it feels so good I let out a horny groan.

"Whew," Abbi sighs. "It's suddenly really hot in here."

I don't respond, because I'm watching her flushed face on the screen as she licks her lips. She likes this. A lot. Then I see her slide a hand up under her top.

"Are you...oh *hell* yes." She's touching her breasts under her shirt. I see the form of her hand circling her nipple. And now her eyes are going dark and dreamy.

Damn this is fun. And I love pushing Abbi's boundaries just a little bit.

A few minutes ago I'd called myself slutty. Except I've never done this before. I haven't had a girlfriend since high school, and therefore nobody to get freaky on camera with.

I pump myself and realize two things at once. The first is that this isn't going to take very long. Abbi's heated gaze is burning me up.

The second is that this only *looks* slutty. It's actually just the opposite. You have to trust someone an awful lot to stroke your cock while she watches. You have to trust that she'll find it hot instead of ridiculous. And that she won't take screenshots and post them on the Internet.

Abbi would never do that. I know it with perfect confidence. Just like I also know that I haven't trusted anyone else like that in a *long* time. I haven't wanted to. I haven't seen the point.

But suddenly it's clear as day that I do trust her, as I tip my head back against the tile and work my slick hand up and down my shaft. Then I drop my free hand down to tug on my balls.

Abbi lets out a little moan when I do that. And I swear the sound is what starts to push me over the edge. "Fuuuuck, honey. Miss you." My hand pumps away. Release is calling my name.

"Miss *you*, Weston," she whispers. "Wish I could show you how much."

And that's what gets me off. My balls go tight and then sweet relief finally arrives. She gasps as I come on my chest. My jaw is locked tight as I milk it for all it's worth.

But then I sag against the porcelain. I feel strangely wrecked. Now I'm just a messy guy in a cooling tub, who wishes he could curl up in a bed with the bright-eyed sweetheart on the screen.

If I wasn't ridiculous before, I am now, right? This is why they never show you the aftermath in porn. I look red faced and crazy eyed. And I feel almost hung over.

So I reach up and turn off my camera. Then I lift the phone to my ear. "Well, I hope that was better than what's on TV," I say casually.

Abbi lets out a hungry moan in my ear. "That was..." She swallows. "Wow."

I smile through my unexpected embarrassment. "Sunday night, then?"

"You know it," she says with a little laugh.

"Eight o'clock," I whisper.

"Okay," she agrees. "I might bring the ingredients for a cake."

"Is that a euphemism?"

"No. But you like cake, right? I'm not sleeping with some kind of psycho?"

"You know I like cake." I open the drain on the bathtub. "But I don't know how much sleeping I'm going to let you do. Bring your toothbrush anyway."

"I will. Good night, Westie."

"Good night, Abbster. I'll dream about you." That's another thing I've never said before. I'm racking up all the firsts tonight.

We sign off, and I stand up and shower myself off. I feel a little skittish now, and it's hard to say why. It's just a little fun with Abbi. No big deal, right?

Right. No big deal.

I turn off the shower and grab a towel. Yup, just an ordinary Thursday night in South Bend. Nothing to see here.

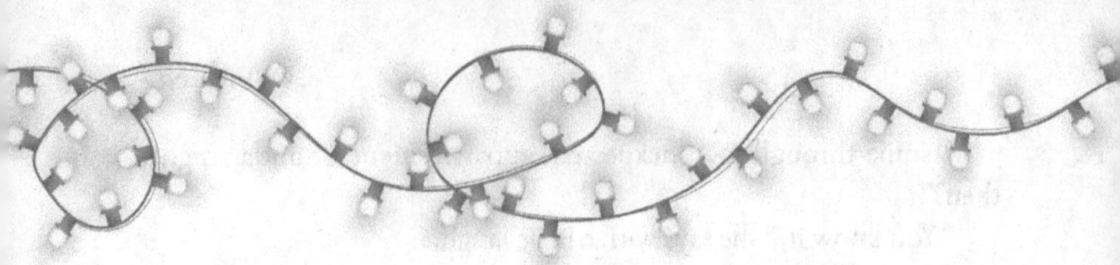

CHAPTER 22
WHERE THE MAGIC HAPPENS

ABBI

Working a double shift always seems long. But Sunday's seems to drag on forever. I'm excited to see Weston. *Really* excited. I tell myself that it's just the sex, which is epic.

But it's scary how much I really like him. And the fact that he seems to like me too is giving me all kinds of romantic ideas that I shouldn't be having. Whenever I catch myself daydreaming about him, I want to slap myself.

He hasn't offered me a future. But he did offer me his kitchen. So earlier today I bought the ingredients to make a huge vanilla cake with pecan praline icing, just like my mother used to make.

Meanwhile, I'm waiting tables on what has turned out to be a hellishly busy Sunday. Carly is in a surprisingly bad mood, too. But it's been too crazy for me to corner her and figure out why.

There's finally a lull at quarter to eight, and I catch up to her by the soda machine. "Hey," she says, a tired look on her face. "Any chance you want to close for me?"

"Oh, crap. I really can't. I, um…"

She laughs. "You have plans with a certain defenseman who won against Notre Dame last night?"

"I do," I whisper. "But keep quiet about that."

"Of course. And I'll stick it out here." Carly's expression droops.

"Are you okay?" I press. "If you really need me to stay, I will. You worked for me on Thursday."

"How did it go in New York, anyway?"

"It's hard to say." I tell her about my dodgy interviews on Thursday. "And then on Friday I interviewed for the marketing teams at two fun, girly brands."

"That sounds better."

"You'd think," I grumble. "But they just want social media coverage." And they were intimidating in a completely different way. At both interviews I was asked which were my favorite designers.

I'm way too poor to have favorite designers. So I'd had to twist the question around and explain which clothing brands were doing the most interesting things on social media. And that worked pretty well, I guess.

I don't think I stuck the landing at either company. And I came home feeling defeated. "But enough about me," I say. "What's got you down?"

She shakes her head. "I'm fine, Abbi."

"You don't seem fine," I argue. "Seriously. Will you tell me what's bothering you?"

She opens her mouth and then closes it and shakes her head. "I don't want to stress you out with my drama."

"But that's what friends do, right?"

Carly looks torn. And I'm mentally tearing up my evening plans to close for her if she needs me to. "I had a run-in with Price," she says.

My stomach drops. "Oh no. When?"

"Yesterday afternoon."

"But bouncers don't work afternoons. Where did you see him?"

"Here." She winces. "He's training to be a bartender. You know how they train people on the lunchtime shift?"

"You are *kidding* me!" I yelp. "This is terrible."

She nods grimly. We both know that Kippy is strapped for bartending help. One time Carly and I offered to train as bartenders, because the tips are better. But Kippy prefers men. And he had the balls to tell us right to our faces that he wouldn't let us try it because we're the best servers he has.

Neither of us wants to argue ahead of our bonus anniversaries, either.

"It gets worse," she hisses. "Price made a point to tell me that he'll be seeing a lot *more* of me. Then he grabbed my ass when I was standing at the touchscreen working on an order."

"I hate him," I whisper.

"Two more months," Carly whispers back. "That's all I have to stick this out until my bonus check. Let's not panic yet," she says, although she looks to be doing that very thing.

"Okay," I agree just as the bartender on shift dings his little bell. "That's my last drink order for the night. I've already dropped the check, too."

"Go," Carly says, shooing me. "Go be with your man. I'll be fine, Abbi. We both will."

I'm sure she's right. I've survived Price before. I can do it again.

———

The hockey house is a big, multipeaked Victorian home just off campus. The lights are blazing from inside as I climb the stairs to the big porch. My arms are weighed down by a shopping bag full of groceries, and I'm feeling a little foolish.

Lots of women go to parties at the hockey house. It's just that I've never been one of them. The total number of college parties I've attended is a pretty low number. I started college less than a year after my mother's death, when I still lived in Dalton's home. Both grief and a long commute prevented me from becoming a partier. That was a dark time, and I'm lucky I got decent grades and stayed in school.

So it almost feels like I'm visiting a foreign country as I approach the door.

Before I can reach for the doorbell, the door flies open, and Weston's smiling face appears. "Abbi! You made it! Let me take that." He opens the screen door and takes the bag with one of his strong arms.

And then? He uses the other one to scoop me into a kiss.

A really good kiss.

Top-notch.

When he pulls away, it's too soon. "Somebody's been hard up for a week," I whisper. And I might mean me.

Weston doesn't reply. His warm eyes crinkle at the corners as he smiles, and I get one more kiss on the temple. "Come in. I made the freshmen clean the kitchen, just in case you were serious about making a cake."

"Oh, I was dead serious."

"Awesome. Come on, let me show you the place." He turns to carry my grocery bag into the house.

I straighten my spine and follow him into the living room, where a dozen or so hockey players and various women are perched all over the furniture. The Bruins game is playing on a giant TV on the wall.

"This is where the magic happens," Weston says, indicating the whole first level of the house with a sweep of his arm. "If by magic you mean a lot of debauchery and smack talk."

"Noted." I peel off my coat and Weston hangs it on a coat rack. And I swear every head in the room swings around to stare at us.

"Uh, guys. You remember Abbi from the Biscuit."

"Hi, Abbi," several voices call out in unison.

"Tonight she's our guest, yeah?" Weston says. "That means her glass is never empty."

"Got it," says a freshman who's seated on the floor. I guess the furniture is for upperclassmen.

"Good," Weston says. Then he takes my hand and leads me into the kitchen.

He hadn't been joking. It's a great kitchen—not fancy, but spacious. There's a big table with eight chairs, too. And my favorite appliance—the mixer—gleams in the corner. "Wow. Time to cream some butter and sugar."

"Cream? Oh honey, *yessss!*" He lets out a salacious moan.

"You perv."

He grins. "How about I help you with this cake? Then I can perv out later."

"Don't you have a game you're supposed to be watching?"

Even as I say these words, a loud chorus of groans erupts in the living room. And one lonely cheer.

"You hear that?" Weston points over his shoulder with his

thumb. "I think I can follow the game from here. The Bruins just got scored on."

"Someone was happy," I point out as I unpack butter, sugar, and flour from my bag.

"One of the freshmen is a Rangers fan." Weston makes a face.

"And you allow that?"

"We tolerate it. Nobody's perfect."

You are. Ugh. It's inconvenient how much I like Weston. I know we're just a temporary thing. But I am going to miss him fiercely when I move away. "Will you preheat the oven to 350?"

"Sure." But he doesn't do it. Instead, he moves to stand behind me. Then he lifts my hair and kisses my neck.

My body flashes hot, and goose bumps rise up on my arms. He kisses me again, his lips soft and yet insistent. "Westie, don't take this as a criticism. But it's hard to make cake when you're so distracting."

"I know." He sighs. "Okay. Put me to work. Keep my hands busy, or I'm going to have to find other uses for them."

"Right. First the oven, and then..." I pull a printed copy of my mother's recipe out of my coat pocket. "Can you measure out three cups of pecans? We have to chop them and then fry them in butter."

"You got it," he says.

The living room lets out a sudden cheer.

"Ooh, score!" Weston says, pulling open the bag of pecans. "Let's do this."

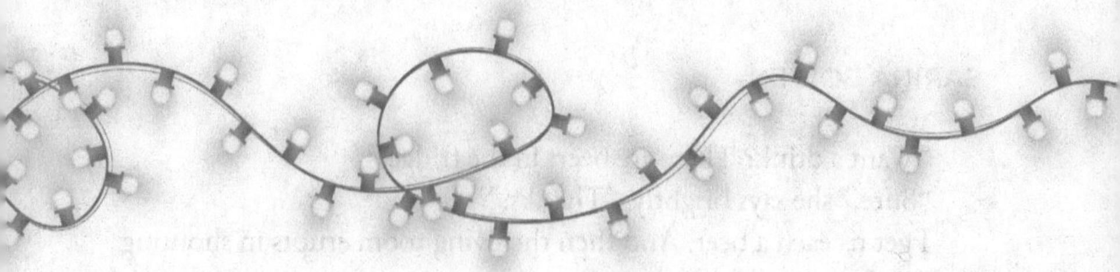

CHAPTER 23
THIS MIGHT TAKE A WHILE

WESTON

I've lived in this house for a year and a half, but I've never baked a cake in this kitchen. That seems like a mistake now, because the house smells *amazing*. And it's surprisingly fun assisting Abbi with her mixing and scraping.

Once the cake is in the oven, and the timer is set, I have an easier time stealing kisses. I push Abbi up against the counter and take her mouth with the same furor that I usually save for stealing the puck.

Abbi melts against my body. Her mouth softens under mine, and her arms wrap around my neck.

I'm just wondering whether there's enough time to drag her upstairs for a quickie before the oven timer dings, when she pushes me away with gentle hands. "Westie, I have to make the frosting. Caramelization takes some time. Do you have a skillet?"

"Yes, ma'am," I say, because it's more polite than ripping her clothes off. Then I find the woman a skillet.

Abbi melts another stick of butter in the pan and then tosses the pecans in. She stirs them continuously and takes frequent sniffs of the pan.

"What is that for?" I ask.

"My mom's instructions say to cook it until it smells 'caramelly,' and then start adding the powdered sugar. This might take a while."

"Want a drink? There are beers in the fridge."

"Sure," she says brightly. "Thanks."

I get us each a beer. And then the living room erupts in shouting and confusion.

Hmm.

"You'd better go see what just happened," Abbi says. She gives me a little push on the hip. "Sounds like a bad call from the ref."

"Right back," I tell her.

"Take your time. I got this."

As I head for the living room, I glance back at Abbi. She's humming to herself and stirring the pecans. She looks happy.

I feel pretty damn happy, too. I've got hockey and beer and the sweet scent of cake. And—even better—I've got more of Abbi's kisses coming at me later. I can't wait to drag her up to my lair and show her how much I've missed her.

"What do you look so happy about?" Tate asks on a growl when I arrive at his side. "The ref just gave this game away."

"Look on the bright side," I point out. "At least he didn't just give *our* game away."

"I guess," he grumbles. "There's still ten minutes in the period. We can rebuild it."

Due to an unfortunate glance at my news feed this morning, I already know that we didn't, in fact, rebuild it. But I'll keep my trap shut, and I cock my hip against the doorway and watch Boston fight for it anyway.

I'm cheering on the goalkeeper when the front door opens and a familiar face appears.

"Hey guys!" It's Amy, a teammate's little sister. She goes to Champlain College—which is the other college in Burlington. And every so often she swings by with a friend or two. In fact, last time that happened I hooked up with—

Uh-oh. After Amy clears the door, another face appears. Her friend is cute and bubbly. I remember we had a good time together. But it was only the one time, of course. But now her gaze locks onto mine, and there's a fire in her eye that spells trouble.

And here I'd thought that a non-Moo-U student was a winning hookup choice. I'd assumed the odds of us coming face-to-face again were pretty low. Not low enough, as it turns out. She tosses her coat onto a hook and makes a beeline for me.

Oh shit.

Even though I'm always up-front with my hookups, this happens once in a while. I make my little speech the same way every time, before any clothes come off. *So, listen, I'm not in a position to start anything serious. But if you're up for one night of fun, I'm your guy.*

Not everyone's hearing is great, I suppose.

"Weston, hey! It's been a while," she says. She holds out her arms, as if expecting me to kiss her hello.

I don't, though. Instead, I stand up a little straighter and give her a smile that's friendly but not encouraging. "How've you been..." It takes me a second to pull her name from my memory. "Kerry?"

"Cara," she says quickly.

Shit. "*Cara*, God. Sorry. Well it's been a while."

"Yeah. No kidding."

I see my buddy Tate start to smile at me from a couple yards away. He can sense my distress. But does he come over here and rescue me?

Nope. No such luck.

Cara moves closer. She puts a hand on my chest. "Anyway, I thought I'd hitch a ride with Savannah and see if you were up for hanging out tonight."

Tate hides his mocking grin behind his beer, and I want to slug my teammate. Because, Christ, this is a train wreck. "Uh, Cara, the thing is..." And then I come screeching to a halt, because this isn't a speech I've made before. *There's someone else.* That sounds like a line from a drama.

I'm still choosing my words when Abbi materializes at my side. "Cake's out of the oven!" she says brightly.

"Oh, awesome!" I slide an arm around her automatically—the same way I've done a half dozen times already tonight.

But Cara goes rigid. And her face turns red so fast that someone should probably call the fire department.

"Could you help me invert it?" Abbi asks. "I need a largish plate if you've got one."

"Plate. Large. Yup," I say, stumbling badly. "I've got that. Baby."

Abbi gives me a sideways glance that seems to wonder if I've sustained a hit to the head. "Okay. It needs to cool for five more minutes, but then it's go time." She kisses the underside of my jaw before peeling away, heading back to the kitchen.

Meanwhile, Cara keeps turning redder. "Looks like you're a little busy," she says quickly. "Take care." Then, before I can say anything, she slips past me and heads up the stairs in the direction that Amy disappeared.

Several of my teammates watch her ascent. And when she's good and gone, they turn to me.

"Awkward," says Vonne. "I sense a story there."

"It's a short story," Paxton chirps from the sofa. "They always are with Weston."

"That's not true," Vonne points out. "Weston has a girlfriend."

"You're a freshman," Tate says. "You haven't seen how it goes with him. We're all a little surprised that he and Abbi have been together these past couple of weeks."

"Right?" another of my teammates puts in. "Weston doesn't date. It's an unwritten rule of hockey."

"You mean, like, the fight ends when your opponent goes down?" Vonne asks with a smirk. "And never step on the logo in the middle of the locker room floor?"

"Like that," Tate assures him. "But Abbi is breaking all the rules."

I give him a withering glance that suggests he should keep his voice down. "Abbi is the exception that proves the rule."

Vonne raises his hand, like a second-grader. "What does that even mean? That phrase makes no sense."

"Sure it does," I bark, even though this whole conversation makes me uncomfortable.

"What it *means*," Tate whispers, "Is that Abbi graduates in the spring. Weston here doesn't have to worry about a real commitment."

"Ooh, an older woman," Vonne says. "Love it."

I roll my eyes at both of them. Tate isn't wrong. It's just that I'm not enjoying listening to my love life being picked apart.

So I leave them behind and head into the kitchen to help Abbi find a plate for her cake. The air here is heavy with the scent of nuts and sugar. "Holy shitballs, that smells good."

"Doesn't it?" Abbi says. "This was the cake my mother made for my birthday every year. It's a straightforward cake recipe, but with this crazy pecan icing. You can only eat a small slice before you start to slide into diabetic shock. So a whole cake would last us a week in the refrigerator."

"I give it a half hour in this joint," I tell her. "So cut yourself a nice slice. You have to look after your own needs at the hockey house."

"I'm starting to understand that," she mutters to herself.

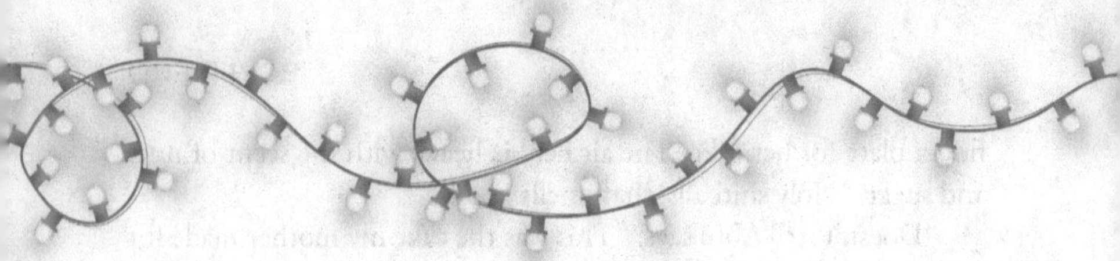

CHAPTER 24
A LOT OF BROKEN HEARTS

ABBI

I'm on my back in Weston's bed. He's hovering over me in the plank position, languorously thrusting, while I pant against his tongue and try not to moan too loudly.

"Fuck, Abbi," he curses. "I don't want it to end. You get me so hot."

He says this as if I might not understand. As if I'm not the one who's splayed naked on his bed, legs wide apart, worshiping at the altar of Weston's dirty talk and growly kisses.

Is this real life?

"Touch yourself, baby."

"W-what?" I whisper.

"Touch yourself and let me watch." He looks down at me, eyes gleaming. "I did it on camera. You can do it in bed, right? There's nobody to see but me. And I *really* want to see."

He punctuates this big idea with another steamy, brain-bending kiss. And I can't think anymore. I can't remember who I was before I became Weston's plaything. And I can't remember why I should ever leave his bed. Everything is perfect here.

"Go on," he rasps. "I want to watch."

So I don't even hesitate. I reach down between our bodies and slowly stroke myself, while Weston presses himself up on his delectable arms and drinks in the sight of us merging together.

"*Fuuuck*," he breathes. "Get there for me, Abbi. I need to hear you come."

And I do—instantly—and it's probably because my fragile little heart heard those first three words the loudest: "*I need you.*"

If only he truly meant it.

Afterward, we lie together in a blissed-out, sweaty heap. This must be what heaven is like. We've had cake. We've had fantastic sex. And even now, Weston is stroking my back, staring into my eyes, looking at me like I matter.

I want to believe him. So badly. But the problem is that I know better. Tonight has been great. But it's also offered me a painful reminder of how things really are.

Weston's kitchen provides near perfect acoustics into the living room. So I'd heard that girl arrive—Cara. And I'd happened to peek out of the kitchen, watching and listening while he blundered her name.

He'd felt bad about it. Weston isn't an asshole.

But maybe I am. Because something propelled me to step out and claim him. I could blame hormones, I guess. The truth is that I feel a giddiness at being Weston's woman of the hour. And when he'd slipped an arm around my shoulder, I felt like a queen.

But then? When I'd gone back into the kitchen, I'd also overheard Tate and Vonne ribbing Weston about his allergy to commitment. That had been hard to hear, even if I knew it was the truth.

Weston and I will be separated the minute after I graduate. He'll become my nicest memory of my time at Moo U. But I already know that he won't become my long-term boyfriend—either fake or otherwise.

Still, when I'm able to live in the moment, life is pretty great. After Weston and I had inverted the cake onto a big platter he'd found in a cupboard, I'd iced it with my gooey pecan frosting. Then I let it cool a little so the icing could set.

Weston had suggested we watch the end of the game before treating a house full of hockey players to cake. And I'd sat tucked against him in the living room. Together we'd watched the last half hour of the game. And every fifteen minutes, a freshman refilled my soda glass, just as Weston had ordered.

That'd meant I needed to pee. So when the game was nearly over, I'd climbed the stairs to the second floor to use Weston's bathroom.

As I walked along the carpet runner stretching down the hallway, I'd heard voices spilling out from behind a door that was open a crack.

"I'm such an idiot," the girl had sobbed. "I really thought he liked me."

It was Cara. And I'd frozen in place, shamelessly eavesdropping.

"Even though he never answered your texts?" her friend had prompted gently.

"I thought maybe he changed numbers."

"Oh, Cara."

"I know, okay? I *know*. It's just hard to understand. We had a *great* time that night. Not just a hot time. I felt a real connection. We talked half the night. And the sex was over the top."

"Oh honey. I'm sorry. Weston is..."

I'd stopped breathing.

"He leaves a lot of broken hearts in his wake. It's not intentional, I bet. He just has this talent for making everyone feel special. But connection isn't his end goal. It's fun."

"I *am* fun," her friend had sobbed.

"Right, but you live across town, so he's already forgotten how much fun you are. He avoids entanglements, Cara. He lives in the moment."

"Ugh," she'd said, and I'd heard copious nose-blowing. "It just stings. I've been thinking about him since November. But he didn't spend any of that time thinking about me."

Then she'd dissolved into tears again, and I'd hurried toward the bathroom.

That poor girl. My heart breaks for her, because I'm pretty sure her friend has it exactly right. Weston is just like she said—a great guy who lives for fun, with a talent for making everyone feel special.

Right this moment he's massaging my shoulder with a loving hand. I feel the same wonderful connection between us that Cara had. But one day soon I'll *be* Cara. I'll be sitting in my tiny New York apartment, wishing he'd return my texts.

Or maybe I'll run into Weston someday at a reunion. He'll call me Amy or Annie. "*It's Abbi,*" I'll say.

And he'll feel bad that he's forgotten. But he *will* have forgotten. Just ask Cara.

"Abbi," he says suddenly. And I startle, as if my thoughts are so loud that he might overhear them.

"Mmm?" I say casually. As if any of this were casual for me. Maybe Weston doesn't know how to do commitment, but I'm just the opposite. I crave commitment. And love. A family, and a place to call home. All the things I don't have in my life.

"Where did you go?" he asks.

"No place at all," I assure him, lifting my face to smile at him. "I'm right here."

It's just that I wish I could stay. Even though I know I can't.

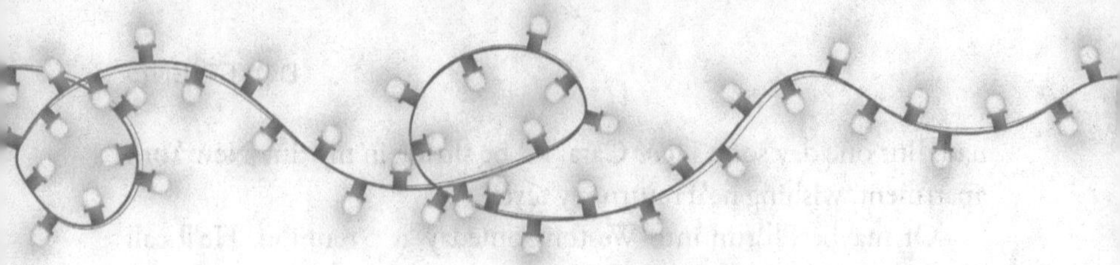

CHAPTER 25
PROPERTY OF ABBI AND WESTON

WESTON

I wake up in an empty bed. Rolling over, I look around for Abbi. But she's not here.

Her phone is, though. In fact, I think her ringing phone is what just woke me up. When I grab it off the bedside table, the screen says: *Caller is DALTON.*

Even though the call has already gone to voicemail, I decide that it could be important. So I heave my groggy self into an upright position and don the Westie pants Abbi gave me for Christmas. Then I start looking for her.

It's just after seven a.m., so the house is quiet. Abbi is the only one awake. She's seated herself at the kitchen table, where the last two remaining slices of cake are positioned with a card I'd printed before going to bed last night: PROPERTY OF ABBI AND WESTON. DO NOT EAT UNDER PENALTY OF DEATH.

"Cake for breakfast, huh?"

She startles. "I didn't hear you come downstairs." And when she meets my gaze, her eyes are red-rimmed.

"Hey, are you okay?"

"Of course."

Hmm. "Your eyes are red."

"That happens sometimes. I made coffee. I hope that's okay."

"Of course it's okay." I put her phone on the table. "This says that Dalton called."

"Oh! Sorry. Hope it wasn't too loud."

"It's fine, baby." She seems a little brittle, but I can't quite put my finger on why.

"I'll check to see if the coffee is done. Here's a fork." She positions the cake plate between us.

"Thank you."

Then she takes the phone and heads to the other end of the big kitchen, tapping the phone to make a call as she goes. "Hi Dalton," she says in a hushed voice. "Sorry I missed your call."

Her polite tone tears at me in a way that's hard to explain. Dalton is the only family she has left, but she speaks to him like he's the school principal. *I'm sorry I missed your call*. It's not even eight o'clock, for chrissakes.

"Noon. Sure. Thank you. I'll be ready. What's that?" Her eyes cut to mine. "I'm ninety percent sure he has class. But I'll double check. Of course." She reaches for two coffee mugs in the drying rack. "Thank you. Lunch is fine, really. I have to work at dinnertime. See you soon."

She hangs up the call and pours two cups of coffee. I'm watching her, trying to decide if I should ask her what that's all about, when I realize I'm letting her serve me a drink in my own damn home.

I leap up and grab the milk out of the fridge. "Thank you for the coffee. Now come and sit with me."

Abbi returns to the table and takes a fortifying gulp of coffee. But she still doesn't quite look like her normal, chipper self.

"Big plans with Dalton today?"

"I'm meeting him at noon," she says in a flat voice.

"Special occasion?" I press.

She sighs. "It's the third anniversary of my mother's death. We go to the cemetery every year."

My heart drops. "Oh Abbi, I'm sorry."

"Yeah, uh, thanks. It's just a shitty day. We get through it."

"Should I come along?" I hear myself ask. Because I'm pretty sure I heard Dalton make that invitation.

"No," she says quickly. "It's not fun."

"Well of *course* it isn't," I agree. "But neither was watching my family implode over Christmas."

Her eyes search me without really seeing me. "Dalton is taking me to lunch after. But you must have class today," she points out. "And then practice."

"Well, yeah," I admit. "And I have to get fitted for a tuxedo before my sister murders me."

She flashes me a quick smile. "Weston, you're busy. It's okay. Really." Then she ducks behind her coffee cup.

I feel uneasy. This is, to be fair, the kind of quandary that ride-or-die single guys avoid. I honestly don't know whether I'm supposed to insist on being there for Abbi, or not. "What about Price?" I ask. "Will you have to duck him today?"

Abbi shakes her head vigorously. "Price wouldn't dream of showing up to a cemetery. You don't have to do the fake boyfriend thing today."

Well, ouch. Because I guess I'm not showing up to one either. I really do have class, and it's a review session for a test I'm taking in two days.

"Okay," I say quietly. I pick up the fork and take a bite of cake. "This is really good stuff."

Abbi's smile is a flash, and then it's gone. "Thanks."

"It's awesome that you have her recipe."

"Yeah." Abbi picks up her fork and looks at the cake. But then she puts the fork down again. "I'm not, uh, hungry. You can finish this. Actually, I've got to run."

"But..."

Before I even manage to finish that sentence, she's on her way out of the kitchen.

Five minutes later she reappears with her backpack. She gives me a kiss on the cheek and reaches for her coffee mug. "I'll wash this before I head out."

I clamp down on her hand. "Leave it, Abbi. I can wash the damn mug."

"Okay," she says quickly, her eyes flashing with an emotion I can't quite read. "Later."

And then she's gone, and I'm sitting here feeling unsettled.

"Someone's an early riser," mutters Tate as he shuffles into the kitchen. "Your girl get you up early for sexy times?"

"No." I let out a sigh. "I might have screwed up with her."

"Might have?"

"Yeah. I'm not sure."

"Hmm." Tate points at the cake. "You eating all that?"

I pass him Abbi's clean fork. "We can go halfsies. She ran out of here without eating it."

"Hmm." He takes a bite. "You two have a fight?"

I shake my head. "I just don't know where the boundary lines are, you know? Abbi doesn't have an easy life."

"Do any of us?" Tate asks.

I know for a fact that Tate's family farm is struggling, and he somehow does chores there, works an extra job, and still makes it to hockey practice.

So the man has a point. "I guess everybody has their moments. But this is a bad moment for Abbi, and I don't know what I'm supposed to do."

"I thought it was casual with you two."

"It is," I insist.

"Then what are you worried about?"

"I'm not sure," I lie, and then I shove another bite of cake into my mouth. "Honestly, I'm starting to feel like Abbi deserves better than me. I'm a commitmentphobe with a busy schedule. She needs a guy who wants to go the distance. A real partner."

"She seems like a great girl," Tate says. "But she's graduating, right?"

"Right." I feel relief just saying it. "I won't let Abbi down, and she won't let me down. We'll just go our separate ways."

Tate's eyebrows lift. "Hang on, though. Did Abbi *say* she wants more from you?"

"Well..." I try to think. "No, she never said so. It's just a feeling I have." Don't most women want more of me?

Christ, maybe I'm just an egomaniac.

"See, you don't actually know." My friend shrugs. "She might not even be looking for a long-term thing. Maybe she's just as relieved as you are that it's off the table."

"Hmm." I sit with this idea for a moment. But it doesn't quite feel right. "Abbi keeps her cards pretty close to her chest. But I get the feeling she can't let herself expect more from anyone in her life. She's really alone in the world."

"Like how alone?"

"An orphan. She has a stepdad, but he remarried. And there's a new step-stepbrother who sexually harasses her."

"Wait—that bouncer at the Biscuit?" Tate asks.

"That's the guy."

Tate makes a face like he's tasted something foul. "That guy is a tool."

"Yeah, and he's the reason she can't even live in her stepfather's home. She's got a lot on her plate. And life has already disappointed her so brutally..."

"You don't want to be the next thing that goes wrong for her," Tate suggests.

"Exactly."

He shakes his head. "That's tricky. Because you got your issues, but Abbi's got more. She's not a starter girlfriend."

"A *what?*"

"She needs a pro, right? Not someone who gets itchy about commitment."

"Right," I agree.

"Hmm," Tate says. "Did you end up inviting her to your sister's wedding in May?"

"No, I didn't," I say slowly. "I doubt Abbi will still be around by then."

"Maybe that's for the best," Tate says. "It sends a whole other message, you know? Weddings make people crazy."

"Yeah? I'm pretty sure marriage makes people crazy. But weddings just make people drunk and horny."

"I dunno, man." Tate grins. "Be careful who you take to a wedding. All that devotion and commitment is, like, contagious. Not that there's anything wrong with that. But you gotta be ready to receive that pass when the winger sends it."

"Yeah. Thanks for the advice." I drain my coffee. Devotion and commitment are not a good look on me. Sad but true.

Does that make me an asshole for spending time with Abbi?

I only wish I knew.

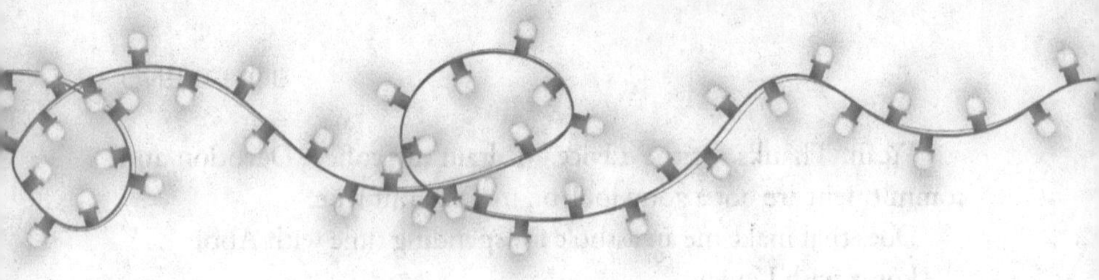

CHAPTER 26
NOT THINKING BIG ENOUGH

ABBI

Dalton picks me up in a car that smells like roses. On the back seat waits a beautiful bouquet of multicolored flowers in a sturdy basket. I stare out the window at the overcast sky as he drives to the cemetery.

These past three years I've learned that grief is like a chronic disease. Some days are good days, and you barely think about it at all. But then there are the flare-ups, when you feel terrible and can't imagine ever feeling happy again.

Today it hurts. A lot. And I can't think of any reason why the pain should stop.

We arrive at her gravesite before I'm ready. Because I'll never be ready. And we climb out of Dalton's car into an empty parking lot.

Last year the snow was knee deep. But today there's only patchy snow and ice on the ground as we pick our way through the soggy, winter-brown grass.

This is a quiet little cemetery halfway between Burlington and Shelburne. But as I approach her headstone, I feel so much emptiness. My mother isn't really here. She's gone from this world. And this plot of brown, snow-clotted earth—with a generous hunk of granite carved with her name—is just a place that we go to have somewhere to put our sadness.

We need this place, though. Especially today. I take the roses out of Dalton's hands and place them carefully in front of the stone. They're beautiful, but I don't believe that she can actually see them.

Only Dalton and I can, as we shiver here under the winter sky, trying and failing to think of the right things to say to each other. I watch Dalton swipe a tear away, and I have to bear down to avoid my own from springing forth. If I cry right now, I might never stop.

It's excruciating. And yet I still see the point of this exercise. We either come here to purge ourselves of a small amount of our pain, or else we'll drown in it alone. I don't like it. But I understand it.

Next year, though, I probably won't be here. I'll be in an office somewhere in a distant city. Dalton will call me and tell me he delivered the roses. And I'll thank him.

Dalton is a good man. He loved my mother. He saw the joy inside her. He used to take her dancing. He even tried to teach her to play golf, but she couldn't seem to get the hang of it. So he switched her country club membership to "pool only" with a cheerful shrug.

I'm glad she had his love in her life, even if she was robbed of the years she deserved to enjoy it.

Mom, I guess you quit while you were ahead, I say inside my mind. *But I'm taking a serious deduction from your score for that terrible dismount.*

"Shall we?" Dalton says eventually, saving me from my awkward internal monologue.

"Yup."

We traipse back to the luxury car with its leather seats and the radio tuned to Vermont Public Radio.

But the scent of roses lingers all the way back to town.

———

Dalton takes me to The Farmhouse on Bank Street for lunch, where I discover that I'm famished. I order the burger with bacon and an excruciatingly locavore salad, and eat everything on my plate.

My lunch companion has a crab cake and a craft beer. We are shoring ourselves up, I suppose. But after the plates are cleared away, our conversation is still flagging. I feel as hollow as the environmentally correct paper straw that I keep worrying with my fingers.

Then Dalton breaks the silence with small talk about Vermont Tartan. "Taft said he hired you for some extra part-time hours after your internship ended."

"He did," I agree. "I was happy to do it, and his recommendation will help me get a job. Hopefully."

"He'll give you a glowing recommendation. But I don't understand why you two aren't going to work together after graduation."

I feel too weary to explain all the ways that social media jobs can be a trap. I'd be stuck taking pictures of Taft's dogs forever. "But it's such a small business," I point out. "It's Taft and Connie's baby. There's no room for me to do more than the social media stuff that they hate."

"Well, I told Taft that he's not thinking big enough," Dalton says. "Maybe they need someone like you to help them strategize for capturing a younger demographic."

"That's nice of you to say. But their daughter is coming aboard this summer, so they already have some new help."

"Alexis?" Dalton looks surprised. "I hadn't realized she was moving back to Vermont."

"True story." I've already met Alexis. She has two really cute toddlers and a perky outlook that is probably just what the business needs.

"Okay. Any other good job prospects?" Dalton asks.

"Let's not make this day any more depressing than it already is."

He shakes his head and gives me a smile. "All right. But if you need me to shake the trees at the country club, just say the word. Somebody will have something. Even if it's just temporary."

"I will absolutely keep that in mind," I say. Although it would feel like a huge step backward if I end up doing the bookkeeping for one of Dalton's doctor friends and picking up extra shifts at the Biscuit. I want a fresh start so badly.

"Some company is going to be very lucky to have you, Abbi. Just hang in there. And if you need to move back home after graduation, you know you could have your old room back."

My eyes fly to his in surprise. I don't even know what to say right now. Moving in with him is *not* an option. But it's nice of him to think it is.

"Your mother isn't here to look after you," he says gently. "The least I can do for her is to make sure you're okay."

"Thank you," I squeak. There's a new lump in my throat now.

"I know you'd prefer to be independent. Lord knows Price doesn't mind leaning on me a little. There's no reason you shouldn't do the same."

I swallow hard. And I'm *this* close to telling him why I can't live in a house where Price lives.

But then I remember what that would mean—driving a wedge between Dalton and his new wife. I know Dalton pretty well by now. If I were forceful, he'd listen. But then I'd have to follow through. Dalton would probably make us all sit down as a "family" and talk to Price about boundaries.

Some people never learn boundaries, though. Price is one of those people.

The best thing to do is to stay the course. There has to be a good job out there somewhere for me. There are still three months until graduation. I'll find one.

I'll have to.

———

The very next day I get a rejection letter for the competitive training program in New York. Then I get a rejection from one of the social media jobs too.

And since I'm already a little depressed, I sink further into sadness.

This happens every winter. It's hard to keep my head above water during this time of year, with my mother's death looming so large in my mind. I'll never be able to look at the half-melted snowbanks without thinking about the day Dalton called me, voice shaking. *There's been an accident.*

I'm not very good company. But since the playoffs are coming, Weston is super busy. We're exchanging frequent texts and we speak occasionally on the phone. But we don't manage to spend time together before Weston heads out on another road trip to play Boston College.

I could really use a little distraction. Even my shifts at the Biscuit feel extra long.

"You look tired. Are you okay?" Carly keeps asking me.

"Sure," I respond. Because I will be eventually. At least I hope I will.

"We're overdue for a girls' night out," she insists. "Get out your phone. When's the next time neither of us is on shift here?"

The answer to that question does not improve my mood. We discover that our next opportunity to see each other outside work is three weeks out. "Better late than never, right?" she says. And we make a plan that's practically a lifetime away.

The following week, table seventeen comes in for dinner right after practice. Weston gives me a big, happy smile. Even though Carly has their section tonight, I feel my mood lift just from seeing his face.

An hour later, hockey players start trickling out the door again. And Weston waves me over. "Hey, girly. Should I study at the bar and then walk you home?"

I check the time, and realize I don't get off work for another two hours. "Didn't you tell me you have a paper due tomorrow?"

"Yeah." He makes a face. "Sad but true."

"Go home," I decide. "Write in peace. I'll catch up with you this weekend."

"About that," he says. "My family is driving up Saturday for the Merrimack game. We're eating out first. Want to come?"

"Sure," I say immediately. "I haven't been to a game all season."

"Better late than never! I'll text you the details." He looks over both shoulders, scanning the room. And then he leans in and kisses me quickly. "Oops, I slipped. But Kippy isn't here. Bye, baby."

"Bye, Westie," I say in a dreamy voice I haven't used in a week.

Pleased with himself, he strides out.

Sending him off to study was the right thing to do. I'm awfully tired. Even if he came home with me, I might not be any fun. My feet ache from waiting tables. And my heart aches, too. I don't feel the least bit fun or sexy tonight. And I'd hate to let Weston down.

Forty minutes later, I'm waiting at the end of the bar when a hand slides across my ass.

I jump about a foot in the air and spin around to find Price grinning evilly at me. "Hey, Abbi. Where's your boyfriend now?"

"Fuck you," I spit. "What does it matter where he is? I'm not yours to touch. And it doesn't matter what you ever do, or ever say, I will *never* be yours to touch."

I hadn't meant to react. Ignoring him is my usual strategy. And now Price has murder in his eyes. Suddenly I'm in a terrifying staring contest with my least favorite man in Burlington.

Until Kippy barks my name. "*Abbi.* Table eight needs their check."

I whirl around and head for table eight, my heart in my mouth.

From now on I'd better watch my back.

———

I sleep terribly that night, and wake up Friday feeling light-headed and tired. But I head off to Vermont Tartan to help them sort out their social media accounts again.

But when I get there, the new intern doesn't show up. "Where's Margie?" I ask Taft after saying hello.

"She called in sick," he says. "There's some flu going around."

I fight off a shiver. Margie and I sat elbow to elbow the other day, working on VT's Instagram account. "So you want me to just dive in?"

"If you wouldn't mind," he says. "Alexis left you some photographs of the spring line in your cloud folder. She loved what you and Margie made last week."

I sit down at the computer and open up the graphics software I'd asked Taft to subscribe to when I began my internship. And I start pulling in the new photos.

Alexis did a good job with the shots. They're well lit on pale-colored wood backgrounds. Very springy. So I begin experimenting with lighthearted graphic embellishments to try to produce a string of posts for a week's worth of content.

I'm a little tired, though, so I don't even notice Alexis behind me until she claps her hands together and startles me so badly the computer mouse flies off the edge of the desk.

"Oh my word!" Alexis hoots. "I apologize."

"No, it's fine," I say, clamping a hand over my suddenly pounding heart. "I just didn't hear you."

"That's good work, Abbi." She pulls out a chair and sits beside me. "I really like your content. It's so fresh."

"Thanks. I didn't use the photo of the slippers, though." I flip the screen to show her the picture that I mean. "The colors don't really pop here, and I didn't want to make the product look murky."

"It *is* murky," Alexis grumbles. "Those are stodgy, and no photo filter could fix it. All our slippers have that elderly look." She wrinkles up her cute nose.

"Tell us how you really feel," her father says from across the room.

"Dad, you know I'm right. We need some new looks."

"Felted wool slippers are in," I point out. "I think they'd fit the vibe without being too edgy."

Alexis blinks. "I was just thinking about those, too."

"Yeah?" I tap the computer screen, where I've got a photo of a plaid blanket enlarged. "I can see them paired with patterns like this."

"Good eye, Abbi," she says thoughtfully. "Tell me this—would a Gen Z kid wear felted wool slippers?"

"This one would," I say with a shrug.

"Interesting." She taps her lip. "Interesting."

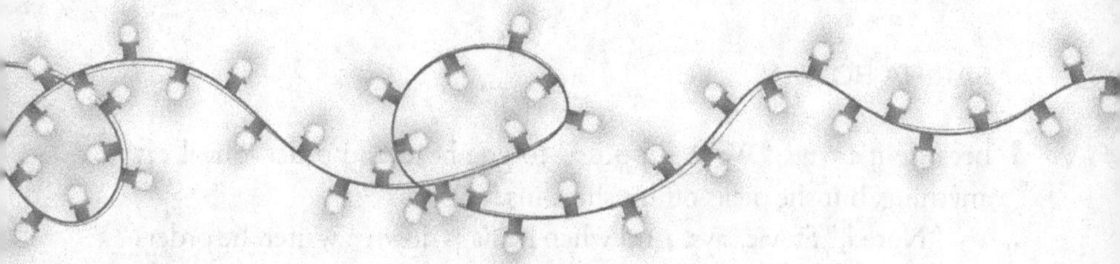

CHAPTER 27
A LOVERS' QUARREL
WITHOUT LOVERS

WESTON

Abbi is late for dinner.

She texted to say she was running late, so it's all good. But I find myself bouncing in my chair at the pizza place, watching the door for her.

Sometimes a guy just gets hyper. And tonight's my night. There's a lot riding on these two games against Merrimack. They're the only league team left that we haven't played. We'll play them back to back, two nights in a row. And if we were to lose *both* games, our playoffs spot is endangered.

So we can't let that happen.

Obviously.

Furthermore, my dad and my siblings finally drove up for a game. Not to mention Abbi's appearance—her first game of the season. This is why I'm practically levitating in my chair, waiting for Abbi to walk through that door.

"Maybe she's with her real boyfriend." Stevie snickers.

"Oh shut it," I grumble. The idea of Abbi finding a real boyfriend irritates me so much. It shouldn't. But it does.

I can't stop glancing at the door. Every time someone comes through it, I stare. "She's just running a few minutes late," I insist, because it's true. "We're supposed to go ahead and order. She'll eat anything, but she picks off mushrooms."

"Noted," Stevie says. And when he flags down a waiter, he orders three different pizzas.

"Three? For five people?" my sister argues. They bicker about it some more while I watch the door.

But it isn't until the pizzas are actually being delivered to our table that Abbi finally appears. I haven't seen her in a few days, but it feels like forever, so I drink her in. Her hair shines in the lamplight. She's wearing a dress and—fuck me—lipstick.

Which makes me focus on her mouth. And all the places on my body where I'd like to see it.

Now I might not survive this meal with my family. I'm thinking about sex instead of pizza or hockey, which is unfortunate because my near-term plans include only those last two things and not the first one.

Abbi spots me, probably because I'm shooting her a hungry gaze. Her eyes find mine. And then she walks bravely toward the family who made Christmas so very awkward.

"There you are, baby!" I pop out of my chair as she approaches. "Save me from these crazy people."

She gives me a shy smile as I pull her in for a hug. She smells like cold air and sweet perfume. "I dig the dress, but you didn't need to dress up for a hockey game."

"Hey, look!" my father crows. "It's the new bag in action. You look very professional, Abbi. Makes a statement."

"Thank you," she says, her smile warming up. "And I'm sorry I'm late, but I didn't wear this dress for you, Weston."

"Oooh, burn!" Stevie chuckles.

"I was actually interviewing for a job."

"No way!" I say. "Where?"

"Let the girl sit down," Lauren complains. "What kind of a boyfriend are you?"

Stevie snickers again.

My sister is right, of course. But I give my brother a little punch in the arm anyway, and then I pull out Abbi's chair and plate up two slices for her. "What would you like to drink?"

"Just the water," Abbi says, pointing at the glass already awaiting her. "Thank you."

"Now tell us about this potential job," my dad says as I hand Abbi the plate. "How did the interview go?"

"Really well," Abbi says. Then she gives me a nervous look that I don't really understand. "I mean—any job offer is good news at this point. Today I got two, actually. When it rains, it pours."

"*Yes!*" I'm so happy for her, because I know she's been stressed out about this. "Let's celebrate. What are the jobs?"

She chews a bite of pizza before answering. "Well, one of them is in New York. I got an offer from a mortgage bank."

"Mortgages are important," my dad says. "Everyone needs a house to live in."

"True," Abbi says, but she looks hesitant.

"Hang on," I hold up a hand. "Is that the place where the guy kept looking down your shirt?"

"Yeah," she says quietly.

My sister groans. "That doesn't sound like a great workplace. I've had managers like that. They never learn."

"Which managers?" my dad asks. "Who do I have to maim?"

"Easy, killer," Lauren says. "This was back in high school. The guy who owned that ice cream stand was kind of a creep."

"Damn, Lauren. How come you didn't say anything?"

She shrugs. "The tips were good, and I didn't want you and Mom to make me quit. I stayed out of his way. But it only worked because the summer was short. If I were depending on that man to advance a career, it could have been ugly." My sister turns to Abbi. "Do you know anyone else who works there? Like, a friend you could ask about the manager?"

Abbi chews her lip, then shakes her head. "That job is in New York, though. If I hated it, I'd be in a good location to look around for something better."

"But you'd also have a pricey lease," Dad points out. "You might not feel like you could quit."

Abbi blows out a frustrated breath. "Yeah, I did think of that."

"What if we don't try to plan Abbi's life before at least feeding her pizza?" I suggest, reaching for her hand. It's surprisingly warm for someone who's just been outside.

She interlaces her fingers with mine and squeezes.

"What's the other job?" my sister asks, because nobody in this family knows when to shut up.

"That's, uh, something that came up unexpectedly." She slips her hand from mine and takes a big gulp from the water glass that's on the table in front of her.

"Unexpectedly?" Now my interest is piqued.

"I had this internship last semester," she says.

"At the flannel place," my dad offers. "Great slippers, by the way."

She flashes him a tiny smile. "That's the place. They asked me if I'd interview with the whole family today, for a permanent job. And we talked for two hours, which is why I'm so exhausted." She takes another gulp of water. "But it was a really good meeting, and they gave me an offer letter and everything. There's even a signing bonus."

"*Nice*," I say, because I don't want Abbi to work for a sexual harasser.

"No *way!*" my sister yelps. "That's amazing. You wouldn't have to move to New York."

"Right," she says, giving me a quick sideways glance. "But I still have a couple of resumes in various places. I haven't made up my mind yet. It's a tiny company, so it feels risky to me in other ways."

I take a big bite of pizza and chew. It's really good. But I feel unsettled all of a sudden.

Abbi might stay in Burlington. That idea is just starting to sink in when my sister pipes up again.

"Omigod! If you're still in Vermont, you can come to my wedding! This is great!"

Uh-oh. Fuck. I never even told Abbi the date of Lauren's wedding. And now I can feel her eyes on me. Her gaze is giving me a sunburn all of a sudden.

"She should come to the wedding either way," Dad says. "Nobody goes to the office Memorial Day weekend. Why isn't Abbi on the guest list, Weston?"

"We uh..." I swallow a bite and try to figure out what to say.

But Abbi finishes my sentence. "We thought I might be moving." She licks her lips nervously. "Like, frantically unpacking my new apartment before my job starts the following week."

"But not if you're staying in Burlington," Lauren points out. "Tell us about this job."

Abbi's face is suddenly flushed. "Well, the daughter of the founders wants to create a whole new business line for younger shoppers. But it's a big deal for them, so it would happen slowly. I'd spend the first year learning about their supply chain and working on logistics."

"That's fun," Stevie says.

"It does sound like fun," I grunt. So why haven't I heard about this? Not even a single word?

Abbi puts down her slice of pizza and wipes her fingers on her napkin. "Excuse me a second." She gets up from the table and heads toward the back of the place, where the bathrooms are off a dark little corridor.

And even as my family watches me with curious eyes, I stand abruptly and follow her. "Abbi, wait," I say as I practically chase her across the big room and toward the bathrooms beyond.

She halts in the corridor and turns around. Even in the dim light, I can see her eyes are troubled. "What, Weston?"

"What the hell is going on here? You didn't tell me about that interview. And now it's already a job offer? But it's a big secret? You haven't been answering my texts."

"My week was crazy. The job was kind of sudden," she says. "And honestly? I thought you'd be weird about it. Kind of like you're being right now."

My head jerks back at this verbal slap. "I'm not being weird. I'm just asking you how your week was."

She licks her lips nervously. "You and I are supposed to be *fun*, right?"

"Right," I agree, but I feel like I've lost the thread.

"My life isn't always fun. Looking for a job has not been *any* fun. And you made it clear that we weren't part of each other's futures. It's the same reason I was never invited to your sister's wedding, I suppose?"

Oof. "It's true what you said. I never thought you would be in Vermont over Memorial Day weekend."

"Well, I might be. Sorry if that's an inconvenience."

"Abbi—"

"You should have seen your face when your sister brought up the wedding. And that I'd be in Burlington. It wasn't joyous, Weston."

"I was *surprised*."

"Me too," she says with a sigh. "But it shouldn't matter, right?" She waves a hand between the two of us. "This, whatever it is, can still reach its natural end point. Tell Lauren we broke up. You don't have to fake it anymore. Or do I have that wrong?"

"No," I say, but I feel so confused.

"Then why did you invite me tonight, anyway? If I'm past my expiration date?"

"I just wanted to see you. But, uh, I didn't think it through."

Her face falls. "Well, I *did* think it through. And I'm tired of faking it with your family. It was funny until I got to know them a little. It isn't funny anymore."

"Okay," I grunt, feeling like an asshole. But I don't even know what I'm agreeing to right now. "Sorry."

"Now go eat your pizza. I'll be out in a second." She disappears into the ladies' room.

I go back to the table feeling deeply conflicted. This is why I don't do relationships—I don't want to fight with anyone. And I'm terrible at it. Abbi made a lot of good points.

It's true what she said—I've been jerking her around. I didn't mean to. But somehow it happened.

When I slide back into my chair, everyone eyes me warily. "Did you fuck up?" Stevie asks gleefully.

"Possibly."

He shakes his head. "I used to think you guys weren't a real couple. But obviously you are. Can't have a lovers' quarrel without lovers."

I take a big bite of pizza and try to tell myself that I didn't just fuck everything up.

It doesn't work.

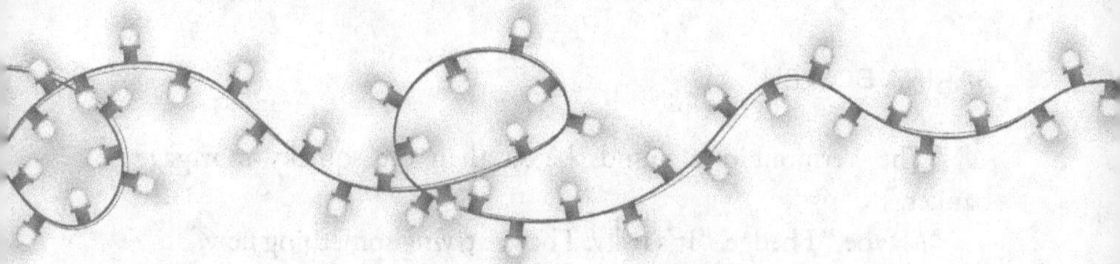

CHAPTER 28
SOME BONEHEADED THING

ABBI

I stare at myself in the bathroom mirror as I wash my hands. I see flushed cheeks and tired eyes. I feel so *off* tonight. Like the world is too bright and too loud.

There was really no need for me to pick a fight with Weston. I don't know why I lit into him for being a little stunned that I have a job offer here in Burlington. For months I've been telling him that I wanted to move to Boston or New York.

But it's hard to ignore the inevitable. I know he doesn't want a real girlfriend. I hadn't expected to change his mind. So it was almost a relief to force the issue.

And—fine—it hurt to hear that I hadn't been invited to Lauren's wedding. It's coming up so soon. My life is happening in fast forward. Graduation is just weeks away. I'm supposed to take one of these jobs and sail into the future.

The future seems scary and lonely, even if I never say that out loud. Even if that's not Weston's fault.

"Hey, Abbi."

I swivel to see Lauren walking into the bathroom, and I'm so tired that it hurts my eyes to move them. "Hey."

"Congratulations on the job offers. Both of them."

"Thanks," I whisper.

"The Vermont one sounds better than the squicky mortgage banker."

"Maybe," I hedge. "It's risky. They're trying something new."

"But trying new things is important." She cocks a hip against the sink. "I know my brother freaked out a little. Weston isn't good at this stuff. But I think he's really into you."

I give a slow blink, because I am just not in the right head space to discuss this with his sister. I think she's wrong. But I don't know what to say to shut this awkward conversation down. "I'll keep that in mind."

She grins. "You already know how ugly things have been for my family. You saw it yourself. The next time Weston does some bone-headed thing, just remember that he's gun-shy."

"I'll try," I say. "Thanks."

Then I leave the bathroom and go back to the table. Weston pulls my chair out for me as I arrive. He even gives me a tentative smile. Like he realizes our snit is stupid, and he's sorry.

He's so damn polite. He's such a good guy.

But he's not *my* good guy. And I'd better remember that.

Weston is the first to leave the restaurant, because he's required to arrive at the arena ninety minutes before the game. He kisses me on the cheek and I wish him good luck.

"Come out to the ice cream place with us, Abbi," Mr. Griggs says. "We can all walk over to the game together."

"I thought I'd run home and change before the game, and leave my favorite designer bag at home," I say instead. "Maybe I'll see you there?"

"We'll save you a seat," Lauren assures me.

Leaving them behind, I head home. The February chill slices through me as I walk uphill toward my apartment. Inside, my place is freezing. So I wet the cloth and toss it up onto the thermometer valve again. It's time to put on a pair of jeans and my *Griggs* sweatshirt for the game.

But I just don't feel like it. My head is achy, and my throat is scratchy. Instead, I make a cup of mint tea and climb into bed wearing Vermont Tartan pajamas.

I honestly don't know what to do about this sudden job offer. They want to pay me a real salary that's about eighty percent as much as the New York job. With benefits, too. Burlington is cheaper than New York. I could move into a nicer apartment here on a smaller paycheck than I could ever afford in New York.

So it's a great offer, but I'm still unsettled. I hadn't pictured my future here in Vermont. I thought I'd escape to a city and start over from scratch. But that's proving harder than I thought, when every day already feels like starting over from scratch.

Is it a sign of weakness that I'd rather walk into the tiny flannel company every day and see the faces of people who appreciate me? Does that make me smart, or does it mean I'm not ambitious?

I sip my tea, hoping the hot liquid can make me feel less confused. Less shaky and sad.

As the start time of the hockey game inches closer, I just can't make myself get up and go to the game. Thinking about Weston makes my heart ache. He told me he's not a relationship guy. He's always been up front about that. The problem is that I'm not capable of keeping up our fling without wishing for more. Does that make me a cliché? The clingy girl who agrees to be casual and secretly pines to be the one who changed his mind?

How did I let this happen?

I watch the clock. My eyes feel dry and achy. I must be overtired as well as overwhelmed. I've got too much on my plate.

Maybe it would be better to end things with Weston right now, on my own terms. At least without him at the forefront of my mind, I can make my job decision with cool, calculated logic. It will be my decision alone. As it always should have been.

Soon the clock tells me that it's ten minutes until the puck drops. So I pick up my phone and begin to compose a breakup text.

Then I delete it. A text is too impersonal. I'll leave him a voice message instead.

My heart thuds with tension as I tap the microphone. "Weston, I'm sorry to snap at you tonight, but I made a decision." As I pause to choose my words, I feel the first hit of grief. "We should just stop seeing each other now, before it gets too strained. I've had more fun with you than I've had in years, no lie. But there are things I have to focus on now that aren't super fun. So I'm going to make the difficult choice to do that. There's no point to drawing out the inevitable. Be well and have a great time in the playoffs."

My throat seems to be closing up, so I'll have to leave it there. I tap the stop button and send the message before I lose my nerve.

And, yup, I'm already sad. When I scroll up, I see the lengthy string of cheery texts between Weston and me.

And I just ended it. Forever.

Ow.

I force myself to lock my phone and set it down on the nightstand. Weston won't get that message for hours. He's busy with his team. I can picture him in his hockey gear, his bright eyes flashing as he concentrates on the game.

Now I know the warmth of that gaze when its full power is focused on me. It's more potent than I ever would have guessed. And I'll feel so chilly when it's gone.

But what was the alternative? A few more weeks of his loving touch, followed by an awkward parting?

It's better this way. A clean break.

I slip down into the bed and sigh. Someday I'll look back on this time with joy, though. I'll remember when Weston got me to sing with him in the car on the way to Thanksgiving dinner. And I'll remember those gorilla noises he made as he tried to show me how to ski.

I'll have those memories and they'll make me smile, without this terrible ache I feel right now, smack in the center of my chest.

That might be a while, though.

Grief takes time. If anyone should know, it's me.

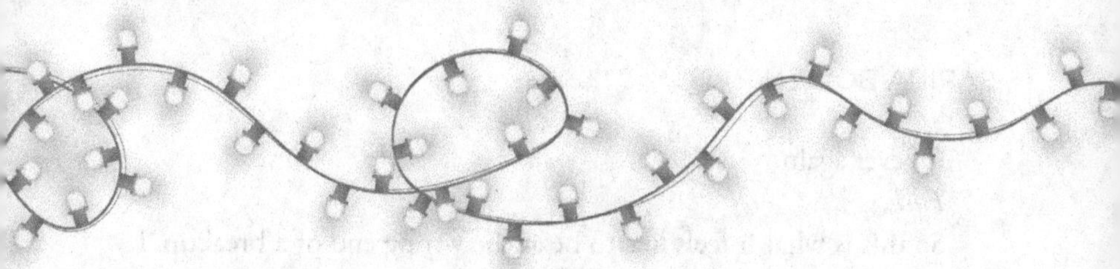

CHAPTER 29
BECAUSE I WANTED TO
SEE YOU

WESTON

It's a great game tonight. Our first line is on fire. And on defense, Tate and I make total nuisances of ourselves, keeping Merrimack away from the crease and holding them to a single goal all night.

My guys put up four goals. It's the best kind of drubbing, and the hometown crowd is a sea of green sweatshirts and cheering. My family is right behind the bench, and Lauren even bought a pennant somewhere. She's waving and smiling whenever I return to the bench.

I don't spot Abbi. But I sure hope she's enjoying herself. And, sue me, I'm hoping she got a little thrill when I stripped the Merrimack sniper during my last shift. I'm too cool to brag about my exploits, but if she happened to witness that, then I'm a happy man.

So I'm feeling pretty great as the boys blast some music in the locker room after the game. And that good feeling lasts about a half hour, until I pick up my phone and find Abbi's message.

My hair is still wet from the shower as I'm listening to her tell me *we should stop seeing each other now.*

Immediately the glow of victory is extinguished. I'm not even sure she attended the game. I looked for her, too. I found my family in the stands, but I couldn't find Abbi.

And she's not coming over tonight.

Or ever again.

Fuck.

So this is what it feels like to be at the wrong end of a breakup. I hate it so much. It's not because it's a blow to my ego, either. I'm going to miss her. A lot. Even though I know Abbi is right. Even if I feel low after listening to her message.

We weren't ever supposed to become a real couple, although it was starting to feel like we were. Tonight she'd asked why I invited her to have pizza with my family. And the answer was so easy— *because I wanted to see you.*

But that isn't fair, is it? That was abundantly clear when my sister started spouting off about the wedding. The one I never invited Abbi to.

Note to self—the fake boyfriend thing is only fun until one or both of you forgets that it's fake. And who knew I'd be the one to forget?

Abbi didn't. She cut me loose, and I ought to be grateful.

So why do I feel so blue?

"Yo, Griggs," Tate says. "Whatcha doing standing there? Let's go play some Beer Jenga and get our drink on."

"*One* beer," Coach says from across the room. "Don't celebrate yet. Gotta beat 'em again tomorrow night, boys. And what the fuck is Beer Jenga?" Coach asks. "Wait—never mind. I don't wanna know."

"Right, Coach," Tate agrees. "Good call." He grabs me by the elbow. "Let's party."

I follow him out the door. But I don't feel like partying.

———

The next couple of days are rough. My brain goes in circles, like a dog chasing its tail. I vacillate between knowing this break with Abbi was inevitable, and a guts-deep feeling that I've just made a huge mistake.

Either way, it feels wrong to me to end things on a bad note. So I try to call her. Twice. But she won't pick up.

Then I try texting. ***Hey, I know you're a little mad at me,*** *and you made a few good points. But can we at least have a talk?* But I get no response.

And now I'm just plain irritated.

"How bad was this argument?" Tate asks as I sit on the bench in the locker room, checking my texts for the millionth time.

"It wasn't that bad! I had no idea Abbi was so damn stubborn."

"Then maybe it's better that you broke up," Patrick suggests.

"Maybe," I grunt. "But I'm in such a pissy mood. I feel so..."

"Dismissed," Paxton, Patrick's twin, says. "Prolly the same way the girls usually feel when you're done with them."

"No way," I argue. "They know the score going in."

"Do they?" Paxton mutters.

My shoulders slump. It's starting to dawn on me that I have inconvenient feelings for Abbi. If it weren't true, I wouldn't care so much that she's done with me.

Shit. How did this happen?

"Time for dinner," Tate says. "Let's go to the Biscuit."

I let out a low moan, and the whole locker room laughs.

"Aw, Griggs!" Tate says, patting my back. "Maybe this is just what you need. Your girl can't ignore you face-to-face."

I'm sure he's right. And I really want to talk to Abbi. But I'd rather do it without an audience.

"Come on, man." Patrick slaps my shoulder. "Back on the horse. Maybe you can find another playmate for the night. Someone to take your mind off her."

"That's not happening," I snap. Not only am I not in the mood, I'd never do that to Abbi.

"He's right." Tate says. "Our guy has to be discreet at the Biscuit after this. What if we lose our table?"

"What if the entire waitstaff turns on us?" someone else asks.

"Then no more wings and beer," Patrick says sadly. "Didn't we warn you about this already?"

"I'm not ready to switch to a steady diet of pizza," someone complains.

"Fix this, Weston," Tate says. "Do it for the team."

"Okay, guys," I sigh. "Let's go to the Biscuit."

I feel tense as we walk through the door. And part of me expects to see the lacrosse team newly installed at table seventeen, gloating while we try to find adjacent booths in the dining room.

But, no, our table is waiting. I take my usual seat and look around. Maybe Abbi will emerge from the kitchen and smile at me like she always does. Can't we at least stay friends? At least I'd have that.

But the minutes tick by with no sign of her. And it's that lazy manager, Kippy, who finally swings by to drop off waters and menus. As if anyone at table seventeen needs a menu. "Someone will be with you in just a couple of minutes," he says. "We're short-handed tonight."

That's when I feel the first twinge of concern. And it only gets worse when a harried Carly hurries up, pen and pad in hand, and works her way down the table scribbling down orders. But the whole time she's shooting me curious glances.

And when Carly reaches me, she doesn't ask for my order. "Where is Abbi?" she demands instead.

"What do you mean?" I fire back. "I was going to ask you the same thing. Abbi won't take my calls."

Carly blinks. "You're kidding. She won't take mine either. She didn't show up for work last night or tonight! And it's her one-year anniversary." She glances over her shoulder before continuing. "Kippy won't give her the bonus she's worked so hard for," she hisses. "He said she blew it by going AWOL. But Abbi would never *do* that."

My stomach bottoms out. What the hell happened to Abbi?

"I've been calling her every ten minutes for the past two hours," Carly says. "And she doesn't answer. I'm going to go knock on her door on my break."

But I'm already pulling on my coat. "Let me do it."

"What about dinner?" Paxton asks. "Should we put in your order?" I don't even bother to answer him. I'm already headed for the door.

But I pull up short as I pass the bar. That cretin Price is behind it, cutting limes into wedges. "Have you seen her?" I bark.

"Seen who?" he says with a snake-like smile.

"Abbi."

He makes a show of shrugging. "Thought you were the boyfriend. Isn't that your story? Aren't you sticking with it?"

I want to punch him in the throat, but I'm in too big a hurry. So I dart out of the restaurant and start hoofing it uphill toward Abbi's place.

Thought you were the boyfriend, Price said. *Aren't you sticking with it?*

I had been, if I'm honest. I'd stuck to it until two nights ago. And I'd been happy, too. Playing the part of Abbi's boyfriend—and then becoming Abbi's boyfriend—had suited me just fine.

Then I freaked out when she said she might stay in Burlington. And now it's hard to remember why. If something has happened to her, I will lose my shit.

I'll lose it at myself, I guess, because I'll be the one to blame.

I break into a run and make it to Abbi's front porch in record time. Her car is parked at the curb, which is a good sign, right? I lean on the buzzer to her apartment unit, and then I try the doorknob of the front door. It's usually open.

But nope. Not tonight.

Shit.

I buzz again, and I start pounding on the front door until I see someone descending the stairs. It's another college student, I think— a skinny guy with round glasses.

Stepping back, I try to look nonthreatening. Although he's eyeing me warily when he opens the door. "Hey man," I say. "My girlfriend didn't show up for work two days in a row, and I'm panicking. Can you let me knock on her door?"

"Uh..." he says, looking a little unsure.

"Or let me talk to your landlord? Abbi said the old lady lives on the first floor, and never turns up the heat."

"Well *that* is certainly true," the dude agrees with a snort. "Abbi is right here, no?" He points at the door just behind him.

"That's right, and I'm really worried about her."

He bites his lip. "Okay, come in."

I leap past him and knock on the wooden door to Abbi's little studio. "Abbster, honey. Please open the door. I'm worried about you."

There is nothing but silence. I even press my ear to the door and hear nothing.

"Maybe she doesn't want to talk to you," the dude suggests.

"I can see why you'd suggest that," I agree. "But I'm telling you—something is wrong."

He sighs. Then he turns and heads down the little corridor toward the back of the building. A moment later I can hear him knocking on a door that's just out of view. There's a whispered conversation, and a tiny elderly woman with gray braids coiled on top of her head emerges with a huge number of keys on a giant ring. She's like something out of Dickens.

"Knock again, please," she warbles. "I don't make a habit of breaking in on my tenants."

I take a fist to Abbi's door and knock urgently. "Abbi, honey. We're worried about you. Open up."

Nothing.

"Step aside," Miss Havisham says, wielding one of her many keys. She unlocks the door and opens it slowly. "Oh dear," she says, and my heart plummets. "It's very cold in here. Like a refrigerator."

I lose all patience, pressing the door open further and sliding past the lady as fast as I move to evade an on-ice opponent. Abbi's room is dark, but I can make out a form in the bed. It's ice cold in here, and I stop breathing as I approach the too-still lump on the mattress.

"Abbi. *Honey.*" I sit down and place a hand on the flannel of her pajamas. My heart is in my damn mouth until she shifts under my touch. "Hey beautiful," I say in a broken whisper. "What's the matter, sweetheart?"

"Sick," she rasps.

"Oh no," I croon.

"Hurts," she mumbles, curling more tightly in on herself. "*Cold.*"

I press the backs of my fingers to her forehead, which is burning up in spite of the chill in the room. "We're going to fix you right up," I say gently. "Everything is going to be okay."

It has to be.

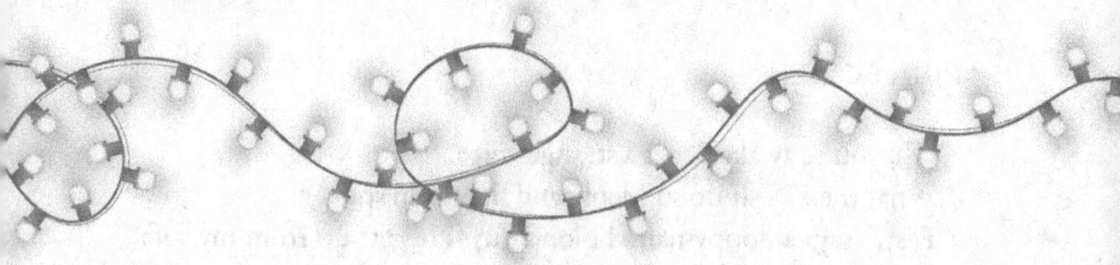

CHAPTER 30
YOU AND I ARE ALREADY BUDS

ABBI

When I'd said I never wanted Weston to leave me, it may have been a miscalculation.

Because he's *so* bossy. *Wake up, Abbi. Drink this, Abbi.*

Can't a girl get the flu in peace?

Not to mention that I probably look terrible—like someone who's been dipped in the fry basket at the Biscuit. Nobody wants the world's hottest hockey player wiping sweat off her forehead. Not if he's doing it only out of guilt.

Even if it feels really nice.

Especially when he kisses my forehead so gently afterward.

Damn it.

At one point I wake up and Dalton of all people is here. He's fussing with an ear thermometer and calling in a prescription. "Make sure she's getting fluids," he says to Weston.

"Yes. I will, sir."

And then we're back to *Drink this, Abbi,* and *Swallow this pill.* But I just want to sleep for a week.

Finally, I wake up again, and there's sunshine streaming in the window. That means it's late afternoon. It's quiet, too. Weston isn't sitting on the bed anymore, or fussing over me.

I roll over and groan into the silence.

"Oh, you're awake," says a strange voice.

"What the…" I sit up suddenly and the room spins.

"Easy," says a floppy-haired blond guy. He gets up from my sofa and approaches me slowly, on a set of crutches.

I squint, because he looks familiar. "You're a hockey player," I mumble. "What are you doing in my apartment?"

"Well, Weston had to go to practice. It's the playoffs, you know. But I couldn't go." He points to a cast on his leg. "So I'm here to make sure you're okay."

"I'm okay," I slur, falling back onto the pillow. "You can go."

"No way. I'm on duty."

"What?" My throat is sandpaper, and nothing makes sense. "What are you talking about?"

"Weston sent me to make sure you're okay. I'm supposed to message him every half hour. If I'm late, even by a minute, he blows up my phone."

"Um…" I try to swallow. "And how long have you been doing that?"

"Since noon."

"And it's…?" *Please say twelve thirty.*

"Four p.m."

"You've been watching me sleep?" I squeak. "I don't even know you. That's creepy."

"Nah, I'm Weston's teammate. Cooper. So you and I are already buds," he says, crutching past me on the way to my kitchen, opening my cabinet and locating the glasses on the first try. "You sound like you need a drink." He opens the fridge. "Ginger ale, fresh squeezed orange juice, Gatorade, or water?"

"What? I don't have any of those things."

He opens the door wider and shows me a full complement of beverages, plus a plethora of unfamiliar food items. "Weston stocked you up. After you have something to drink, you'll have your choice of soups, along with toast if you're feeling up to it."

I blink.

"So what will it be?"

I'm so confused right now. "I'd love some juice, I guess." But how is he going to carry it over here ? I start to get up but he grabs the juice bottle, shoves it into the big front pocket of his hoodie and closes the refrigerator before coming back to me.

"Thanks," I say, taking it from him. But then I can't get it open. My hands feel weak and ineffective as I tug at the lid. And I have the sudden urge to cry.

My unlikely caretaker sits down heavily at the edge of the bed, grabs the juice, and has it open with a quick turn of his wrist.

"Thank you," I squeak. Then I take a sip, and it's cold, sweet nirvana. Seriously, it's a miracle. Like I've never tasted juice before. I'm starved for it.

"There you go," he says. Then he pulls a phone out of a pocket of his shorts and points it at me.

"Whoa!" I shield my face with one arm while the other holds my precious bottle of juice. "Do *not* take my picture."

"But it's proof of life!" he insists, and I hear the shutter noise. "Maybe Weston will calm down if he sees you're conscious. Seriously, that guy was *freaked* that you were sick."

"Cooper!" I bark. "Do not send that to Weston."

He chuckles. Then he tosses his phone down. "Fine, fine. But Weston loves you. I don't see what's the big deal."

I let out a sigh. Of *course* he doesn't understand.

"Look—I've never seen Weston spend time with any girl but you. And I've *really* never seen him bolt out of the Biscuit like his ass was on fire like he did when he thought something happened to you."

"Why did he think that?" I ask cautiously. After getting feverish the night before last, I'd holed up at home, dosing myself on NyQuil.

"Carly said she was worried about you. Apparently you didn't turn up for work two nights in a row."

"Two nights in a..." Horror dawns inside me. "What day is it?"

"Tuesday."

My heart stops. "Oh my God."

"Yeah, you slept for three days."

"Oh my *GOD!*"

"You mentioned that."

"You don't understand!" I shriek. "I'm going to get fired. I won't get my bonus." The juice bottle wobbles in my hand.

He takes it from me. "Breathe, Abbi. They'll understand."

"They won't."

"How about some food?" Cooper's phone dings. He picks it up and reads a message. "Weston said practice is over. He'll be here in an hour."

"I need a shower."

Cooper frowns. "That's not on the list of things that Weston said you could have."

"Are you kidding me?" I sputter. "If I want a shower, I'll take a shower!"

"Sure, sure," he says, setting the juice bottle down and then heaving himself up. "I'll be over at your desk, facing the other way."

"You could just leave," I point out.

"No can do," he says, picking up his crutches again. "Weston wants me to stay, so I stay."

I let out a groan. I don't understand why Weston is calling the shots. He probably feels really guilty. I told him we should end things, and then I got the flu. It's just a coincidence, but the man took it personally for some reason. So I need a new plan.

Step one: Shower so I don't look like a leper.

Step two: Thank him for the juice and send him home.

Step three: Go straight to the Biscuit and beg Kippy for patience. Cry, if necessary.

It's not like I don't feel weepy when I think of my annual bonus snatched away from me.

———

Showering takes all my strength. After I manage to shampoo and dress in clean clothes, I want to curl up in a ball and sleep for another three days. But I won't let Weston see me look defeated. So I wrestle the sheets off the bed and stuff them into the hamper.

Remaking the bed feels like a marathon, though, and Cooper takes pity on me and helps.

"You don't have to do that," I say. "But you're awfully good at hospital corners."

He just shrugs. "Are you going to dry that hair? Weston will yell at me if he thinks you look cold."

"Oh for God's sake!" I hobble back into the bathroom and spend a few tiring minutes with the blow dryer. Then I brush my teeth. That done, I throw my clean self on the clean bed and moan, because my heart is pounding like I just ran a marathon.

"Aren't you the picture of health," Cooper says. "Maybe this will help?" He's inched his way toward me with a bowl of soup in one hand and a crutch under the other arm.

"You really don't have to wait on me," I say, grabbing the bowl as it wobbles. "That's dangerous."

"Yeah, because you look so competent yourself." He chuckles. "Eat the soup, Abbi. Why do you hate getting help?"

"I don't," I snap, but it's only half true. Help is wonderful. But you should never get too used to it. I look down at the bowl. It's full of steaming chicken noodle. "Thank you," I manage.

"Don't mention it." He pulls a spoon out of his pocket. "Mind if I have some, too? There's more."

"Of course not. Dig in."

"Just don't tell Weston," he says.

"I won't. Cross my heart."

The floppy-haired surfer boy gives me a smile and crutches back to my kitchen.

———

After we manage to get the dishes cleared, it's time to face another problem. I locate my phone on the floor under the bed, and warily unlock it.

I find a couple of missed calls from Weston, of course, and some text messages asking me to call him. But the most frantic messages on my phone are from Carly. ***Where are you? What's wrong? Kippy is so mad! Call me.***

Oh boy. That can't be good.

I'm terrified to open my email. The first thing I spot is a polite message from Taft at Vermont Tartan, asking if I've had a chance to make a decision about the job. Then there's a follow-up message explaining that he'd heard from Dalton that I was ill, and to take my time.

Then, in a complete study of contrasts, I find a pissed-off email from Kippy at the Biscuit. ***Abbi, this is unacceptable. Two shifts blown without a phone call? We have terminated your employment. Your last check will be issued within 10 days.***

"Oh my God," I breathe. Then I let out a tortured groan.

That's when the door pops open and Weston enters carrying my keys. "What's the matter? Why is Abbi moaning? Cooper, what have you *done?*"

"Calm down, Westie," I say, dropping my phone onto the bed. "I was groaning at an email."

Weston stalks over to me, setting my keys on the night stand, and sitting on the edge of the bed. His beautiful eyes find and hold my gaze. "Cooper, you're dismissed," he says without even a glance at his teammate.

"Yes, sir." Cooper chuckles. Then he rises, grabs his crutches and heads carefully toward the door.

"Thanks for the, um, help," I manage.

He flashes me a quick smile before he disappears.

Even after the door shuts, Weston continues to stare at me with clear, serious eyes. "How are you feeling?" he whispers, taking both my hands in his.

I don't know what to do with that penetrating gaze, and it rattles me. "I'm, uh, doing fine. Nothing to see here. Thanks."

Awkward much? Yikes.

Nonetheless, Weston leans in and gently kisses me on the forehead. His lips linger, and I stop breathing. "Don't think you're feverish anymore."

"Right. Yep."

Next, the soft brush of his kiss lands on my nose. And this bit of tenderness makes my eyes feel hot, and my chest ache with a sudden pang of longing.

"Abbi," he says gently. "I'm sorry I was a dick."

"It's nothing," I insist. "I get it."

He shakes his head once. "No, I don't think you do. You mean a lot to me. I was afraid to say so before."

Oh boy. "Weston, I'm really fine. Don't feel bad for me. There's no tragedy here. Everybody gets sick."

"Yeah, but everybody isn't you." He swallows roughly, still gazing into my eyes. "I realized something this week, Abbi."

"What's that?" I ask, trying not to fidget. All this attention is uncomfortable for me. I know I'm pale and have bags under my eyes.

"I love you," he whispers.

Wait, what?

"I love you," he repeats. "And I'm sorry I had so much trouble admitting it. I tried really hard to keep things casual, but I failed. And when Carly told me you didn't show up for work, I finally understood how much I need you."

"Weston," I breathe. "I'm sorry for the drama. But just because you got worried for a minute doesn't mean you—" I almost can't even say it out loud, because I want so badly for it to be true. "Love me."

"Oh, it does," he says with a bashful smile. "I'm the one who said we should just be friends who also have sex. But now I can't remember what that even means. When you're really close friends, and you also have really hot sex, that only adds up to one thing. At least for me, anyway. It means you're my person, Abbi. And I want to keep being friends and keep having gratuitous amounts of sex for years to come."

We're just staring at each other now, and I might be in shock. "Gratuitous amounts?" I repeat nonsensically.

"Well, yeah." Then Weston wiggles his eyebrows. Because he's Weston, and he's fun even when he's being serious.

A weird half-giggle escapes my throat before I choke it back. Then my eyes fill. "I could, um, get behind this idea."

"Could you please?" he whispers.

"Y-yes," I say shakily. Although I have to wonder if my fever has caused some kind of delirium. If I wake up and realize that Weston didn't actually just say all those wonderful things, I'm going to be inconsolable. But just in case this is actually happening, I'd better tell him how I feel. "I love you so much," I gasp. "I tried not to."

"Same, same." He smiles, and pulls me into his arms. I rest my cheek against his flannel shirt. "So this all worked out just like we planned, no?"

"No," I agree, and he laughs. I hear it in stereo as I burrow a little further into him.

"I fought it hard," he whispers, "because I didn't think I was good enough for you."

"What?" I yelp. "You're the best man I know."

He shrugs, then kisses the top of my head. "But you deserve the best, Abbi. I thought you deserved someone who wasn't all twisted up after watching his parents betray each other. I thought you needed a pro-level boyfriend."

"But you are," I insist.

"Nah. Those don't exist. There's only flawed guys who try hard. That's me. Just promise me one thing."

"What?"

"You'll come to my sister's wedding with me. If you're going to be my real girlfriend now, I need a date to this thing. And not just because you have a way with my dad. I'm in it for the arm candy." His smile is incandescent.

My heart flutters. "Sure," I say easily. "I'd love to come, although I think your dad will be okay this time. And Weston?"

"Yeah?"

"Just for the record, I don't find either of your siblings the least bit attractive."

"Good to know," he says, rocking me against his sturdy chest. "Good to know."

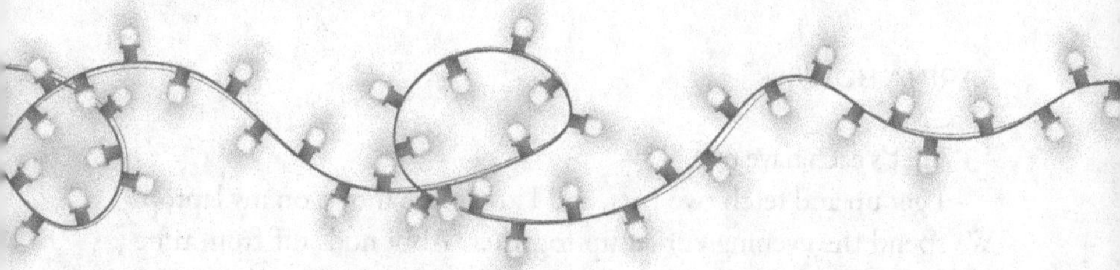

CHAPTER 31
ALL THAT GRATUITOUS SEX

WESTON

Abbi is still pretty wiped out by the flu. "You probably shouldn't be this close to me," she says as I hold her tightly. "What about the playoffs?"

"I had a flu shot," I mumble, hoping that actually matters. "There's no way I can leave you alone right now. I miss you too much. Just deal with it."

"Yes, sir."

"That's more like it. Can you eat some more? We need to build you up."

"For all that gratuitous sex?" she asks.

"Exactly," I say gruffly. But it's a lie. I just want Abbi to be okay. "How about a frozen fruit bar? I got a box for you at the grocery store." Plus a hundred other things. That's what a distraught guy does when the woman he loves has a fever.

Abbi goes still. "You brought me frozen fruit bars?"

"Yeah, and then I had to jam the box into your tiny freezer. Please don't tell me you hate them."

She shakes her head slowly. "I love them. That's what my mother used to buy me when I had a fever."

Oh, man. See? This flawed, jaded guy really can do a thing or two right once in a while. "I think they're mixed berry. Want one?"

"Let's each have one."

I get up and fetch two bars, and I also put a movie on my laptop. We spend the evening curled up together. Abbi nods off from time to time, her soft hair tickling my chin. But I wouldn't trade this for anything.

When you love someone, reruns and fruit bars are all the fun you need in your life. It's more than enough.

———

The next night, though, I don't go over to her place after practice. After a grueling pre-playoffs practice, I send her a delivery of hot soup and a series of texts to make sure she's doing okay.

Totally fine here, Westie. Getting bored, though. I want to call Kippy and beg for my job back, but I think I should write a letter instead. Dalton says he'll give me a doctor's note.

A paper trail is a good idea, I reply. But the truth is that I have a few ideas of my own.

After practice, as we're all toweling off in the locker room, my teammates bring up the Biscuit as a matter of course. "You coming?" Tate asks, snapping his towel in my direction. "Maybe we should send Abbi some takeout."

"I got that covered already," I admit. "But I was planning on stopping by the Biscuit anyway. I need your help with something, guys. Listen up, okay?"

They gather around me, and I lay out my plan.

———

A half hour later, we're assembled around table seventeen, as usual. Carly—after inquiring about Abbi's progress—has dropped off glasses of water and reeled off the specials. But when she comes back to take our order, I ask to speak to the manager instead. "We have something to say to him. Can you let him know?"

She blinks. "Of course. Just don't get me fired."

"I would never."

Kippy arrives a couple of minutes later, his eyes shifting around the table, looking for problems. "What can I do for you gentlemen?"

"Well, we were doing some math earlier," I say. "According to my credit card bill, I've spent nine hundred dollars here in the last few months. And I'm not the only one. Guys?"

"I spent a thousand," Lex says.

"I spent seven hundred," Tate chimes in.

"I don't do math if I can help it," Patrick says. "But I get drunk more than most of these guys, so you better assume my bill is the highest."

"He spent twelve hundred and seventy-seven bucks, and I spent eight hundred," his twin says.

Around the table we go, as the numbers mount. Kippy holds up a hand to stop us. "Okay, I see the trend. What are you looking for? A free basket of fries? I could stomach some kind of unofficial rewards program, if you're quiet about it."

"No, man," I say, trying to keep the anger out of my voice. "This is not a shakedown. We were perfectly happy to spend our cash here —until you fired Abbi for getting the flu. By email, no less."

"That's *cold*," Tate adds.

Kippy frowns. "But she didn't even *call*."

"Yeah, that's how *sick* she was," I say, my hands in fists. "Didn't you stop for a second and wonder why your most reliable employee —tied with Carly here, who we also think is great—didn't show up? Wouldn't a decent boss *worry* a little if that happened?"

Kippy's nostrils flare, because I've just called him out for being an asshole. "I don't have time to babysit my staff."

"Sure," I say with a shrug. "But we don't have time to drink beer and eat wings here until you offer Abbi her job back. With the one-year bonus intact."

His ears redden as he glances around the table.

Eleven hockey players look back at him with solemn expressions. "We like pizza, too," Cooper says. "Pretty sure they could find room for us next door."

"And for our entourage, too," Patrick adds. "The hockey lovers of Burlington come to the Biscuit for us, you know."

I never knew Patrick's ego could be so useful, because Kippy blanches. Then he swallows hard. "Abbi can come and see me tomorrow," he says. "We'll work something out."

"That's not good enough," Tate chirps. "Call her right now. She's probably worried about her job. She's conscientious, sir. You don't let a good employee go."

Slowly, with a trapped look on his ugly face, Kippy reaches into his pocket for his phone.

"Here," I say cheerfully, handing him a Post-it note. "This is her number."

Scowling, he starts tapping it into his cell. Then he puts the phone to his ear. "Er, hello, this is Kippy at the Biscuit. How are you, uh, feeling?" he stammers, like it might kill him to care.

I guess that used to be me, though. I thought it would kill me to care too much for Abbi. Yet loving her is the best thing that ever happened to me.

"You, uh, can have your job back. And your bonus will be waiting for you. I'll write the check tonight."

He goes silent, listening to Abbi's response.

That's when I nod at Carly, who's beaming. "All right, let's do this order! I'll have the—"

"Thai spiced wings?" she guesses. "And a Coke?"

"Yup," I say, handing over my menu. Because some of my habits never change, and that's okay.

A few minutes later, I'm just taking my first sip of soda when my phone starts pinging with texts from Abbi.

OMG you will not BELIEVE what just happened!!!! Kippy called me. I got my job back, and my bonus!

That's great, baby, I reply.

In other news... I've decided to take the job at Vermont Tartan. Tell me how you really feel about me staying in Burlington. Be honest.

I feel great about it, I tap out quickly. *Less phone sex. More real sex*. I add a string of eggplant emojis because I'm classy like that.

Well that clears things up, she says.

Eat your soup. You're going to need the energy. What are you going to spend your bonus on?

The deposit for a new apartment. Somewhere with a full-

size freezer, where you don't have to trick the heating system to stay warm.

I liked keeping you warm, I admit. ***But I agree about your pad. Tell that landlady you're outtie.***

No more bad jobs or bad apartments. She agrees. ***It's the end of an era.***

And the start of another, I add. Then I follow it with a bunch of heart emojis, because I'm turning into a big sap.

But I think I like it.

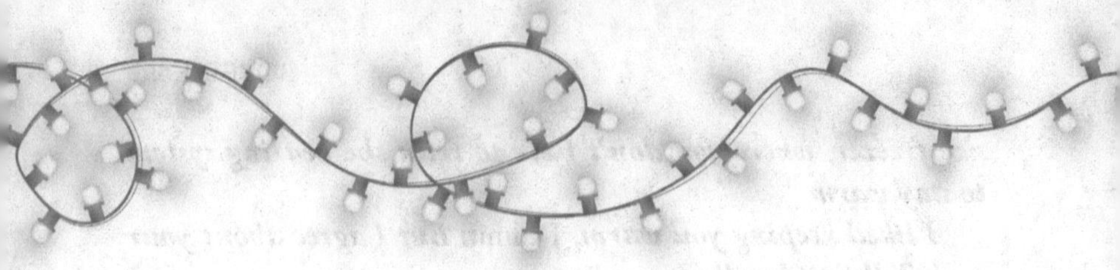

CHAPTER 32
SHOOT!

ABBI

"Omigod. Omigod! SHOOT!" I scream as Weston rushes the net.

But he's blocked! There's a tussle, and Weston manages to keep the puck off the enemy's stick by firing it back to Tate.

I scream again.

Cooper laughs. He's seated on my left, eating popcorn and watching me freak out during the third period of Weston's game against Boston College.

On my right sits Carly. She has to go to work later. But this is a day game, so she can see the hockey team in action and then serve their supper afterward.

She won't, however, have to fend off Price while she does it. Carly told me earlier this week that my step-stepbrother has been fired from the Biscuit.

"I saw the whole thing go down, Abbi, and I'm sad there's no video. But he stole a bottle of premium vodka from behind the bar," she'd told me gleefully. "Then he put it in his pants on the way out. The new bouncer stopped him. He said—I swear to God—'*There's no way your dick is that big.*'"

I'd laughed so hard that Kippy gave me the stink eye. Not that I care much anymore about what that guy thinks. Now that my bonus check has cleared, I feel less pressure to take every shift he offers me. That's why I'm watching this hockey game with Carly on a Friday afternoon. I don't need to kiss Kippy's ass anymore.

Actually, I feel less pressure about *everything* except this hockey game. My semester will wind down in a few weeks. I'll graduate on the quad at the end of May. And then my full-time job will begin at the flannel factory.

My new apartment is already waiting for me, too. I'd started hunting while I was recovering from the flu. And I'd found a sunny renovated one-bedroom in a walk-up brick building off of Church Street. It was available immediately, however. So I called my landlady, who said she'd end my lease early if I wanted. "I finally got a buyer for this place," she'd said. "He can find his own tenants."

So that was an unexpected stroke of luck. My new place is sitting empty, though, until I move in there ten days from now. I can't wait.

From the new place, it will be a short walk to work in one direction. Or, in the other direction, I can walk uphill to meet Weston on campus. He's spending the summer in Burlington too. He's got a nine-to-five job working as a clerk in the hospital.

"To burnish my stellar resume before I apply to med school," he said. "But we can drive to my dad's lake house on the weekends. How do you feel about paddleboarding?"

"I'll learn," I'd told him, "especially if you'll make gorilla noises while you demonstrate."

"Nah. Dolphin sounds this time." Then he'd made the sound of a dolphin's snicker, and I'd laughed so hard I got the hiccups.

I'm really looking forward to the summer, and not just because I'll get to see Weston in a bathing suit. I've got so many things to look forward to—a new job. A new apartment. More time with Weston and Carly.

And I won't have to smell like Buffalo wings every night anymore. Those days are almost behind me.

But first we've got to win this game before I die of excitement. It's the third period, and the score is 3-3. There are eight minutes left on the clock, and it's a struggle not to leap out of my seat every time we touch the puck.

"Ooh, penalty," Cooper says.

"On who?" I scan the ice, full of anxiety. But then a BC player heads for the penalty box, and the announcer calls the penalty against him. "What's high sticking?" I ask my companions.

"I don't know, but it sounds wonderfully dirty," Carly says.

Cooper almost chokes on his soda. "I could demonstrate later."

"Nice try, freshman." She reaches over and takes his popcorn, helping herself to a handful before passing it back.

I decide I don't need to know what the penalty is for. I just need us to capitalize on this power play. "LET'S GO, WESTON! Put the biscuit in the basket! And I'm not talking about the restaurant!"

"He can't hear you," Carly says.

"You don't know that."

And Weston already told me how happy he was that I could attend this game. "Even if we don't make it any further than round two, I'm psyched you're coming," he'd said.

Now we have a power play, and I'm vibrating with excitement. The speed of play picks up the moment the puck is dropped. Moo U takes possession, and they begin a patient game of keep-away.

BC mobs their own net, of course. They need to avoid giving up a goal until they're full strength again.

There's sweat dripping off Weston's face as he and Tate pass the puck back and forth. Time ticks down, and I feel each elapsing second like a penance.

"They're so calm," Carly says. "I'd be freaking out."

"You gotta have patience," Cooper says. "Gotta wait until fate gives you that chance. Kinda like Abbi waited for Weston to get his head out of his ass."

"Aren't you deep?" Carly snorts.

"No, I'm smart."

I don't hear the rest of their bickering, because there's a flurry of activity down on the ice. Lex Vonne makes a fast pass to Weston, who wings it toward the net so fast my eyes can't keep up.

The goalie twitches, and I see the puck smack into his stick. But then I lose track of it until Carly lets out a shocked gasp.

"What just happened?" I yell as the lamp lights.

"Rebound off the goalie, into the net!" She lets out a whoop of joy.

My heart leaps. "Omigod. Was that a goal for Weston?"

"Nah." Cooper laughs. "They'll credit the poor goalie and give Weston the assist."

I clap anyway. "We'll take it. I think Weston and the goalie just won the game together."

"Don't jinx it," Cooper says. "There's time on the clock."

But sometimes things just go right for a change. And a few minutes later, Weston's team has won the game.

It's funny how I've become one of those girls who stands around outside the locker room and waits for the team to come out. But here we are. The hallway is crowded with families and girlfriends and even some sports reporters. It's madness.

Eventually the players begin to emerge one by one, to loud cheers from everyone in the hallway. And when it's Weston's turn, the cheering is deafening. There are back slaps and fist bumps, and I wait patiently for the hullabaloo to die down.

But when our gazes finally lock, Weston smiles.

God, that smile.

"Abbi," he growls, weaving toward me. "Thank you for coming."

"Wouldn't miss it." He scoops me up and lifts me clear off my feet. I can smell the shower soap and feel the scrape of his whiskers against my face.

"God, it's crazy here." He chuckles, glancing around the hallway. "And I really want to get the hell out of here with you. But there's, uh, a quick press conference."

"Really?" I laugh. "So fancy."

"I know, right?" His grin is self-conscious. "Coach wants me there because of that crazy goal at the end."

"It *was* crazy," I say, dazzled by his blue eyes. "You take your time. But I'm going to hustle over to my new place, okay? Dalton wants to drop off my boxes before he leaves town for the weekend."

My stepfather has put three cartons of my mother's books in the trunk of his car, because my new apartment finally has enough room that I can shelve them. And because Lila wants them gone.

"I was going to carry those for you." His forehead wrinkles with concern. "Won't they be heavy?"

"Dalton will help me," I say, hugging Weston quickly. "Go and be important and come over when you're done."

"Okay." He gives me a single kiss, but there's a lot of expectation built into it. Weston is always fired up after a win.

We're going to have a *great* time tonight. I'm looking forward to it. "Did you know I'm having a new mattress delivered tonight, too?"

"Baby, I'm counting on it." He gives me one more scorching kiss before I peel myself out of his arms and make myself go.

———

Thirty minutes later I'm walking slowly around my new apartment. It even has that new place smell—fresh paint and optimism.

Night has fallen already outside my window. My footsteps echo against the wood floors of the empty living room as I wait for Dalton to show. I'm lucky that he's willing to stop here at six on a Friday before he starts his weekend.

You might find on-street parking, I text him. *But if you don't, I'll come down and get the boxes so you don't have to find a lot*.

And then I'll probably just stand there on the sidewalk with three heavy boxes and wait for Weston to rescue me. But that's not the end of the world.

Don't worry, Dalton replies. *My new assistant will carry them up*.

That's a lot to ask of an assistant, but I'm not going to complain.

Twenty minutes later, someone buzzes the door downstairs. I press the button to admit him. It might even be Weston. I'm not sure how long press conferences take.

Two minutes later, I hear someone slowly climbing the steps. So I block the door open to make this easier. "Over here! Thank you!" I cry as two of my boxes come into view.

But my heart drops as I get a better look at Dalton's new assistant.

"Fucking heavy," Price curses.

"Just put them down," I say quickly. "Doesn't matter where. I'll take care of it."

He squats down and I say a quick prayer that he won't strain his back—only because I know he'd blame me if he did.

"*Fuck*," he says again. Slowly he straightens up. "Not my job to haul your shit around, princess."

"Right," I agree nervously. "Thanks, though."

He takes a step closer to me. "You can do better than that."

"Better than…?" I take a step back. "Never mind. Go home, Price. Don't worry about me."

"I need a real thank-you," he says, his smile mean. "Show me some gratitude."

"You want a tip?" I snap. "Heard you aren't getting those anymore after you were fired from the Biscuit."

He makes an angry sound, and I instantly regret saying anything. How dumb am I? Now he's stalking toward me with fury in his eyes. "You stuck-up little bitch. Always gotta rub my nose in it."

"In what?" I babble, edging to the side. The door is still open. I just need to get past him.

"Fuck you," he sneers. Then he lunges.

I leap forward, almost getting clear of him. But he catches me by the wrist.

As soon as I feel his thick fingers close tightly around my arm, fear washes through me. Bile climbs up my throat. I've really done it now.

He shoves me against my clean white wall, both his hands on my arms. "Now I've got you where I want you."

"Where's D-Dalton?" I stammer. "He'll be w-waiting for you."

"Let 'im wait. I'm busy here." Price releases one of my arms, only to put his meaty hand around my throat.

It's not tight, but I've never been so scared. The threat is there. I open my mouth to scream, but I gag instead.

And he *laughs*.

That's what snaps me out of my inaction—anger. This fucker

doesn't actually want me. He just wants to be terrifying. We're standing so close together that I don't have much room to move.

Still, it's enough. I lift one foot off the ground and knee him between the legs.

It's not a direct hit, but he still lets out a shout of surprise. "FUCK, Abbi. You fucking CUNT!"

I lift the other foot, preparing to try again, when I hear a crash in the doorway—the sound of a box of books being dropped too quickly onto a wood floor. "What the hell are you doing?"

Dalton. My God, I have never been so happy to see anyone in my life.

Price has already released me. "Nothing. Just fucking around."

This is the moment when I should start yelling. I should let both of these men know how bad it really is, and how I'm not going to take it anymore.

Instead, I put both my hands around my throat and start shaking like a paint mixer at the hardware store. A sob escapes from my throat.

"Oh God. Abbi," Dalton says in a hushed voice. "Oh God."

I sink slowly to the floor. I'm fine now, right? How come I can't even hold myself up?

"Hey guys!" Weston's voice says from the doorway, and I lift my head from my hands, like a seedling toward the sun. "Whoa. What the fuck is *he* doing here? Abbi?" Weston crosses the room in a flash, lowering himself to his knees in front of me. "Abbi, hey, what happened?"

I'm pulled against his chest in gentle arms, and I take my first real breath in ages.

"Get out," Dalton barks, presumably to Price. "Get out of my sight."

"Call the police," Weston says. "Not joking."

My apartment door slams, which is probably Price's doing. And a moment later Dalton is also kneeling on the floor in front of me. I let out a terrified sob, and it echoes in the empty room.

"Why didn't you tell me?" Dalton pleads.

"She *tried*," Weston says through clenched teeth. "You brushed her off."

I look up at Dalton, whose mouth is opening and closing like a fish. "She said he pestered her, but I never..." His mouth flops around some more.

The thing is, I don't know exactly what I said to Dalton. I don't remember the precise words I used. "It was him or me," I whisper, knowing that I'm not making a lot of sense right now.

"She thought you'd take your new wife's side," Weston says. "Can you really blame her? It's not like she has a lot of family to spare."

"*Shit.*" I don't even know if I've ever heard Dalton curse before now. "Abbi, I'm sorry. You should have—" He swallows. "I should have asked you more questions."

"You *know* he's a troll," I bite out. "Can't finish a sentence. Can't hold down a job. So you just *hired* him after he got fired *again?*" My voice is shaking.

Dalton groans, scrubbing his face. "You're right. I don't know what to do about him. I don't have a damn clue. I was just trying to go easy on him for Lila."

"He doesn't need someone to go easy," Weston growls. "But I guess you know that now. That asshole kept Abbi on the run from her only *home.*"

"Jesus." Dalton goes pale. "Abbi, I'm so sorry."

"It's okay now," I croak. It's not like I want to move back in. "But I refuse to be around him again. Not even on Thanksgiving."

"Okay, okay." Dalton sits heavily on the wood floor, looking uncomfortable in his suit pants and white shirt. "Can I take you two to dinner? I feel terrible."

I *almost* say yes. It's on the tip of my tongue. But I don't want to go out with Dalton. I want a night just with my boyfriend. "That's a nice offer, but we have plans," I say quietly. Because I'm finished being the girl who works too hard to stay in Dalton's good graces.

I've got to stop being afraid to ask for what I need.

"All right," he says heavily. "I'll leave you two alone." He glances around the room. "Is it pushy of me to ask if you have plans to get some furniture? You said no when Lila asked you if you wanted to look in the attic."

"What if she said no because that meant dealing with Price?" Weston asks.

Dalton blanches. "Did you, Abbi?"

"Maybe," I admit. "Can we talk about it another time?"

"Of course," he says, rising to his feet and dusting himself off. "Please take care of yourself, and we'll talk soon."

"I will. Thank you."

Dalton lets himself out, and the sound of the door closing echoes in my empty space. "Wow," Weston says. "There's some drama for your Friday. Are you okay? What did Price try, anyway?"

I lean back against the wall and close my eyes. "Intimidation," I mutter. "Humiliation. He pinned me against the wall just to be terrifying."

Weston makes a very unhappy noise, and I hope he's not plotting Price's murder right now. "What do you need?" he asks after a deep breath. "How can I make this better?"

"You know what?" I wipe my hands on my jeans and will my body to relax. "You already are. It's Friday night. My mattress isn't due to show up for..." I check the time on my phone. "Ninety minutes. I asked them for the latest time slot, because I didn't know if there was a team dinner you'd have to go to."

Weston shakes his head. "I'll see them tomorrow."

"Can we go sit down at a restaurant on Church Street? I just want to go out with you. I want to have *fun*." There's that word again, although it's growing on me. I haven't made enough time in my life for fun.

I could start now.

"That we can do." Weston gets to his feet, then holds out a hand to pull me up. "Let's see... Sushi? Ramen? Burgers? What are you in the mood for?"

"Just you," I whisper. "I don't care what we're eating. I just want to have dinner with you."

Weston stops in front of the door and turns around. His smile is tender as he pulls me into his arms. "That's easy, isn't it?"

"Yes," I agree as he gives my cheekbone a slow kiss. "I'm easy to please."

"You know what else is easy?" he asks, kissing the corner of my mouth.

"What?" I brush my knuckles against his evening stubble.

"Me," he says, nipping my ear. "I'm easy. And I will show you how easy about fifteen minutes after that mattress shows up."

"Will you, now?"

"Bet on it, girl. Bet on it."

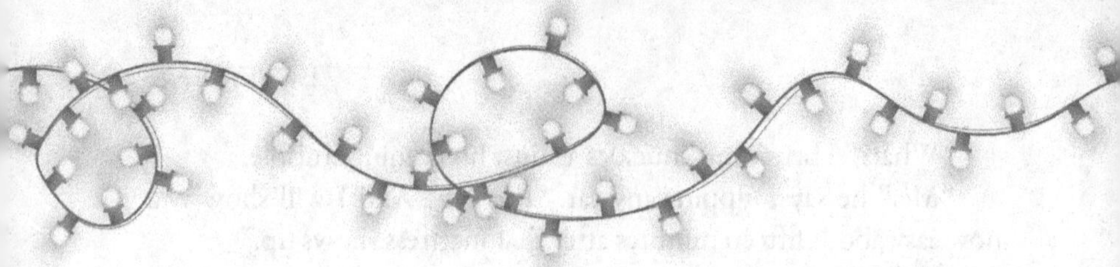

CHAPTER 33
EPILOGUE: TOTALLY WORTH IT

WESTON

"Westie, what room are we sleeping in?" Abbi asks as we drive through the back roads of Fairlee toward my father's house.

"Oh baby, we're taking that double bed again. Stevie and Tamar can take the bunk room."

"Hmm. Are they down with this plan?"

I shrug. "Doesn't matter if we get there first."

"Devious, Griggs. I like it. I don't know if we can make sex noises this time, though."

"What?" I gasp. "It's a tradition. Besides, they'd be *real* sex noises." I nudge her with my elbow, because I'm subtle like that.

"No way," she says. "I have to be able to look your brother and Tamar in the eye over the turkey tomorrow."

"You're forgetting something, though. Stevie and Tamar might be making their own sex noises. They won't even hear us."

Abbi thinks this over. "Maybe if we're *very* quiet."

"Uh-huh," I agree. The old bed squeaks like a piglet on cocaine, but I'm too smart a man to point that out right now. "Five more minutes until we get there," I say instead. "Just enough time for a singalong. Cue up the Avett Brothers?"

Abbi claps her hands. "'Ain't No Man!' Yes! Another tradition."

She taps furiously on her phone, and a few seconds later the intro kicks in, and then we start to sing.

I actually slow down the car so that we won't arrive before the song is over. We really go for it, too, singing loud through the chorus and into the verse.

Tomorrow is Thanksgiving Day, but this year I didn't hang up my sign to advertise for a date. I already have the perfect date.

Although we're not on our way to Dalton's house this year. And I'm no longer avoiding family holidays. This year we're headed to my dad's. And this way Dalton can host Price—who no longer lives in his home—and keep peace with his wife.

Dalton had asked Abbi first, though. He'd extended an invitation, explicitly stating that if we wanted to join him for Thanksgiving, that Price would not be included. Dalton and Lila have finally figured out how "tough love" for that asshole works, but I hear that it wasn't easy.

The Price situation actually sent Dalton and Lila to marriage counseling for a little while, until Lila learned how not to be her son's enabler. But I guess things are better now.

Abbi gently turned down Dalton's Thanksgiving invitation, though, telling him we were already spoken for. And so Dalton is taking us out to dinner on Sunday night, "just to catch up," he'd said.

Dalton and Abbi are in a good place lately. And neither of us needs a fake boyfriend or girlfriend anymore. We're just in it for the turkey and the stuffing this time. And Aunt Mercedes's cheesy mashed potatoes. And whatever pies my father bought from the bakery, because that man doesn't often cook.

I love Thanksgiving. Always have. But I love it even harder today, with my best girl singing her lungs out in the passenger seat beside me.

Even the car is different this time. Three months ago we traded in Abbi's heap of a car for a used Subaru Outback.

Yup, we bought a car together, which is a pretty big commitment. But next year—if everything goes according to plan—we'll probably live together, too. I'll be in medical school, and moving out of the hockey house. She'll be working her way toward world domination in the flannel industry. Sharing an apartment just makes sense.

I honestly can't wait. We spend most of our nights together anyway.

The final chords of the song resonate as I turn into the driveway and park behind my dad's car.

"Whew!" Abbi collapses against the seat. "That was a good one."

"The best," I agree, killing the engine. There's no snow on the ground yet, and the lake shimmers between the distant trees. Abbi and I came to stay here a few times over the summer. We had some fun swimming in the lake and roasting marshmallows in Dad's fire pit.

And I made gorilla noises on the paddleboard, just for old time's sake.

Abbi removes her seat belt, but I grab her hand before she can climb out of the car. "Happy anniversary, baby."

She turns to me with wide eyes. "It's sort of true, right?"

"You know it." I lean over and kiss her quickly. "I'll never forget knocking on your door on Thanksgiving last year. When you opened it, I was so surprised to find out that the hot waitress from the Biscuit was my date."

She rolls her eyes, like I'm humoring her.

"Believe it, girl. I totally wanted to take you home that night, too. Remember how I said we should save the other bottle of wine for later?" I wiggle my eyebrows.

Her smile widens. "I do remember. And then it didn't happen."

"Oh it *happened*, honey. Just not that night. We had some issues to work through."

"We did," she agrees.

I swivel around and reach into the back seat for something I stashed back there in secret. "Happy anniversary, honey." I hand her a wrapped present, which I'm sure she can guess is a wine bottle. "We'll have to chill this so we can drink it later."

"Oh! Who's a fun guy?" She rips the paper away and pulls out a bottle of champagne. But I've covered the label, with my own hand-lettered version. In brightly colored Sharpie it says: A BOTTLE

FOR LATER. BUT NOT TOO MUCH LATER. BECAUSE I'M A MAN WITH NEEDS.

Abbi lets out a snort of laughter. "Subtle, Westie."

"I know, right?"

She gives me a kiss on the jaw. Then she pulls something out of her purse—a greeting card, with WESTIE on the envelope, and a drawing of a West Highland Terrier. "This is for you."

"Aw! Thanks." I slit the envelope with my thumb and pull out the card. On the front there's a cat in a turkey costume. Inside, I find twenty-five dollars in cash. And Abbi has written only: TOTALLY WORTH IT.

"Oh baby!" I say, laughing. "I love you so much. You're hilarious." Then I have to kiss her.

And we're still there, entangled in each other, until my dad taps on the window. "Did you know you're steaming up the car?" he yells through the glass.

Abbi, embarrassed, quickly opens her door and climbs out.

When I follow her a moment later, my dad is laughing at us. "You know, your brother used to have this dumb idea that you two were only pretending to date."

"Is that so?" I ask, unbothered, while Abbi makes herself very busy pulling her duffel bag out of the back.

"Yeah." Dad shakes his head. "Love that kid, but sometimes he's a dingus."

"Total dingus, I agree."

Abbi gives me a wide-eyed stare. And I just wink back at her.

THE
END

———

BLONDE DATE

A NOVELLA

A blind date. A nervous sorority girl. A mean-spirited fraternity prank. What could go wrong?

As a sorority pledge, there are commandments that Katie Vickery must live by. One: Thou shalt not show up for the Christmas party without a date. Two: The guy shall be an athlete, preferably an upperclassman.

Unfortunately, Katie just broke up with her jerkface football player boyfriend. She'd rather hide under the bed than attend a party where he'll be.

Yet staying home would mean letting him win.

Andrew Baschnagel is living proof that nice guys don't finish first. He's had his eye on Katie since the moment her long legs waltzed into his art history class. So when her roommate sets Andy up to be Katie's date, he'd be crazy to say no.

And maybe he can prove to her that not all guys are like her ex...

PART ONE

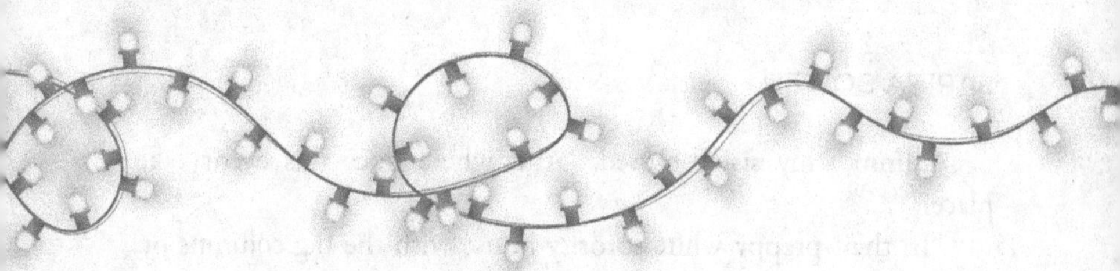

CHAPTER 1
ANDY

With a growing sense of panic, I pawed through the clothes in my narrow little dorm room closet. For five long minutes I'd stood there inspecting my shirts, tossing them one by one on the bed. That was four more minutes than I'd usually spend trying to decide what to wear. But I still didn't have a freaking clue.

It was time to call in the big guns.

Luckily, my older sister answered on the first ring. "I need a consult," I said. Delia was in med school, and you got further with her if you spoke in medical terms.

"Where does it hurt?" she asked.

"I have a date, and I don't know what to wear."

Her laughter was so loud that I had to hold the phone away from my ear. "How old are you?"

"Old enough to ask for help when I need it."

"Fair enough. What's the occasion?"

"That's the tricky part. First there's a charity bit, where I'm helping a bunch of sorority girls with their community project. Setting up a Christmas tree, or something."

Delia laughed again. "What do you know from setting up a Christmas tree, Jew boy?"

"How hard could it be? But there's also a tree lighting, and, like, cocktails."

"Hmm," my sister mused. "And where does this event take place?"

"In their preppy white sorority house with the big columns on the front."

"Well... This really could go either way. Casual or dressy."

"That's what I was afraid of. How should I play it?"

"Who's the girl? Anyone special?"

Why yes. But I wasn't going to tell my sister that just hearing this girl's name gave me a thrill. *Katie Vickery*. When she'd called to invite me to this thing, she'd opened with "you don't know me..."

But she'd been wrong. Very wrong. I knew *exactly* who she was.

In the first place, if you were a lonely junior at Harkness, noticing the frosh girls was like your job. And she made my job easy. I'd picked out those long legs the very first time they'd walked into my art history lecture. And — lucky me — summer's warmth had held on an extra week or two this year, treating me to a steady parade of Katie's short skirts every Monday, Wednesday and Friday morning.

The most attractive thing about her, though, was her laugh. It was deeper and huskier than you'd expect from someone so slight and fair. I loved the sound of it. Whenever I heard her laugh, my brain took a short trip around the block.

God, she was hot. But she also had *unattainable* practically stamped on her forehead. Because Katie was the sort of girl that *everyone* noticed. And I wasn't even a little bit surprised when she started sitting with the football crew during lectures.

I didn't dwell on this. Girls like Katie Vickery were out of my league, and I didn't bother to sit around wondering why. Some things just *were*.

As the fall semester wore on, Bridger, my next-door neighbor, started spending a lot of time with Katie's roommate, Scarlet. So I overheard updates on Katie. Scarlet mentioned that they sometimes went jogging together. After that, Katie's long legs began loping through my dreams in spandex shorts.

But that wasn't a premonition, or anything. It was just the work of a shy guy's subconscious. In a million years, I'd never thought I'd be standing here, dressing for a date with her. And if she hadn't invited me out of sheer desperation, I wouldn't be.

"Um, earth to Andy!" my sister prompted. "I asked you a question. Is the girl anyone special?"

"We don't really know each other," I admitted. "She dumped her football player boyfriend a few weeks ago and needed a date for this thing. Enter me."

"So this is a date of necessity. But how did *you* get the nod? She must not know your track record with women. Not that there's anything wrong with that." My sister snickered.

"Come on, now, D. If I wanted to be mocked, I would have called my *other* sister." Our younger sis was kind of a bitch. "You remember Bridger?"

"Who could forget him?" Delia asked. My neighbor was kind of a stud with the ladies.

"Well, this whole thing was his girlfriend's idea."

"I knew I liked that guy," Delia said. But of course she did. All the women did. "And his girlfriend has good taste, too."

"In me? Or in Bridger?" I teased.

"Both. And this sorority girl is going to love you. You're pretty cute for a skinny guy."

I didn't have time to argue with her. But even if it was true, *pretty cute for a skinny guy* probably wasn't going to be enough to win me Katie's undying affection. I'd been invited on this junket because the newly single Katie was apparently done with football players. "And jerks of all stripes," Scarlet had explained. "I told her, 'Andy is absolutely not a jerk.'"

For a second I'd felt awesome about that. But then I'd realized that being *absolutely not a jerk* also wasn't enough of an endorsement to fill the utter void that was my love life.

Oh, well.

"Are you going to help me or what?" I prodded.

"Of course. So you want to impress her, but you don't want to look like you're trying too hard," my sister said.

"Exactly. So tell me what to wear. While I'm young, if possible."

"Well, when the Jewish kid goes to the Christmas tree lighting at the WASPy sorority house, he should always wear nice pants."

I looked at the three pairs I'd draped over my desk chair. "Won't that be too dressy?"

"Not if they're khaki-colored. How about the ones you wore when we saw that show in Boston?"

How did she even remember that shit? If Delia asked me to name three items of clothing that she'd ever owned *in her lifetime*, I couldn't do it.

I lifted the pants off their hanger. "All right. What else?"

"The shirt should be a dark color. Dark blue, maybe? With the collar open. Whatever you do, *don't* button that sucker all the way up. Wear a t-shirt underneath, and it's okay if the t-shirt is visible at the collar. That takes you one notch back toward casual. And no tie."

See? This was why a guy called his sister. I hopped into the pants using one hand. "And the shirt is tucked in, right?"

"Tuck it in! Absolutely. Unless you really don't want to get laid."

I laughed and had to grab the phone to keep it from hitting the floor. "That's not happening."

"Are you saying that because you're talking to your sister? Or because you really believe it?"

"Uh, why? Are you doing a psych rotation at school, or something?" I pulled a clean t-shirt over my head.

"I was only teasing about your record with girls. You know that right? You're a catch, Andy. As long as you tuck your shirt in."

"That must be what I've been doing wrong."

My sister laughed. "Your only real problem is confidence."

I stuffed my feet into a pair of shoes. "Am I wearing a jacket, too? Or just my coat?"

"Your plain black sport jacket. It still fits, right? God, I hope your arms aren't getting any longer. Because you're already kind of like an orangutan."

"And you wonder why I don't have any confidence," I mumbled.

"Kidding! But seriously, if the jacket sleeves are too short, then skip it. And you need to shine your shoes."

"I don't have time."

"What? When is this date?"

"Ten minutes."

"Andrew Isaac Baschnagel! Did you shower and shave?"

"Yes, Mom."

"Hang up and go meet your girl. Crap. I wanted you to send a picture before you left. In case you need tweaking."

"No time for tweaking. Bye, Delia! Thanks."

"Bye, orangutan." Then she clicked off. Delia loved getting the last word.

But never mind. I put on *exactly* what she'd told me to. I hung up the pants that hadn't made the cut. Then, shoving my keys and my wallet into a pocket, I ran out the door and down the entryway stairs. Checking my phone, I saw that I had plenty of time. It was a two-minute walk to Katie's dorm, and I had twice that.

My phone buzzed with a text from Delia. *Good luck with the WASPs, string bean.*

Holding up my phone and grinning like a dork, I took a selfie and sent it to her.

The clothes look great. But you're hopeless, she replied.

That was probably true. And I'd never admit it to my sister, but she wasn't totally off base with her remark about my confidence. Some guys just had a kind of swagger that worked for them. My neighbor Bridger? All he had to do was walk into a room, and the girls hurled themselves at him, like moths at a window screen on a summer night.

But what was swagger, really? It came from the belief that hot girls wanted to take you to bed. So, to acquire it, you'd need at least a little evidence that this was true.

Yeah. I didn't have that. All I had was evidence that a hot girl needed a date for a party. But that was better than nothing, right? And I'd have a couple of hours in the company of the lovely Katie Vickery.

Life could really be worse.

Apparently Delia wasn't done with me, though. When my phone buzzed again, she'd written: *Ask her out again on your way home tonite. Don't chicken out.*

I hadn't thought that far ahead. But my sister was a smart girl. *Okay. If things go well, I'll do it*, I replied.

If you do, I'll buy you a sundae at Lou's. If you chicken out, I win a sundae.

That seemed like a perfectly good incentive to do something that I already wanted to do. *Deal*, I replied.

CHAPTER 2
KATIE

After much deliberation with myself, I'd straightened my hair until it hung in golden sheets around my shoulders. It was a kick-ass look on me. Straightened hair said: *I'm here to shine, and I will go that extra mile. So don't you dare mess with me.*

Actually, it probably only said: *I am handy with the straightening iron.* But whatevs. Either way, it gave me confidence, and confidence was in short supply this week.

Unstraightened hair, on the other hand, made a different statement. It said: *I am an effortless beauty, and you'll just have to take me as I am.* But nothing felt effortless lately. And "effortless" was just a little too close to "careless" for my comfort. And tonight I could *not* appear careless. So I'd spent an hour on my hair, and now it was straight enough to be featured on somebody's geometry exam.

I pushed the hair off my bare shoulders and assessed my outfit. "What do you think?" I asked my reflection in the mirror. "Is the neckline too much?"

My reflection didn't answer. But my suitemate Katie did. "There's no such thing as too much. You look hot in that dress."

"Thanks, K2."

"Any time," she said, plopping down on my bed and making herself comfortable.

During the first week of school, a smokin' hot lacrosse player had nicknamed us K1 and K2 because we were both named Katie. "But why does *she* get to be K1?" the other Katie had asked at the time, employing the flirtiest pout *in the world*.

"Sweetheart, K2 is an awesome nickname," the LAX guy said. "Because K2 is a big mountain. And, well..." he broke off on a chuckle, his eyes *right* on her ample cleavage.

The other Katie had grinned, then hitched up her bra. "I guess I can wear that name with pride."

"You wear it well," the guy had said, leaning in to kiss her cheek. About fifteen minutes later, they were lip-locked against a tree in the back yard of the frat house. And I, in my A-cup bra, was totally envious.

And that LAX player wasn't the only one who thought of us as a pair. Our roommate Scarlet called us Blonde Katie (that's me) and Ponytail Katie. Others simply referred to us as The Katies. Together, we'd hit the party scene hard these past three months. I'd begun the year with a kind of I-am-freshwoman-hear-me-roar attitude. I loved college, and it loved me back.

I'd thought so, anyway.

But seven nights ago I'd hit a sour note, and his name was Dash McGibb. Even though I was a generally upbeat person, my bad experience with Dash had left me feeling uncertain about everything — my choices, the company I kept.

This dress.

I fiddled with the silky, draping neckline, wondering if I should change. I probably wouldn't, though. I'd already tried on everything in my closet. Selecting a pink lipstick, I pursed my lips for the mirror.

"I can't believe you're going to this party with a *basketball* player," K2 scoffed from my bed. "The team record so far this season is one for *four*."

The lipstick prevented me from answering her immediately, which was a good thing. It gave me time to reconsider my snarky reply, which would have been to ask Katie how *her* basketball game was looking this year. (She and I ran three miles exactly once per week. Neither of us was athletic. We only jogged on Sundays as penance for our chocolate chip cookie addiction.)

"Is it?" I asked instead. "Then losing is something that Andy and

I will have in common. Because my dating record this year is zero for two."

She rolled back onto my bed, her skinny knees pointing the ceiling. "Just because both of your boyfriends turned out to be duds is no reason to sell yourself cheaply."

"*Jeez*, Katie. I'm not a horse up for auction." Her words ricocheted inside my brain. Especially one of them. *Cheaply*. My stomach gave a little lurch at that word. My mother used it a lot. *Cheap* was not how the Vickery women were supposed to behave. But I hadn't heeded this guidance, and now I was paying the price.

K2 gave me a wounded look. "It's just an expression."

"I know. Sorry." I tried to change the subject. "Have you seen my eyeshadow stick?"

"Um, whoops." She got up and ran off to her own room in our little suite.

The first week of school, I was positive that Katie and I, with our matching names and our matching Prada suitcases, were primed to take over the world. We'd both ruled our high schools. We were also in agreement on exactly which sort of guys we wanted to date — athletes, of course. We were here to party with whoever did it best, and whoever was the best looking.

In contrast, our third roommate, the tight-lipped Scarlet, had seemed a lot less fun. I'm not proud of it, but I'll admit that I'd kind of written her off by the third week of the semester. But recently I'd learned that she'd had damned good reasons to be cautious and quiet. And tonight I found myself wishing that it was Scarlet who was home with me. The attack of insecurity I faced right now was bigger than a fashion crisis. I needed the support of a friend who knew about *life*, and not just what to wear for it.

I hadn't told a soul yet about the crappy little thing that had happened to me last week. And now that I was primping to go to a party where I'd probably end up face-to-face with the jerks who'd embarrassed me, I could have used a pep talk.

K2 came back into my room with my eyeshadow. And when my phone rang, she grabbed it off my dresser to look at the screen. "It's your mom."

"Crap."

"So don't pick up." She did another belly flop onto my bed.

"But I've been ducking her." I took the phone from Katie and answered it. "Hi, Mom."

"Hello, sweetie. Getting ready for your date?"

"I am." *And if you knew that, why would you call me now?*

"I've been making plans for the holidays. We're having the Iversons visit for the weekend before New Year's. And then I thought we could pop into the city to see a play," my mother said.

"Mmm hmm," I said. "Sounds fine." But my attention was still on the full-length mirror I'd installed on the back of our closet door. Specifically, I was trying to decide if the pearl earrings I'd put on made my dress look less slutty. Or had I only managed to convert the look into "slut with pearls"?

"Have fun tonight," my mother said. "Are you wearing something pretty? The girls of Tri Psi knew how to throw a good party in my day."

"Thank you, I will have fun," I said, ignoring the question about my outfit. One had to wonder what my mother's idea of a good college party had been. Surely alcohol didn't enter the picture, at least not for the girls. And my mother would never sanction any activity that might rumple a girl's twin set. Mom was a first-class Good Girl. And in spite of massive evidence to the contrary, she assumed that I was one too.

"Is this boy who's taking you to the party a gentleman?"

"Of course he is," I said. And it might even be true. Though gentlemanliness had never been high on my list of important qualifications for a date.

And last week I'd finally paid the price.

"Good," Mom said.

"Yeah," I said, distracted.

"Say *yes*, darling," my mother corrected. "*Yeah* sounds cheap."

"Yes, Mother," I intoned. "I should go. He'll be here in a minute." At least I hoped he would. It would stink to be stood up tonight of all nights. But after all that had gone wrong this week, I probably wouldn't even be surprised.

I hung up the phone and spun around. "Okay. Last call, here.

Are you sure this dress doesn't look slutty?" My fingers worried the fabric between my breasts.

Gently, Katie swatted my hand away. "First of all, we don't use the word 'slutty' when referring to ourselves. And that dress looks *sexy* as all hell. In the best possible way. I hope your basketball player brought a hankie to wipe up his own drool." She got up off the bed and turned me around by the shoulders, so that I was facing the mirror again. "The dress is navy blue, K1. It's an anti-slut color. And the contrast with your hair is just awesome. Use your eyes, babe."

"Thanks," I whispered, trying to see things her way. The dress I'd chosen was cut in a halter style. Until tonight, I hadn't ever stopped to wonder why we were dressing up for this weeknight party, where charity work was supposed to happen, too. But sorority girls, I'd discovered, were always looking for an excuse to get dolled up.

Yet when guys were around (which was always) we were supposed to be grateful if they'd worn khakis instead of sweats, and a button-down instead of a faded Harkness t-shirt. In fact, if they wore their baseball caps frontwards instead of backwards, that was dressy.

Double standard, much?

I dabbed the eyeshadow applicator into the silver shadow and skimmed it across one eyelid and then the other.

Once more I squinted critically at the girl in the mirror. The dress showed a lot of shoulder. But it wasn't too short, which was important. I needed to be able to bend over tonight without giving anyone a show. And the halter top had just enough coverage that I wouldn't expose my cleavage if I leaned forward.

"You look great. Now go," Katie prompted, swatting me on the rear. She gave me a smile in the mirror and slipped out of my room.

I slipped my feet into my most authoritative shoes — black suede Prada pumps with a three-inch heel. Then I took one last look in the mirror. Katie had been right. This dress was perfect. It was sexy without showing off. And my hair looked fabulous, and the jewelry was subtle.

Fine. I looked *fine. Not slutty*. I stood there a little longer, willing myself to believe it.

Usually I didn't think so hard about these things. I *liked* to look sexy. And, to be perfectly blunt, I liked sex. A lot. I'd never been afraid to admit that to myself. Not until last week, anyway.

For the most part, coming to Harkness — and getting out from under my conservative parents' roof — had been liberating in all the best ways. In high school, sex had to be sneaky. It's hard to get your freak on when you're listening for footsteps outside your bedroom door. Or — God forbid — in the backseat of your boyfriend's little BMW convertible.

At Harkness, sexy times weren't so fraught. And although I'd had to train my roommate Scarlet to watch out for the bandanna on the doorknob of our room, the logistics were a lot easier.

For the first two months of the semester, I'd had a blast. In September, I'd dated a freshman tight end. He had an eight-pack like you read about and gorgeous, muscular thighs. But he wasn't much of a conversationalist, so I'd had to let him go. Then there was Dash, who I should probably start calling The Fullback Who Shall Not be Named. He was another freshman with lickable abs. But I broke up with him in November, because he wasn't very nice to me when we had our clothes *on*.

I'd meant to take a break from football players after that. After all, it was hockey season now. And in the spring there would be lean, muscular lacrosse players to cheer for and party with.

But then a week ago I'd run into Dash again. And I'd done something so incredibly stupid that the humiliation was going to follow me to my grave. A few stupid hours had turned me into someone who second-guessed her wardrobe, her makeup, her life choices...

My phone buzzed with a text. *Evening! I'm downstairs in your courtyard. Andy B.*

Be right down, I replied. It was sort of cute that he'd added his last initial, as if I might have forgotten who I'd invited to this little party. Andy Baschnagel was a basketball player. I didn't, as a rule, do basketball players. The sport just wasn't sexy to me. Those long baggy shorts and even longer arms? Eh. Maybe if I went to Duke or Michigan, I'd understand the appeal.

Anyway, I hadn't invited Andy B. to this party because he was a basketball player. I'd done it because he wasn't an asshole (I hoped). And because I'd pledged Tri Psi and could not show up at one of their events without a date. And for extra points, he had to be A) an athlete and B) an upperclassman. With Andy, I could check both of those boxes.

No matter that I was suddenly having trouble remembering why I cared about checking those boxes. It was too late to wonder about that now. I had a party to survive, and a guy waiting downstairs. It wasn't his fault that I would rather hide under the bed than face the people at this party. And I'd absorbed at least *some* of the ladylike manners my very proper mother had taught me.

It was time to march down there and make the best of it.

—————

When I reached the courtyard, Andy was standing there texting someone, a smile on his face.

He looked friendly enough. And he was pretty cute for a skinny guy. But still, all that attention to his phone was not an auspicious sign. I was sick of guys who spent the whole evening texting their buddies, calculating everyone's odds of getting some action later.

"Hi," I said carefully. He still hadn't noticed me.

His head jerked up, his face guilty. "Sorry. Hi." He offered me his hand to shake. "I'm Andy."

For a second, I didn't step forward. I mean... what guy under forty shakes hands like that? Recovering myself, I took his hand, which was warm even on this cold night. "Hi. I'm Katie."

"I know," he smiled. Then he shoved his phone into his pocket even though it chimed with an incoming text.

"Don't you have to get that?" I asked. It was a little bitchy of me, honestly. But I needed to know what I was going to be dealing with.

"Nah," he said. "She can stuff it."

"Who can?" I couldn't help but ask, even as his phone rang in his pocket.

He grinned. "My sister. Sorry. Let me get rid of her." He jerked the phone out and swiped to answer. "Delia. Go dissect a cadaver or something. I'll talk to you tomorrow." There was a pause. "I love you too, even though you're bossy like a drill sergeant. G'night."

I laughed in spite of myself. "I think you got the last word."

"It's only a temporary victory. She always wins eventually. But that's okay, because she's already doing me a big favor."

"What kind of favor?" Together we walked out of the Fresh Court gate, heading down College Street, toward Fraternity Row. I kept our pace slow, and it wasn't even because of my three-inch heels. I was dreading this party.

"Well, Delia is going to med school. Every Jewish family needs a doctor, see. And now the pressure is off me."

I laughed again. That was, like, twice in two minutes. "Really? Are your parents doctors?"

"Nope. Dad is an accountant, Mom is a librarian. But that doesn't matter. It's a cultural thing. The deli by our house even has a platter on their catering menu called the 'My Son is a Doctor' plate."

"But they won't be ordering it for you?"

"No. I might go to law school, though. That's second best."

"Interesting. My mom doesn't care what I do, just as long as I look pretty doing it." I shouldn't have said that. It was really too much sharing for the first ten minutes of a blind date.

"Well..." he cleared his throat. "At least one of us is a shoo-in for meeting the parental expectations."

My face burned a little then, because I'd made it sound like I was fishing for compliments. "That's nice of you," I said quietly. "Do you have just the one sister?"

"Nope" he said cheerfully, giving me another smile. When Andy smiled, his angular face softened up, taking him from ordinary to pretty damned attractive in one leap. It was kind of spellbinding, really. "I have another sister, too. Spent my whole life getting henpecked and waiting for the bathroom. I thought I came to Harkness to get away from them. But then I couldn't figure out why my freshman bathroom was so gross and smelly all the time."

"See, girls aren't so bad," I said.

"True dat."

We were within a hundred yards of the Tri Psi house now, and I had slowed our pace practically to a crawl.

"Do your feet hurt?" Andy asked, looking down.

That made me smile, because it was so obvious that Andy did

have sisters. "My feet are fine. I'm just having second thoughts about tonight, that's all." I stopped walking altogether.

Andy stopped too, folding his arms. "Yeah?"

"Yeah," I sighed. (Even though "yeah" sounded cheap. Sorry, Mom.)

He stood very still, studying me. "Look," he said, tugging on an ear. "Is it me? I mean, if you changed your mind..."

"What?" *Oh, hell.* I reached out to put a hand on his arm, giving it a squeeze. "Jeez, no. You are *not* the problem. This is all on me."

But he was still frowning, and his brown eyes were filled with concern. "Then what's the matter?"

"Well..." my eyes drifted toward the big white house on the corner. I'd always had fun there. But tonight I didn't want to set foot in the place. "I'm pledging that sorority. And we just spent a whole lot of hours setting up a holiday toy drive. The party for the kids is tomorrow. And tonight we're supposed to wrap the gifts, which should be fun, right?"

"Sure?"

"But the Beta Rho guys are setting up our tree on the sun porch. And I really don't feel like seeing them tonight, that's all."

"Is one of them your ex, or something?"

I let out a big old sigh. "Yes. But also his friends... There are *several* guys that I don't want to see."

Andy looked toward the house, and then down at me. "Do you mind if I ask why? I mean... are they scaring you?"

I shook my head. "It's not like that. It's just..." The moment stretched out, because there was no way I could actually tell him why. It was deeply embarrassing to me, and if he knew what I'd done, he'd stop looking at me the way he was looking at me now. His eyes were soft, and he'd given me his complete attention. He looked at me as if I were important. And I didn't want to see how that expression would change if he heard the stupid thing that I'd done.

But he was waiting for an answer. And I owed him one, because I was the idiot who had us standing out here in the cold.

"Okay," I tried. "My mother has a saying that you shouldn't do anything you don't want reported on the front page of the *New York Times*. And I've never been very good at following that rule, although I wish I were. Because my ex and his pals weren't very nice about… a recent embarrassing episode."

Again, Andy's brown eyes darted over to the sorority house and then back. But his frown lost some of its depth. With what I'd just told him, he would probably assume that I'd gotten drunk and puked all over the place, or something. "Well, okay. Going in or not is your call. We could always just go for ice cream at Scoops instead. I saw on Facebook that they made a new batch of salted caramel today. That's my favorite flavor."

I reached across to give his arm another squeeze. "I like your style, Andy. And it's tempting. But then they win, right?"

Andy shrugged. "You could look at it that way. Or you could just say that life is too short to spend even ten minutes with assholes."

Aw. This guy! I liked him already. "You are a very smart man. But I spent a lot of time on this charity thing, and if I don't see it to completion, I'm going to feel bad about that, too. So tonight I'm going to put on my big girl panties and give it a shot."

"Fine." His face lit up then with another winning smile. "But if you change your mind, what's the word? Give me a code so I'll know when to help you bail out."

"How about 'scoop'? As in ice cream."

"Deal. If you say 'what's the scoop?' we're outie." Then he held out his arm in that formal way, as if escorting a lady to dinner inside the pages of a Jane Austen novel. That was even weirder than shaking my hand. But so what? I took his arm, and in we went.

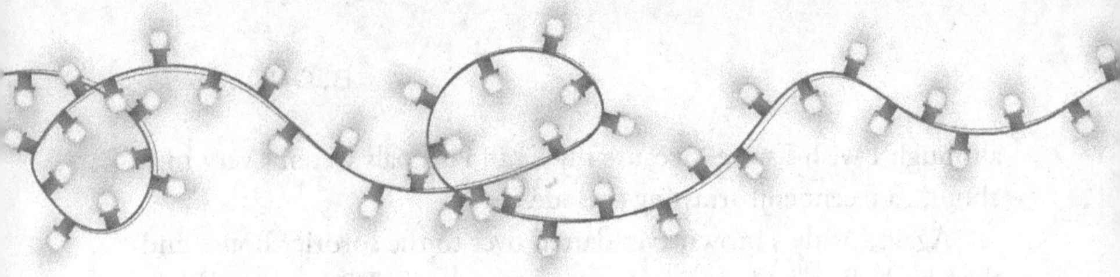

CHAPTER 3
ANDY

Together, we climbed a set of wide steps, passing a perfect row of rocking chairs on the porch. Until tonight, I'd never been inside of a sorority house. To me, they were mythical places, where the toilet seat was always down and the air smelled of flowers instead of feet. I opened the door, then stood aside for Katie.

And then we were inside, and the place did not disappoint. Like so many of the buildings at Harkness, Tri Psi had been built about a hundred years ago. The big front room had high, beamed ceilings. On one wall rose an oversized stone fireplace, where orange flames licked the air behind an iron metal grate.

All around the room, shiny-haired girls buzzed like bees. It was just the sort of estrogen-fueled chaos that reminded me a lot of my sisters.

Katie tagged one of the girls on the elbow as she flitted by. "Amy?"

She turned to look over her shoulder, smiling at us. "Hey! You look gorgeous. And have I met your date?"

I was introduced to Amy, who seemed to be in charge. She rattled off a bunch of instructions to Katie at warp speed — there were tables to set up and rolls of paper to find and toys to wrap. Katie nodded along at this barrage of details. But when Amy moved on, Katie turned to me with a smile. "First things first." She sidled up to a table bearing a metal tub full of ice, with dozens of bottles of beer nested inside. This was obviously not a keg-and-red-plastic-cup affair.

"Thanks," I said when she handed me a cold beer. "What's next? You can put me to work." Honestly, I was thrilled that this party had a mission other than small talk or — God forbid — dancing.

In high school, I was the scrawny nerd who never got invited to parties. Even though I'd grown into my long legs and stopped getting shoved into lockers years ago, I had never mastered small talk. And we won't even *talk* about what kind of a dancer I was. Because that way lies the abyss.

College had been much more fun for me than high school. Except for my nonexistent love life, I was happy at Harkness. Although our basketball team kind of sucked, my teammates were happy to have me. And on a basketball court I always knew what to do. I knew to always be ready to catch the pass. To find an opening and go for it.

But at a party? It was like I'd never received the playbook that everyone else got at birth. A party with Katie Vickery was double trouble, because her hotness made me into more of a bumbler than usual. A job was just what I needed.

Katie shifted her weight from one long leg to the other. "Well... most of the guys will be in that room," she tilted her head toward an arched doorway at the side. "They're putting up the tree. But if you wanted to stay here with me, you could help with the wrapping."

For a second I wasn't sure what to do. I didn't want to be underfoot. But there was something hesitant in in Katie's expression. As if perhaps she could use a little backup. "I'd just as soon help you, if that's okay," I said.

I knew I'd made the right choice, because the most beautiful smile lit her face. "Awesome. Then will you help me set up a folding table? Last time, mine fell down on one end, like a wounded camel. And all the Halloween pumpkins went rolling off."

Well, okay then.

There was a stack of collapsed folding tables leaning against one wall. I grabbed one and let Katie show me where to set it up, which took about sixty seconds. Then I drank my beer while she went running off for wrapping paper and tape. The beehive was in full swing around me. There were girls on the old wooden staircase, wrapping strands of Christmas lights around the banister, and girls toting boxes of Christmas cookies through the front door.

Katie returned with three enormous rolls of wrapping paper. "I'll just grab the first stack of gifts," she said.

"Are you sure I can't help with that?" I asked.

She waved me off. "It's mayhem back there. I'll be right back." True to her word, she soon reappeared with a stack of boxes. They were rainbow looms — those things that little kids used to make bracelets out of rubber bands.

Measuring the boxes, I began cutting pieces of Santa Claus paper to size. Functioning as an assembly line, Katie and I became a wrapping machine. I cut. She folded and taped. Working side by side made it easy for me to admire Katie. As she moved, her silky hair fell over her shoulder like a curtain. It made me want to sift my fingers through it, to see if it was as soft as it looked. And the way her dress skimmed her hips was making me a little bit crazy. In a perfect world, I would have loved to fit my hands around her waist.

Down, boy. I lowered my head and cut another rectangle of wrapping paper instead.

When every box was wrapped, Katie disappeared for a minute into a closet, returning with a towering stack of... basketballs! Some of them were ordinary basketballs, and pretty good quality. Others were meant for little kids, with cartoon pictures drawn all over them.

"Now we're talking," I said. "Those are some lucky kids if they're getting these."

"Glad you think so," she said. "But they're not going to be easy to wrap."

I saw what she meant. The balls were in half-boxes, which meant that one side would cave in a bit when we taped it. "It will work," I told her. "This is just karmic payback for all those years my mother had to figure out how to wrap basketballs for me in blue and white Hanukkah paper."

Katie gave me a killer smile. Then she unrolled a long span of wrapping paper, this one in plain green. Then she grabbed a ball — there were bears on this one — and set its oddly shaped carton onto the paper.

"Hold up…" I gave her the hand signal for time-out. "We can't wrap the kiddie balls in that plain paper, unless you're putting name tags on each of these. The paper should signal what's inside, right? A guy who chooses the green wrap can't end up with Disney characters on his basketball. He's going to get his ass kicked."

Katie's hands stilled. Then she and Amy, who was wrapping stacks of teddy bears nearby, both began to laugh. "Omigod, so true!" Katie said. She swapped the ball for a plain one. "The bigger question is, did I screw this up? Should I have not bought the decorated ones at all?"

I shook my head. "Those are good for little kids, because the bigger kids won't steal them. No cool dude is going to bring a ball with pandas on it to his pickup game."

"These are all good points," Amy remarked. "And now I'm thinking that we should put age ranges on everything. We could write, 'a sporty gift for up to age six.' Would that work?" She raised her eyes to me.

"Well, sure."

While Katie's sorority sister ran off to find some paper to make the tags, Katie touched the cuff of my shirt. "You are really good at this. Thank you for helping."

I shrugged. "I had lots of experience getting my ass kicked. I know all the scenarios."

Giggling, she touched a warm hand to my back for a second as she reached for the tape. Every time she put one of those slim hands on me, I felt it everywhere. And she smelled incredible. Like strawberries. I don't know what it was — a lotion? A fruity shampoo? Whatever it was, it was making me crazy.

"I really wasn't sure what to buy for the boys," she said, leaning over the next gift. "I hope these have a shot at making someone happy. There were trendier toys at the store, like action figures. But I went with sturdier things, and I hope it was the right call. These kids don't get to make a list and choose."

I cut the next piece of wrapping paper, thinking about that. "Even when you get to choose, gift-giving is never perfect, right? I asked for a lot of stuff as a kid only to find out it wasn't as good as it looked on TV."

"Ha! That is *so* true. My EZ Chef Oven never baked the cakes all the way through. I just hope that something here makes somebody's day, you know?"

"It has to," I told her. "There's something a little magical about getting a wrapped gift, especially if it's unexpected. The experience is bigger than the thing that's inside."

She didn't answer for a second, and I didn't quite know why. But then she spoke, and her voice was quiet. "You're a smart guy, Andy B.," she said, catching another piece of tape on her slender forefinger. "And we've been here an hour, and so far I haven't had to use the secret code word."

Her eyes flicked toward the arched doorway then. The sound of male voices had been coming from that room for a while now. She didn't look happy about it.

"That offer still stands, though," I whispered.

"And I do appreciate it," she breathed.

———

Eventually, we got everything wrapped except for one basketball — a pink one, with ducks on it. This last ball had a torn box around it and a black ink mark on its surface. "What do we do about this one?" I asked. "Ditch the box? Tape it up?"

Katie regarded it with a frown. "This one they gave me at the store, because it's damaged and because all our purchases were for charity. But I don't think I want any kid to get a damaged gift. That's just not right."

"Without it, do you have enough toys?"

"We do."

"Fair enough." I tore the ball from its box and tossed the cardboard onto our recycling pile. Then I spun it on my fingertip. Holding a basketball — even a pink one with ducks — always made my head feel clearer.

The Christmas tree setup next door must have been almost finished, because the sound of male laughter grew louder, and guys began to wander in, beers in hand. Their new role seemed to be smirking and drinking. Katie kept her eyes glued to the gift-wrapped packages which she was busy tagging. But I noticed that her body drifted a few inches closer to me.

And I didn't mind one bit. I was flattered, honestly. If my job tonight was to provide some kind of cover, I could do that.

Now, nice guys usually got friend-zoned. That wasn't only true in movies. I was living proof. And there were days when that got depressing. But tonight I was just where I wanted to be. I didn't mind being needed by this fabulous creature. Because, what a view! And these girls had good taste in beer.

Really, things could be worse.

With her laser focus, Katie leaned over another gift tag, that silky hair cascading off her shoulder and into her work, where I saw the ends begin to adhere to the tape in its dispenser. "Hang on," I said, hooking the pale strands with my thumb. "You don't want to tape yourself to that present." Gently, I released her hair from the adhesive. And then there was nothing left to do but sweep the whole bunch of her hair back and over her shoulder, where I smoothed it down where it belonged.

Her eyes locked on mine. "Thank you," she whispered.

"No problem," I said, but my voice was thick. Because touching her had made my brain take a day trip to Atlantic City.

I gathered up a stack of wrapping paper scraps and went looking for the recycling bin.

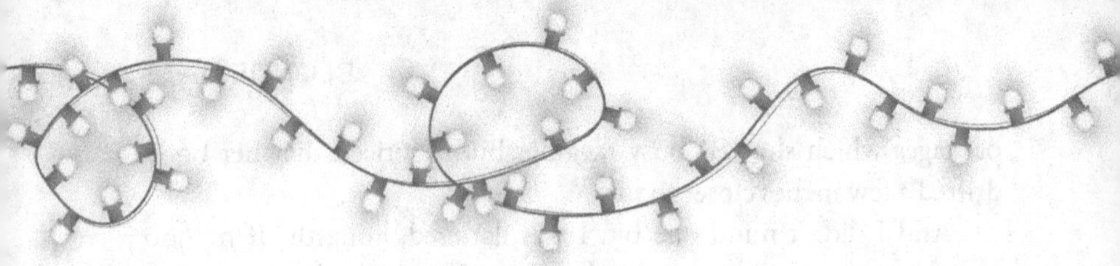

CHAPTER 4
KATIE

So far, so good.

The gift wrapping had gone even faster than I'd hoped. And Andy was good company. I didn't feel like I had to be on script with him. There was a social dance I'd learned at my mother's heel. "Ask his opinion," Mom had taught me. "A man wants someone to validate his worldview."

Even at frat parties, between games of beer pong and funnels, I'd stuck to a version of the script. Flirt and dodge. Toss the hair. I knew how to listen in a way which expressed interest without giving too much away.

It was exhausting, really. And tonight, I didn't have it in me. But it seemed not to matter. Andy's quiet companionship didn't demand anything of me. That was all for the best, because I was too freaked out by the sounds of laughter bleeding in our direction.

Some of that laughter was almost certainly directed at me.

Since the gifts were wrapped and tagged now, the next step was stacking them beside the Christmas tree in preparation for the kids' party tomorrow. But I didn't do my share, because I was putting off going into the next room. Instead, I grabbed another beer for Andy, and then planted myself right next to him. I looked up into his big brown eyes and just let him ground me. "Are you ready for the exam in European Paintings?" I asked. The test was in three days.

"Not yet," he said. "I think the baroque art is going to be the hardest to memorize," he said. "All those dark canvases. They're blending together on me."

"True," I agreed. "I'm so far behind, too. I didn't make it to the last two lectures, when he reviewed the final list of artworks. I'm probably going to memorize the wrong ones."

Andy shrugged. "I copied down the entire list in my notebook. I'll make you a copy if you want."

My heart gave a little bounce. "Could you?" This guy was going to save me *twice* this week — once from being dateless, and once from being clueless.

"No problem."

Across the room, one of the brothers stood on a chair, banging a spoon against a beer bottle. It was a beefy guy that they called Whittaker up there, looking for attention. "Ladies and not-so-gentlemen!" There was laughter all around me, but I did not laugh. Neither did Andy, actually. Even as the chuckles died down, I glanced upward, over my shoulder. He met my gaze with the world's most discreet eye roll.

"...The girls of Tri Psi ought to know that this year's tree was a three case effort. That's right. It took seventy-two beers to cut this sucker down and stand it back up on your porch."

There was another smattering of laughter, but I still wasn't feeling the love. Nothing was as light and funny as it would have been a week ago. To my new, jaded eyes, the peculiar mating ritual where a bunch of big strong boys put up a tree for the sorority princesses just hit me wrong. I mean, why couldn't we put up our own freaking tree? How hard could it be? And what were we supposed to owe these bros in exchange for their labor?

Gah. I was thinking too hard again.

"...So come on in, ladies, and let us light her up for you." He hopped off the chair and lumbered into the porch room. The sisters began to follow him.

But I did not. Because I hadn't seen Dash yet tonight, though I was sure I'd heard his rasping chuckle more than once. Rationally, I knew that I was going to have to face him down at some point. I had *seven* semesters left at Harkness. And pledging this sorority meant that I'd encounter him frequently. I needed to just get past it.

Yet something stuck my Prada heels to the floorboards. I just couldn't make myself go in there. And a full-body shiver started in my shoulders and worked its way down.

A warm hand landed lightly on my back. "Katie, are you okay?"

Yes?

No.

God.

I spun around and looked up (*way* up — he must be 6'-4") into his chocolate eyes. "I think I'd like to go outside for a minute."

He blinked once. Then, without a word, he turned toward the front door.

———

Like a fool, I'd run out onto the porch without my coat. So immediately I broke out in goosebumps. But the cold air felt good in my lungs. I needed to calm down. Like *right now.*

"Should I get your coat?" Andy asked. "Do you want to go?"

I shook my head. As stupid as I probably looked right now, I wasn't quite ready to bail. *Jeez.* If I let myself get this freaked out about seeing all those jerks from Beta Rho, what a long year it was going to be. "Crap," I swore. *Get it together, girl.*

"Are you going to tell me what's wrong?" As Andy said that, he draped his sport coat over my bare shoulders.

"Thanks," I stammered. "I'm not usually such a drama queen."

His eyebrows arched. "Well, maybe you have a good reason."

There was curiosity in his eyes. But it wasn't judgmental. "I don't like the way they look at me," I blurted, before I could think better of it.

"Why?"

Right. The reason was much too embarrassing for polite conversation. So instead of answering, I just looked down at my shoes.

"Let's just go, then?" he suggested. "You look a little... traumatized, actually."

That's when I let out a big sigh. Because there were people in the world who had good reason to feel traumatized. But I wasn't one of them. I hadn't been raped, or injured, or abused in any way. I'd just been stupid. Very, very stupid. "Ugh," I said. "If I leave, I'm giving him too much power."

"Maybe not," Andy challenged. "What did he do?" After asking, Andy immediately clapped a hand over his own mouth. "Sorry. It's none of my business. But you have me imagining the worst, here."

Ouch. Now a nice guy was worried about me, and I didn't even deserve it. "That's the stupid thing! Everything that went down..." *Gah!* I cringed at my unfortunate choice of words, "...between Dash and me was voluntary. I wasn't even drunk. Not very, anyway."

This explanation did not seem to appease Andy. When I looked up, his face was still full of concern. I hadn't meant to talk about this tonight, or maybe ever. And certainly not with him. And now he'd know that he was on a date with someone who was crazypants.

I took one more deep breath of cold air, which helped. A little. "Okay, I broke up with him because he didn't seem all that interested in me as a person. All he wanted to do was play video games with the brothers, but I was supposed to just hang around and watch until bedtime. Like a good little woman."

"Charming."

"I know, right? In my defense, I realized pretty quickly that he wasn't worth the effort, and I told him we were through." What I might have added was the fact that Dash didn't seem very broken up about losing me. And that should have been a big clue. But I'd missed it.

The story should have ended there. Because my instinct about him had been dead on. But it *didn't* end there. And that's why I'd been hearing a chant playing inside my head all week. And the mantra was: *Stupid... stupid... stupid...*

Andy was watching me with patient eyes, waiting for an explanation. It was silent there on the porch. And somehow I kept talking. "So, last week I went over to the Beta Rho house for a few minutes, just to drop off a bin of Christmas decorations for tonight. It was quiet there that night — the usual video games but no party." I'd been telling this part of the story to my shoes, but now I looked up to find Andy watching me. God, this was going to be embarrassing. "That night, for the first time, he made a big effort to talk to me. You know, the full court press."

Andy smiled at my basketball reference, but he didn't say a word.

"He got me a glass of wine and asked me a lot of questions about my classes, and pledging Tri Psi, and..." I rolled my eyes. "Ugh. I just sort of fell under the spell. He was so sweet and patient, telling me how much he missed me..."

"So far, so good." Andy pressed. "What went wrong?"

Yikes. I hadn't told a soul about this, not even my roommates. And tomorrow, I would probably regret telling Andy. I really didn't need even more people to know this story. But I was *angry*. And I wanted someone to *know* what pigs they were.

"Okay, he played me like a hand of poker," I sighed. "After my second glass of wine on an empty stomach, and two hours of heavy flattery, he wanted me to come upstairs with him. Fool that I am, I went." I looked down at the porch floorboards again. "He took me into one of the brothers' rooms. And we..." I cleared my throat. "We fooled around a little bit."

Andy dropped his voice. "But you didn't want to?"

He was about to get the wrong idea. "That's not it. See, I didn't mind at the time. I didn't start feeling bad about it until two days later. But that night I heard some voices in the hall. I heard a couple of the brothers laughing. But the door was shut, and I didn't think anything of it."

"Oh, *shit*," Andy whispered.

I looked up quickly, catching a wince on his face. "What?"

He closed his eyes for a long moment. And when he opened them, he said, "please tell me that this was not a hole-in-the-door situation."

My stomach dropped. Was I the only one on the planet who didn't know any better than to fall for Beta Rho's pledge ritual? Slowly, I nodded.

Andy's face sagged. "I'd always just assumed that was a myth."

"Apparently, it's not." I tried to say this with nonchalance. But I don't think I pulled it off. Because my eyes began to sting. And that was no good, because, you know, *mascara*. Carefully I pressed my fingertips against my tear ducts. "I wouldn't have even known, except that I overheard a couple of them talking about it. I was studying at one of those carrels in the stacks. Have you been up there?"

Andy nodded. The main library held twelve floors of books, and each floor had a row of old oak study desks with little walls attached. When you really needed to study — as opposed to picking somewhere with good people-watching — the stacks were the place to go.

"I heard these two guys carrying on, and I was going to walk over there and complain. But then I heard them say his name." I swallowed then, and my throat was thick. "So I listened. And one of them had been in the hallway that night. He was telling the other one exactly what he'd seen..." I had to stop there. Not only did I not want to speak about the details, I didn't want to think about them, either. When you're getting busy with somebody, you do not want to spend your time wondering what the expression on your face looks like when you're giving a....

God. Just shoot me.

I cleared my throat. "So, thanks to me, Dash's place in the pledge class is secure." And now I was done talking about this nightmare.

Andy pressed the fingertips of both hands against his brow, as if he had a sudden pain there. "He earned *pledge points* for letting the other guys *watch.*" He let out an angry noise. "That's disgusting."

When he said that, the weight of my outrage grew a tiny bit lighter. All week, I'd been carrying this embarrassing secret around. And it was awfully heavy. The sound of Andy's displeasure made me feel as if I'd just handed off a portion of my anger, letting someone else carry it for a moment instead.

"I'm still an idiot," I said, because it was true.

"No! *Shit,* no. That is the lowest of the low. That is..." Andy took a deep, slow breath and let it out again. "You know all those brochures about consent that the college passed out during the first week of school?"

"Sure." They were pretty funny, actually. My roommates and I had a few giggles reading the flyers out loud to one another. Some genius had written out a script for hookups that was supposed to guarantee that both parties had consent for every sexual act. So the bullet points read like a porn film. *Do you want me to put my hand here? Does it feel good when I do this? Can I touch you here?*

As funny as that was, it didn't really apply. "But... I, uh. I consented."

Andy shook his head. "No, you didn't. Because if you had, you wouldn't feel afraid to go in there right now." He jabbed a finger toward the door.

I had absolutely no response to that. Except that the pressure in my chest loosened another percentage point or two.

Andy didn't wait for a reaction from me, though. He was on a roll. "I mean... forget common decency. Don't any of them have *sisters?* God."

"At least there wasn't any evidence," I said quietly. "When I was eavesdropping, I actually heard the brother who wasn't there ask if there were pictures. And the other one said no, because that would make it into a code violation."

"How *thoughtful* of them to avoid violating the code," Andy spat. "Are you going to report it anyway?"

That was something I'd thought about all week. "It's not like I don't feel the urge. But as far as I can tell, they didn't break any rules, let alone laws. So it would be a waste of time. Not to mention that everyone would know how stupid I was."

Andy moved fast, then. He stepped forward to wrap his arms around me, giving me a quick, fierce hug. "You weren't stupid. Trusting, maybe. But that's supposed to be a good thing to be."

I was too shaken up to decide whether or not he was right. But I did notice that Andy gave first-rate hugs. Those long arms were good for something besides dunking basketballs, I guess. Come to think of it, he was probably only hugging me for warmth. We'd been out here awhile, and I had his jacket on. "I'm sorry to dump this on you," I said into his shoulder.

He released me, stepping back. "Sorry it *happened* to you. Want to go home? You don't owe it to him to be civil."

"But I can't avoid him for four years! And it's not just him! I don't know who was standing on the other side of that door. So I don't even know who to avoid. I'm lucky it's *not* on the front page of the *New York Times*. Mom was right."

Andy stuffed his hands into his pockets, and began pacing the porch. "She wasn't, though. I don't think your mom has thought that through."

"What do you mean?"

He stopped walking and turned to me. "We all do things that we don't want to see in a newspaper. I mean, she probably has sex with your father, right?"

"Ew."

He grinned. "Sorry, but you get my point. She doesn't want *that* pictured in the *Times*, even though there's nothing wrong with it. And you didn't do anything remotely wrong, either. At the risk of sounding very pre-law, you have a reasonable expectation of privacy if you follow a guy into his room to..." he broke off the sentence, and there was an awkward pause.

"...Put some lipstick on his dipstick?" I supplied. And then I laughed. I actually *laughed* about my nightmare. Because now that I was breathing just a little bit easier, I could see just how fricking ridiculous the whole thing was. And humiliating. But still... *funny* in a way.

God, I was probably losing my mind.

But I'd made Andy's lips twitch too with my crude description of what had happened. He was trying not to laugh now, but sometimes holding it back only makes it worse.

"Go on," I told him. "We might as well laugh about it. It's either that or crying."

He let a chuckle escape. "You want me to punch him for you? I've never won a fight in my life, but this seems like a good cause."

"Well, okay," I teased. "So long as you think a trip to jail is a good use of the rest of your night."

He grinned. "With my luck, it would be a trip to the hospital, and *then* a trip to jail. But seriously, I have two sisters. The thought of someone doing that to you makes me want to deck him."

"That's really..." I swallowed hard. "Thank you. I needed to hear someone say that. I've spent the week telling myself, 'hey, it's just sex, right? No big deal.' But I'm embarrassed. And it's not the same as if we were fooling around and somebody walked in by accident."

"Of *course* it's not the same. Intentions are everything." As he said this, I saw him shiver.

"Come on," I said suddenly. Here I'd been struggling to find a reason to go back inside the house, but there was a perfectly good one standing right in front of me. I opened the door. "You're going to freeze, and catch pneumonia, and miss our art history exam. And then I won't have anyone friendly to sit next to. So we're going back in."

"If you're ready," he said.

"I'm as ready as I'll ever be." I took Andy's cold hand in mine and pulled him inside. There was nobody in the parlor anymore. Keeping hold of Andy's hand, I tugged him through the room and into the big old sunroom.

In front of us rose a giant Christmas tree with about a million white lights on it. And now I understood why the girls put the tree in here. Those lights reflected in the many windowpanes circling the room. Lifting my chin, I gazed up at it, unblinking. I'd done this ever since I was a child — I'd stare at the lit Christmas tree until my vision went slightly askew and the lights blurred before my eyes. The tree was even more beautiful when you didn't focus on each pinprick of light, but saw the whole thing at once.

"Nice," Andy whispered beside me. "The kids at your party tomorrow will love it."

"I hope so. Otherwise those three cases of our beer that the Betas drank went to waste."

My date snorted, and I squeezed his hand a little tighter.

Of course, I couldn't stare at the tree forever. Or cling to Andy. Eventually, I had to look around, and even make eye contact. And it wasn't going to get any easier if I put it off.

The brave thing to do would be to just say hello to Dash and his stupid friends, as if nothing had happened. They'd forget about the little show I'd put on eventually, right?

Gah. Okay. Deep breaths.

"Let's get you another drink," I suggested. "I know I could use one." Still clutching Andy's hand like a security blanket, I steered the two of us over to a table against the wall. I had to let him go to pop the tops off of two bottles of Moosehead Lager.

"I like this beer," Andy said, taking his. "Thanks."

I took a swig of mine. Maybe a beer or ten was the right way to go. Tonight I couldn't exactly get wasted to dull the pain. And not because I'd worry that Andy would take advantage of me. It was just the opposite — poor Andy already had already shored me up once tonight. He didn't need the trouble of escorting a drunk girl home, even if I did feel like getting numb.

Now, at close range, I heard a familiar chuckle.

Steeling myself, I turned. And there he was, a beer in hand, grinning at his pledge brothers. Dash's eyes slid in my direction. They seemed to lock on me for a nanosecond, then jump to Andy. Then, just as quickly, they slid away.

Okay, that wasn't so bad. I was just about to exhale when the guy beside Dash elbowed him, a knowing smirk on his face. Lowering his beefy head to Dash's ear, he said something which made my ex-boyfriend grin.

My pulse kicked up, and I felt hot all over. Maybe I couldn't do this after all. Maybe I should duck out of a party for the first time in my *entire freaking life*, and then transfer to another college. On another continent.

That sounded like a plan.

Turning my back, I squeezed past Andy and out through the door we'd come in not five minutes ago. I trotted across the parlor, skidding to a stop in front of the fireplace. Meanwhile, my heart bounded along inside my chest like a cartoon rabbit.

"Shit," I whispered to myself.

I heard footsteps, and a few seconds later Andy appeared at my elbow. "Forget something?" he teased. But I saw worry in his face.

Looking down into the fireplace embers, I tried to think. "They're probably laughing at me right now."

"They're not," he said. "I overheard them talking about hockey, actually."

"Figures. That's all they live for. *Games*. They made my life into one of their crude little games."

Andy made an irritated noise. "They did. And that sucks."

"He acted like a pig," I said.

"He is a pig. But what would make you feel better? An apology?"

I considered that idea. "I want him to wear a t-shirt every day for a week that reads: *I am a pig*."

Andy laughed. "You should consider law school, Katie. You'd make an interesting judge."

I looked up at him then, and his warm brown eyes were smiling at me again. "That's just the sorority girl solution, Andy. Haven't you heard the joke? How many sorority girls does it take to screw in a lightbulb?"

He cocked his head like a puppy. "How many?"

"Six. One to change the lightbulb and five to make the t-shirts."

He touched his empty beer bottle to mine. "Good one, sister. Is there a frat version of that joke?"

"Sure. It takes eleven frat boys to screw in a lightbulb. One to hold the bulb, and ten to drink enough that the room starts spinning."

He gave me the hot smile again. "You are a total hoot when you're stressed out."

"Why, thank you. I'm almost as fun when I'm not stressed out." But of course he wouldn't know that, because tonight he was keeping company with a total head case. "I have to walk back into that room. The only alternative is transferring to a school in South America. Or Europe. I hear Spain is nice this time of year."

Andy winced. "They made your visit to their house into a game, but it was a game you didn't know you were playing. And now you're supposed to go in there and be social, and pretend like it never happened. Another game."

"And not knee him in the balls, or throw up, yes."

He set his empty beer down on the mantelpiece, which is probably exactly what that space had been used for since the beginning of time. "So maybe what you need to get through the next half hour is one more game. A harmless one, though. You and I can play a game with them, only they won't know they're playing."

Now I was lost. "What game?"

"Well..." he tapped a finger on the mantel. "We'll try get each guy to say the name of an animal in conversation."

"An *animal*?"

"Sure. That's what you called him. And if you're focused on that, you won't stop to worry whether they're looking at you funny."

"Andy, they *will* be looking at me funny. Because I'm going to have to have some pretty weird conversations to get an animal name out of them."

He just grinned. "Who cares? I'll be doing it, too. For points. Whoever gets the most animals wins. And no repeats."

It was the most ridiculous idea I'd ever heard. And maybe the most brilliant. "So, this is competitive?"

"Unless you're afraid to take me on."

I giggled. "*Please*. Sorority girls are *made* for this game. I'm a Division One small talk champion. Bring it, basketball dude. And maybe I can get Dash to say the word 'pig.' Since he is one."

His eyebrows shot up. "That's a good twist, honestly. It's like a trump card. A trump animal."

"Right! If I get Dash to say 'pig,' I win automatically."

"He doesn't have, like, a pet pig that I don't know about? Am I being gamed, missy?"

I shook my head. "If either one of us can get anybody to say 'pig,' we win. So it's a little like catching the golden snitch."

"Okay. I'm in. But they have to say 'pig,' and not some similar word. Because how hard would it be to get a frat boy to talk about how much he likes bacon?"

"Good rule. Should we shake on it?"

With a smile, Andy offered me his hand. When I took it, we shook. Then he pulled me in for one more quick hug, which lasted only a fraction of a second. "Remember, 'scoop' is still the escape word."

"Oh, I remember," I told him. "But now I want to win this thing."

He gave me a gentle shove toward the porch. "Lead on, then. But you should know that I won't *let* you win. You're going to have to earn it."

"Do you always talk smack before a game?" I asked him. Now I was actually flirting with him. If you'd asked me two hours ago if I'd find the energy to flirt tonight, I would have said you were crazy.

"Basketball is at least fifty percent smack talk. The way my team plays, anyway."

He gave me one more of his killer smiles, and together we headed back in there.

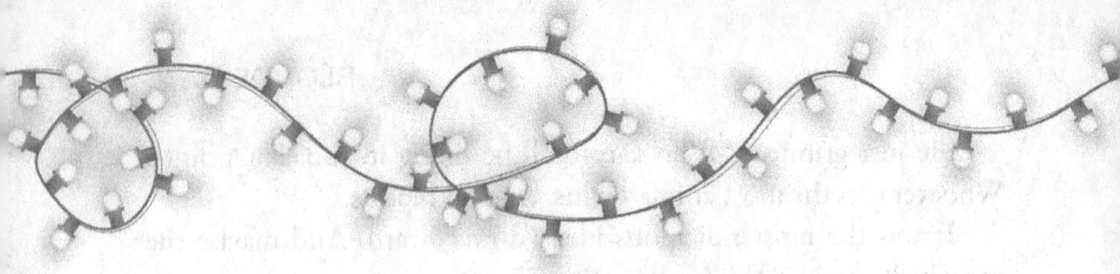

CHAPTER 5
ANDY

Katie's step had a new swagger as she marched back into the party. She stopped to shed my sport coat, handing it over without a word. Then she squared her bare shoulders as if going into battle. (A really sexy battle.)

I shrugged the jacket on, then stooped to pick up the pink basketball I'd been playing with earlier. It had been abandoned in a corner. Tucking it under my arm, I followed Katie into the party, where one of the Beta Rho brothers was standing in front of the drinks table opening beers. Katie asked him to pop one open for me.

"Sure thing, cutie," he said.

"That would be *Katie*," my date corrected, her voice frosty.

"Right. Just like I said." The guy opened another bottle of beer and handed it to me.

"I like this lager," I said, holding up my bottle. "I don't think I've had it before."

"It's all right," he said with half a shrug. "I think we started buying Moosehead because our treasurer is Canadian."

"*Ah*," I said, reaching over to give Katie's elbow a meaningful squeeze. The game wasn't even a minute old, and I'd already scored a point with "moose."

Katie's eyebrows shot upward. Then she grabbed my hand and tugged me over to her side. Standing on tiptoe, she admonished me in a low voice. "That was clever, tall man, but it was low-hanging fruit. Don't get too used to winning."

I took the risk of putting a hand onto one of her deliciously bare shoulders and leaned down toward her ear. "You talk a big game, lady. But I don't see any action."

Her eyes flared then. And she stood up a little straighter and stalked toward her friend Amy, who was chatting with two fraternity brothers beside the tree.

Katie was a smart girl. She'd picked a target rich environment. I followed, dodging a few people. The party was in full swing now. All the work had stopped, and guys and girls stood around in twos and threes, drinking beer and munching Christmas cookies.

Katie's eyes were darting around the room, as if she were looking for something. But what? I'd already clocked Dash, her ex — and who calls himself "Dash" anyway? — about ten feet from Katie. Then I saw her swoop down and gather something up. When she stood up again, there was a sparkle in her eye. And a cat in her arms.

She gave me a victorious glance, then tossed all that gleaming hair over her shoulders. I maneuvered closer to her, so that I could hear whatever went down.

Katie waited for a pause in Amy's conversation with the two beefy guys before her. "Careful," Amy said, turning to Katie. "Mr. Whiskers is going to scratch your dress."

"He wouldn't dare," Katie said. "Cats like me." With an innocent face, she looked up at one of the guys in front of her. "How do you feel about cats?"

"I'm more of a dog person," he said, swigging his beer.

"Are you now?" Katie said, throwing a meaningful glance over her shoulder at me. She bent her knees to release the cat. Mr. Whiskers disappeared under the Christmas tree. Then Katie gave a big sneeze. "Excuse me a moment," she said.

I followed as Katie made a beeline for a box of tissues on a side table. "I'm allergic to cats," she said, blowing her nose. "But that was totally worth it."

"So you threw yourself on the sword for that point?"

"I did," she agreed, blowing her nose.

"Well, as Teddy Roosevelt said, 'greatness is the fruit of toil and sacrifice and high courage.'" God, I was such a dork. But Katie was still smiling, so it didn't really matter.

"I'm winning this thing," she said.

"You're *tying* this thing. The score is 1–1, smack-talker."

With a fiery look at me — one which I felt in some very inappropriate places — she marched off again.

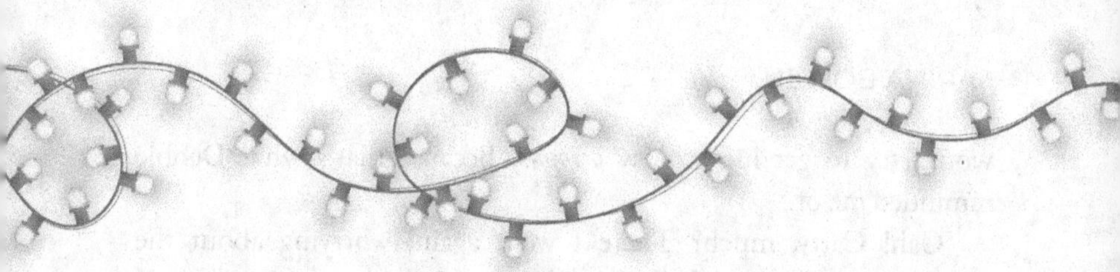

CHAPTER 6
KATIE

The room was more crowded tonight than I'd anticipated. Everyone was taking this last opportunity to have a beer with friends before we all hunkered down for exams. As I waded back into the thick of things, I was halted by the sight of a girl's limbs wrapped around Dash.

That was fast.

Peeking through the boughs of the Christmas tree, I snuck a closer look. When the girl shifted her face from one side of him to the other, I recognized her. *Debbie Dunn.* She wore an unhealthy amount of eye makeup. And was staring up into Dash's face, and practically rubbing her boobs on his oxford shirt.

My first thought was: *Ew.* My second was: *Have I ever done that? And did it cause someone else to say 'ew'?* My third thought was: *Do I care? Am I actually* slut-shaming *Debbie Dunn because she's wearing gloppy mascara?*

My fourth thought was: *When did I start over-thinking absolutely everything? And how can I stop?*

Abruptly, I moved around the Christmas tree, looking for someone else to talk animals with. Andy had been right about one thing. It was hard to second-guess yourself to death when you were trying to come up with a reason for your neighborhood frat boy to say *hedgehog.* Or *platypus.*

For now, I steered a wide path around Dash. Later, maybe I

would try to get him to say *octopus*. Because that's what Debbie reminded me of.

Gah! Catty, much? There I went again, worrying about the wrong things. Because, hell, the girl was actually doing me a *favor*. If Dash was busy allowing Debbie to slither up his body like a sea creature, he couldn't exactly make any crude comments about me (or my recent performance) to his pals.

I should thank her. I should buy her flowers. (Because Dash never would. That was for damned sure. He wasn't a fan of "romantic shit," he'd said once.)

And anyway, a few yards from where I stood, Andy was busy talking to Dash's pledge mate, the one they called Ralph. "You're from Chicago?" I heard Andy say. "How do you like your football team this year?"

Crap!

"The Bears look pretty good going into the playoffs," Ralph said.

Andy's eyes flicked over to me, and I saw a corner of his mouth turn up in satisfaction. Then, after he and Ralph exchanged a few more words, Andy actually *moonwalked* backwards a few paces, as if in victory. Now, someone as tall as he was really couldn't moonwalk without making a spectacle of himself. And I saw a few eyebrows lift in his direction. But Andy seemed not to care, and that made me smile.

Once upon a time, I'd felt that way, too. In high school, I'd found it easy to be the silly one. I had a lot of good friends, and a solid standing in the social group of my choice. And were I to have moonwalked (not that I'd ever wanted to) through a party, nobody would have cared.

Somehow I'd taken a wrong turn these past few months. I cared too much about the opinions of people who cared too little about me. That was something I was definitely going to mull over later. But right now, I had work to do. Because Andy was a point ahead of me in our weird little game.

And there was never going to be a better time to face the music. So I marched up to stand among the group of fraternity boys which included Dash, and also Whittaker.

"Evening, Katie," Whittaker said. A little smile played on his lips, making me almost certain that he'd been in on Dash's stupid little prank.

Just breathe.

"Evening, Whittaker," I said. "Are you ready for the art history exam?" He was one of Dash's football cronies in that class. I used to sit beside them every Monday, Wednesday and Friday. I'd felt smug about that, too. As if one seat in that lecture hall was better than another one. It seemed quite ridiculous now. Some other stupid girl could have that seat. Debbie, or a whole team of Debbies. I was done with it.

"Still have to memorize all those paintings," Whittaker said.

"Yeah," Andy put in. He slid in behind me and put a hand on my bare shoulder, giving it a gentle squeeze. "I'm taking that course, too. And some of those paintings are a little gruesome. You know, those Renaissance scenes? Especially that one from right after the hunt?"

Crap again! I knew where Andy was going with this. The hunt painting had a very dead wild boar in the foreground. But no way was he going to win this thing by getting Whittaker to say "boar." It had to be *pig*. No substitutions. I leaned my shoulders back against him as a silent message. *Don't think this will work for you, pal.*

He gave my shoulder another squeeze, as if to say: *don't you wish you'd thought of this?*

Whittaker scratched his head. "I don't think I know that one yet."

"Bummer," Andy said. "Add that one to your study list, then." I tipped my head back on his shoulder so I could see his face. He winked at me, and I had to bite the inside of my cheek to keep from giggling.

When I faced forward again, I found Dash watching us, and Whittaker, too. Maybe they were wondering why Andy and I kept giving each other significant glances. Or maybe they were remembering exactly how ridiculous I looked during what was supposed to be a private moment. God, I hoped it was the first thing, and not the second thing. Weirdly enough, though, I didn't care quite so much as much as I had about an hour ago.

So that's something.

"Anybody have any good plans for winter vacation?" Andy asked.

"Sailing in Fiji," Dash bragged. God, he was such a tool. I can't believe I ever thought he was a catch.

"Doing some skiing," Whittaker said.

"Yeah?" Andy perked up. "What's your favorite mountain?"

"We're heading to Utah," Whittaker answered. "Gonna hit Alta and Snowbird."

"I *love* Snowbird," Andy agreed, giving my shoulder yet another squeeze.

He would. Because now I was down by *two* points. The party would breaking up soon, too. My chance for victory would soon be over. I looked around the room, wondering how we were going to fit fifty kids in here tomorrow. "I'm glad it's not my job to set this place up in the morning. It's going to be mayhem, right?" There was another committee for that. (Sororities loved committees.) I wasn't due to help out until the party started at eleven.

Dash shrugged. "I don't think I'm going to make it over here. You girls seem to have it covered. Amy had a checklist, and shit."

The hair on the back of my neck stood up, and not because of Dash's dismissal of a party for fifty indigent children. But because I had my Hail Mary idea. "It must be really hard to plan parties," I said in a wistful tone. "I mean... where is Amy going to find all the tables and chairs that we need? Does anyone, like, deliver those things?"

I felt Andy stop breathing. Because he saw where I was going with this.

Dash gave another indifferent shrug. "She probably just called a party rental company."

"Huh," I said slowly. "Like that one with those trucks I see around campus sometimes? Those bright ones with..." *Take the bait,* I prayed. *This is for all the marbles.*

"Yeah," he drained his beer. "With the pink pigs on 'em."

Andy's hand closed firmly around my elbow, as if to say, *I can't believe you pulled that off.* And I gave him a subtle bump with my hip. *Take that, tall guy.* I felt rather than saw the smile that he ducked his head to conceal. When he let out a nearly silent chuff of laughter, his nose grazed my hair, and his breath at the back of my neck gave me goose bumps. In a good way.

And through it all, Dash just stood there in front of me, looking half bored and half uncomfortable, worrying the label on his beer bottle. And then Debbie slithered up to him again, plastering herself against his side. She shot me an ornery look.

"Welp!" I said, turning toward Andy. "I think I'm done here. After I duck into the ladies' room, do you mind if we head out?"

"Not at all," he said, spinning the pink basketball on one finger.

"Back in a jiff," I promised. I crossed the room, which was already beginning to thin out. It was still early, but exam week wasn't the best time to party, even for this crew. And tomorrow the sorority was hosting fifty kids. A hangover would not be welcome in the morning.

I crossed through the parlor to the big old bathroom. Like so many buildings at Harkness, it was a blend of old-world grandeur (the marble tiles) and awkward 1970s renovations (the creaky metal doors on the toilets).

After I took care of business, I emerged from the stall to find Debbie in front of the single tiny mirror, refreshing her lipstick. Washing my hands, I began to feel philosophical. "That spot where you're standing," I said to Debbie, "is where we usually have elbow-jousting matches. Primping is practically a blood sport around here."

"If I had your face, I wouldn't bother primping," Debbie said in a low voice.

I stared down at the paper towel in my hands. On the one hand, I really didn't understand why she'd say that. But we girls put ourselves down often enough, even if we don't usually do it for people who aren't already our friends. I didn't know what to say.

But while I struggled to figure it out, Debbie spoke again. "I don't know why he broke up with you, either. If you lasted a month, I'll probably last a week."

"Whoa. Hey now," I said, hands on my hips. "Don't you dare give him all that power. Maybe he doesn't get to decide."

She gave me a sullen glance. "Of course he does. They already have the power."

"Debbie."

She turned to me, her eyes dark.

"He isn't worth it, okay? Go out with him if you want. Or not. But treat yourself right. Because he's not going to look out for you."

She gave me a little eye roll. "Everybody gets dumped, Katie. Even you."

"But I didn't. I broke up with him."

"Sure you did," she said immediately. Her words had dismissed me, but her eyes were interested.

"I did. And then he decided to teach me a little lesson."

"How?" she whispered, unable to hide her curiosity.

"I was stupid. I fooled around with him one more time..." God, I didn't want to say this next part out loud. But she deserved to know what she was getting herself into. "Without my knowledge, he let some people watch."

Her eyebrows shot straight up, disappearing into her bangs. "Like, through a hole in the door?"

Kill me now. I really was the only naive idiot left on this campus, wasn't I? Slowly, I nodded.

"That is so wrong," she hissed.

"You think?"

She stuffed makeup products back into her clutch purse. "You know, fuck it. I'm just going to sneak out and go home. He's been giving me a not-so-nice vibe all night. And that is just too much." She jammed the bag under her arm. "Good night."

Without another word, she stormed out of the bathroom.

Then it was just me alone with the little mirror. And I felt an instinctual pull to go over to it and check my makeup. Because you never know when your eyeliner has smeared...

No, I coached myself. *Andy's waiting. And he doesn't care about your stupid makeup.*

I pushed open the bathroom door and went to find him.

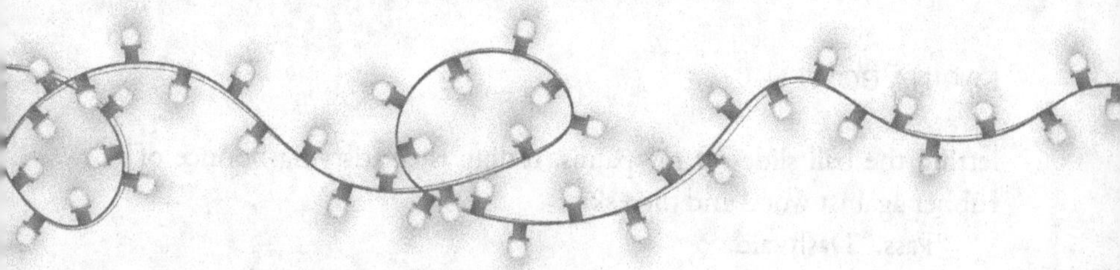

CHAPTER 7
ANDY

When Katie departed for the bathroom, it left me standing there with Dash and his thick-necked pals. I'd had enough to drink. So instead of reaching for another beer, I began to noodle around with the outrageous pink basketball I'd been carrying around. I rolled it up the back of my hand and along my arm. Then I dribbled it a couple of times on the old wooden floor beneath me.

"Nice ball you've got there," Dash muttered. "Is your team switching *teams* this season?"

A gay joke from a frat guy? *Shocker.* "You know, it's not nice to make fun of a guy's balls," I quipped. Nothing he could say right now could ruin my mood. I still wouldn't have minded landing a punch right in the middle of his smirk. But I wasn't going to do it. Because fighting Dash and his crew was a pretty bad idea, one which would surely mess up the plan I had to walk Katie home and ask her out.

Eyes on the prize, and all.

Ignoring Dash, I toyed with the ball, spinning it on my finger and dribbling through my legs. This always relaxed me. Whenever I was stressed out about something, I took the ball in my hands and began to calm down.

Still, I could feel him watching me. Maybe he thought I was showing off, but it wasn't really like that. If I wanted to show off, I'd do these tricks twice as fast. I was just taking things nice and easy, letting the ball slide off my palms, feeling the satisfying bounce of rubber against wood and then skin.

"Pass," Dash said.

Really, dude? You have to get competitive? Maybe he didn't enjoy the fact that I was friendly with his ex-girlfriend. What a tool.

I passed him the ball. He palmed it, then bent his knees to execute a couple behind-the-back bounces. Then once under the knee. And then he bounced it back to me.

You want to show off? Fine. For the next fifteen seconds, I gave it to him: bang-bang under one leg, followed by a scissor cross, a few strokes of walking the dog, and then a quick bounce back to him.

He fumbled it, which made me irrationally happy. Then he did a little handiwork with a triangle dribble around his right leg (and I'd bet money he couldn't do his left) before a fake and a snap back to me.

The fake and the snap were exactly what I thought he'd do. So I took that ball as if I'd been waiting for it all my life. Slowing it down, I dribbled around my body a few times, spinning it on a fingertip after that. "Stay ready," I warned him.

He lifted a brow, irritated that I'd warn him like that. As if he were a bumbler. (Even if he was.)

I dropped the ball low in front of me, pounding the dribble for four or five strokes. Then I let go. The ball ricocheted up... and *straight* into Dash's crotch.

Three-pointer! So to speak.

"URMMFFF!" the guy groaned, catching the ball and bending over in the time-honored position of a guy whose eggs had just been scrambled.

It took all my effort not to laugh. "Ouch," I said.

"You *ass*," Dash muttered. And when he straightened up, his face was red with anger.

My heart rate kicked up a couple of points, but I held his gaze. "That hurts, right? When you think you've signed up for a simple game of one-on-one, but then it turns out that someone else had different plans for you?"

His face did something interesting then. It locked up tight in surprise. And then guilt crossed his features. His mouth sagged, and his eyes looked away from me. He swallowed uncomfortably.

"You can call me an ass if it makes you feel better," I said in a low voice. "But you leave Katie alone."

Dash didn't acknowledge me. He just set the ridiculous pink basketball down on a wicker chair, and then picked up a sport coat that had been lying over the back of it.

"You get me?" I pressed. That's when I heard the sound of high heels tapping toward me. "Hey!" Katie said, skidding up to me. "Sorry about that. I got caught up chatting in the bathroom."

"No problem." I turned to give her my full attention and was basically walloped all over again by how attractive she was. Her silky hair slid over her bare shoulders as she moved. And those kissable lips gave me a little smile. "Are you ready to head out?" I asked, hoping the answer was yes.

"Sure! We can grab my coat on the way."

A frat brother nudged Dash, whose face was still red and ornery. "Let's hit it, bro," he said.

Dash cleared his throat. "I was waiting for Debbie. She might still be in the bathroom."

Katie paused, her hand grabbing mine. "She left," she told Dash. "What?"

Katie's grin took on a devilish glint. "She said she had more important places to be. Or something like that. G'night." She gave my hand a little tug, and we left the room together.

PART TWO

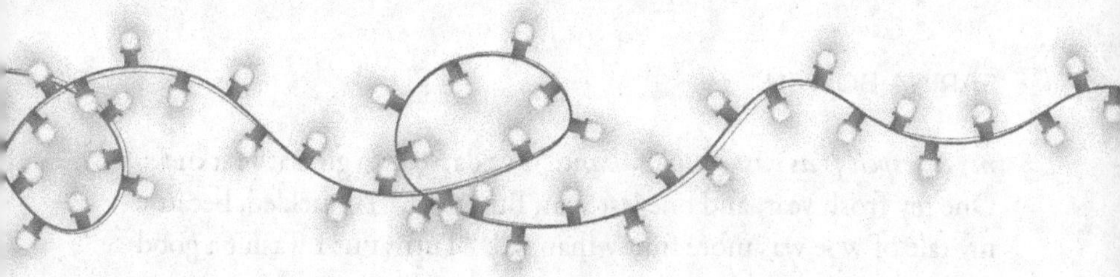

CHAPTER 8
ANDY

When Katie had put her coat on, she'd had to drop my hand. Now that we were walking along the sidewalk together, I wanted it back. *Your only real problem is confidence*, my sister had said. What would a confident guy do in this situation?

As casually as I could, I reached over and took Katie's smooth hand in mine. She laced her fingers in mine, just like that.

Huh. *Thank you, Delia*.

"Your game saved me tonight," Katie said. "But what on earth inspired it?"

"Ah," I said, as my thumb skimmed her palm. "During the summer, I work at a boys' sleep-away camp in the White Mountains. And we're always having to think up games to keep them from fighting with each other before dinnertime."

"So you *counseled* me, like one of your nine-year-old campers?" She was smiling again, which I loved.

"Well, they're twelve. But, yeah." Maybe I was a sap, but tonight I felt truly connected to someone for the first time in a long while. Katie might not remember this night except as a blip on her way toward feeling better about the shitty thing that happened to her. But I wasn't going to forget it any time soon.

"So, you know my tale of woe," she said. "What's your story? No girlfriend, I guess?"

"Not at the moment," I said, because it sounded smoother than *my dry spell is as vast as the Sahara.* "I've dated two girls at Harkness. One my frosh year, and one last year. But, um..." I chuckled, because my tale of woe was more funny than sad. "Turns out I wasn't a good match for either girl."

"Bad breakups?" she guessed.

"Nope. I'm still friends with both of them, actually."

"But you got your heart broken?"

"Not exactly. There wasn't a whole lot of spark there in the first place. That was the problem. Both of my ex-girlfriends decided — right after dating me — that they would rather be with women."

I watched Katie's face as she took that in, waiting for the inevitable reaction. Her eyes flicked toward mine, and she bit her lip, trying to fight off her amusement. Those pretty eyes were sparkling now. "Go ahead," I told her. "You can laugh. Everyone else does."

"Oh, Andy," she giggled. "Both of them?"

"Yep."

Her giggle became an unruly belly laugh, and we had to stop on the sidewalk while she pulled herself together. She took a deep, gasping breath and wiped her eyes. "You know that had nothing to do with you, right?" she said eventually. "You didn't turn those girls gay."

"Yeah, I know it. But my friends are pretty amused anyway."

"*Both* girls," she tittered.

"Yep!"

We had almost arrived at Fresh Court, and the inevitable end of the night. This was the moment when I had to screw up my courage and ask her if we could go out again some time. But how to phrase it? Some guys were smooth and could ask for anything.

I was not one of them.

"Wait." Katie tugged on my hand just as we were about to walk underneath the Fresh Court gate. "Are you going to copy the art history notes for me?"

I paused. Did she mean tonight? "Any time. My printer makes copies."

"Can I get them now? The test is only three days away."

"Well, sure." I changed direction, steering us toward Beaumont. Katie's fingers gave mine a squeeze, which I returned. That little exchange made me ridiculously, irrationally happy. I walked on, as if it were the most ordinary thing in the world to have Katie Vickery stop by my room. But inside, I was dancing a jig.

Calm down, idiot, I chided myself. *The girl is just very serious about her art history exam.*

Even at the pace of someone walking on high heels, the trip from the gate to my entryway only took a few minutes. But that was plenty of time to fret about the condition of my room. For once I'd made the bed. *Yes!* I'd straightened it out, anyway, because I needed a surface on which to lay the evidence of my not-very-masculine fashion crisis.

Wait — I'd picked all those clothes up afterwards, right?

Uh, oh. This was going to be bad.

But it was too late to worry, because we were already arriving at my entryway stairs. Katie followed me up to the second floor, where I unlocked the door. Peering into the room, I gave a split second prayer that either things weren't as bad as I remembered, or else elves had come by to tidy up while I was gone.

No such luck. The bed was covered with my clothes. Stepping into my room behind me, my date laughed. "Looks just like my room."

"I was in kind of a hurry," I said, lamely.

"See? That's what I tell Scarlet when she complains about the mess. But apparently I'm *always* in a hurry."

Embarrassed, I went over to the desk to find my History of Art notebook. Flipping through the pages, I said, "The review lecture took me six pages. But it will only take a couple of minutes to copy."

"No rush," she said, sitting down in my desk chair, which was mercifully clean.

No rush, my brain repeated, listening for clues.

Stop, I ordered myself. Don't fuck this up. Give the girl her notes, walk her home, ask her out and count your blessings.

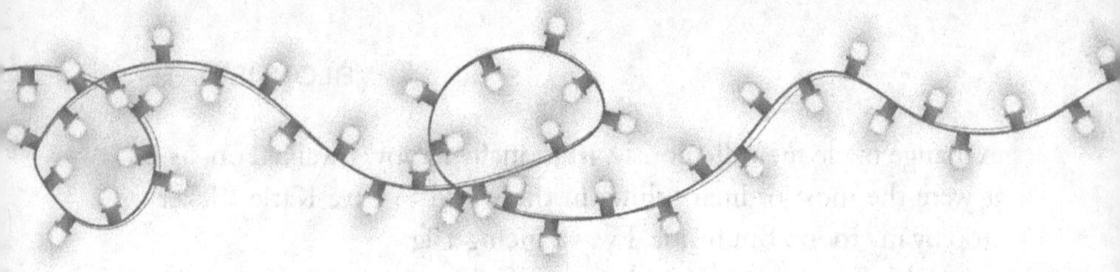

CHAPTER 9
KATIE

I watched Andy fumble with his printer. While it warmed up, he moved over to the bed and grabbed an armload of clothes. Most of them were shirts, still on their hangers. These he ferried to the closet, jamming them onto the bar and shutting the door. If another guy did that, I would assume that he was trying to clear off the bed, in order to steer me onto it. But Andy didn't give off that hey-baby-come-upstairs-to-see-my-trophies vibe. And it was refreshing. I was so *done* with guys who had big expectations and very little gratitude.

In contrast, Andy reminded me a bit of a chocolate lab puppy — cute and clumsy. He even had big puppy feet.

As I watched him frowning over his art history notebook, I found myself wondering what it would be like to kiss him. Tonight it had dawned on me that I'd approached the dating scene at Harkness all wrong. Someone like Andy, who didn't carry himself like God's natural gift to women, probably had a whole lot of untapped passion.

Now, conventional wisdom said that confidence was a turn-on. And that was true, but only up to a point. Because confidence implied experience. And I was learning that experience wasn't all it was cracked up to be. Both my football players had plenty of experience. But neither one had ever made me feel as if our moments together were truly special.

Except for that last night with Dash. That was the only time he ever convinced me that I made a difference. And that had turned out to be a big fat lie.

Ugh.

It's just sex, I reminded myself. But I liked sex, and I'd often enjoyed it with him. Both of my football players had had beautiful bodies and plentiful stamina. In fact, if someone had asked me to draw a picture of the kind of guy I thought I wanted, I would have ended up with a likeness of them.

But it hadn't been enough, had it?

Andy handed me the first page of notes, still warm from the printer. "Have a look at this, and tell me if any of the handwriting is inscrutable," he said.

I scanned the page. Each painting's title was listed carefully, along with its artist, approximate date of creation, and sometimes the materials used.

He leaned over my shoulder, and for a weird moment I wondered if he was looking down my dress. And I kind of hoped he was. Judge me if you will.

But no. His long fingers touched the page in front of me. "Wherever I didn't write down the materials, that's because it was oil on canvas," he said. "There are a lot of those. And I may have misspelled Caravaggio. That's kind of embarrassing."

"No, that's right," I said. "One R and two Gs."

He flashed me a smile that said "friendly" more than it said "do me." Then he went over to flip the notebook around in the printer. "Good thing."

When I received the second sheet, I found a little drawing in the corner. "What's this?"

Andy sat down on the bed and folded his long arms onto his knees. "That is an X-wing fighter. Don't judge."

Aw. "I would never!"

His warm brown eyes smiled back at me again. "Good. Because there may be some rebel ships on the next page. I had to amuse myself while that blowhard in the Knicks hat asked seventeen questions."

I knew exactly which student he meant. And the guy really was a blowhard. But I teased Andy anyway. "Now, now. Do you hate him because he always wants to talk about Cubism? Or because he wears a Knicks hat?"

Andy gave me a full-on smile this time, and it was really pretty hot. "Both."

"Who's your team?" Not for nothing had I learned how to talk sports, even when I didn't give a damn. But boys? They loved it.

"I'm a Celtics fan. Not that it's easy."

"They're not a good team?"

He put a hand to his chest in mock distress. "Katie, they're the best team. It's just that they lose most of the time."

"How is that possible?"

Andy blinked at me with wide eyes. Then he leaned over the printer to copy the last two pages of notes. "Aren't we surrounded by evidence that the people who win are not always deserving?"

Interesting. I was pretty sure he wasn't talking about basketball anymore. "Thanks for your notes," I said softly. "It's going to make a huge difference."

"Don't mention it." He stapled the sheets together and handed them to me. And that was the moment when I no longer had a reason to stay there, chatting with the nicest guy I'd met in forever.

We'd reached that moment. The one which concluded the predictable chapter of our evening. Now a page would be turned. And we might find "THE END" stamped there. But I found that I wasn't really ready to hear those words. I'd taken a big gamble telling Andy my uncomfortable little story. And trusting him with it had been the smartest thing I'd done all week. He'd let me get mad, and he didn't think I was an idiot. I'd know it if he did. Those big eyes were just too expressive to hide it.

I wanted a little more of Andy. Truly I did. I stood up, then, and turned to him.

Unfortunately, he didn't catch the look of intent I was trying to give him. "I'll walk you back," he said quickly. He grabbed his jacket and shrugged it on.

Andy was truly adorable. And lovably uncalculating. Even *gentlemanly*. (Look, Mom! I found one.) But that would simply not do.

Not at all.

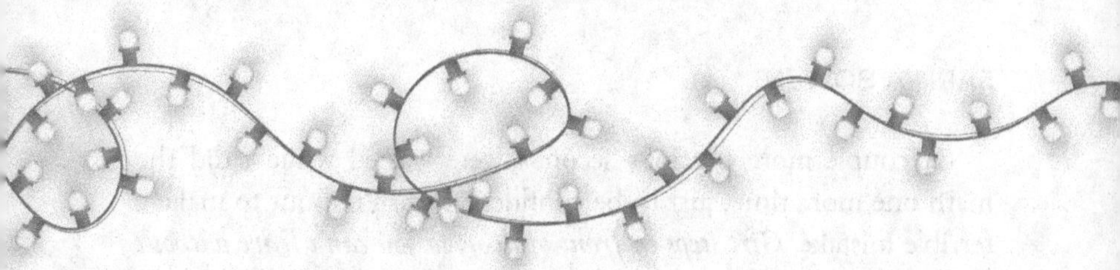

CHAPTER 10
ANDY

Katie moved slowly over to the door of my room, but she didn't open it. "Thank you for the notes. And for taking me to that wacky party. And for inventing a game that distracted me from feeling like a moron."

I smiled at her. In fact, I'd been grinning like a mental patient all night, probably. But she had that effect on me. "You're welcome. For all of it. Best sorority party I've ever been to."

She gave me a teasing eye roll. "Very funny. You told me earlier that it was the *only* sorority party you'd ever been to."

"That doesn't mean it's not true."

For a second, I got lost in the happy look on her face. Also, I expected her to move away from the door. But she didn't. Katie put her back against the door instead. Raising her chin, she looked up at me with soft eyes.

Hold up. Those weren't just soft eyes. They were eyes that asked for something.

Whoa. Time out.

I'd heard Bridger use the phrase "fuck me eyes," before. But it was a safe bet that I wasn't getting "fuck me eyes" from anyone. Like, *ever*. And I wouldn't know them even if I saw them. These, however, seemed to be "kiss me eyes."

I was pretty sure, anyway.

Oh, hell.

A couple more precious seconds were wasted while I did the math one more time, just to be confident I wasn't about to make a terrible mistake. *Girl steps in front of door, so you can't leave without pushing her out of the way. Girl stops, head against your door, mouth tilted up toward yours...*

Okay. Not too many ways to read that.

I stepped closer. Then, stalling, I lifted a hand to smooth that silky hair away from her face. She leaned into my hand slightly, and that tiny gesture gave me the courage to tip my face down to hers. Even then, I almost chickened out. I'd wanted to kiss this girl since the first time I saw her. This couldn't possibly be happening.

But it was.

Our lips met softly. My heart was a freight train in my chest, urging me on. But I fought the impulse to rush. Because Katie deserved better than that. I kissed her slowly. Teasingly, even. Once. Twice.

It was glorious.

She made a sweet little noise of approval, and the sound shot through me like a sonic boom. Feeling bold, I deepened the kiss. I scooped one hand into the silky hair at the back of her neck. And when she opened for me, the first slow slide of my tongue against hers sent my brain on a week-long sailing trip around the Caribbean.

Leaning in, I lost myself in Katie's sweet mouth. She tasted like wine and honey. Her hands slipped around to my back, and I practically died of happiness.

Still, after the most amazing ninety seconds of my life, I made myself pull back. Because all my blood had departed the thinking regions of my body to run south. And I needed my brain to come back online, before I somehow found a way to wreck this perfect evening. "Katie," I said, my forehead resting against hers. "Thank you for this awesome night. You are excellent company. I hope we can do it again sometime."

God, I hoped that was the right thing to say.

She was quiet for a moment. "Andy?"

"Yeah?" I whispered, my voice thick.

"Can we do it again right now?"

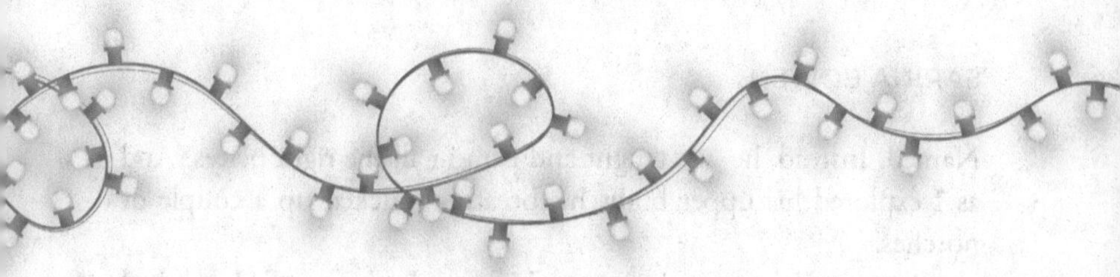

CHAPTER 11
KATIE

I saw Andy take a long, slow blink. For a second there, he looked like he was trying to remember a formula for his physics exam. But then he gave me the cutest smile. And there was more warmth in his face right then than I'd *ever* seen in my jerkface ex's expression. For a moment I worried that he was going to be a gentleman and beg off. But once again, Andy proved that he wasn't a stupid man. His hands came up to cup my jaw, and then his mouth slanted over mine again.

This time, his kiss was filled with the most delicious tension. There was plenty of hunger in that kiss. When our tongues met, he made an achy little sound. But wrapped around his obvious need was a sweet layer of restraint. He wanted this. I could taste how much. But he wasn't going to lunge at me. He did not grab me or press me against the door.

That left us taking kiss after long, slow kiss. Each one felt a little harder to control than the last. The big hands which were so gently cradling my jaw were actually trembling.

Hottest. Thing. Ever.

If I'd been a good girl, like my mother had hoped, I wouldn't have taken this as a challenge.

I was not, however, a good girl.

I reached for him again, my palms grazing his ribs, venturing down to his waist. The feel of all that solid boy flesh under my hands was divine. He wasn't bulky like The Fullback Who Shall Not Be

Named. Instead, he was taught and firm in all the right places. And as I explored his upper body, his breathing kicked up a couple of notches.

Because I've never been good about backing off, I reached around, cupping his ass. With a tug, I pulled him against me. And gabardine doesn't hide much. His belt buckle was not the only thing suddenly stabbing me in the belly.

The feel of him just lit me up. This smart, kind boy knew all the dumbest things about me. He'd received my ugliest secret without judgment. And now I was kissing the stuffing right out of him.

And he was really into it.

He broke our kiss with a groan. His lips wandered down my jaw next, and onto my neck, dropping kisses in their wake. When he moved, the part of him which was currently straining inside his pants brushed against the silk of my dress. And the result was a single and wholly unsatisfying drag of friction between my legs.

I didn't bother to hold back my moan of frustration.

At the sound of it, Andy's lips ceased their travel down my neck, and his body went completely still. Carefully, he rose up to his full height again, pulling me into a gentle hug against his chest. Into my ear, he whispered, "Katie, you are making me completely crazy. That's why I think it's time to walk you home."

In the silence which followed, I could hear only two beating hearts. "Just tell me this," I said finally. "Do you really want me to go home?"

He gave a strangled chuckle. "What I want is for you to wake up tomorrow and say, 'I had an unexpectedly great time last night. In fact, I want to see that skinny guy again.'"

"Unexpectedly great?" I whispered.

"Well, yeah. Or good. I could work with good, too."

I smiled into his neck. "Mmm." I had no trouble thinking up a few things that would feel unexpectedly great. His skin against my skin, for example. Sex had just always made sense to me. I treasured that communion, whether it was slow and sweet, or hot and wild.

The guys I'd dated weren't really fond of showing much emotion. So getting them naked had always been my go-to method for getting a glimpse of their unguarded selves. Andy wasn't like the others, though. He didn't mind sharing how he felt. But that only made me hungrier for him. All evening he'd been funny and generous. Without clothes, I imagined more of the same. Only much more intense.

That sounded *delicious*.

Still... I felt myself hesitate, and it wasn't a sensation that I was used to. Perhaps second-guessing myself was going to be a new habit. I nuzzled into his collar, where I could feel Andy's pulse ticking against my nose. I took a deep breath. He smelled like clean laundry and strong, steady boy. At that moment, I could swear that I'd known him for years.

"See," I said to his collarbone. "The last time I did something impulsive with a guy, it was a total disaster. I've spent the last week telling myself that I'm a big idiot."

His arms tightened protectively around me then, and I loved him for it.

"But I don't want to be embarrassed anymore. And I don't want to feel guilty about wanting you right now."

He took a deep, slow breath, and then let it out the same way. "I want you, too. But I'm willing to wait."

"I know." It came out as a husky whisper. "But that's why you don't have to." Reaching up, I undid the first button on his shirt. Teasing the collar apart, I stood on my tiptoes and began kissing his neck. This brought my body closer to his, and I did not waste the chance to brush against the bulge in his trousers.

Andy let out a groan that could probably be heard the next town over.

Suddenly we were lip-locked again, and simultaneously stumbling out of our shoes. Without my heels on, I was a lot shorter than him. Andy had to lean down fairly far to kiss me. So I gave him a little shove toward the bed. He took a couple of awkward steps back, until the bed collided with his legs.

Down he went, bringing me with him. Reacting fast, he tucked my head under his chin as we landed with a mutual "oof."

"Are you okay?" he laughed.

Scrambling into his lap, I said, "Yes." *Kiss.* "I." *Kiss* "Am. And I'd be even better if we could lose some of these clothes."

Andy's eyes squeezed shut. "That's... um..."

Uh oh. "Don't you want to?" I whispered. A little wave of insecurity splashed over me then. Although Andy had the flushed, lusty look of a turned-on guy. And I loved that look. The face that said: *You have my complete and undivided attention.* So I didn't really know why he'd hesitate.

He flopped backward on the bed. Instead of looking me in the eye, he pinched the bridge of his nose. "I just spent the evening hoping you could recover your appreciation for the male species. So it seems wrong to pounce on you the minute you're feeling okay again."

I leaned onto one elbow, looking down on him at close range. "The male *gender*. You are not a different species," I teased him. "Even if you all act like it sometimes."

But he did not smile. "Sorry," he murmured. "Not thinking too straight right now. I just don't want you to hate me tomorrow. Because it wouldn't be worth it." He reached for one of my hands, taking it between his two, kissing my palm.

I admired his long fingers. There was affection in his touch. I'd been basking in it all evening, whether I'd realized it or not. "I'm never hating you tomorrow," I told him.

In answer, he pulled me closer, until my head came to rest on his chest. His long fingers skimmed my hair. I had only an oblique view of his face, and he seemed to be thinking hard. Maybe too hard.

"You said something tonight about receiving a gift," I prompted him. "That there was something a little magic about receiving something from another person. That it was bigger than the thing itself."

He chuckled. "Sounds like something I might say to a pretty girl I was trying to impress."

I picked my head up. "I think it worked. And if I tell you one more time that you're thinking too much, will you believe me?" I hiked myself up farther onto his chest, looking down into his face. And then I waited to hear his answer.

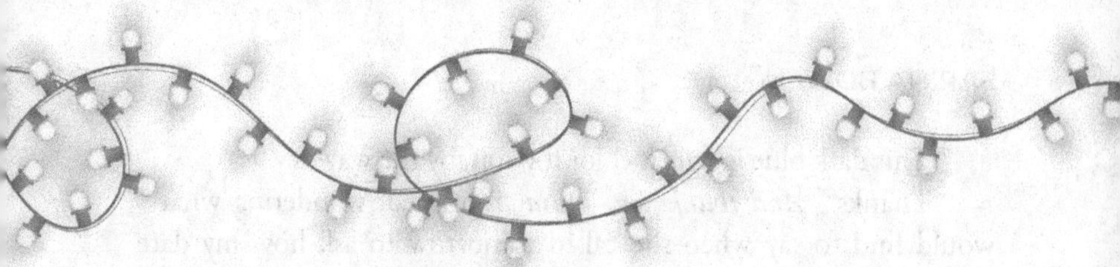

CHAPTER 12
ANDY

I opened my eyes and looked up into Katie's stunning face. Her smile wasn't naughty like it had been before. It was happy. Somehow, on this bonkers night, I'd made her happy. And no matter what happened next, that felt like a big victory. I tugged her head back down on my chest. Her silky hair brushed my chin, and her sweet, fruity scent was doing a number on my self-control. "I've been told that before," I said.

"What?"

"That I think too much."

"There are worse complaints."

"Mmm," I said, kissing the top of her head. We were basically living out part of my fantasy life right now. Katie Vickery was lying *on my bed*. My desk lamp cast a yellow glow onto the wood paneling. From where I lay, it felt as if we were the only two people in the world. Seriously, Katie lying in my bed didn't make sense under any other construction of reality.

She sat up a little bit and finished unbuttoning my shirt. Then she kissed my neck, just below my ear. "You know better than to argue with a girl who's undressing you, right?"

"Yep," I said immediately. Because I am not an idiot. Ask anyone. I was going to let this happen. Because if I didn't, I'd regret it for the rest of my life. And everyone in this bed was there willingly, and nobody was drunk. Check and check.

"This dark blue is a great color for you, by the way."

"Thanks." *And thank you, Delia*. I grinned, wondering what I would find to say when she called tomorrow to ask how my date went.

"...And your smile is hot," Katie said, finishing the buttons.

"Your *everything* is hot," I said, sitting up. I ditched the shirt. And what the hell. I ditched the t-shirt beneath it, too.

Katie's eyes flared. And then she lowered her head, and began kissing all the recently exposed skin that she could reach.

"Arrraaahhhrrrgh," I gasped. Because I'm sexy like that. And because she'd begun working open my belt. And just the *proximity* of her hands to my groin had me throbbing.

I reached for her, finally allowing myself to run my fingers down the sides of her satiny dress, past her waist, which fit entirely into my two hands. I stopped when her hips slid into my grip. *Yesss*. She felt amazing. And then she yanked on my pants, and my boxers, too. I lifted my hips and let it all fall away.

Oh hell, pinch me. I was *naked with Katie Vickery*. Except for my dress socks. Because dress socks looked great on a naked guy.

Fail.

Quickly, I ditched my socks, and then wrapped Katie into a kiss that was probably going to last until New Year's. And then she wrapped her hand... *Oh, God*. Okay. Nothing was going to last until New Year's. Or even five minutes, unless I got a hold of myself.

So I shifted away from her ambitious fingers and carefully lifted her dress over her head. But that only made me hotter. Because now I had a full-on view of the sexiest bra that had ever made an appearance in my (real) life. It was lacy and black, and my eyes were probably bugging out just looking at it.

Katie wiggled out of a pair of stockings, revealing the smallest lace panties ever manufactured. Seriously, the physics lab up on Science Hill could attempt to split them like an atom in the particle accelerator.

I think I stopped breathing.

My brain took a sabbatical to Tahiti.

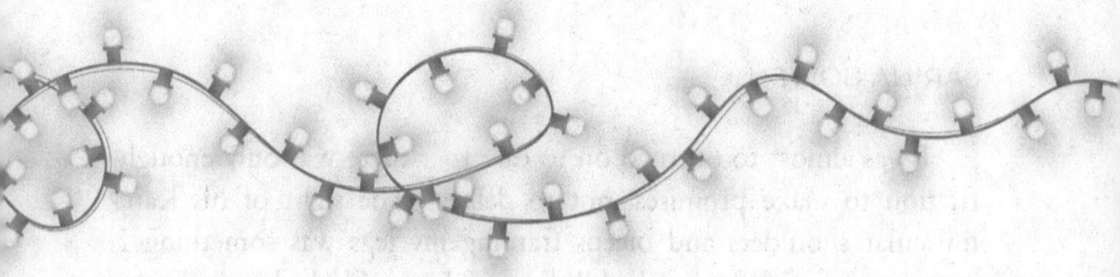

CHAPTER 13
KATIE

Okay, who knew I'd become a basketball fan tonight?

After his big hands scooped my dress up over my head, Andy stretched, elongating that powerful torso as he reached over his head. I was almost too busy drooling over his tight chest to notice that he'd taken care to lay my dress over the chair.

I reclined on the bed, and Andy propped himself up on his elbows over my body. Dropping his head, he began to trace the outline of my strapless it-fits-under-every-dress bra with his tongue.

My modest cleavage had never been my best attribute. But as he kissed me, Andy made the kind of low, happy noise of a man who had just been given exactly what he craved. And as if that wasn't sexy enough, he raised his eyes to mine, his expression burning hot. I didn't know if he was asking for permission or merely trying to torture me. But I'd never felt quite like the center of someone's universe before. The slow slide of his lips coupled with that heated gaze had me tingling. Everywhere.

His lips skimmed lower, and then lower still. He began dropping soft, open-mouthed kisses just at the top of my panties. He lifted those eyes again, and the coal-dark stare was back, its intensity redoubled. I began to practically squirm with desire. In a second, I was probably going to start begging. At last, he dropped his mouth onto the lace between my legs and kissed me gently. All without breaking eye contact.

I was almost too turned on to care that there was only enough friction to make promises, not to deliver. The sight of his lean, muscular shoulders and biceps framing my legs was something I won't soon forget. I panted while he teased me with the barest touch. And when he pressed his lips against my body and groaned, I thought I would *die*.

Okay, enough with the teasing.

I plunged my fingers into his hair, then gave his head a little tug. He came willingly, all that firm skin and muscle covering me like I wanted it to. And then we were kissing again, so deeply that I tasted more of Andy than of myself.

The heavy beat of a dance tune began to pulse on the other side of Andy's wall. For a second I was under the illusion that the sound was my own heartbeat, amplified. Because I was throbbing. *Everywhere*. And then — hallelujah — he hooked the bikini strap of my panties with one thumb and dragged them down.

We made out with incredible urgency, as if a meteor were about to obliterate the earth. Our two bodies moved together, the hot beat of his neighbor's music urging us on.

"Katie," Andy breathed between kisses. "Should I find a…"

I gave him one more hard kiss, and then a shove on the shoulder to encourage him. "Go. Hurry."

He was up like a shot and rifling through his top dresser drawer. But after ten seconds of fervent scraping around, I began to get nervous. It was all well and good to be with the sweet sort of guy who didn't expect you to put out. But when push was ready to come to shove, having the necessary equipment was awfully important.

Luckily, he found what he was looking for.

A half second later, Andy was back on the bed and sheathing himself with hands so eager that they shook. I saw him take a deep breath and gather himself together. Instead of climbing on top of me, though, he gave me a little nudge and lay down beside me, pulling me into his arms. He inhaled deeply again and let it out slowly.

I trailed my hand down his chest. "Second thoughts?" I asked, hoping he wouldn't say yes.

He shook his head. "No way. You?"

"Not a chance." But even as I said it, I had the first quiver of uncertainty I'd ever experienced just before sex. A little voice in my head said: *Really, Katie? Shouldn't you feel shame for this? Other girls would.*

This stopped me for perhaps two seconds.

Oh, *shut up!* I ordered that voice. Those other girls didn't know what they were missing. I was not going to let The Football Player Who Shall Not Be Named ruin this moment for me.

Andy shifted into position over me again. But he didn't make it happen yet. Instead, he lifted his long hand to cup my face, and he kissed my forehead tenderly. "I've had a thing for you since the first art history lecture," he said.

"What?" With all his warm skin over me, it was hard to track any conversation.

"You sat in front of me with a friend," he whispered, kissing my nose. "You told her you'd always wanted to visit the Louvre and the Prado. But you were happy to take the course first. You were wearing a pink t-shirt and a denim skirt. Your friend was looking at Facebook for the whole lecture. But not you. You took notes. Your hair was held back in a pink scrunchie, and I wanted to pull that out and let your hair fall down loose."

Somewhere in the middle of that little speech I'd stopped breathing. "Wow," I gasped. I was blown away. Gone.

Above me, Andy just smiled. "But no pressure, right?"

Looking up at him, I giggled suddenly. And all the tensions of the evening fizzed up, shaking my stomach with laughter. For a second I thought that I was going to totally lose it, the way that laughter sometimes grabs a hold of you and won't let go. It was entirely possible that I was about to become hysterical.

But Andy just smiled wider. Then he lowered his grin to my jaw and kissed me there. And then he kissed the sensitive spot under my ear. And my neck. And my collarbone.

The laughter died in my throat, and I relaxed onto the bed.

"Is this okay?" he whispered, bringing his body close to mine.

"Yesss..." I breathed.

As he fitted us together, Andy groaned like a man in pain. But he moved like a man in love.

I wrapped my arms around him, drinking in his kisses.

"Katie..." he whispered, his breath catching. And the sound of it was the same sound you'd make if you'd just unwrapped an unexpected gift and found just what you'd wanted inside.

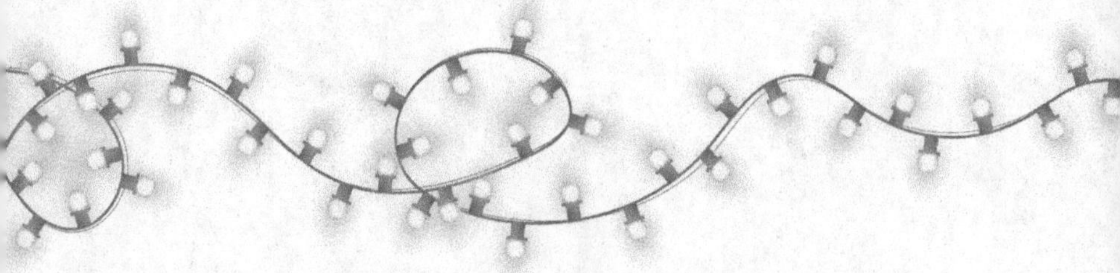

CHAPTER 14
ANDY

Oh Jesus. Pinch me. Seriously.

This couldn't really be happening. Not to me. In fact, any minute now I was going to wake up in some library somewhere, face down in a puddle of my own drool. With my physics notes pasted to my face. And when they peeled off, I'd have equations tattooed all over my cheek in blue ink.

A good dream was the only plausible explanation for this moment.

And *why the fuck* was I thinking about physics notes right now? I needed to memorize this moment. Because if it was really happening, then the world was probably ending. Maybe there was a rip in the space-time continuum. Which meant that the polarity of the earth was in jeopardy. And... um...

Ohhh...

Wow.

Ohhh...

Wow.

Jeez...

Wow.

This.

This is...

So much wow.

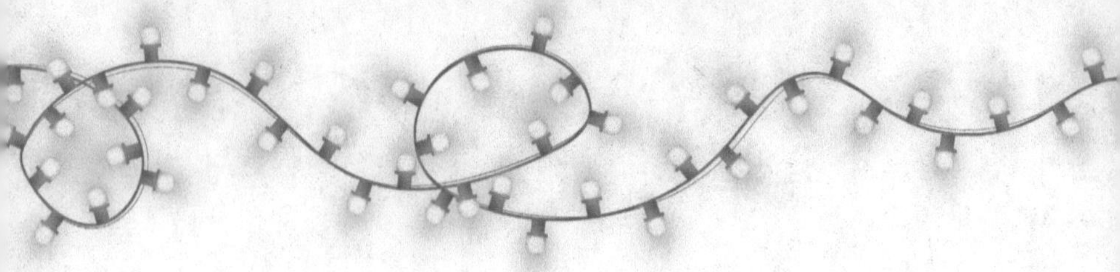

CHAPTER 15
KATIE

Beautiful creature
A single bead of sweat at your neck
Your agonized huff of breath
As you try to hold yourself back

We have brought each other here
To this place of slicked skin against skin
Torturing each other so perfectly

"More," I beg you, because I can't help myself
And you close your eyes with gratitude
For this pretty moment

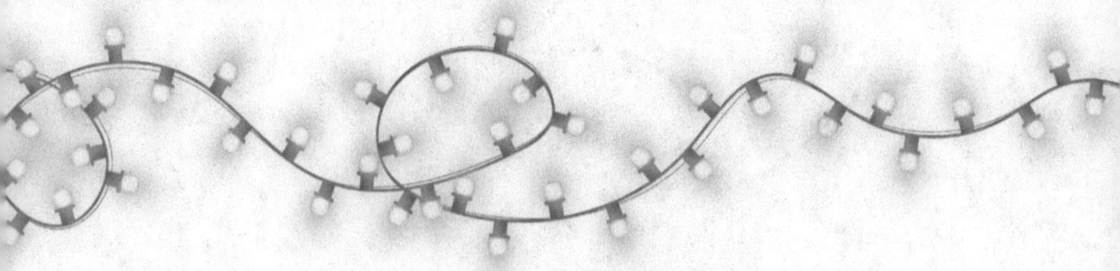

CHAPTER 16
ANDY

Oh.

Oh yeah. Oh boy.

Yesyesyesyesyes.

More? Rawr...

Wow. Good. Too good. Red zone, here.

DANGER.

Quick! Picture Mrs. Dunlop's neck. Warty 5th grade teacher to the rescue!

Okay. I've got this. Except... Oh my God. Oh... wow. Just... so sexy. So sexy. I've never made anyone moan before. *Oh,* that *sound.* Oh, hell. It's coming, and it's going to be good.

But is she going to...? I need her to...

Oh God, please let her just...

Time for a Hail Mary maneuver. Maybe if I reach down and touch her there. Wait... how do guys do this? My arm is stuck. I can't get out of my own way. Wait. Okay. Right *there.*

Winning! Yeah!

Almost.

C'mon, Seabiscuit!

But... ahhhgghhmmm. Feels incredible for me, too.

Mayday! This train is pulling out of the station.

Can't. Hold. Out. Much. Longer.

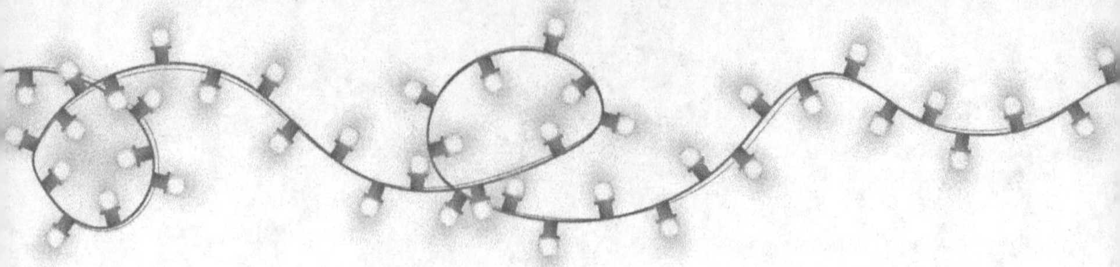

CHAPTER 17
KATIE

The look on your face
Sweet and intense
Shreds my heart
Now I'm tilting fast
And spinning hard
All of me
Is lost to you

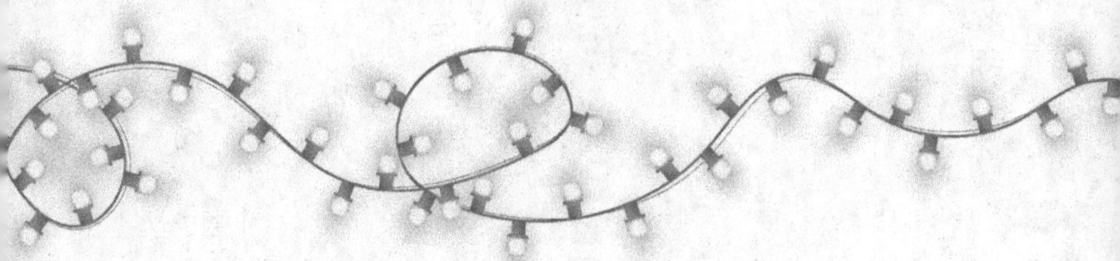

CHAPTER 18
ANDY

COMPLETE LOSS OF BRAIN FUNCTION
Please stand by...

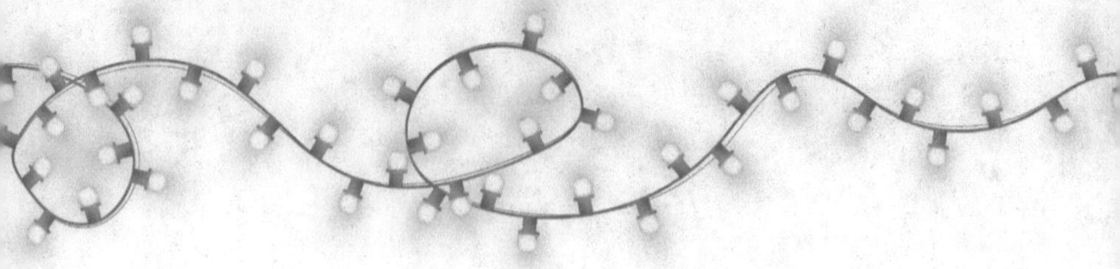

CHAPTER 19
KATIE

For a few minutes we just lay there, breathing hard, while dance music continued to vibrate the bedroom wall. Andy's face was stuffed half into the pillow, half into my hair. I could feel the rapid rise and fall of his chest against mine.

But eventually the music stopped, and the silence seemed to bring the two of us back into focus. It was quiet enough to talk now, only I didn't know what I wanted to say.

Even for someone like me, who really liked sex, the part afterward was a little awkward. There was always that uncomfortable moment when your brain came back online and reminded you that you should probably untangle yourself from this sweaty boy and go on with your life.

The realization that special moments didn't last was always a disappointment. And the more special they were, the bigger the letdown.

This one was kind of a doozy.

Andy had gotten his breathing back under control, and was now playing with a lock of my hair. "Can I ask you something?" His voice was muffled.

"Yeah." Or *yes*. (Sorry, Mother. Though, come to think of it, after what I'd just done — stripping this boy naked and practically leaping on him — the use of "yes" versus "yeah" was a moot point. Right, Mom?)

"What I need to know is…" he hesitated. "Do you feel a sudden compulsion to begin dating women?"

What?

"*Oh!*" I began to laugh.

"Be honest," he said, turning his head to show me his smiling eyes. "Do you have an urgent desire to run out for a copy of the *Sports Illustrated* swimsuit edition?"

Laughing, I realized that this boy was just going to keep on surprising me. "Well, now that you mention it… I do find myself wondering whether I should date someone who shares my taste in lipstick."

First, he gave my ass a pinch. Then he pulled me close, and I snuggled into his neck. For a few minutes, his hands gently skimmed my back. But eventually, he smoothed my hair down and sighed. "I really don't want to move. But I have to get up and get rid of this, um…"

Condom. Right. I released him, though I didn't want to.

Rolling off the bed, he grabbed a tissue from the box on his desk, then stood in front of the wastepaper basket, his back to me. I used the moment to marvel at how long his legs were. And the fact that he had a really nice butt for someone so slim. Go figure.

"I should really go," I said.

When Andy turned around, he was frowning. "Oh, no you don't," he said, giving his head a little shake. "Not so fast." He came back toward me, and I tried not to stare at his nakedness. There was something really sexy about that long, lean body. He was built as if only the best, most essential parts had been added to his frame. As if any extra would just be a distraction.

On his way over, he snagged his boxers off the floor and stepped into them.

I'd pulled the sheet up to cover myself, and now he gave me a little nudge to move over for him. Dorm beds were pretty narrow. But I scooted toward the wall, and he slid into the bed, rolling onto his side to face me. "Hi," he said.

"Hi." I clutched the sheet against my chest. I was feeling very naked all of a sudden.

"I thought if I trapped you in here, you wouldn't go."

"You'll want me to, eventually," I pointed out. "If I'm still here a week from now, that would just be weird."

"Well," he cleared his throat. "If you say so. But we could probably compromise on tomorrow morning, no?" Beneath the sheets, his toes wandered over to be with mine. He trapped the arch of my foot between both of his and gave it a squeeze.

I didn't know what to say. My football player boyfriends had always complained that they couldn't *possibly* spend eight hours crammed into a tiny bed with me. "You won't sleep well. And there are exams to study for."

He gave his head a shake. "That's not the point. I want the whole package. We're supposed to have that tricky night's sleep, where I'm trying not to give you a black eye when I roll over. And I believe I'm entitled to some awkward conversation in the morning."

"Seriously?" I fought off a grin.

"Seriously." He leaned over to kiss my eyebrow, and then had to turn away so he could yawn.

It was catching, so I yawned too. "The problem is that I only have a dress to wear. Walking home tomorrow morning..." I let the sentence trail off. Because he'd understand what I meant. Anyone who saw me would know I was doing the Walk of Shame.

It was called that for a reason.

Andy frowned. "I have sweats you could borrow."

I pointed across the room at my spike heels, lying on the floor where I'd shed them so hastily a little while ago.

He chewed on his lip for a second. "Okay. I'll walk you home right now, if that's what makes you the most comfortable," he said. "Otherwise, I can set my alarm for seven. But we'll probably wake up then anyway, after elbowing each other all night." He gave me a shy smile. "And we could walk you home before anyone else even thinks about waking up. Then I could wait at the coffee shop while you shower and change. And *then* we'll get the earliest possible start on memorizing two hundred European paintings."

"Hmm," I said, as my heart gave a little flutter. That all sounded too good to be true.

"There won't be a soul outside at seven in the morning. Especially during exams," he pointed out.

"You really want me to stay?" He was probably just being nice. He gathered me up in his long arms. "I really, really do."

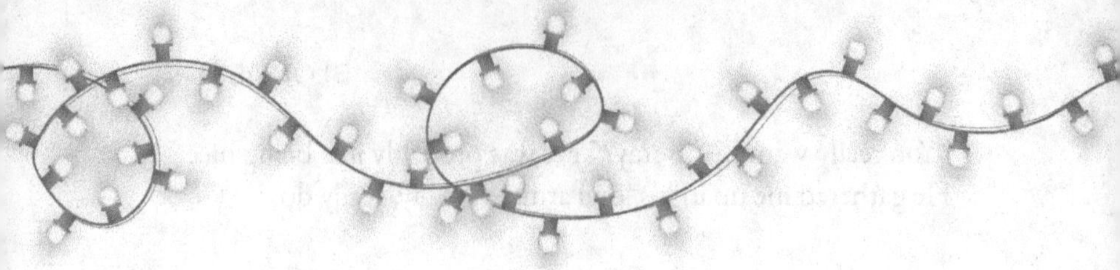

CHAPTER 20
ANDY

I found a t-shirt for Katie to wear. Actually, I picked out my favorite one, which had an X-wing fighter on the front of it. And that made her laugh. And I *loved* her laugh, because it sounded a little bit out of control. Here was a girl who usually matched her hair band to her sweater. She looked pristine and put-together every time I saw her. But the sound of her giggle gave her away. It was riotous.

And *man*, my X-wing t-shirt had never looked so good as it did with her long legs sticking out from under the hem. I found her an extra toothbrush, too. And then I checked to see if the bathroom was empty, and it was. So Katie did the mini Walk of Shame into the bathroom to brush.

"Do you want the inside or the outside?" I asked when she returned, pointing at the bed.

"You first," she said.

I shut the lamp off and then climbed in, scooting all the way over to the wall. She got into bed then, gingerly. First, I pulled the covers up. Then I put my hands on her hips and pulled her closer to me. "Let me show you how this works best," I said, angling the pillow just so. I positioned Katie's back against me so that her head was level with my sternum. That way we both had some breathing room.

"Mmm," she lazed against me. "Okay. I think I get it."

Luckily it was dark, and she was facing the other way. So she couldn't see how big my dorky smile was just then. Seriously, you could probably see my teeth from space. Because I'd never been happier than I was right then. I had the girl of my dreams in my bed, curled up against me. I was optimistic that maybe this would become a thing. But that was probably getting ahead of myself, right?

I wasn't going to lie here and worry about it, though. No matter what happened tomorrow, I would always have this night.

"So," I prompted. "Which European paintings are we going to memorize first?"

"The medieval ones," she said immediately. "There aren't as many of those as in the Renaissance section."

"Good point," I whispered, smoothing my hand down her hair.

"I'm a little worried about the modern stuff," she confessed. "He covered it really fast. The Russians... I don't remember what any of those paintings look like."

"Like... *The Knife Grinder*? We can tackle those," I said. "You know that little sofa in the back of the coffee shop? I'll park my butt on that puppy while you're changing. We can sit there and flip through the paintings on my laptop."

There was a pause, and I hoped she wasn't about to tell me that she'd rather study alone. "We are going to rock that test," she said instead. "We are going to kick its ass."

Again, I grinned in the dark. "We are going to send it home, crying for its mama." Katie giggled again, and I felt it in my chest.

Then it got quiet for a little while, and I wondered if she'd fallen asleep. I wasn't sure I even wanted to fall asleep. Because I didn't want to miss a moment of being with her.

"Andy?" she asked suddenly.

"Yeah?"

"Have you ever had a one-night stand before?"

Now there was a tricky question. "Well... I'm not sure I can say."

She turned to peek at me over her shoulder. "Never mind. That was a really personal question."

I dropped my arm around her waist and gave her a squeeze. "That's not the problem. It's just that I'm not sure. The answer is no. Unless I'm having one right now, and I was really hoping that wasn't the case."

After I said it, my heart nearly failed. Was that too much, too soon?

"You're definitely safe," Katie whispered.

Whew. I dropped my nose into her hair and took a deep breath of her. "Good to know," I said.

Her slim fingers gently stroked my wrist for a few minutes. And then she began to breathe deeply. I lay there smiling in the dark for awhile longer, until I fell asleep too.

And I had very, very good dreams.

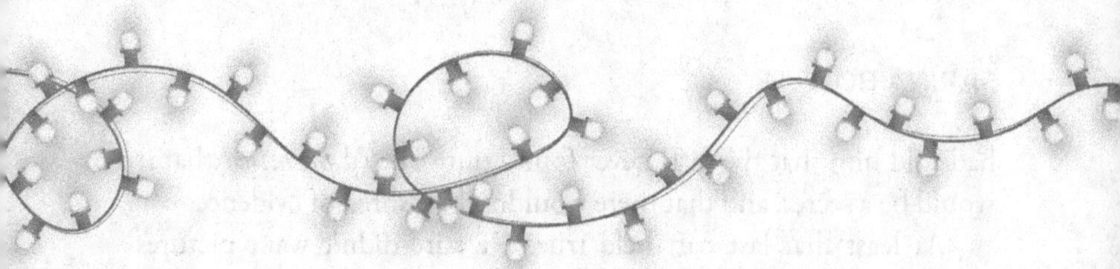

EPILOGUE

Dash McGibb had a way of flipping his pen up in the air and catching it again. He did this while sitting in one of the old wooden lecture hall seats, waiting for the exam to begin. He flipped the pen a dozen times. Flip. Catch. Flip. Catch. It helped take his mind off of two uncomfortable things.

The exam was one of them. He'd taken this course because it had sounded easy. Looking at paintings — how hard could that be? And football season had ended only two weeks ago. That had taken up most of his time.

This test? It might go badly.

Also, there was the matter of the empty seat next to his. Until a week ago, that seat was always occupied by the most attractive girl in the freshman class. But Katie Vickery had not appeared in class for the last two lectures. And Dash guessed that he was the reason why.

The other night at the party, she had seemed okay. She'd even spoken to him a little bit. (Something about party planning trucks with pigs on them?) He'd hardly been able to concentrate on their discussion, because he'd been freaking out.

Because she *knew*.

Somehow, she'd figured out the ridiculous prank they'd made him pull. He'd seen the knowledge of it on her face the moment she appeared beside the Christmas tree. Even though his frat brothers had told him that the girls never found out. They'd *promised* that it would be a secret, and that there wouldn't be a shred of evidence.

At least that last part held true. He sure didn't want pictures floating around campus of him getting...

Shit. It was such a stupid thing that he'd done. So colossally stupid.

And for what good reason?

She must have figured it out immediately. Because Katie wasn't the sort of girl who would skip the last two lectures. All he could do about it now was watch the door, hoping that Katie didn't blow off the final exam just because he'd been the world's biggest asshole. He didn't want that on his conscience.

There was plenty on it already.

The minutes ticked by, and he waited. At the front of the room, the teaching assistants set up a projector. They would show sixty paintings, pausing thirty seconds on each one. There had to be a few easy ones in there, right? He was hoping to see the Mona Lisa's odd smile, or maybe *The Last Supper*.

At last, Katie hurried through the door, her gaze sweeping the crowd. He lifted a hand to wave to her, to let her know that he'd welcome having her as his seatmate. Even though she probably hated him.

Her gaze slid right on past.

Dash watched as Katie scanned the room, a ripple of uncertainty on her face. Then that ripple broke into a shy little smile, which she directed at a lanky boy two rows up. Wait — he was the basketball player. Her date from the other night.

The guy sat up straighter as she approached. Katie had that effect on people. They wanted to be just a little bit more of whatever they were when she was around. Dash had felt the same way. It's just that he'd never figured out what to do about it. Katie scared the shit out of him most of the time. That's how he always ended up slipping into the lowbrow humor of his frat buddies. He knew it wasn't the right way to talk to her. It's just that he'd never figured out what to say instead.

Looked like he'd never get that chance, now.

She scooted into the row where the basketball player sat. Following exam day rules, she didn't take the seat next to his, but left an empty one between them. Still looking a little awkward — maybe even sheepish — Katie lowered her bag onto the empty chair, then turned to face him.

The basketball player reached a long arm behind the empty chair to give her ponytail a playful tug. And Dash saw Katie's smile melt into something warmer and less self-conscious than it had been a few seconds before.

"I wanted to ask you to lunch," the guy said. "But my bossy sister is going to be waiting for me in her car after the exam. She's my ride to New Hampshire."

"We'll go for lunch after the break," Katie said. "Three weeks from now."

"Yeah," he agreed. "But that sounds like a long wait to me."

Her face got soft then. And Dash didn't recognize that expression. He wondered if she'd never shown it to him, or if maybe he hadn't recognized it when he'd had the chance.

"I almost forgot," her date said, reaching to the floor for what turned out to be a tiny little gift bag. "This is a good luck present. For the exam."

Her eyes sparkled as she took the gift in two hands. Reaching inside, she removed two long, thin objects. "They're... a lightsaber pen and pencil?"

"Those are really good luck."

Katie giggled. "Because the force is with me?"

"Now you're getting it. There's one more thing in that bag."

Katie reached inside one more time, removing a little green thing, which she balanced on her palm. "It's Yoda."

"He's wise. And he also erases," the basketball player said.

She laughed. "That's... they're perfect. Thank you."

"It's nothing," was his reply. But obviously that wasn't true. Because Katie arranged those funny things on the little wooden writing arm of the lecture hall seat, then smiled at them as if she'd been given a set of crown jewels.

Dash flipped his very ordinary pen up into the air again, puzzling over what he'd just seen. He knew that girls liked flowers, which he'd never really understood. Flowers were expensive and they looked really sad when they began to wilt. But a Star Wars pen? *What the everloving fuck?*

It was almost exam time, though. A graduate student had passed a stack of test booklets down the aisle. Dash took one and passed the rest of the stack onwards.

"Quick," Katie said. She handed the basketball a bulging gift bag.

From inside, he pulled... that awful pink basketball he'd been playing with the other night. Then he put a hand over his mouth and laughed.

Katie beamed at him. "It made me think of you. Sorry. There's something else in the bottom of the bag."

He pulled out a large bar of gourmet chocolate. "Hey... salted caramel!"

"Because we didn't make it to the ice cream shop." After she said that, her ears began to turn pink.

"Right," he chuckled. "I was really broken up about that."

"I'll bet," she said, looking toward the proctor, who was passing out the actual test now.

"Thank you, Katie," the basketball player said. He put his gifts on the floor and smoothed the test down onto the tiny desk in front of him. "And good luck."

"May the force be with you," she replied.

Dash looked down at the test he'd just been handed. It was time to stop worrying about Katie, and start worrying about European art. The painting identifications were tough, but probably not a total disaster. The essay question he chose took a long time, though. And by the time he'd finished comparing the Baroque period to Renaissance painting, he was one of the last people left in the room.

Tired now, Dash gathered up his things and turned in his exam booklet. He shook out his cramped writing hand and headed for the door.

He had managed not to think about Katie for ninety minutes. But that streak ended when he exited the building.

The basketball player was just tossing a duffel bag into the back of a car. Then he chucked the pink basketball inside too. Turning to Katie, he opened his arms.

With a sweet smile, she stepped in close and hugged him.

Looking away, Dash punched the traffic button to activate the crosswalk. (And did those buttons really do anything, anyway? Or were they just a way of asking for your patience while cars kept rolling by?)

Out of the corner of his eye, Dash could still see Katie and the tall guy. They were kissing now. But "kissing" didn't even do it justice. They were kissing each other as if they'd just invented it. She'd risen up onto tiptoes to reach him. And his arms encircled hers as if he were holding a rare and precious thing.

The look of pure absorption on the guy's face did something to Dash's gut. He'd once held five feet and four inches worth of perfection in his arms, and he hadn't tried even half as hard to hold on to it.

Now that seemed like an error. A big one.

The car that the happy couple leaned against gave a loud and impatient blast of its horn. They broke off their lip-lock, laughing. "I'll call you," the guy said.

"I hope you will," was Katie's answer. "Now go, before you get in trouble."

"I'm already in trouble," he said, opening the passenger door. He winked, folded himself into the car and closed the door. Katie gave him one more wave.

Dash glared up at the traffic light, willing it to change. Finally, it did. But he hesitated for a second anyway as Katie closed the distance to the corner.

I'm sorry. The words formed themselves on the tip of his tongue as she approached. He could say that, right? That was the thing he really needed to do.

Pedestrians moved forward, stepping off the curb. Including Katie. So Dash followed her, readying himself to speak to her once they'd crossed the busy street.

"Katie?" he said.

But she didn't turn around. She hadn't heard him. And now the trill of a cell phone rang out. Katie pulled her phone from her pocket, answering even as she walked down College Street. "Hi there." He could hear a smile in her voice. "I didn't think you meant you'd call *right away*," she giggled. Without a backward glance, she kept right on moving, her long strides carrying her up the street. Away from Dash.

He watched her until she well and truly disappeared.

THE
END

———

CROSSROADS
A TRUE NORTH NOVELLA

A story of missed connections, broken dreams and two hearts that just won't quit.

Damien Rossi drives a taxi but dreams of more. Specifically, he dreams about Nicolette Overland, his favorite client, a lonely beauty who lives in an actual mansion on a hill.

Nicolette can't stop thinking about the hunky guy with the soulful brown eyes, either. She looks forward to every Christmas holiday when she knows he'll be waiting for her at the airport. But when she screws up her courage to finally tell him how she feels, it might be too late...

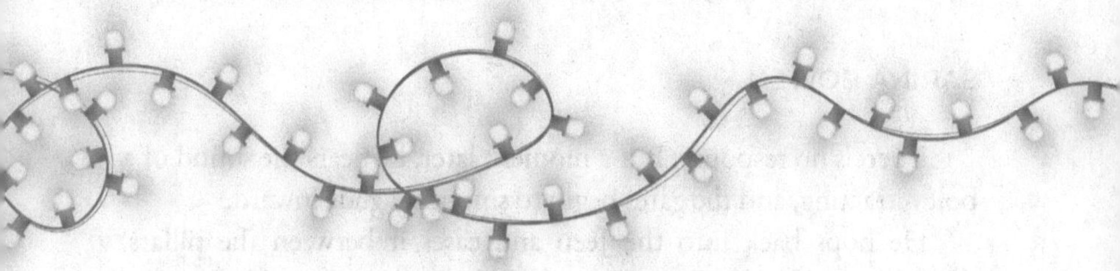

CHAPTER 1
ON THE RADIO: "SHE WILL BE LOVED" BY MAROON 5

"No way," Damien whispers as he pulls up to the address on Old Route 16.

He's lived in this area all his life and never has to look at a map, but it hadn't occurred to him that the address he'd scribbled down in his date book would bring him to *this* house—the one you can't see from the road. The one with the sleek metal gate flanked by stone pillars and old-growth trees. Like something out of a James Bond flick.

He's been passing this spot his whole life, wondering what was hidden beyond the gated entrance. And now he's about to find out.

Maybe. If he can actually get in.

He gets out of his Jeep Grand Cherokee and contemplates the gate, which is striking in its simplicity. It's bracketed by pillars that are part of a larger stone wall that encircles the property, exuding a sense of time-tested strength and privacy. The gate itself is made of heavy, dark metal with clean lines and a no-nonsense design.

It takes him a minute to find the keypad camouflaged in the black metal. He doesn't know the code, but beneath the number pad is a single red button. He presses it.

"Yes?" says an older woman's voice almost immediately.

"I'm the taxi driver," Damien says, clearing his throat. "Picking up Mr. Michael Overland."

There's no response. But a moment later, he hears the sound of a bolt retracting, and the gates begin to smoothly glide inward.

He hops back into the Jeep and eases it between the pillars. Ahead lies a steep, curving gravel road, swallowed up by looming maple trees. As he begins his ascent, he notices in the rearview mirror that the gates are slowly closing.

Okay, that's a little creepy. Hopefully The Overlands aren't hiding a meth lab up here. Damien is a fan of *Breaking Bad*, but he doesn't want to live it.

Following the drive around a curve, he isn't quite prepared for the way the treeline falls away, revealing a vast, grassy hilltop and a sprawling contemporary home, all impressive timbers and stone angles.

"Holy crap," he whispers under his breath. Maybe he should have washed the car this morning. He's hoping the Overlands will become repeat customers.

He slows to a crawl, taking in the property, which is arguably even more impressive than the house. He can see half of Vermont from up here. It's a good thing it's not his job to mow this place. Even on a tractor, it would take all day. Weeding the garden must be another massive project. Lavender and daylilies bloom from some of the longest flower beds he's ever seen.

The house—or is it a mansion?—sits at the crest of a circular drive, so he pulls right up to the front door. He cuts the engine and hops out, wondering if Mr. Overland has a lot of luggage, and whether he's supposed to ring the bell beside those imposing oaken doors and offer to help.

Before he can decide what to do, the front door swings open to reveal a middle-aged white woman in a maid's uniform—like the kind you see on Masterpiece Theatre. She hefts a huge, wheeled suitcase out the door.

Damien hurries over to take it from her. "I can get that, ma'am," he says.

"Margie!" cries a female voice from inside the house. "You don't have to lift that. I got it."

Damien looks up when a young woman steps outside, and then he almost trips over his own feet. She's tall, with long, sun-kissed hair that falls just right, framing her face like she's stepped out of a summer love song. Her eyes are a striking shade of blue—pale with a darker ring around the iris.

She's just...perfect. Like, movie star flawless, except for a spray of freckles across her cheeks and the bridge of her nose. The freckles give her beauty a down-to-earth quality. They make her seem real.

And now she's staring at him, too, while he grips the suitcase and forgets why he's here at all.

Eventually, the woman in the uniform clears her throat. "I want a *proper* goodbye," she says.

The girl turns with a laugh and holds out her arms. "Bye, Margie. Thank you for *everything*."

"Be well, my precious. I want pics of that dorm room, or I'm not sending cookies."

"Okay!" She laughs again.

Damien recovers himself, opens the back of the Jeep, and hefts her suitcase inside. It probably weighs more than Ms. Overland, but he doesn't care. Maybe she'll notice how strong he is.

He closes the back hatch and waits patiently while the two women finish their goodbyes. When the house's door finally closes, the beautiful blonde approaches the Jeep.

"Hi," he says. "I'm Damien. You don't look like Michael Overland."

It's a struggle not to inspect her cleavage. In a tank top and a cardigan, she's not even trying, and she's stunning.

"Everyone says that," she announces. "But my parents named me Michael to toughen me up."

Oh shit. "They...wow," he stammers. "Um, I'm sorry."

She tosses her hair. "Gullible much? I'm just kidding." Then she smiles, and his stomach does some kind of swooshing thing. "Michael is my father. I thought he'd be here to say goodbye." She looks at her watch. "He said he'd probably be back in time."

Probably? That's a little harsh.

"We can wait a minute," he says, leaning against the car. She looks a little anxious. "And you still didn't tell me your name."

"Yeah, it's..." She frowns.

"Tricky question?" he prods, because it would be a crying shame if he didn't get this girl's name. "If you're headed to college right now, I'm a little worried for your GPA."

She laughs suddenly, and the sound reverberates in his chest. It's a little wild and unbridled. "Okay, okay. Sorry. But I've been thinking about this all day. This is my first year of college, and I've been Nicky my whole life. But maybe it's time to introduce myself with my real name. Nicolette."

"Nicolette," he says slowly. "I don't know any other Nicolettes. But I know other Nickys."

"It's different, yeah. That's a plus, don't you think?"

"Sure. But if you want to ease into it, you could start with Nicole and work your way up."

She lets out a playful snort. "I suppose I could. It's a family name. My grandfather was Nicholas Overland."

"Does it have an interesting meaning? And I ask this as someone whose name literally means demon."

"Does it?" Her smile brightens even further. "Maybe I should change *my* name to Damien, because that's pretty cool. Nicholas is two Greek words pushed together, and it means victorious people."

"Huh," he says. "A name for an overachiever. And it's kinda militant—the kind of name they give you if they expect you to conquer the world."

"That's what the Overlands are supposed to be, I guess." She checks the time again. "You know what? Let's just go. My father wouldn't want me to miss the plane just because his lunch ran late."

Damien thinks that's a little sad. Then again, his own father left town a couple years ago and never came back. So who is he to judge?

"All right. It's your call. Hop in." He opens the rear door for her, then seats himself behind the wheel and starts the vehicle.

"The code for the gate is 1980," she says, scooting toward the right-hand side of the backseat. "But if you pull up close, I can reach it from this side."

"1980. Your birth year?" he teases, mentally filing away the number, just in case he needs it later. Like if Nicolette comes home from college and invites him over for croquet in front of the mansion. Or, you know, sex.

"1980 is the year my father made Managing Director," she says with a sniff. "He's not a very sentimental person."

"Nice taste in houses, though," he says as the gate swings open for them. "Did you grow up here? I thought I knew everyone in the county."

"It's complicated," she says. "We have a place in New York City and used to live mostly there. But I spent my summers in Vermont when I was little. And then my mother died when I was about ten, and my father moved us up here. But I went to boarding school in Massachusetts."

That certainly explains why she never turned up at the high school in Colebury. He definitely would have noticed, even if she's a year younger than he is. Which she must be, because Damien's friends departed for college last August. "So where are you flying out to?"

"Raleigh-Durham. I'm starting at, um, Duke."

"*Sweeeeet!* Great basketball team. I mean, it would be better if they had a hockey team. But I guess you can't have everything." He accelerates onto the highway.

She laughs. "I had the same thought. I played hockey in high school."

"Shut the front door," he says. "So did I. Were you any good?"

"Not really," she says with a laugh. "You?"

"Nope!"

They both laugh uproariously—the way you do with someone you've known much longer than five minutes. Damien sneaks another look at her in the rearview mirror, and notices that laughter takes her from pretty to blazing hot. There's a blush across her cheeks and her collarbone.

Christ. He better stop looking in the damn rearview, or they're going to end up in a ditch.

"My dad went to Duke, too," she says eventually. "And law school at Harvard. I'm supposed to follow in his footsteps at both places."

"Supposed to?" he asks, even though it's none of his business. "What happens if you don't?"

"I'll never know," she says quietly. "Duke is great. But it would have been nice to have a choice. And don't listen to me—I'm just panicking. I haven't had to be the new girl for years."

Damien, keeping his hands at ten and two and absolutely not peering into the rearview mirror again, thinks this over. "I haven't been the new guy pretty much ever. But I can see why that's stressful. You're starting over."

"Yeah." She sighs. "I just have the first-year jitters."

Damien silently curses Mr. Michael Overland, who couldn't even be bothered to see his daughter off.

Nicolette must be tired of talking about herself, because she changes the subject. "You've always lived in Vermont?"

"Always. Along with my four siblings—three brothers and a sister."

"Wow!" she says with genuine delight. "Where are you in the pecking order?"

"Second. There's my older brother Matteo, my younger brother Alec, and the twins—Benny and Zara. You have siblings?"

"Well..." She clears her throat. "Not really. My father is dating a woman who has twins. They're sixteen, and I hardly know them. My father's girlfriend hates me, though, and I'm kind of scared that I'll be getting two awful stepsiblings."

"That bad, huh?" He risks a glance in the mirror only to find her looking right at him. "Maybe it's a twins thing. Benny and Zara are a lot to take. And they fight all the time."

"These two don't fight. It's weird. It's like...they're too pretentious to fight or do anything normal. And I say this as someone who went to *boarding school*. Somehow, they have zero personality. It's like all three of them are doing a lifelong impression of Edith Wharton characters. All manners and no heart."

Damien hasn't read Edith Wharton but would rather not admit it. "At least they're not at Duke. What are you going to study?"

"I'm supposed to be pre-law. So maybe history or poli-sci. But I'm going to take a lot of writing classes, too."

"What do you want to write?"

"Books."

"What kind of books?" he pesters. And how are they already on 89? He needs this ride to last for hours.

"YA Horror. I want to write creepy shit that keeps you up all night."

He feels a tingle on the back of his neck. Because that's not very far off from his own hobby—sketching a graphic novel about vampires. "Okay, let's hear it. What book are you working on?"

There's a brief silence. "I don't usually tell people. In case it sounds stupid coming out of my mouth."

"Oh, please. Some of my favorite things are stupid."

She lets out a nervous laugh. "Fine. It takes place in an old house beside the cemetery. The heroine has just moved there with her family. And her room is haunted..."

Before he knows it, he's putting on his blinker to exit the highway.

"God, are we there already?" she squeaks. "I'm not ready. What if my roommate is mean? What if they serve steamed cabbage at every meal? What if my dorm room is in a creepy house beside the cemetery?"

"Deep breaths, Nicky Nicole Nicolette. Deep breaths."

He has her laughing again by the time he pulls up to the airport. This is Burlington, and the airport is tiny, so any door will do, no matter which airline she's flying. He gets out and removes her giant bag from the back, while she hops from foot to foot nervously.

"How about we take a breath for a second," he says, leaning against the Jeep. "You want to step inside and check the monitor? Do you know if your flight is on time? I don't want to strand you here if there's a problem."

"Good idea," she says. "One sec?"

He watches her retreat inside, briefly wondering what it must be like to have her life—flying off to live with strangers and study for four years. He doesn't think he's college material, but like she said earlier—it would be nice to have a choice.

She darts back out a moment later. "The flight's on time. Boarding in an hour." She puts one hand across her breastbone. "I've never been this nervous. I have no chill."

He smiles at her, because that's such an easy thing to do. "It's going to be fine. How long is your flight?"

"Two hours and ten minutes." She licks her lips. "Do you know any way to become more interesting in, say, two hours and ten minutes?"

He cracks up. Then he puts his hands on her shoulders. "Listen, Nicky Nicolette."

She smiles suddenly, and he wonders how anyone could have such bright eyes. Does she know they're beautiful? Or do they just look normal to her, because she's seen them every day of her life?

"This Duke thing is going to work out fine. Your roommate could turn out to be a bitch, but only if she's the kind of girl who can't handle the fact that you're prettier than her." Her brilliant eyes widen. "And if your dorm is haunted, it's probably only by Civil War soldiers. Just smile at them and ask them to move along. It's. Going. To. Be. Fine."

Her eyes dip for a moment before returning to his with a new spark in them. "You are really the best, Damien. Thanks for getting me here safely and then talking me off the ledge."

He drops his hands from her warm shoulders even though he'd rather hold on. "You're welcome. Want my card? I could pick you up at Christmas."

"Sure. Of *course*," she says with such enthusiasm that it makes his heart feel lighter.

He digs a card out of his wallet. He designed it himself—it's a line drawing of the Jeep, with his name and phone number in the middle. "Call me any time," he says, handing it over.

"Hey, cool card." She admires it for a moment then tucks it into her purse. "Thanks, uh, again." She grabs the handle of her big bag.

"You take care," he says. "I'm going to want an update at Christmastime."

Her smile is so pretty, it's almost a gut punch. "Will I need a perfect report card to get a ride home?"

"Hell no. The grades don't matter, Miss Nicky Nicole. Just try to have a fun time."

The smile becomes bashful, and then she looks away. "You're the only person in my life who'd say that to me. So thank you."

"You're welcome. Have a safe flight."

She gives him one more devastating smile. And two seconds later she's gone.

He drives away from the airport feeling oddly bereft.

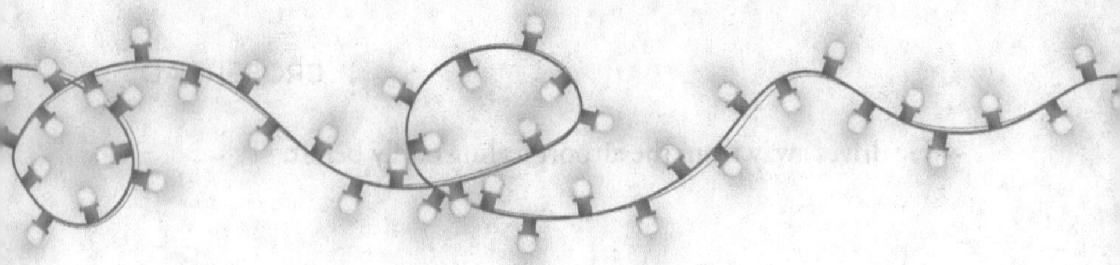

CHAPTER 2
VOICEMAIL FROM NICOLETTE (19) TO DAMIEN (20)

Hi. This is Nicolette Overland. You probably don't remember me, but in September, you drove me to the airport when I was leaving for college.

I was the nervous wreck with the super-heavy bags?

Anyway, I'm hoping you're available to pick me up on Thursday at the airport for Christmas break. But I have a complication. I'm in the middle of exams and haven't had time to do any Christmas shopping, and I can't arrive home empty handed.

So I can either hire you to drive me home from Burlington, and then borrow a car and drive right back to Burlington to shop before the stores close.

Or—and you can price this however you would price a really weird job—you could drive me to the Church Street Mall before you drive me back home? I can shop fast.

Probably. I mean, I'll try.

I need to find a gift for the father who has everything, his girlfriend who hates me, and her two weird teenaged twins who are deep into classical music the way some people are into drugs.

Oh God I can't stop talking.

Sorry.

Beep.

VOICEMAIL FROM NICOLETTE TO DAMIEN

Damien! This is Nicolette again.

I forgot to say that I decided to go by Nicolette, not Nicky or Nicole.

If you have any sense, you'll delete this message and pretend you never got it.

Or—this would be helpful but still preserve your sanity—you can make a weird excuse, like you are going to be busy shampooing your cat, and helpfully connect me with a Burlington-based taxi service.

So...yeah. If I don't hear back, I'll know why.

Oh—wait! My flight is American Airlines from Washington D.C., arriving Thursday December 23rd at 2:35. I should have led with that. Um, bye!

Beep.

VOICEMAIL FROM DAMIEN TO NICOLETTE

Hey Nicolette! I totally remember you. I'll start adding a few extra sets at the gym this week so I can handle your luggage.

Also, my cat was recently shampooed, so we're all set for Thursday. I'll pick you up and take you over to the mall. I could stand to do a little Christmas shopping myself. I have a lot of nosy siblings, so I tend to leave it to the last minute, anyway. No closet is safe for surprises.

Just call me if your flight seems like it's going to be late?

I'll see you Thursday.

Beep

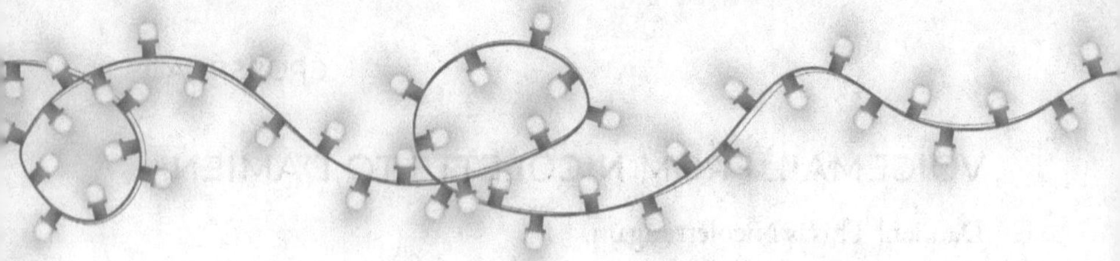

CHAPTER 3
ON THE STORE'S SOUND SYSTEM: "ROCKIN' AROUND THE CHRISTMAS TREE"

"Okay, which one?" Nicolette asks, her tone a little anxious. "I can't decide."

Damien studies the two shallow, handmade bowls she's considering. They're both beautiful, although their purpose, apparently, is just for show. "They're both cool, but the glaze on the green one is special."

"It is, right?" She runs a fingertip around the rim of the bowl. "I love it. But blue is her favorite color, so..." She sighs.

Indecision puts a little furrow in her perfect brow. He's not quite sure why she's struggling. At their first stop—a bookstore—she'd chosen a gift for her dad inside of three minutes. "Coin flip?" he suggests. "Rock paper scissors?"

"Sorry I'm so indecisive," she murmurs. "I just want to get it right."

"Because your...step-whatever is a great gift giver?" he asks.

Nicolette laughs, and then gives him a sideways glance that, in spite of its brevity, still makes his breath catch.

He'd thought he'd remembered how beautiful she was. But he hadn't. Not really. Since picking her up an hour ago, he's felt a little tongue tied. And overwhelmed.

It isn't just the perfect curve of her cheekbones, or the bottomless blue of her eyes. It's her energy. It's the sunny sound of her voice and the way she listens with her whole body. Like he's someone who matters. Nobody else looks at him like that.

"Actually, she's *not* the best gift giver. I mean—her taste is fancy." She makes a face. "She'll probably give me a designer fragrance that I'll forget to wear. Or a big silk scarf. The last time I tried to wear a scarf, I looked like someone who'd just lost a wrestling match with a tent." She smiles, and her eyes crinkle in the corners.

"So then why are you sweating this?" He waves a hand over the two bowls. They're both made by the same Vermont artisan, and they both cost over two *hundred* dollars. If he ever bought a bowl for that price, it had better include a wish-granting genie.

She runs a hand lovingly across the green bowl again. "This woman is the first person my father has dated since my mother died. So it's important to try."

Ah. "Get the green one, then. If it calls to you, maybe it will call to her, too."

"All right," she says. "Why not?"

By the time they make it to the check-out desk, Damien has picked up a couple of gifts, too.

The young man behind the counter wraps and boxes the green bowl with more care than Damien imagines donated organs receive before they're put onto the Life Flight helicopter. He estimates that half the attention is due to the bowl's price tag and half to Nicolette's attractiveness.

Honestly, he doesn't blame the guy. See also: the taxi driver who's assisting with Christmas shopping.

"Thank you for your help!" Nicolette tells Damien when the transaction is done. "I really appreciate it."

"No problem," he says, feeling more than a little gobsmacked by her smile.

"All right, one more stop," she says, turning for the door.

"I can carry the bag," he says, reaching for the handle as they emerge into the chilly air of the Church Street Marketplace.

"No way," she says, holding the bag out of his reach. "You are a saint for putting up with me. A *saint*."

"Like I didn't procrastinate, too?" He's just purchased a set of candles for his mother and a throw pillow for his sister in the precise shape of a goldfish cracker.

"I still think you should have bought those singing refrigerator magnets." She bumps his shoulder with her own. "The world needs more rude lyrics for Christmas carols."

"You're a menace. Do you know how loud our house is already? With five people?"

House isn't even the right word for where he lives. Nicolette has almost certainly never been inside a cramped double-wide trailer, and he's not about to describe it to her.

She shakes her head. "I'm an only child. Lots of silence. And, well, classical music now that Veronica's twins live there during all their boarding school vacations."

He can't even imagine living in a home where two or three simultaneous arguments aren't the norm. "You still have to find something for them, right?"

Her forehead creases. "Yes. I don't have *any* ideas. Maybe I'll have to go with something from that chocolate shop. But that's lame, isn't it?"

It's hard for him to concentrate when he badly wants to kiss that wrinkle between her eyebrows and make it go away. "Lame is a strong word. Who doesn't like chocolate?"

"But, ugh," she complains. "What in the world would they want from me? They wear brands I've never heard of. And they like classical music, which I don't understand."

"Hmm," he says, trying not to stare. Her blue eyes are so expressive that it almost hurts to look at her. "There's a violin shop across the way. Maybe they know what musicians want?"

"Wait, where?"

He puts one hand lightly on her shoulder and steers her across the pedestrian mall. It takes a moment because the place is so full of shoppers.

"Okay, yes!" she says, admiring a window display that says *Gifts For the Music Lover*. "You're a genius."

That is sadly not true, but Damien appreciates the compliment anyway.

"I'm buying *that*." She points at a book in the window. The cover indicates it's about the history of Bach's cello suites. "They play those pieces all the time. And maybe one of those." She points at an ornate book of Christmas carols. "I'll be right back, okay? Then we can finally get out of here."

"Cool," he says. Although he wouldn't mind if they stayed here all night. Shopping with Nicolette is the most fun he's had in weeks.

He'd like to see more of her, but he knows better than to ask. She's probably dating some college guy already. Some guy who's also going to be a lawyer.

Some guy with money and ambition.

He wanders over to a giant Christmas tree in the middle of the pedestrian walkway and stares up at the lights. He does that thing where you let your vision blur, so that you're seeing something without really seeing it.

As a rule, he hasn't spent much time on deep thoughts about his future. But spending time with Nicolette invites him to see himself from her perspective. She makes him wonder what it would be like to be a college guy. To think bigger.

"Nice tree, isn't it?" she asks a few minutes later, startling him with a stealthy approach.

"Yeah," he says, glancing over to find that she's gazing up at the tree in much the same way as him. The white lights reflect in her clear eyes, making her look even more angelic than ever. "Got what you need?"

"Mm-hmm," she says dreamily, still gazing at the tree. "I wish I were one of those people who just loves Christmas. But the truth is I don't."

"It's a lot of pressure," he says.

"It is. But also, my mother loved Christmas so much. And since she died, this time of year always makes me miss her more. It's always a little hard."

Ouch.

"How about you?" she asks. "Big fan of Christmas?"

He looks up at the tree again, considering the question. "It's all right. But I don't have, like, ye olde happy childhood memories. At my house, Christmas always meant stress. My mother always wanted to celebrate, and my father couldn't take the pressure."

"Did they fight?" she asks, still gazing at the lights.

"Sometimes. Or he'd manage to lose his job a couple weeks before Christmas and disappear for a few days. So she was always in distress, trying to make everything seem jolly when it wasn't. I'm one of the oldest, so I was one of the first to realize that Santa wasn't real. She used to recruit me and my older brother to help her make it magical for the little kids."

"Your older brother... Matteo, right?"

"Wow. Good memory. Yeah. One year we went with to, uh, Toys for Tots to help her choose gifts. The toys are free. And everyone who volunteers there is so nice, but I was so embarrassed."

God, he doesn't know why he's telling her all this. Like he's secretly hoping she'll recoil from this story, so he can stop wanting to kiss her senseless.

She turns to him, and that forehead wrinkle is back. "Christmas is just the *weirdest* holiday, isn't it? There's this entire mythology for children, all based on lies. With colossal expectations. We all run around trying to pick the perfect gift for everyone like it's a blood sport."

"Yeah." He chuckles because it's true. "I think you played a solid game, though. Great hustle. Good footspeed. It's a silver-medal performance at least."

She bonks him gently with her newest shopping bag. "Let's buy some wrapping paper and go."

"Wrapping paper?" He isn't sure where to find that.

"I saw some at a store by the parking garage. If they also have ribbon, maybe I can win the gold medal. You probably need some too."

He supposes she's right.

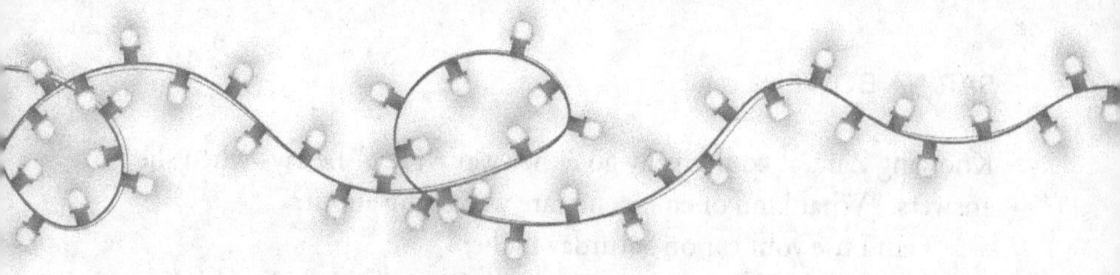

CHAPTER 4
ON THE RADIO: "IRREPLACEABLE" BY BEYONCÉ

It's snowing. Hard. This is why Damien has four-wheel drive and the most expensive wiper blades you can buy. After crossing the river and entering New Hampshire, he makes the turn onto Airport Road and feels the car downshift to take the snowy hill.

He climbs steadily, passing the main entrance to the municipal airport. It's not a popular taxi destination, and until today, he didn't even know that there was a second airport terminal behind the regular one. A *private* terminal.

Lebanon, New Hampshire isn't exactly a destination for million-aires. It's just a place Vermonters visit to buy cheap booze at the liquor outlet and shop at Target.

But sure enough, the road curves around the top of the hill and brings him to a small parking lot in front of a compact terminal building. There's a wreath on the door, and beyond the front windows, orange flames flicker in a fireplace.

So this is how the other half flies. He cuts the engine and sits back to wait for Nicolette.

Since it's her, he's five minutes early. He'd never want to make her wait. He pulls out his phone and checks it for messages just in case her charter arrived already.

But no. The only message is from his eighteen-year-old sister, Zara. "Call me back!" she says. "Emergency."

He hits the redial button in case it's an actual emergency.

Knowing Zara, it could really go either way. "Hey," he says when she answers. "What kind of emergency are we talking about?"

"Can I use your car on Saturday night?"

He closes his eyes wearily. "Probably not, buddy. The holidays are my busy time." He needs to drive drunk people around and earn tips. "You know this."

"But there's a party, and everyone is going."

"If *everyone* is going, then finding a ride ought to be easy."

"But Damien—"

Her complaints escalate, but he tunes her out, spotting a glow in the distant sky. The glimmering spark grows larger and more defined as the jet approaches. The lights on the wings and fuselage blink rhythmically, blurred by the gentle snowfall.

"Hey, Zara?" he says when she takes a breath. "I've got to go. My fare is here."

"What if you could drop me off at the party?" she asks. "And pick me up later? I'll do all your laundry or something. We could barter."

He sighs again, because he gets it. He really does. She doesn't want to ask one of her friends to drive all the way out to the trailer park to pick her up. She doesn't like to remind people where they live if she can help it.

"Let's see how Saturday shapes up," he says.

"Okay!" she says quickly.

"And please don't use the word emergency unless it really is."

"Well..."

"*Zara.*"

"Okay, okay." She sighs. "Bye, Demon. I hope you get a big tip."

"Thanks, buddy."

He tosses his phone aside. Then he reaches into the glove box and pulls out a Santa hat, tucking his head into it before getting out of the SUV.

The jet is coming in for a landing now, its engines a low hum that gradually increases in volume. The landing lights cut through the darkness, illuminating the runway in a stark white beam. He can see the sleek body of the aircraft now, its nose slightly tilted up as it prepares for the landing. And then the wheels touch down smoothly, a dusting of snow flying up around them.

How much fun would that be? Damien asks himself as the jet brakes tidily to a stop and taxis toward the little terminal. *Driving a taxi in the sky.*

A ground-crew member, bundled in a heavy coat and hat, approaches the aircraft with a light wand in hand, guiding it into its final position as the engines slow and then quiet.

Damien feels a hum of expectation. This will be the fourth or fifth time he's driven for Nicolette. His raging crush has only gotten stronger over the past couple years. Picking her up is not a job anymore—it's an event. He loves hearing her stories from college. Or any stories, really. She's always full of life and adventure.

She's as sweet as she is exciting. And that's just so rare.

The jet's cabin door opens with a mechanical whir, and a set of stairs extends down to the tarmac. The interior lights illuminate a uniformed flight attendant at the top of the stairs. She looks around briefly then steps back inside.

Damien feels his pulse kick up with expectation. He doesn't even know if this is the right jet, but he's walking toward the fence like a moth to the flame.

A moment later, Nicolette appears in the doorway, wearing a wool coat and jeans. She starts down the stairs, then spots Damien and grins widely. Her feet speed up, and he winces internally as she trots toward the snowy ground, bumping her suitcase down each step behind her.

Careful. He's well aware that she doesn't know how to pack a suitcase that weighs less than fifty pounds. At the bottom of the little stairway, she all but skids toward him at the fence. "Hi!" she calls. "Great hat!"

"Thanks," he says, grinning back like a fool. "Did you plan on climbing that fence? Or is there another way out of there?"

She looks up at the top of what must be a ten-foot chain-link, as if actually considering it. "Good point. Hold on." She smiles again and then turns for the little terminal building, dragging her case through the snow.

Damien strides into the terminal to meet her there. It is, of course, part of his job to carry her luggage. That's what he tells himself as he practically sprints inside to see her. The bounce in his step has nothing to do with Nicolette's smile or the squeal she makes as she drops her bags and leaps toward him.

Somehow, he manages to catch the hug that's hurtling his way. "Hey!" he says uselessly. "Good flight?"

"I'm so glad to see you!" she squeals. "And I'm also really glad exams are over."

He laughs and lifts her up off the ground playfully. "And here I thought I was special."

"Oh, but you are," she says. "You're definitely the most fun thing about this evening."

"Because...?" He sets her down and grabs her suitcase and carryon. As predicted, they weigh as much as a small car.

"Because of the Step Monster's caroling party." She makes a face. "It's awful."

"Not a fan of caroling?" he asks as they head toward the parking lot.

"Oh, caroling is fun. But this party is misnamed. It's actually a concert—her and the Twins of Evil."

Last summer her father eloped with the woman Nicolette refers to as the Step Monster, and so now she has two step-siblings.

"They play instruments and sing. All three of them. Which should be fun, but somehow isn't." She skips through the parking lot, kicking up snow. "So drive slowly, okay? I might be able to miss the first half. I can tell her the roads were slick and unplowed."

Damien opens the passenger door for her. Last time he drove her to the airport, she'd waved off the backseat and climbed in front with him. "Kind of silly of me to sit in back, right?" she'd said. "Makes it harder to talk to you."

And, yeah, it also makes it easier for him to get way too invested in the hour or so they share together. But it's the best kind of torture.

After she's tucked safely into the car, he opens the hatch and hauls her luggage into the back. "I didn't even know luggage could weigh this much. What do you have in here?"

"Gold bars. Weapons. The bodies of my enemies."

"Right." He closes the back and then climbs into the driver's seat. He starts the engine and notches the heat up, but then turns to her without putting the car in gear. "You know," he says quietly. "On my way down, there was an accident in the northbound lane. Traffic was stopped. But it's probably taken care of by now."

"Bummer," she says. Then she grabs his wrist suddenly, and a zing of warmth runs up his arm. "God—am I a terrible person? I don't *actually* want someone to have an accident so I don't have to listen to my step-mother warble her way through Greensleeves."

"But what if nobody had to die?" he suggests with a smirk. "You could just *say* we got stuck waiting for the accident to clear. And we could, I don't know, get a pizza at Lui Lui." He points out the window. "It's not even a mile from here."

Nicolette sits back in her seat suddenly. "Damien Rossi, you are a *genius*! What do you like on your pizza?"

"Just about anything."

"We're doing this!" She rubs her hands together. "I'm starving. And at home she's probably serving something like saddle of rabbit in fig sauce."

"Huh," he says, navigating out of the parking lot. "Sounds a little fussy."

"She *invented* fussy," Nicolette scoffs. "And she makes it very clear that I don't measure up to her standards. There are all these little comments about my clothes. My hair. My lack of makeup. While her kids smirk at me in their designer wear."

"Hmm." Damien has a few thoughts about that, which he should probably keep to himself. But he'd bet any amount of money that Nicolette's Step Monster is jealous of a girl who looks ready to star in a Hollywood role after exam week.

There can't be many women in Vermont prettier and more enchanting than Nicolette.

If there are, he's never met one.

———

Thirty minutes later they are seated in a booth, finishing their shared Caesar salad, and waiting for their pizza. The place is packed, but they were shown to the last available booth, which is in view of the open-jawed pizza oven where flames dance cheerfully inside. George Michael sings about giving his heart away over the sound system.

"God, I needed this," she says, rubbing her eyes. "Calories are necessary before I face the family. I'm *so* tired. I crammed for my poli-sci exam until three o'clock in the morning."

"Did it go okay?"

She shrugs. "I guess. I know a lot more about the differences between Mexican, Canadian, and American democratic principles than I ever wanted to."

"And your writing?"

"What writing?" Nicolette grabs her straw and takes a sip of Coke. "I can hardly remember the plot of my book. There's just no time to work on it. But what about you? Do you have your sketchbook?"

"It's in the car," he dodges. Last time they were together, he shared some of his pages, but it made him feel self-conscious.

"Where in the car?" Before he can even process the question, she slides out of the booth.

Seriously? "Don't go out in the snow. It's not worth it."

"I beg your pardon." She leans on the table, looming over him in a sweater that looks as soft as a cloud, and a body that does things to him. She meets his gaze with her bright blue eyes. "I will absolutely get a little snow in my hair to find out what your broody vampires have been up to since September."

Damien sighs. The vampires aren't all that inspiring. But he can't say no to her. It's just not a thing he can do. "Sit," he says, sliding out of the booth. "It'll be easier for me to find than you."

She grins up at him triumphantly.

He trots outside, grabs the damn sketchbook out of the glove-box, and carries it back inside to hand it over.

"Don't make that face," she chirps, taking it from him. "I've been reading about voting demographics and French history for two weeks. I need a little vampire mischief. And last time you promised you'd make one of them look like me."

He did, and that's half the problem. The new character is called

Selene Nightshade, and she's *very* pretty, with a perky bust and an impish smile. He wonders if Nicolette will take one look and see right into his horny mind.

Or maybe he's got an inflated sense of his artistic skills. Either way, it's embarrassing.

She opens the book and quickly shuffles to the new material, while he sips his Coke and questions all his choices.

It takes a few minutes, but she lets him know the instant she finds Selene by letting out a squeal. "Omigod, Damien! You made me a badass."

"I tried." He shrugs.

In the story, Selene is a daring vampire who runs an underground network of safe havens for vampires fleeing from vampire hunters. She just happens to do this brave work in lowcut tops and a ponytail.

"Can I have a copy of this panel? I want to put it on my wall at school." She flips the book around and shows him a page where Selene is fighting off a burly human.

He squints at the drawing, seeing only its flaws. "I guess? Makes me worried for your decor, though."

She laughs happily and closes the book. "The only reason your modesty isn't super annoying is because it's real. Who else have you shown this to?"

This question is also embarrassing, because literally nobody else has seen it. "Eh, it's not done, you know?" There isn't anyone else in his life who's demanded to see it, except for his younger siblings, and it's easier to say no to them. He's been practicing for years.

A server turns up just then to slide their pizza onto the table. "Careful, it's *molten*," he says. "If you value your taste buds, I'd give it ten minutes."

That's really no problem for Damien. He'd happily sit here all weekend with Nicolette.

She pushes a lock of straw-colored hair behind her ear and peers at him. "Look. Maybe I'm being nosy, but did you ever think of going to school for this? Vermont is like the only place in the country with a school just for graphic novelists."

He has, in fact, thought of this. The Center for Cartoon Studies is right across the river from where they're sitting now. But they're probably looking for a different sort of student. "I might not be their kind of guy," he says gruffly.

She picks up the book, opens it to a page with an elaborate fight scene, and faces it toward him. "Really? If this isn't their type of thing, then I'd like someone to explain to me what the hell they're doing over there."

"Well..." It won't be easy for someone with a Duke pedigree to understand. "It's not the art. It's...the Rossi family doesn't often darken the door of a college."

She closes the book and puts it down. "College isn't the only way to get ahead in the world, in spite of what my dad thinks. But it *is* the best way I know to meet people who are interested in the same stuff as you. Doesn't that appeal to you a little bit? Meeting a bunch of other people who just want to talk about this?" She taps the book with her finger.

"Well, sure," he admits. "It's not that I'm uninterested. I just can't really imagine it. And I can't really swing the expense." He's already looked at the cost, and it isn't cheap.

"Wouldn't there be financial aid?" she presses.

"Not much," he says quietly. "It's a tiny school. Besides, I work a lot, and my family needs my income right now." It's been a difficult year at home, with lots of unexpected expenses. The twins won't graduate for another six months, and his mother needs to move into a better neighborhood.

Nicolette's face falls. "God, I'm sorry to bring it up. It's none of my business."

"Don't worry about it. I have time. And a few other ideas for paying for school. It's just going to take me a little while to get started."

"So what happens next in the story?" She reaches over the pizza to poke his arm.

And there's that warmth again. Whenever she touches him, he feels it. "You tell me."

"Because you don't know? Or because you want to know if you're sending the right signals?"

He laughs. "It's a little of both. I'm torn between a couple of different ideas."

Nicolette slides out of the booth again, picks up his sketchbook, and then slides next to him. His heart makes an unforgiving skitter.

"Okay, so on this page?" She points to the hero. "I thought Jart was going to attack. But then he gets all coy with the vampire hunter, and it kept me on edge."

"Yeah? Sweet," he says casually. But inside he's bursting, because building suspense is exactly what he'd meant to do.

She goes on to make a couple of other predictions, before setting the book aside. "Do you think this pizza is cool enough to eat now?" She drags her plate to the empty spot on the table in front of her and reaches for a slice. "Guess I'm about to find out."

Damien takes a slice after she does. He let Nicolette choose the toppings, of course, and she went with meatball, onions, and ricotta.

Hell, she really is the perfect woman. The first bite makes him want to weep.

The waiter reappears and smiles down at them. "Does this date night need anything else? A beer or two, maybe?"

Damien, having no idea what to say about this false assumption, balks.

But Nicolette doesn't miss a beat. "Do you want a beer, darling?"

"No, I'm driving," he manages.

Nicolette's smile lights up her whole face. And it lights a fire inside Damien that's almost as hot as the flames from the pizza oven. What he wouldn't do to make her smile.

───────

Unfortunately, it doesn't take all night to eat a pizza. Not thirty minutes pass before the server is asking them if they need a box for the last two slices and dropping the check in its little billfold.

They both grab for it at the same time.

"Hey!" Nicolette yelps when he gets his hand on it first. "You're not paying that."

"It was my idea," he says. "A guy's gotta eat."

She shakes her head, accepts the box from the server, and slips the last two slices inside. "At least take the leftovers. If I took them home, the twins would just scarf them down before I got a chance."

This is probably what will happen at Damien's house, too, but he takes the box anyway.

They head out into the snow, and Damien has to drive fairly slowly when they reach the highway.

"Do you need to call home?" he asks. "It will take us another forty-five minutes to get there."

In the passenger seat, wearing his Santa hat and looking cute as hell, Nicolette pulls out her phone. "No texts. My father probably forgot I was coming home tonight. He always looks a little surprised when I turn up."

Damien is silent for a moment. "I've never met your dad, but I don't have a great impression."

"Why?" She turns to him quickly.

He doesn't speak for a moment, and it's partly because the truck in front of him is kicking up a cloud of snow and partly because he needs to choose his words carefully. "Every time you mention him, he's blowing you off somehow. I just don't get it. You're, like, the perfect daughter. Going to college. Studying hard. Nice to everyone. What the hell does it take to get his attention?"

Beside him, she goes absolutely still.

Crap. "God, I'm sorry. Don't listen to me." He's said too much, and it's none of his damn business.

"Damien," she whispers. "I think that all the time—*what the hell does it take*? I've never figured it out."

Aw. "You still shouldn't listen to me. My dad left when I was a teenager. I'm just painting your situation with my own brush."

"Maybe it's the same brush, though." She pulls off the Santa hat and smooths it on her lap. "My dad is still *physically* in my life. But after my mother died, it's like he forgot that I exist. And now he's got this *new* wife and *new* kids and..." She presses a hand over her mouth, as if to stop herself from saying more.

"Eh, I knew he was an ass," Damien murmurs. "What he does to you seems almost more cowardly than what my father does to his kids. Like, yours will stick around, but he'll freeze you out because you remind him of his dead wife."

She lets out a little gasp. "That's what my therapist said. Almost word for word."

He snorts. "Well maybe if this taxi thing doesn't work out, I can become a therapist." He puts the blinker on to exit the highway.

"Yes!" She cackles.

Grinning, he eases onto the off-ramp. He's just begun to decelerate when a flicker of movement registers in his peripheral vision. A deer, stepping onto the road.

For a nanosecond, all he registers is the snow-globe beauty of the swirling flakes in the headlights and the big brown eyes of the doe. But then Nicolette gasps, and his reflexes kick in. He jerks the wheel to the right.

The tires lose grip momentarily, sending the Jeep into a slide. Damien feels the vehicle's rear end slip. His right hand shoots out to brace Nicolette against her seat.

A surge of adrenaline fires inside him as the Jeep fishtails. But he steers into the skid with practiced ease, the way his father—the same complicated fucker who made his childhood so confusing—taught him to do on these same snowy roads.

The tires catch traction, and he countersteers again, bringing the vehicle back under control in a matter of seconds.

After they stop safely at the end of the ramp, it takes him another second to realize he's got his whole arm pressed against Nicolette's chest. He quickly removes it. "You okay?"

"Uh, yup," she replies with a nervous laugh. "Nice driving."

"Thanks." He takes a breath. "Wasn't really a close call, though. I actually paid that doe to do that so I could cop a feel."

She barks out a shocked laugh, which makes him laugh, too. And then they're both in hysterics, the kind that a harried moment can cause.

Eventually he remembers how to breathe, and another car winds down the ramp to stop behind them.

Looking both ways, as cautious as a granny, he pulls out onto the road to drive her home. The last few miles are uneventful. The only thing that's odd is that the Overlands' gate is standing open.

He pulls up the winding path to find the driveway mobbed with cars and the magnificent house positively blazing with light. There are Christmas trees in every front-facing window and a giant wreath on the front door.

"Holy shit," Nicolette breathes. "It's like the North Pole threw up on the house. And whose cars are these? She must have invited half of Vermont."

Not my half, thinks Damien. He spots a Land Rover, a BMW, a Mercedes, and a Porsche Cayenne.

"Hey, you want to come in?" she says suddenly.

He looks over at her, startled. He's dying of curiosity, and he'd follow Nicolette anywhere.

For a moment, he allows himself to picture it. His hand on her back as they navigate the room. Her smile lit by candlelight and the glow of a Christmas tree. A shared glance when the music gets particularly awkward.

And then a kiss goodnight.

But a second later, reality creeps in. Her picky stepmom won't be any nicer to Nicolette if she invites the taxi driver in his jeans and his North Face ski jacket to her party.

"I shouldn't," he whispers. "It's a weekend at Christmastime. That's, um, prime driving hours."

"Oh," Nicolette says. Then, with a jerk of anxiety, she peers at her watch. "Oh *geez*! You should have said something! How many rides did you miss? We didn't have to stop for pizza..."

"No, it's fine," he says quickly. "My idea, remember?"

But she's already scrambling out of her seatbelt and opening the door. "Thanks for everything."

He has to hurry out of the car to catch up with her as she fumbles for her luggage. He manages to lift the bags out, but before he has a chance to say anything, she's tugging them up the walk toward the house.

"Happy Christmas, Damien," she says from the porch.

"Take care," he says, feeling helpless and all wrong. He watches her yank the rolling suitcase over the threshold. "Call me anytime."

Should he have just said yes to coming in? But to what end?

You don't belong at this party.

An elegant woman swans into view in the open doorway. She's

wearing a floor-length cranberry-colored dress. She gestures wildly at Nicolette's bags, as if urging her to clear them away.

Nicolette turns around, though, and manages a smile and a wave at him before someone else closes the heavy wooden door.

Tightly.

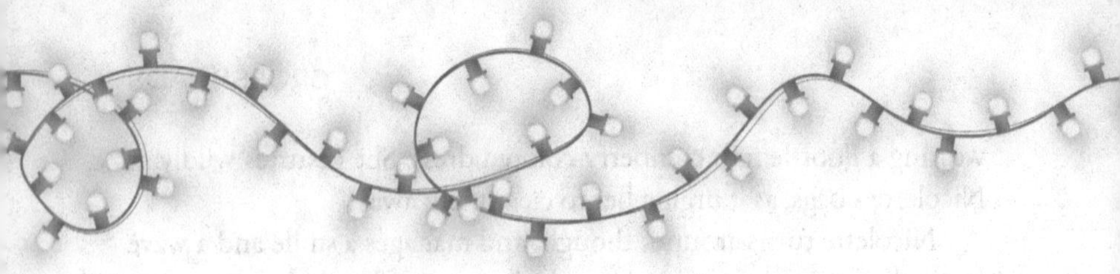

CHAPTER 5
ON THE SOUND SYSTEM: "APOLOGIZE" BY TIMBALAND, FEATURING ONEREPUBLIC

Nicolette is holding a glass of pink champagne at an impossibly chic New York City Christmas party. She's seated on a banquette, smushed together with her best friend, Cici. They were boarding school roommates for six years.

Cici's parents have rented out this edgy room at the top of a hotel called The Standard, filling it with investment bankers, socialites, and friends of their two grown children. The food is smashing—little bites of roast beef en croute with horseradish. Smoked salmon with creme fraiche. Tiny meatballs served on toothpicks. Cheeses. Strawberries dipped in dark chocolate.

The only thing Nicolette doesn't like is the mulled wine, but possibly that's not the venue's fault. Maybe putting spices into wine is just a bad idea on principle. At the first opportunity, she abandoned her glass on a grand piano and took a glass of bubbly off a passing tray.

Now she's trying to follow the deeply involved conversation two prep-school friends are having about the plot of *Lost*. She loves these friends but can't follow the conversation. She's just come off another grueling exam season and hasn't watched TV in months.

She's just tired, period. When Cici asked her to come to New York right before Christmas, she said yes as a means of getting out of her stepmother's stupid caroling party. She didn't realize she was saying yes to three days of shopping and dining out and partying like a *Mean Girls* character.

Tomorrow, at least, she can fly home and spend the rest of Christmas break reading and skiing. Her stepmother Veronica is sending the twins off on a New Year's cruise with their father, which will get them out of Nicolette's hair.

It's pretty much perfect, except for one problem. She texted Damien *twice* today, hoping to set up a ride home from the Burlington airport. But the texts won't go through.

At first, she'd chalked it up to bad connectivity in Vermont. Cell phones just don't work there as well as they do in the rest of the world. It's one of the things she loves about the place.

But her third attempt didn't work, either. She's running out of time, and she really wants to see his face. She looks forward to it every time she goes home. That rugged smile. Those flannel shirts rolled up onto forearms that flex when he lifts her bags.

And those soft brown eyes. That's what she misses most of all. And the way he listens with his whole body when she speaks.

He's the best thing about Christmas. So where is he?

Nicolette slides off the banquette and heads for a quieter corner in front of the floor-to-ceiling windows. The room has sweeping views of lower Manhattan and New Jersey. Since it's nighttime, there are glittering city lights in every direction, split by the dark slash of the river.

It's intensely beautiful, and she wishes Damien could see it. She wonders if he's ever been to New York.

After pulling her phone out of her clutch bag, she texts him again. *Message not delivered* is the response a few seconds later.

It's so confusing. Every time Damien drops her off, he says, "Call me anytime." He wouldn't have changed his number, right? What taxi service does that?

Unless he lost his phone recently, and is in the process of getting a new one...

"You're looking smashing this evening, Nicolette. Want a brownie?"

She looks up to find Cam, Cici's older brother, standing before her, and it's startling. Cam has always startled her. He's blond and beautiful, just like his sister, with Hollywood features and carefully tousled hair.

Tonight, he's wearing a deep-blue shirt that makes him look a little dangerous. "Are they ordinary brownies?" she asks. "Or are you up to your old tricks?"

He laughs. "They're honestly just brownies. Although I might have snuck the platter out of the kitchen uninvited." He extends a tray which contains a couple dozen bite-sized brownies. "Help me hide the evidence?"

Her smile is automatic, because it's Cam. "Thank you." She takes one and pops it into her mouth, causing Cam to grin, displaying perfect teeth to go with his perfect face.

Nicolette spent all of middle and high school praying that Cam would notice her. If he'd ever crossed the dining hall at Andover to offer her a brownie, she would have died of happiness.

Now she's just a little weary. And also distracted by the Damien issue.

"Listen, a few of us are going out to 1 Oak after this," Cam says. "Want to come?"

Nicolette's smile brightens again, because it's Cam after all. But now she has a problem. She's not very interested in clubbing and probably can't fake it. She'll fall asleep in a corner somewhere and demonstrate once and for all that she's not a fun person. "That sounds wild. But Cici and I were going to head back to your parents' place. It's our last chance to hang out together before I go back to Vermont."

Cam doesn't look offended, because why would he? He's hot and rich, and the monied twenty-something women of New York fall at his feet.

He does, however, look thoughtful. He tilts his perfect face before he speaks again. "You realize, Nicky, that you don't really *have* to go back to Vermont, right? You could just stay uptown with us for another week. I know you aren't a fan of your father's new wife."

For a moment, Nicolette is too stunned to speak. This observation is far more startling than the offer of a brownie or the invitation to tag along to a club. Until tonight, he'd never shown any sign of paying attention to anything she'd ever said.

"Thank you. But I have to go home," she says. "Because if I don't..."

On second thought, she doesn't actually want to verbalize the rest.

"If you don't?" he prompts.

"Then she wins. Then Veronica pushes me out of my own house." And that isn't even the worst of it. If she doesn't go home, she's also ceding her father—what little part of himself he bothers to share with her—entirely to his new wife and stepkids.

Cam nods, his expression grave. "Yeah, okay. Can't let the bitch win. I approve."

Again, Nicolette's smile is automatic. But it's a little thin.

"Maybe another time?" Cam adds, and then his perfect eyebrows do a flirty thing that she's seen him do before—just never aimed at her. "A bunch of us were thinking of going to St. Barts for spring break."

"That *does* sound fun," she says, although spring break feels a million years off.

"If you come, I'll make sure that it is," he says. "Want another brownie?"

Stunned again, Nicolette shakes her head. He gives her another flirty smile and then finally moves on to talk to another girl in an even shorter dress. The whole interaction had lasted maybe three minutes. Five, tops.

Still, it's odd. She shakes herself. And then she pulls out her phone again to check the screen, which is still dark.

"What did my brother want?" Cici asks, sneaking up on her.

Nicolette looks up, startled. "They're going to some club. He invited us, but I told him we were going to chill together instead."

Cici's gaze travels over to her brother and then back again. "*Interesting.*"

"Which part?"

"All of it? For starters, Cam remembered we exist. And then you actually turned him down?" She lets out a throaty laugh.

Nicolette feels a flush climbing her cheeks. "It's been years since I mooned after Cam," she says, because denying that she ever has wouldn't be very credible.

"I know, and thank God. But he probably took one look at you decked out in that dress—" Cici waves a hand at the Marc Jacobs minidress on Nicolette. "And he said to himself, 'Wait, isn't that Cici's friend? She used to be invisible, but now she's got long legs and tits! I'd better hit that.'"

Nicolette gives a sniff. "He's just making the rounds. And there's no way I'm going clubbing. My feet are already killing me."

Cici shakes out her golden curls. "You don't have to convince me. Just prepare yourself to fend him off again next time. The fact that you actually turned him down means he'll be back. Cam can't stand to hear 'no.'"

Nicolette just shrugs, because she has trouble believing that Cam is capable of insecurities. And also because she's busy pulling out her phone again for another glance at the screen.

"Hold on," Cici says, her voice rising with delight. "Nicolette Chelsea Overland, why do you keep checking your phone? Are you waiting to hear from a *guy*? Do you have a boyfriend, and you forgot to tell me?"

"God no. I wish."

"Then why do you keep staring at that screen? I've seen you do that all night."

"Sorry." Again, a denial would probably not be very credible. "I've just been trying to reach the driver in Vermont. The one who always picks me up from the airport."

"Ohhh," she says with a sigh. "The dreamy one? Damien? You told me all about him. Last summer when we drank all that schnapps on the boat."

Nicolette shudders. Because boats and schnapps don't mix, and that night hadn't ended well. But it had been a rainy weekend in the Hamptons, and they were bored. Secondly—and far worse—she's embarrassed to have brought up Damien like that.

"I'd never call anyone *dreamy*. What a stupid thing to say."

"You absolutely did. And then when I suggested you have a summer fling with him, you got all sniffy. You said he wasn't fling material."

"He isn't," Nicolette says quickly. "We're just friends."

"Friends who also want to bone." She shrugs. "I know you don't really do casual. But Christmas vacation is, what? Three weeks? A fling is all you have time for."

It's true that Nic has never managed to figure out casual sex. Either a guy isn't interesting enough to bother, or she likes him too much to be casual about it. The only time she had a one-night stand, it left her feeling cheap and lonelier than ever.

And then there's the problem that she's a chicken. Propositioning Damien—handsome, strong, self-possessed Damien—sounds utterly impossible.

"I just...can't," she admits. "Besides—if I scared him off, I don't know who would drive me home from the airport. There aren't a lot of taxi services in central Vermont."

Instead of agreeing with her, Cici makes a sad face. "When's the last time you really had it bad for a guy, though? Someone you couldn't stop thinking about?"

"I don't know," she lies, because it's easier than admitting that Cici's brother is the only other guy who ever drew her interest for more than a minute. And the two men are so different. It's hard to imagine that Cam and Damien are even the same species.

"Oh honey, I get it. You're always so afraid to get attached. You can blame your parents for your attachment issues. But what if it doesn't have to be such a big deal? When you see Damien again, just tell him, 'Hey, when you have a night off, I'd love to go out for pizza again. We had fun that time.' And see what he says?"

"It sounds so easy when you put it like that."

"Because it is?" Cici shrugs. "Just try it. You never really go after the things you really want."

That's depressingly accurate. Then again, when Nicolette tries to picture herself asking Damien out on a date, she feels herself blushing all over.

On the other hand, she literally owns a coffee mug that reads: *Do one thing every day that scares you*. And does she follow this advice? Nope. Never.

"Fine. If I agree to do it, can we go home now?" Nicolette asks. "I need to be well-rested to humiliate myself."

Cici lets out a whoop. "I'll find our coats."

———

Nicolette wakes up in a graciously appointed spare bedroom in the Wentworth family mansion the next morning. The first thing she does is reach for her phone to look for a text from Damien.

There's nothing, which is awfully weird and not exactly confidence-boosting. Is he really blowing her off? Is he too busy for the airport pickup and doesn't care enough to say so?

That doesn't sound like him, though. He's always happy to see her. This past May, when he'd picked her up in Burlington, they'd hit a coffee-shop drive-through and then sat in the parking lot catching up before he drove her home. She'd demanded his sketchbook again, and he'd gamely pulled it out from under the seat to show her.

He doesn't drink coffee with her out of pity, right? That's not how taxis work.

So where is he?

She picks up her phone and hits the Call button. Texts are their usual MO, but her flight lands at two, and it's nine a.m. already. She's got to get a hold of him.

Damien's voicemail picks up right away, and she holds her breath so she can hear the low scrape of his voice better.

"You have reached Damien's Taxi Service," his message says. "Unfortunately, I've stepped away from the business for a while, and I'm out of town. So please dial Rose's Taxi at 802-238-4135. She'll get you where you need to go."

When the message ends, Nicolette has to call back, because she was too surprised to write down the number for Rose's Taxi. And what does *stepped away* mean, exactly? That he got a better job?

She can't help it. She feels stung. Not because Damien isn't driving anymore. That's probably a good thing. But he could have said something.

"Nicolette?" comes Cici's voice from the corridor. "I got the good bagels, with smoked salmon!"

She looks up from her phone and takes in the beautiful room, with the silk curtains and the thick carpets. "I'll be right there," she says sheepishly. "Thank you."

Dropping her phone onto the bed, she lets out a quiet groan. Every day—all day—she lives her life surrounded by outrageous privilege. She thinks of herself as a person who takes nothing for granted, but that's a lie, right? It's absurd to think that Damien should phone his clients to inform them of his career decisions.

You are ridiculous, she chides herself. *Stop it*.

It's just that Cici was right. Nicolette never lets herself get very attached to anyone, because they always disappear. Like her mother—gone from a brain tumor when she was ten. And her father, who can't be bothered to pick her up from an airport himself.

Damien picked her up because it was his job, but it always felt like more than that. She imagined they had a real connection. That he was as interested in her as he was in the sixty-dollar fare.

Maybe he found a way to go to art school, though. She should be happy that he's chasing his dreams.

She picks up her phone one more time and calls Rose's Taxi.

———

Seven hours later, she gets off a plane in the Burlington Airport—the first place Damien ever dropped her off. It's Christmas Eve, so there's a Christmas tree in the corner on the rugged carpeting. It's the kind with industrial tinsel and presents that are probably just wrapped empty boxes.

Nicolette feels a little hollow inside—like one of those fake gifts. And even though she knows he's not coming, she glances around for Damien at the baggage claim.

There's no sign of him, and she feels a fresh wave of disappointment.

Her bag trundles toward her on the carousel, and she yanks it off the conveyor belt and extends the handle. If he were here, he'd tease her about how much the bag weighs. *How many bricks did you bring home this time?*

She drags the bag out to the curb and eyes each car until she spots one that has *OVERLAND* scribbled on a cardboard sign in the window.

As she approaches the car, a middle-aged Black woman with short salt-and-pepper hair climbs out to meet her. "So you're Nicolette," she says with an appraising frown.

"Um, yes?" That strikes her as an odd introduction. "Are you Rose? Thanks for picking me up on short notice."

The woman looks her up and down, nods, and then heaves her bag into the car's trunk in one fluid motion. "Got bricks in there?"

Nicolette sighs. Then she climbs into the backseat, the way most people ride in a taxi. But it feels all wrong now.

Luckily, Rose doesn't try to make conversation. Instead, she turns up the radio, which is set to a news channel. It doesn't help Nicolette's mood to hear about the recent North Korean nuclear tests. Or fighting in Afghanistan. *Intense clashes between NATO forces and Taliban insurgents have resulted in the heaviest casualties seen this year...*

If Damien were here, they'd be singing along to Christmas tunes by George Michael and Whitney Houston. She'd be nagging him to see his latest vampire drawings.

And maybe—just maybe—she'd have been brave enough to ask him out for a drink after Christmas.

"Got something for you," says Rose from the front seat.

"Sorry?"

"Here." Without taking her eyes off the road, Rose lifts a white envelope and offers it over her shoulder. "He left this for you."

"Damien?" Nicolette asks stupidly.

"Of course, Damien," Rose says gruffly. "It's not from Santa Claus, is it? He gave me this letter and said to give it to you when you called."

Nicolette takes the envelope and smooths it across her lap. *NICOLETTE* it reads in dark black ink. There's a little drawing of Selene Nightshade—the vampire inspired by her—grinning beside the letters.

Her eyes begin to sting. Because he didn't forget about her after all.

She carefully slides her thumb under the flap, taking care not to rip the envelope. She pulls out two sheets of paper and begins to read.

Nicolette—

Happy Holiday vacation! I hope you manage to avoid your step-monster's caroling party on your own this year, because I can't be there to help. I'm not sure where I'll be when you get this letter. Maybe Texas. Or maybe Afghanistan or Iraq. I've enlisted in the army, because I can earn a good living and then go to school on the G.I. bill. It's the best way I could figure out how to move my life forward.

Maybe you're reading this and wondering why your taxi driver felt like he had to explain his disappearance. And you'd have a point. Except you're the one who pushed me to try for school, and nobody else in my life has done that. Literally nobody. I just thought you'd be interested to hear that it made a difference to me. I realized that I don't always want to be a taxi driver who draws on the side. I'd like to be an artist who also drives a taxi.

So thanks for that.

Sincerely,

Damien Rossi

P.S. Part of our training is going to include running up and down hills with a seventy-pound pack. I figure after handling your luggage, I already have an edge on the rest of the guys.

In the back seat, Nicolette lets out a combination laugh and sob.

"Everything okay back there?" the driver asks.

It's really, really not.

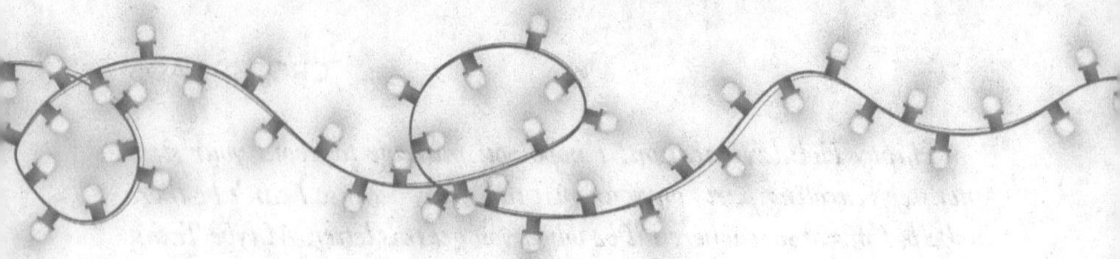

CHAPTER 6
ON THE RADIO: THERE IS NO RADIO

"Don't take this the wrong way, but you're not as pretty as the day I first met you."

Damien looks up into the smirking face of his buddy Jarvis, who's perched on the edge of the next cot. "Oh fuck off. You're no looker either."

Jarvis lets out a low, infectious laugh. "I think I'm too tired to shower. I'm just going to sit here and solidify in my stench."

Damien understands. Another brutal day on patrol has left both of them as heavy as concrete blocks, every muscle weary.

"Mail!" yells Staff Sergeant Thompson.

Damien doesn't turn around because that would require too much energy. Besides, he got a letter from his mother only two days ago, so he's not expecting anything.

He leans over and unlaces his boots, dirtying his hands. The dust here coats everything—every piece of gear, every stitch of clothing. The inside of his nose. Even after a shower, he knows he'll still be able to taste it.

"Rossi! You got a package here. Christ, it's heavy." Thompson's voice carries a hint of humor.

For him? Really? Damien rises, his quads complaining. He turns around to see Thompson holding a big, square box. He ambles over to take it. And it *is* heavy. That's weird.

"Whatever you got, don't forget to share," Thompson says.

"Yessir."

Damien carries the box back to his cot and sets it down.

"Whatcha got there?" Jarvis asks. "Can I have some?"

"Hold your horses." It's definitely his name on this box, but the handwriting is unfamiliar. Then he notes the return address is Old Route 16.

No way. It can't be.

He pulls his knife out of his pocket and slits open the heavy layers of packing tape. Mindful of all the nosy faces turning in his direction, he opens the flaps carefully and peers inside, finding a fat plastic bag secured with a fancy gold cord.

He tugs off the cord, and a bark of exhausted laughter scrapes out of his chest. Inside the bag are an outrageous number of individually wrapped chocolate bars and Oreo snack packs. He plunges a hand down into the goodies, feeling like that cartoon of Scrooge McDuck diving into a pile of money.

"Guys?" he says, because there's no way they'd let him keep all this bounty to himself. Not that he'd even want to. "Snack time!"

Jarvis lets out a whoop, and half a dozen soldiers surround Damien immediately. He spends a pleasant few minutes handing out cookies and miniature chocolate bars.

"Who'd you blow to get all that?" someone demands.

"It's from a friend," he says.

"Nice *friend*." Jarvis snickers.

Damien just shakes his head. He opens a baby Snickers for himself and bites down into the rich, sticky, nutty goodness. A candy bar in the desert is life affirming. It really is.

Only one thing could make it better. He gathers the edges of the candy-filled plastic bag and carefully lifts it out of the box, looking for a letter. And sure enough—he finds an entire second layer beneath. There's another plastic bag. But first, there's a white envelope with *DAMIEN* printed carefully on its face. He snatches it out of the box and hastily slits it open. It's a letter, dated January ninth, which means the box took more than a month to reach him. That's not surprising.

For a second, he just holds it in his hands, stunned that a piece of paper touched by Nicolette made it all the way across the world to find him in this hellhole.

He reads.

Hi Damien—

Happy holidays from Vermont! I live near Boston now, though. I graduated from Duke in May. Seems like a minute ago you were dropping off my freaked-out teenage self at the airport.

Anyway, after all this time I'm sure you weren't expecting to hear from me. Rose gave me your letter two years ago, but there was no return address.

Then, right before Christmas this year, a friend and I went out to a bar near Tuxbury called The Mountain Goat. There was a young woman waiting tables, and her name tag said "Zara."

And I thought—Damien has a sister named Zara! And she looked like you, only prettier. So of course, I asked her if you two were family.

She said: "I don't always admit being related to Damien. But I miss his grumpy ass, so what do you want to know?" And then, in between serving beers to the entire bar, she told me that you're doing okay, and that you already signed up for a second tour.

I guess that's a good sign? You wouldn't do that if it was horrible and dangerous, right? I have to say that I'm a little obsessed with reading about Afghanistan now that I know you're there. I realize they only write articles about the worst stuff that happens. So could you do me a favor and stay out of the New York Times? I'd really appreciate it.

You're getting this box because I talked Zara into

*giving me your mailing address. She said you can receive
packages, and that she sent you a chocolate bar for
Christmas. So I hope this box finds you. Bear in mind
that I have never been to an Afghan army base. So if
you find this stuff weird or unhelpful, please blame the
internet. I googled "what to put in an army care package"
and this is what Google suggested.*

*Oh—the one weird item is my lucky marble. It's a
marble from Rutland. I got it on a summer camp trip
when I was eleven. But I decided you needed luck more
than I do right now.*

With love from Vermont,

Nicolette

*P.S. I know I pushed you to apply for art school, and
I feel weird about that now.*

*P.P.S. Forgot to tell you—this year I applied to five
top law schools and got rejected by all of them, including
my father's. He's barely speaking to me right now. So
that's extra fun.*

*In other words, don't take advice from me. I clearly
don't know what I'm doing. :-)*

With his heart bubbling over with joy, Damien reads the note
two more times in a row.

"Damien?" Jarvis says.

When he looks up, Jarvis snatches the letter out of his
hands. "Who's *Nicolette*?" He whistles. "Nice name. Got a
picture?"

"She's a client. And a friend," Damien says. The way he snatches
the letter back makes Jarvis grin.

"Buddy, *friends* don't mail friends a pile of chocolate all the way
to the sandbox. What else you got in there?"

He tucks the letter under his pillow and looks into the box again.
The second plastic bag is from the Onion River Co-op in Montpe-

lier. Even the familiar logo on the bag gives him a homesick lump in his throat.

It's a damn plastic bag. He needs to get a grip.

He unknots the top, and inside there's a lip balm, a tube of toothpaste, a travel-sized shampoo, some dental floss and a bar of goat's milk soap from a Vermont farm.

"Fancy soap?" Jarvis asks, tickled. "Please tell me this chick is hot. You're getting *very* laid when you go home for leave this summer."

If only. Although Jarvis has a point. Who takes this much trouble to send a present to her taxi driver if she doesn't also have feelings for him?

It's fun to wonder.

In the corner of the bag, as advertised, he finds a single round marble, made from white Vermont marble. It's beautiful, and he tucks it into his pocket immediately.

Then there's a pair of Darn Tough wool socks, which every Vermonter is programmed to appreciate, even in Afghanistan. No— *especially* in Afghanistan.

And last, but certainly not least, there's a folded-up thing made of finely knitted wool. He pulls it out and unfurls it, revealing a small blanket—the size you'd throw over your sofa to keep warm while you're watching a movie. Except it's the nicest blanket ever made, in charcoal gray, and soft as butter. He fumbles for the little tag sewn into a corner. *100% Cashmere*, it reads.

Shit, really?

"What did I tell you?" Jarvis says, running a hand over the blanket. "This Nicolette thinks of you, and her mind goes straight to *bedding*. My wife would pee herself to have a blanket this nice."

Damien rolls his eyes, even though Jarvis has a point. It's quite a spread of presents covering his cot. An embarrassment of riches.

As he sets the cardboard box onto the packed-earth floor, something heavy slides around inside it. Two somethings. The book-shaped objects are heavy and wrapped in brown paper, which is why he hadn't noticed them before.

More? Seriously?

He carefully tears the paper off the first one and finds a beautiful hardcover book. It's a graphic novel called *The Arrival*, and when he opens to a page in the center, the art is outrageously intricate and intimidatingly beautiful.

Then he rests the next wrapped object on his knee and contemplates it. This is already the best gift box he's ever seen on an army base. He runs his thumb under the seam of brown paper and peels it back to reveal a cloth-bound sketchbook. It's navy blue, with paper so thick and creamy that ink would never bleed through.

Stuck between its pages is an envelope addressed to Nicolette in Durham, North Carolina. And two sheets of notebook paper, with a single post-it attached. *Would love to hear from you, if only to know if you received this!*

"Aw," Jarvis says, cutting the crap for once. "Do you believe me now? The lady wants to hear from you."

"Yeah, yeah," he says. But the truth is that two sheets of paper will hardly be enough for the thank-you note he needs to write. He flips through the blank sketchbook pages and imagines himself filling them with new art. Something to take his mind off the stress of endless patrols. Honestly, the paper is almost too fancy to draw on.

But that's what it's for, says Nicolette's voice in his head.

He grins, as if she were right here with him. He hopes this gift is more than just a gift. He hopes it means something. You don't send your lucky marble halfway across the world just on a whim, right?

"Look, I know I like to bust your balls," Jarvis says. "But if you like this girl, let her know, okay? You gotta stick your neck out if you want to get the goods."

Damien rubs a hand over his scruffy face. "Is that what you did?"

"Absolutely. Told my Katie that she was *the one*. Women like a guy who isn't afraid to say how he feels."

"Supper!" yells the Staff Sergeant.

Damien hastily tidies up his treasures, storing everything carefully in his footlocker for later, except a couple candies he pockets for the Staff Sergeant as he heads for the mess tent.

He'll write that thank-you letter after dinner.

Who knew that a thank-you note could be so freaking hard to write?

His first efforts are too bloodless. *I really enjoyed your gift.*

But then he swings too far in the other direction. *You can't have any idea how much this meant to me.*

Too dramatic.

"You finish that thing yet?" Jarvis asks him every night for a week. "It better be epic after all that scribbling you're doing over there."

Finally, after a lot of spinning his wheels, he ends up trading his last packet of Oreos for more paper. And then he sits down to just write the damn thing.

> *Nicolette,*
>
> *Your box arrived at the end of a long, exhausting day when I was feeling homesick. If I'm being honest, that's every day. But your gifts were a bright beam of sunshine. And Google did us both a solid, because everything was perfect. And I'm very popular now because I have chocolate.*
>
> *I miss chocolate. I miss Vermont, and I miss my family. And maybe it's dumb, but I miss driving the taxi. It's a job where you're always helping someone in the moment of need.*
>
> *Also, I miss you. Maybe I'm not supposed to say that. Maybe that's too much, but it's true. The book you sent me is special. Not only because it's a nice book, but because only someone who knows me well could have picked it out.*
>
> *I mean that. I'm not a big talker, but you know as much about me as anyone. And when I come home again, I want to take you out for pizza. Or drinks or dinner. Whatever I'm allowed to ask for, that's what I want.*
>
> *Meanwhile, I've been thinking about your law school disappointments. I don't quite know what you're going*

through, because people never had the same kind of expectations for me like they have for you. But honestly, it's hard to understand. Who wouldn't want <u>you</u> on their team? I just don't get it. Unless—hear me out—in your heart of hearts you didn't really want to go to those schools and somehow they could tell.

If I'm wrong, I'm sorry. And if I <u>am</u> wrong, then you should absolutely try again. You are infinitely smart and capable. If you want it badly enough, I bet you can get it.

I should go now. It's almost time to eat (a pretty bad) dinner. But thanks for making me the happiest (and warmest) soldier in the barracks this week.

Thinking of you,

Damien

By the time he's satisfied with this letter, an entire week has gone by. He folds it carefully and tucks it inside the envelope. When the mail call comes the next day, he's ready.

The Staff Sergeant brings in the bag, and Damien hears his name again. "Rossi! Got something for you. But nobody get excited, it's just an envelope. Not another metric ton of chocolate bars."

There are grumbles around the barracks.

Damien takes his letter and finds that it's from his sister. Addressed to *Demon Rossi*, in the way of bratty siblings everywhere.

The first part is some teasing and gentle whining about his siblings, and it makes him homesick as hell. But then he reads this:

Hey, I hope it's okay that I gave that girl at the bar your address. Nanette or something. Super pretty in a posh way. Hope you know who she is? Ex-girlfriend, maybe? She asked a <u>lot</u> of questions about you! I'm not the only one who noticed, either. Her boyfriend—some douchey guy in a polo shirt—didn't like it <u>at all</u>.

Anyway—hope it's okay! Love you! —Z

. . .

His heart stops. Her *boyfriend*.

It's so upsetting, and not just because she's taken. That is a tragedy, but what's worse is that he feels like an absolute fool. He misread all the signs, possibly from the first day they ever met. She made him feel special. But clearly, she makes everyone feel that way.

God damn it.

God damn everything.

He picks up the letter he'd written—thankfully still sealed up in its envelope—and he rips it right in half.

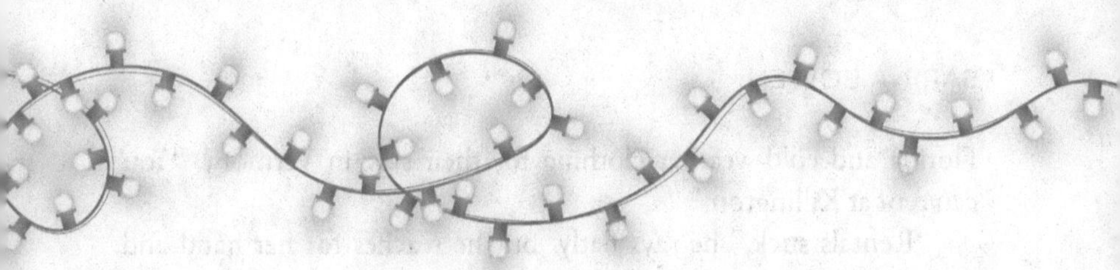

CHAPTER 7
ON THE AIRPORT SOUND SYSTEM: "JINGLE BELLS"— THE MICHAEL BUBLÉ VERSION

"Wow." Cam looks down the escalator with a grin on his handsome face. "You weren't joking. That's the whole airport?"

"That's the whole thing," Nicolette confirms as they descend slowly toward the luggage carousels. "One terminal."

Her husband has been to the family compound in Vermont before, but this is the first time they flew in rather than driving from their apartment in Boston. They've been away on a pre-Christmas getaway together, which had the benefit of shortening the time they'd have to spend with Nicolette's family.

It got her out of the stupid caroling party, which is still going strong even though the twins have graduated from college.

Like Cam, Nicolette is scrutinizing the arrivals area, but her reasons are different. She can't help it, but every time she arrives at this airport, she thinks of Damien. Even if it's been years since she's seen him.

When they step off the escalator, the luggage carousel is already turning. A guy in a Patagonia jacket passes them with a ski bag over his shoulder, and Cam makes a wistful face. "I wish I had my skis and boots."

"We didn't want to carry our skis around Miami," she points out. Cam is a fun time, but he's not a very practical person. It was a challenge packing for the both of them for this trip—resort wear for

Florida and cold-weather clothing for their stay in Vermont. "You can rent at Killington."

"Rentals suck," he says flatly. But he reaches for her hand and gives it a squeeze.

She fixes her eyes on the rotating carousel and tries not to wonder where Damien is right now. In a desert somewhere, maybe. It still smarts that she never heard back from him after she sent him that gift box. It was an unsolicited gift, and he doesn't owe her anything, but God, it would have been nice to hear from him. Just to let her know he's alive.

Obviously, Damien didn't ever feel the same way about her that she felt about him. He must have rolled his eyes when he got the note. And the lucky marble—like a nine-year-old would carry. Every time she's reminded of it, she feels like crawling out of her skin.

"There we go," Cam says. "Isn't that mine?" He points at a navy blue Tumi bag gliding toward them.

"Of course it is," Nicolette says a little more sharply than she meant to. The fact that Cam can't always recognize his own luggage irritates her, even though it shouldn't. She's known him for, what, eight years? Nine?

You're marrying an overgrown child, Cici had said after Nicolette's engagement party. *Never forget that.*

The comment was made in jest, after Cam had opened the dishwasher in the middle of the cycle and sprayed water all over the kitchen. But all humor has a basis in truth.

The fact is that Nicolette *chose* this. She married a fun party boy because opposites attract. And because she was a little stunned that Cam could ever love someone like her. It still seems a little unreal.

Besides, it's not fair to expect Cam to transform his personality just because she's stuck being the practical half of their marriage for the rest of her days.

Cam grabs his own bag off the belt, but not hers, almost certainly because he doesn't recognize her bag, even after traveling with her for a week. Instead of prompting him, she darts around his body to grab it herself, hauling it off the carousel and almost tripping in the process.

"Whoa, tiger," Cam says with a laugh. "Easy. Is someone picking us up?" This is surely the first moment that the question of their transportation has occurred to him.

"I called a taxi," she says, pushing her hair out of her eyes. "Rose is probably waiting outside." At least she hopes so. Cam will be crabby if their ride is late.

"Cool," he says. "Can't wait to kick back with your dad and Veronica, plus Margie's cooking."

They roll their luggage out to the sidewalk, where the late December temperature is below freezing. She scans the few cars in evidence, but Rose isn't among them. "I'm sure it will be just a minute," Nicolette says, pulling out her phone to check for a text. But there aren't any.

Cam pulls out his new iPhone and ignores her, which is a habit of his that she usually detests. But at least it will keep him occupied.

The wind bites Nicolette's face as she stares toward the turn in the road, hoping to see Rose's minivan appear.

Instead, a black Grand Cherokee comes into view, and she stops breathing. It's like seeing a mirage.

The Jeep stops right in front of her, and she lets out a little gasp when she sees the silhouette inside.

Cam looks up suddenly. "Is this our ride?"

She nods, not trusting her voice, as Damien exits and disappears behind the back of the vehicle, where he raises the rear liftgate, all without saying a word.

Nicolette's heart stutters as he finally faces her and Cam. His expression is unreadable, but his eyes meet hers for a brief second before shifting to Cam. "Evening," he says, his tone detached. "Rose is double-booked tonight."

That's all he says. No hug. No acknowledgement that they aren't strangers.

Cam, oblivious to the tension, shrugs. Then he steps away from his suitcase, as if he doesn't have two functional arms to lift it himself, and opens the door to the Jeep's backseat. "Headed out to Colebury, yeah?"

Damien nods. Then he grabs Cam's bag off the pavement and moves it effortlessly into the back.

Nicolette can't stop cataloguing all the things about Damien that aren't the same. He's broader across the chest. More muscular. He looks exhausted. There are dark smudges under both eyes.

And he doesn't smile.

She tries to shake off her surprise, lunging for her bag. But Damien is faster. He grabs it before her hands properly close on the handle, slots it into the back, and then closes the hatch.

They're face to face now, just her and this stranger who looks like Damien but acts like an alien. "Hi," she says, with pointed eye contact.

"Hi," he repeats, dodging her glance. "Good flight?"

"*Good flight?*" she echoes incredulously. "Seriously?"

He flinches, like he's ashamed. Then he opens his mouth to say something more.

Except Cam picks that moment to bark something from the backseat. "Can we pick up the tempo a little, buddy? We're on a tight schedule."

They are not, by any stretch of the definition, on a tight schedule. But Damien reacts as if he's been poked with a cattle prod, snapping to attention and ducking around the other side of the vehicle, where he climbs into the driver's seat.

Nicolette goes in the other direction and finds herself standing next to the front passenger door. From the back, Cam is giving her a funny look. He holds the rear door open for her. "Baby? Come here. I gotta show you something."

She gets into the back beside her husband and closes the door. Damien puts the Jeep into gear and pulls away from the curb.

"Check out this hotel," Cam says, holding up his phone. "My dad still wants us to go to Aruba for Easter. You can get the time off, yeah?"

Her heart drops. "I told you I'd ask, but that's a tricky time. The partners like to get away." She's working as a paralegal at a Boston law firm and trying to decide whether or not to reapply to law school.

In truth, she's stalling. She doesn't want to go to law school, but she also doesn't have a great backup plan.

"Push for it," Cam says. "See this beach? All you'd have to pack is a bikini." He makes his voice sultry. "I'll make it worth your while."

Now she's squirming inside. "Look, Vermont got some snow," she says, turning toward the window.

He wraps an arm around her. "Hope the ski conditions are good. Too bad I couldn't talk your dad into going to Aspen. Vermont skiing is so trashy early in the season. Hell, it's trashy, period."

Nicolette's eyes slide unbidden toward Damien, whose profile is only partly visible to her.

He's staring straight out the front window, back straight, hands at ten and two on the steering wheel. There's no indication that he's even listening to them at all.

She's mortified, anyway. And it's a long forty minutes until they finally arrive at the gate to her family home.

"You need the code, buddy?" Cam asks as Damien lowers his window.

Damien punches it in without comment.

"Guess not, then," Cam says in a snarky tone.

"Cam," she says under her breath.

He makes a face of innocent confusion.

When the car finally arrives in front of the house, Damien opens the driver's door almost before they're in park. Like he can't wait to get away.

Nicolette slips out of the car and waits for him to open the back. As he raises the liftgate, his chunky wool sweater rides up an inch, and she sees a flash of ribcage. Her guilty eyes can't quite look away. But she notices something marring his olive skin. Like a scar. But his sweater slips down before she gets a good look.

"You take plastic?" Cam asks, reaching for his wallet.

"It's already handled," Damien says tonelessly. He lifts out Cam's bag first, setting it with a thud onto the plowed drive.

"Then here," Cam says, peeling a five out of his wallet.

She sees a flicker of hesitation on Damien's face. But then he takes the bill and shoves it into his jeans' pocket. "Thanks," he mutters.

Cam turns toward the front door, where her father has appeared, wine goblet in hand. "Cam! I just opened a 1989 Château Pichon Baron! Let me pour you a glass."

Nicolette hangs back, and when Damien offers her the handle of her suitcase, she doesn't take it from him. "Look," she says. "Seeing you is a surprise. I didn't know you were back."

He glances down at his boots. "Been back a few months. Trying to settle in." There's something heavy about his delivery. Like there's a story there. But he doesn't tell it.

"Well..." She sighs. "I'm glad to see you safely home." After all this time, she still reads every single article about Afghanistan in the paper. Every day.

Finally, he lifts his chin and really looks at her. For a split second, the old Damien is back, eyes blazing with every ounce of intensity that they'd ever held.

But then he looks away again. "Good to see you, Nicolette." He clears his throat. "Merry Christmas."

Then he turns away quickly, before she can go in for the hug. He hops back into the Jeep and drives away.

After he's gone, she realizes that he didn't say, "Call me anytime."

Damien heads back down the driveway, and it's suddenly dark outside. In December, nightfall seems to descend on Vermont instantly—like an inexpertly lowered theater curtain.

The nights are long, and the days are short, which isn't helping his mental health. He doesn't sleep anymore. Not much anyway. When he closes his eyes, he's back on patrol in Afghanistan, watching the distant hills for any movement that might be insurgents setting up for an attack.

His nights are so exhausting that sleep seems pretty futile lately. He feels like a leaky fuel pump—getting by, but just barely. It's been like this for the entire six months he's been home, and hiding it from his family takes every ounce of his self-control.

When he reaches the bottom of the Overlands' long drive, the gate opens on its own. Which means that Nicolette is still standing in the front entryway, watching the video feed and delaying entering the warm house to do this small favor for him.

He looks both ways before turning onto the two-lane highway.

But then the exhaustion overwhelms him, and he pulls off the road a quarter of a mile away. Coming to a stop on the shoulder, he puts the Jeep in park and leans back against the headrest, closing his eyes.

Thank you for the gift box, Nicolette. It meant a lot to me. That's all he had to say to make things right. He just…couldn't. Not with her douchey husband standing there smirking. With his titanium luggage and his shitty opinions.

Besides, it's fine if she thinks Damien's a dickhead. He has nothing to offer her. If she'd asked to see his newer drawings, he couldn't even show her. They're full of darkness and death. And so is he.

Afghanistan nearly killed him. And *nearly* is debatable in that sentence. It didn't kill his body, but it murdered some corner of his soul.

She wouldn't understand. Nobody can. Honestly, he wouldn't even *want* her to understand. He watched Jarvis die during a firefight. Held his hand while the medic worked frantically trying to stop the bleeding.

There was nothing about it that made any sense. Death wasn't anything like Hollywood wants you to think. Jarvis didn't have any brave last words. He didn't even have a chance to say *Tell my Katie I love her.* He just died on the dusty ground, a look of shock on his face.

He'll carry that around with him forever. People like Nicolette and her ass of a husband will never understand. They're lucky not to.

Damien stuffs a hand into his pocket and finds the five-dollar bill. He tosses it into the cupholder. At least it will buy him a shot of whiskey. He shoves his hand into his pocket one more time and finds what he was looking for. The marble Nicolette sent him. It's been halfway around the world and back again, and unlike Damien, it's unchanged. Still smooth to the touch and perfectly shaped.

He carries it with him always.

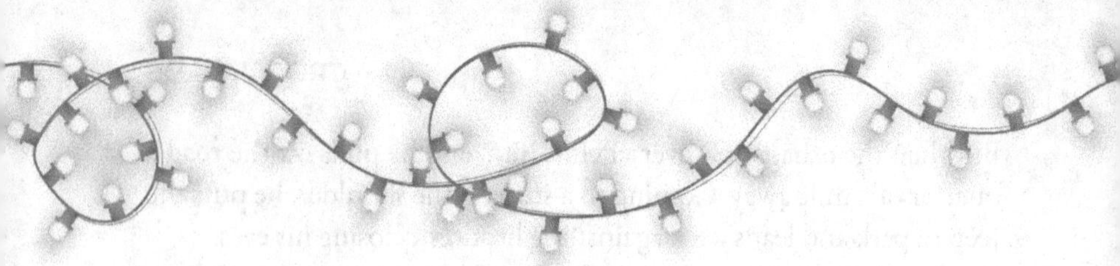

CHAPTER 8
ON THE BOOKSTORE SOUND SYSTEM: "UNDERNEATH THE TREE" BY KELLY CLARKSON

In the name of Christmas shopping, Nicolette is browsing an independent bookstore in Burlington. Her family has so much money that holiday shopping is futile. There's never a thing that anyone really needs.

Still, she's picked out the new Malcom Gladwell for her father and the new Dan Brown for Cam.

For herself, she's getting a nonfiction book and also a copy of Stephen King's *Revival*. She's been waiting for this book for ages, and she's 99 percent sure nobody in her family will have a clue about that. Just in case she's wrong, she'll stash the book in the closet until Christmas morning. And when it fails to appear, she'll be able to read it anyway.

She has other errands to do, too. She has to visit a shoe-repair shop, and her stepmother wants her to pick up several flower arrangements for her annual party. But Nicolette finds herself lingering in the shop, scanning the colorful spines on the shelf. Because books are the most exciting thing in her life at the moment.

After she's shopped the entire store, she finally adds herself to the line of holiday shoppers at the checkout desk, where two cashiers are working furiously.

As the line slowly inches forward, she becomes aware of a tall, dark-haired man across from her who's peering at the books in her stack. Nicolette suddenly gets goosebumps. *Damien*, her mind offers up, even if she hasn't yet seen his face.

She turns and braces herself to see the same bombed-out shell of a person she saw last time at the airport. But that's not what she gets. No, this version of Damien locks her gaze on the first try. And then he smiles. "Nicolette. Wow. Hi."

His hair is longer than she's ever seen it before. He's wearing an unfamiliar puffer jacket. She's relieved he's smiling, because after their last, disastrous meeting, a friendly expression would not be a given.

"Hi," she says stupidly. Then she adds with a little more enthusiasm than necessary, "You look great." She feels herself flush to the hairline. But this is how it's always been. Damien always turns her into a blithering idiot just by showing his face.

It's been, what, nine years since that first day he drove her to the airport? And she's still a babbling mess. But he never seems to mind.

"Listen," he says, cutting through her reverie. "I don't know what you're up to today, but if we ever get through this line, I'd really like to buy you a cup of coffee. You got a half hour for me?"

"Absolutely," she says without even considering it.

Because it's Damien.

———

Her heart runs a race inside her chest as they wait for their coffees at Uncommon Ground on Church Street.

That's normal, right? You see an old acquaintance, and you feel effervescent inside? Like a flute of champagne poured from a newly opened bottle.

You're married, she reminds herself. *Get over your teenage crush.*

"I see a table," he says.

She realizes their drinks are ready. It's too late in the day for coffee, so she'd ordered a decaf. Now she follows him over to a table near the back. This coffee shop is delightfully old school, with wainscoting and tile. She sinks into a chair and takes a sip of her latte.

He settles across from her with a patient smile. "All right. Now catch me up on all the recent episodes of the Nicolette Overland show. I know I've missed a lot."

It's Nicolette Wentworth now, actually. But she doesn't correct him. "Well, to my father's horror, I haven't gone to law school yet. I'm still working as a paralegal in a Boston firm, trying to decide whether to reapply."

He sips his coffee. "If the decision is so hard, maybe that's not what you want."

"Maybe," she agrees. "The problem is that I don't know what else to do. It's not like I'm holding myself back. I'm just uninspired."

"What about your writing?" he asks, raising an eyebrow. "How's that going?"

"Slowly, since you asked." He smiles at her again. "I'm still writing, but it's just a hobby. I don't want to put pressure on my stories like that." Besides, she can't just start referring to herself as a writer. Not with merely a half-finished novel. And nobody else in her life seems to think it's a real career.

"Fair enough. What else is going on? You make it to Vermont very often?"

"Every couple of months or so. Cam and my father both work in commercial real estate, and they have several projects together. So we built a guesthouse on my father's property."

His eyes widen. "*Nice.*"

She wonders if he really thinks it sounds nice, or if he's actually thinking how spoiled she is. Talking to Damien has always made her see her own life differently. He pierces the weird little bubble she lives inside. "We might not get up here much next year, though. Cam—my husband," she clarifies.

He nods.

"—he's exploring a run for congress during the next election cycle."

"Fascinating," Damien says, setting his cup down. "Like a real campaign? Speeches and kissing babies?"

"Yep. Lots of smiley photographs. I now own several pieces of clothing in red, white, and blue."

He chuckles. "Wow. Can he win?"

"Maybe?" The idea makes her feel slightly hysterical. But it would be disloyal to say so. And she already feels disloyal. Cam would hate that she's sitting here with Damien. Not because he's a jealous ogre. He isn't. He'd hate it if he knew how Damien makes her feel.

"So you might move to Washington D.C.?"

"Well, we'd get an apartment there, and also keep our place outside Boston. Life would be pretty chaotic." She feels herself wince. "But that's almost two years away. So I don't have to worry about it yet."

He studies her with calm brown eyes. "That sounds like... a lot. Are you happy?"

It's such a simple question. But an awkward beat goes by before she answers. "Absolutely."

It's the only possible answer, because an Overland doesn't complain.

So she doesn't mention how lonely she is sometimes.

She doesn't explain how Cici has become so distant since Nicolette married her brother.

And she doesn't explain how all her Duke friends are spread all around the world. Or that all their Boston friends are really Cam's college friends. And some of them are snobs.

"I have a steady job, even if it's a little dull," she says. "And a husband who thinks I'm great." *Usually*, she adds silently.

Things have been strained with Cam lately. They've been trying to get pregnant, and it's not working. It's led to some stupid fights. When she suggested they give it a break for a while, because the whole thing stressed her out, he actually said, "I'm in a phase in my life when a man should have children."

And she hurled back, "Do you actually want them? Or would they just make your campaign photos look better?"

They barely spoke to each other for days, and then Cam sent her three dozen roses for their wedding anniversary. They were so beautiful, and she was so tired of being angry that she cried. And then they had sex, and she cried some more in the shower after. Because she didn't want Cam to see.

Now it's almost Christmas, and her stepmother will invariably ask them when they're going to start a family. Like it's any of her business.

Across the table from her, Damien sets down his coffee cup and leans forward in his chair. "Look, it's more fun talking about you than me, but I have something I need to say."

"Okay?" she says, relieved to change the subject. "Hit me."

"First of all, I need to thank you for that box you sent me when I was in the sandbox. It was, like, the best present ever." He gives her a shy smile. "I mean that."

Oh. "You're welcome. I wasn't even sure you'd gotten it."

"Yeah, I bet." He winces. "Look, I need to show you something." He stands up.

She's baffled as he thrusts a hand into his pocket and retrieves something. He sits down again and shows her his palm.

It's her lucky marble. *Right there* in his hand. She barely manages to hold back a gasp.

"I'm sorry," he says quietly. "I got your package. And I started to write you a letter back but..." He looks down into his coffee. "Well, it got heavy. And then I didn't feel I could send it. I've felt bad about it ever since."

"Damien," she says, gobsmacked. "Don't apologize. I'm just glad it reached you."

"It reached me all right." He rolls the marble between his thumb and forefinger. The move looks habitual. Like he's done this many times before. "All that chocolate—I was the most popular guy in the barracks for a week."

Something warm blossoms inside her chest. "That makes me so happy."

He glances up, giving her a fleeting smile. "I'm sorry I let so much time go by without saying so. When I saw you a couple years ago, on that drive from the airport?"

Four years ago, almost exactly, she mentally corrects him. That awkward hour is hard to think about, even after all that time. It makes her cringe to remember the way Cam treated Damien—like the help.

She wanted to snap at her husband, "Don't talk to my friend that way." Except Damien wasn't acting like a friend, he was acting like a robot. She'd tried to forget the whole thing.

"Back then, I wasn't in a good place," Damien says quietly. "It took me a while to, uh, recover from my time in the army. It was ugly there for a little while. I had a full-blown case of PTSD."

"I'm so sorry," she says quietly.

He shrugs. "Don't be. I'm doing much better now. Just wanted to explain myself, because I'm not proud of the way I acted." He glances away, but then meets her gaze again. "You know that book you sent me? The sketchbook?"

"Of course. Did you use it?"

"I did. But I can't show you the sketches. They're gone."

"Oh no. What happened?" She's picturing a bad coffee spill.

"Hard to say. Our outpost was attacked, and I ran out of there to a firefight and never saw my stuff again. My friend died in that battle. The notebook was probably blown up or burned up. Or—who knows? Maybe an insurgent is using it to draw the next great graphic novel."

She doesn't laugh. "I'm sorry, Damien. That sounds terrifying."

"It wasn't great. But I'm here now and a lot of guys aren't. So I can't complain. Or at least I shouldn't." He clears his throat and swallows roughly.

She can feel in the pit of her stomach how bad it must have been to cause him to make that face.

"I think you should take this back," he says, extending the marble. "I think it worked its magic on me already. I'm here in one piece."

Her heart flutters. "All right," she says softly. "I suppose I could use a turn."

He grins as he puts it in her hand. "Here. I'm going to want an update on how this goes."

She pulls a coin purse from her bag and zips the marble carefully inside. "You know, I worried a lot about something happening to you over there. Know why?"

His eyes warm. "Because I'm probably a better taxi driver than a sharpshooter?"

She shakes her head. "No. I'm sure you could do anything if you try. But I gave you that song and lecture about going to school. And in that note you left with Rose you said the G.I. bill was one reason you enlisted.'"

"Overland." He sits back in his chair. "You did *not* make me enlist."

"I know. I know. I don't mean to overstate my own importance. But if you didn't come back, I was going to feel responsible."

"Well, you shouldn't have. I joined up because I didn't want to just...settle. I thought I might look up someday and realize I'm fifty and still stuck in a rut. So, yeah, maybe I got more than I bargained for. It messed me up a little. But I don't really regret it. I saved a lot of money, and I learned some things about myself. And I survived it."

"Well, good. Because it really beats the alternative." She clears her throat.

"No—I meant it in a bigger way than that. Like I *chose* to accept the help that was offered, and let my family take care of me, and then work on myself. And now I can go to school on the damn G.I. bill. If I want to."

"Do you?"

He looks up at the ceiling, thinking. "Yeah, I think I do. But only if I can study art. I'm pretty old for college, so I'll only do it on my own terms, you know? I can study art and drive a taxi. Other people might find that weird, but I don't care what they think. I just need to try."

"You *should* try," she says, startling both of them with her intensity. "I wish I wanted something badly enough to rearrange my whole life for it."

He gives her a strange look. "I guess I'm really good at wanting impossible things."

———

The conversation gets a little less intense after that. The topic moves on to horror movies and books. It's been too long since they compared their favorites.

This is how it's supposed to be, she thinks as he teases her about her taste in B-movies. *Easy.*

It's so easy that she loses track of time. Before she knows it, there're only twenty minutes left to make it to the shop for Veronica's pickup.

"Oh, heck!" she curses. "My stepmother will skin me if I don't come home with her flowers."

"Sorry," Damien says, rising to his feet. "I didn't mean to keep you."

"No! I just lost track of time." She's grabbing her shopping bag off the floor, jumping to her feet. Flustered. "It was so great seeing you."

The hug just happens. Later, she'll try to remember who leaned in first, and she won't be able to decide. All she knows is that she loves the feel of Damien's strong arms around her. He's so sturdy, and it's hard to remember the last time she's been hugged so thoroughly and so well.

But then it's over, and he's leading her toward the door. "It was *really* great to see you," he says. "If you're in Vermont again sometime and you have a free afternoon, call me. We'll hit a bookstore. Have a coffee. Argue about *The Walking Dead*. Wait—" He grabs a card out of his pocket. "In case you don't have my number."

"Thanks," she says brightly. She *really* needs to get to the flower shop, but he's still looking at her intently.

"I've really missed you," he says. "Thank you for taking the time today."

She blushes to her hairline again. "It was entirely my pleasure."

And then she makes herself hurry away.

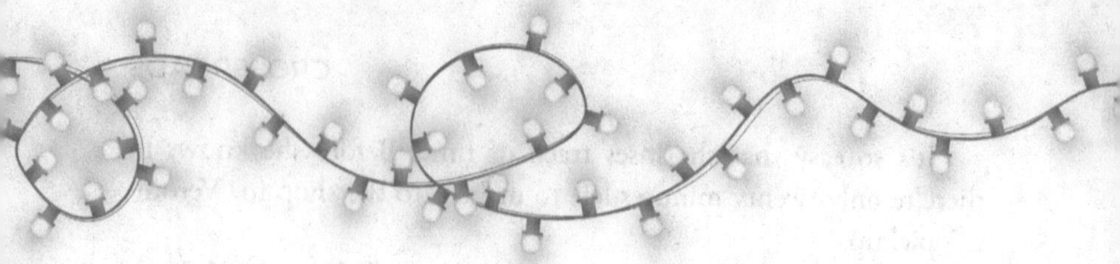

CHAPTER 9
ON THE SOUND SYSTEM: "CHEAP THRILLS" BY SIA

The Gin Mill is a brand-new bar in Colebury, Vermont, just a few miles up the road from the Overland estate. Nicolette has just parked her car outside the brightly lit old mill building with the cheerful neon sign above the door.

Snow and gravel crunch under her feet as she walks toward the front door, and the sound of voices and laughter waft out of the many-paned windows.

She and Cam are in Vermont for the holidays, as usual. One of Cam's college roommates has a ski house at Killington, and whenever they're in Vermont, Cam makes a point to try to see him.

Nicolette, on the other hand, makes a point to stay away. He's not her favorite person.

Tonight, they went to a hockey game over the New Hampshire border—Dartmouth versus Harvard. Nicolette begged off, saying she had some work to finish, and they should go without her.

She spent a lovely few hours by herself, and then forty minutes ago, Cam started texting her, asking her to "show her face" at the bar.

You used to be fun, one of the texts read.

It's a cruel thing to say. But the holidays are just so hard on everybody. Especially when spending time with her father and Veronica means being asked the age-old question—*when are you going to start a family?* As if they haven't ever considered this. As if Nicolette hasn't cried in the bathroom the last two years every time she gets her period.

Cam has been especially irritable since he lost the congressional primary to a statehouse representative who's spent more time in politics. The defeat made a certain amount of sense to Nicolette. But Cam hadn't seen it that way, especially since the candidate was a woman.

That makes it embarrassing, he said to her after giving a half-hearted concession speech to a room full of his supporters. *She's not even pretty*, he added while she cringed inside.

At least he only said it to her. Probably.

It's been a rough couple years, all around.

So tonight, when Cam essentially bullied her into going out, Nicolette gave up her happy spot by the fire in their guesthouse, put down a stack of manuscripts from work and her red pen, and pulled on jeans and a nice top.

The evening has a chance of being fun. She's been curious about the Gin Mill for a while. They're supposed to have a great beer and cider list, with all the local cult brews. So she pulls open the big front door and allows the music and happy voices to wash over her like water.

The inside is charming. A long wooden bar sweeps the left side. There are high-top tables in the center of the expansive space, some booths along one wall, and pool tables along the other. It's not fancy, but the brick walls lend it warmth, and candlelight flickers cheerfully from votives on every table.

Cam and his friend Rick Bellamy are easily spotted at the bar.

"There you are," her husband says when she approaches. "I saved you a seat." He lifts his coat off the barstool between the two of them.

"Thank you," she says.

He makes a show of kissing her sweetly and seating her on the stool. Cam has always been in his element like this—in a social setting, with friends. It's what he does best.

She's always known this about him, too. Cam loves a loud party, while she prefers a cozy dinner with a couple of friends. Or coffee and gossip in a quiet spot. They're mismatched.

She knew this but married him anyway, with the expectation that he'd make her life more exciting. Instead, it's just more exhausting. But that's on her, isn't it?

"Hey buddy!" Cam snaps his fingers at the bartender, and she flinches inside.

Sure enough, when the guy—and he's a looker—finishes up his transaction, he turns to Cam with obvious reluctance. "Help you with something?"

"Can you get my wife a Goldenpour?" Cam says, oblivious. "It's a cult beer," he tells her. "Very hoppy. Lots of citrus and minerals."

She would have preferred to try a cider, but the bartender's mouth is tight, and it's a look she is familiar with. Plenty of bartenders get that look after a night serving Cam. So she doesn't change her order.

When the bartender slides a pint in her direction a moment later, she makes eye contact. "Thank you, sir. I appreciate it."

A hint of warmth relaxes his expression. "My pleasure." Actually, there's something really familiar about this guy, but she can't place it, and she doesn't think they've met.

When she tries the beer, it's interesting. Almost aggressive in its flavor profile. It's not really her thing, but it's still fun to taste something that's been crowned the best beer in the world.

"I like this place," she says, making conversation.

"Yeah," Rick agrees. "It's great to see some new energy in this part of Vermont. We need it so bad."

"Yeah, such a backwater," Cam adds.

Nicolette sees the bartender roll his eyes. He doesn't bother being subtle about it. Hard to blame the guy. She looks away, embarrassed, to study the room. There's a sign on one wall that says, *Jukebox night! Songs $1. All Proceeds Benefit the Colebury Community Skating Rink.*

A few minutes later, an uptempo song kicks off. It's "Cheap Thrills" by Sia, which Nicolette always enjoys.

She's not the only one. The hot bartender picks up an empty beer can—as if he were holding a microphone—and starts to lip sync the lyrics.

The cocktail waitress laughs and bats her eyelashes at him.

Cam and his friend are deep into their hockey talk. When one of them stops to take a breath, she says, "I'm going to put some money in the jukebox. Any particular requests?"

"Anything you want, doll," Cam says, a possessive hand on her back.

"But no girly shit," says Rick, reinforcing her dislike of him. Cam is always the worst version of himself when he's with Rick.

She threads her way through the bustling room toward the jukebox on the far wall. She digs three singles out of her pocketbook and feeds every one of them into the machine. Then she chooses three Taylor Swift songs. Because Rick won't notice. And also fuck that guy.

"Shake It Off" comes on, and she smiles to herself.

But now she's spent all her singles and still isn't ready to go back to the bar. Taking her time, she circuits the big room, taking in the dartboard, where a cheerfully cutthroat game is underway, and then the pool table where a long, lean man is lining up a tricky shot, the cue balanced on the knuckles of one hand.

Her heart recognizes him before her brain catches up. "Damien," she says suddenly.

The shot misfires. He turns awkwardly around. But when he sees who's called his name, his face breaks into the most beautiful smile. "Nicky Nicole! Where've you been all this time?"

Her face heats. Because Damien.

"I never called," she says clumsily. *Although I think about you often.*

Every time she's standing in a bookstore, she thinks of running into him in Burlington, and the lovely hour they spent catching up over coffee. Like a little vacation. She'd felt refreshed and optimistic afterward.

"I noticed that." He leans against the pool table and smiles. "Been busy?"

"I have," she says, leaping on the excuse. "Got a new job, and it's going really well."

His expression lights up instantly. "Whoa, buddy," he says, leaning forward. "Tell me everything. I'm losing this game anyway." He makes a vague gesture toward the balls on the table.

"He forfeits!" says the guy he was playing against. "That's unheard of. I can't imagine what on Earth would make you do that. Oh wait, a woman." The guy grins.

"Shut it, Benito," Damien mumbles.

Nicolette recognizes the name. Benito is one of his younger siblings. She never forgets a detail when it comes to Damien. "Sorry," she says.

Benito grins. "Don't be sorry. This is very entertaining for me. They should serve popcorn here. I'm going to suggest it."

"Let's hear about this job," Damien says, ignoring his brother. "Is it The One?"

"I think so. I'm working as the assistant to a literary agent. The salary is atrocious, but I'm basically paid to read books all day."

His eyes widen. "Great scam, Overland."

"I know, right? It's a bit like diving for pearls. Most of what we're sent is terrible, but every once in a while, I open up a shell and find a treasure." And she loves it. Finally—a job she looks forward to every morning.

"Congratulations," he says, his brown eyes gleaming. She can tell he understands that it's a big deal to her. "You here with your family?"

She blinks. The joy of seeing Damien caused her to forget all about Cam. This is exactly why she never called Damien. She still has that business card. Both of them, actually—the one he gave her a decade ago and the one he gave her last year. But she can't call. It wouldn't be right. You can't just go out for coffee with a man who's always made your heart beat faster.

That's not coffee, that's yearning.

And now he's asked her a question that she's failing to answer. "Yup," she says, several beats late. "I'm here with my husband. You've, uh, met him. And his friend."

Damien nods. And then he swallows. "Well, you have a good night. Always great to see you."

"You too," she says, trying and failing to keep the wistfulness out of her voice.

Then she gives him one more smile. A good one. And goes back to Cam.

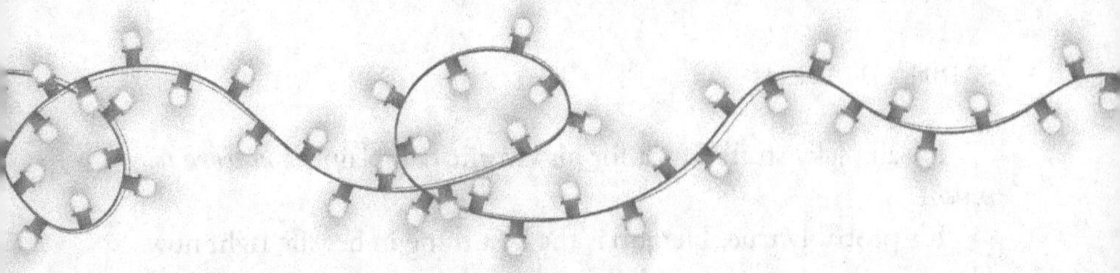

CHAPTER 10
SOUNDTRACK: LONELY SILENCE

On the night after the next Christmas, Nicolette stands at the counter of the guesthouse on her father's estate, pouring herself a glass of sparkling water. It's already eleven thirty, and all the lights are out at the main house up the hill. It's so quiet that she can hear every little crackle of the fire in the fireplace.

With her soda in hand, she returns to the sofa in front of the fire. A book by Stephen King is waiting for her. This one is called *End of Watch*. It's pretty dark, which suits her mood right now. It's hard to stare your troubled marriage in the eye when you're worrying about an antagonist's supernatural talents.

Once again, she bought the book for herself. Her father and step-mother only gift her things that they wished she liked, and books aren't Cam's style. He likes to make splashier gestures—like jewelry and lingerie. Or once, a new car.

It's so quiet that she can hear the bubbles in her soda and the dry sound when she turns a page. Usually, she's a fan of silence. But tonight, she just can't settle.

She and Cam have been fighting again. He's been depressed and anxious ever since losing his bid for congress. And his favorite coping mechanism seems to be picking fights over nothing. He doesn't like her choice of restaurants or vacations. She takes up too much of the closet with her clothes.

It's all picky stuff, except for his favorite complaint. *You work too much.*

It's probably true. Her job is the best thing in her life right now. Her marriage is rocky, and she still can't get pregnant, although they're officially seeking treatment for infertility.

The specialist says she doesn't ovulate as regularly as some women. But part of the problem also lies with Cam's sperm count, and he's become *very* touchy about it.

Nicolette understands. Having a low sperm count doesn't exactly reinforce a guy's manliness. But the issue of their infertility has become a festering wound in their marriage. Instead of bringing them together as a team, it's the crackling tension that underlies every little decision.

She takes a sip of her soda and turns another page. To mark her place in the book, she's using Damien's business card. She found it here in the guesthouse when they'd arrived for Christmas a few days ago.

It's not like she thinks of Damien all the time. But the holidays are an exception. As soon as string lights appear all over New England, she thinks of riding along with him after a flight to Vermont. It was once a tradition—like putting up the tree or making gingerbread.

She wonders whether he went Christmas shopping on Church Street again this year, and whether he thought of her at all.

Once—after they'd had coffee together—she'd actually dreamed about Damien. It was a sex dream, set in the backseat of his Jeep. So ridiculous.

Still, she keeps the business cards. Because you never know when someone will need a taxi. And a crush remains a crush for a reason—it's low-stakes. A crush doesn't have to stand the tests of marriage and commitment. A crush has never eaten the last cookie and left his plate in the sink for you to rinse.

A crush has never gotten so drunk on date night that you tipped the waiter a hundred extra dollars as compensation for his rudeness.

A crush never stopped speaking to you for a week after you got your period again.

She holds the card by its edges and studies the drawing for the hundredth time, admiring the clean lines of the car and the jolly shape of its headlights.

The kitchen door opens suddenly. "*Nicolette!*" Cam bellows.

Guilty, she shoves the card into the book and closes the cover. "In the living room!" She's surprised that Cam has returned home after going for drinks somewhere with Rick Bellamy. She'd assumed he'd end up crashing at the Bellamy house, like he often does.

"Nicolette!" he calls again. "Help me make an ice pack?"

Ice pack? *What the…?* She tosses the book aside and hurries into the little kitchen. "God, Cam! What happened?" His eye is swelled shut.

"Bar fight," he says, struggling against the sleeves of his jacket. And losing.

"Let me get that." She eases the jacket off his body. "What happened?"

"Some asshole just wanted a fight, I guess, and I was convenient. At least I got one good punch in."

She grabs his hands and inspects them for damage. There isn't any, thank goodness. "Did you call the cops?"

He gives his head a drunken shake. "And there's no point. Guy was a townie. He was friends with the bartender, and I'm a flat-lander, you know?"

She does know. Sometimes there's tension between the weekend people and the real Vermonters. And, well, sometimes Cam acts like an entitled nightmare and makes everything worse. But that doesn't mean they can punch him.

"Are you hurt anywhere else? It's not too late to call the police." She gets ice from the dispenser in the fridge and rolls the ice cubes inside a clean dish towel. She offers it to Cam. "I wish we had some frozen peas. I could look in Veronica's kitchen." She glances over to the main house, which is dark and silent.

"This is fine," he grunts, carefully applying her homemade ice pack to his face. "Veronica doesn't seem like the type to have peas in her freezer."

This is probably true. "But you're going to have a shiner. How did you even get home?"

"Bellamy drove me. We'll have to pick up the car in the morning."

"Okay," she agrees quickly. "No problem. I could call the taxi service..."

"No," he barks. "I'll ask your dad. He won't mind."

"Okay," she says again. She takes Cam's handsome face in two hands and studies it. "Your nose looks okay. It's just the eye."

"I'm sorry," he whispers, looking into her eyes. "I know I don't deserve you."

Her heart softens, and she gives his chin a stroke with her thumb. All she ever wanted was for him to look at her just like he's doing now. Thoroughly, and tenderly. "It's okay, Cam. You'll look like Rocky for a few days, but everything is going to be fine."

He gives her a tiny smile, with more humility than she's seen on his face in... well, ever. "I love you."

"I love you, too," she says. And right this second, she really means it.

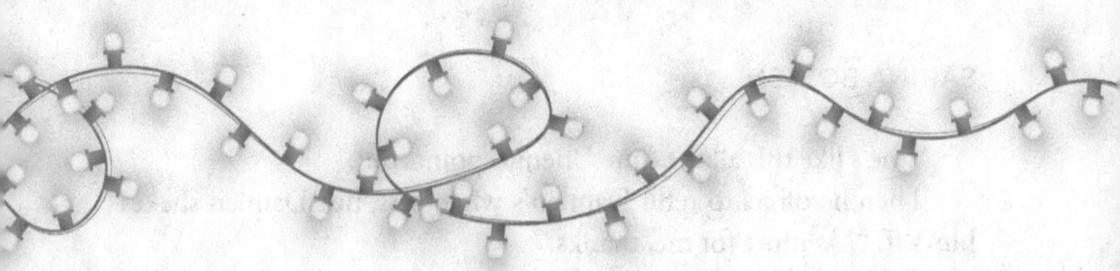

CHAPTER 11
SOUNDTRACK: AULD LANG SYNE, AND ROSSI FAMILY SQUABBLING

Damien is seated at his uncles' dining table, nursing a glass of wine, trying to unwind. It's New Year's Eve, and he's well fed. Everything is fine.

Mostly.

But even under the best of circumstances, a Rossi family gathering is not the most relaxing place in the world. The twins Benito and Zara, who are three years younger than Damien, are bickering over the definition of rock music. Or something. While his brother Alec is trying to convince his uncle Otto to invest in a new brewery business idea.

"I don't want any part of your get-rich-quick scheme," his uncle grumbles. "Talk to me when you have a real plan."

"There's more lasagna," his mother says, offering Damien the serving spoon. "And more sausages."

"Mom, I'm stuffed," he says. Did she not see all the food he just ate?

"I still worry about you," she says.

"He eats plenty, Ma," Benito says, sitting down beside him. "Relax."

"I'll go get the dessert," she says, and Damien groans. He hasn't left room for dessert.

"The holidays make people crazy," Zara stage whispers, grabbing the lasagna pan to clear it from the table.

"She's like this all the time," Benito points out.

Then he offers to refill Damien's wine glass, but Damien shakes him off. "No more for me, thanks."

Benito tops up his own glass and sits down. "You doing okay?"

"Sure," he says, irritated at the intrusion. He has a big, nosy family and they have been asking after his welfare since he got home from his second deployment, battered and sad.

And, yeah, things were bad for a little while there. But they're better now.

Mostly.

"Look," Benito says in a low voice. "I heard about your little adventure the other night."

Damien's stomach tightens. "Who told you?"

"I did," Zara says, reemerging from the kitchen.

"Thanks," he says tightly. "Real helpful." The twins have always been close, though. Except when they're not. He shouldn't be too surprised that Zara spilled the beans.

"Any cops knocking on your door?" she asks.

He shakes his head and glances toward the kitchen door, hoping his mother isn't hearing any of this.

"Are you struggling again?" Benito asks.

Once again, it's not Damien's favorite topic. But he resents the question ten percent less coming from his youngest brother, because Benny tried the army, too. He came home with a knife wound but a lot less PTSD than Damien. "I'm not really struggling, I promise. This was an isolated incident. And, no, I haven't heard from law enforcement."

"Law enforcement?" his mom yelps, appearing in the doorway with a chocolate cake. "Who are the cops visiting and why?"

"Damien got into a bar fight," Zara chirps.

He groans loudly. "Christ, Zara. You said you'd keep quiet."

"Yeah—in front of anyone who'd get you in trouble," she clarifies. "Mom's not going to report you."

"A bar fight?" his mother says. "Damien *why?*"

Great. He's just spent the whole week trying not to think about it. And now his whole family is staring at him, looking for answers.

"It wasn't just a random act of violence," he explains, sounding as sullen as he feels. "There was this guy at the Gin Mill, getting drunk and hitting on a woman."

"That's nothing new," his brother Alec says. And he'd know because the Gin Mill is Alec's bar.

"Yeah, I realize that." Damien sounds tired to his own ears. "The problem is that the guy is married to a friend of mine."

"Sakes alive," his grouch of an uncle says. "Why put your nose in? Sounds like it was none of your business."

Damien already knows that it's none of his business, but he still resents the comment. "It wasn't just flirting, Otto. He was really going for it. They were going to go back to her place. He was trying to get Connor's attention to close out his tab."

"And Connor was totally ignoring him," Zara adds cheerfully. "We've all served this prick before, and we know he's a shitty tipper."

Otto reaches for the stack of cake plates. "Maybe the customers would tip better if you didn't ignore them."

"Maybe you can kiss my ass," his sister says under her breath, and Benito chuckles.

"Who's this friend?" their mother asks. "The one with the skanky husband?"

"She's... You don't know her," Damien says quickly. "She's a taxi customer. Didn't go to school around here."

"Rich girl," Zara says. "Super pretty. Way out of Damien's league. She's the one who asked me for his address when he was in the sandbox."

All their faces swing in his direction again. "Is this an ex?" Benito asks.

"No way. But she's a *friend*, like I said. So I put down my pool cue—"

"He was losing to me anyway," Zara inserts.

"—and told the guy I'd go around behind the bar to help close out his tab, because *his wife must be expecting him at home*."

Everyone cackles.

"You should have seen the other woman's face," Zara says. "I wish I had a video. She clearly had no idea he was married. And now the guy is getting all pissed off, telling Damien he doesn't know what he's talking about. And Damien holds up his phone and offers to call the guy's wife to straighten it out."

"I'm so sorry I missed this," Alec says with a chuckle.

"You should be." Zara hoots. "The dude had no idea who Damien was, either. You could see his wheels turning as he tried to figure out how bad this could get. He got so frustrated he grabbed Damien by the jacket."

"Now that's just dumb," their mother says as she cuts into the cake with a chef's knife. "There aren't that many people tougher than a Rossi."

"It *was* dumb," Zara agrees. "This dude looked like an accountant."

"Real estate investor," Damien mumbles, picturing Cam's Hollywood-smug face. He's all cheekbones and dark gold hair. The kind of guy who always gets the girl whether he deserves her or not.

"Yeah, he looked expensive," Zara says. "But now he's expensive with a big black eye. I hope he doesn't sue you."

"He won't," Benito chimes in. "Because then he'd have to explain it to his wife."

"Good point." Alec helps himself to a piece of cake. "But you could still tell the wife. Are you close to this girl?"

Damien shakes his head. "Not that close."

"Although he'd like to be," Zara says.

He gives his sister a grumpy look. "Don't make assumptions."

"Come *on*. I know you. The whole reason this bothers you so much is that the guy doesn't deserve her."

He closes his weary eyes and sighs. "No, he doesn't. But that doesn't mean I want to tell her that she's probably married to a serial cheater. He had all the moves." *We'll have to go to your place because my younger sister is staying with me.* Damien had felt sick listening to it. The guy probably doesn't even have a younger sister.

"If it was my marriage, I'd want to know," Alec says.

"Like anyone would ever marry you," somebody mumbles.

"Honey, I bet she *does* know," their mother says. "Even if she hasn't admitted it to herself yet, on some level she knows who she married."

That shuts all of them up for a second, because their mother has a lot of experience with bad marriages.

But Damien isn't sure if this applies to Nicolette. If it were any other woman, he might agree. But she's the most open, trusting person he's ever met. She expects the best of people.

Plus—and this thought makes his stomach churn—she bought a pregnancy book that time in Burlington. What if she's pregnant? Hell, she might already have a child.

He puts his elbows on the table and sighs. "What if she didn't even believe me?"

"Wouldn't there be a security video?" Zara asks.

"*Savage*," says Benito, high-fiving his twin.

"There's probably some footage," Alec agrees. "What it shows depends where he and the woman were standing. We can check tomorrow."

Damien buries his head in his hands. God, this is getting so convoluted. Even if there is footage, what is he supposed to do?

Here are some pictures of your cheating husband that I captured off my brother's security system. Sorry I gave him a black eye. After you call a divorce lawyer, want to have dinner?

He looks up suddenly. "There's no way I can tell her this. It's too self-serving. I don't know anything about their marriage. They might even have a baby."

Zara winces. And then her eyes dart over to the corner of the room, where her own toddler is sleeping in a Pack'n Play. "I guess you can't be the one to tell her," she says sadly.

"I don't see how I can," he agrees.

But then she adds something under her breath that he doesn't quite catch. It sounds like "Although maybe someone else could."

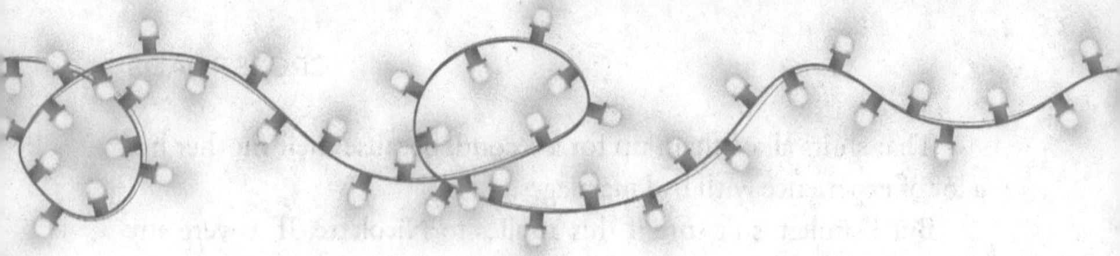

CHAPTER 12
ON THE RADIO: "BLUE CHRISTMAS" BY ELVIS PRESLEY

"Why this song?" Damien grumbles to himself as he sets Zara's dining table. "Isn't it a little early for Christmas tunes?"

"It's Thanksgiving," one of his brothers replies, as if that makes it okay.

He places another fork on another snowy napkin and moves on down the line.

"Look, I need you to trade jobs," his sister says. "The baby is cranky, and I need to get the potatoes in." She holds up his nephew —Micah, five months old—and pushes the baby against his sternum.

"Cranky, huh?" Damien takes the baby and leans him up against his chest. "And you thought of me?"

"Yup," she says unapologetically. "He's fed, but he needs a nap. Dave is on a call. Benito is sharpening my carving knife, and Mom is making gravy. And Alec is...I don't even know. Probably sexting May in a corner somewhere."

Micah starts to cry. *Uh-oh.* "What does Micah enjoy these days?"

"Well, driving. And rocking. Sing him a song. I'll be right in the kitchen."

Damien carries the crying baby in a circuit of Zara's lovely home, while the little guy balls his tiny hands into fists and rubs his eyes.

"*Hush little baby, don't say a word. Mama's gonna buy you a mockingbird,*" he sings. God, it's an odd song. It starts weird, and then rapidly escalates from birds to diamond rings.

Damien would like a word with the composer.

Micah doesn't mind, though. He's gone from full-on crying to merely fussy. And his eyes are drooping.

"You could try putting him in the car seat," Zara calls as he passes through the kitchen. "Or the crib, but he's more likely to protest."

From his pocket his phone lets out a particular ping that means someone wants an Uber. By force of habit, he reaches into his pocket to check on the fare.

Until last year, there were no Uber drivers in this part of Vermont. And now there's only a few of them. Damien was the very first one. And he isn't about to drive on Thanksgiving.

But then he sees the address on Old Route 16 and does a double take. The ride is for *Nicolette O.* And she's requesting a lift to central Colebury, which is only a couple miles from her house.

Nicolette. Hell. It's been almost a year since he punched her husband, and two years since he saw her last. But he thinks about her a lot, as always.

He does another lap past Zara's kitchen fireplace, and the phone chirps again.

"Is that Uber?" Benito asks. "On Thanksgiving?"

"Yeah, I know. But it's *her*."

He doesn't even name her. But every head in the busy kitchen turns to stare.

"No way," his mother says.

"What does she want?" Benito asks.

He shrugs.

"Go," Zara says, making a shooing motion with her wooden spoon. "But take the baby with you. He'll be out like a light."

"Really? You all think I should accept this ride on Thanksgiving?"

They all stare.

He looks at the screen again. Her avatar is a picture of her sweet face. She's smiling.

He hits *Accept Fare* with his thumb.

———

Ten minutes later, he turns into the driveway and finds the gates are standing open. That's a first.

Proceed to the guesthouse in back, the ride order said. So he follows the new driveway around the main house, past a ridiculously large garage, and finds a small home nestled into the pine trees beyond.

It's beautiful, just like everything else on the Overland property. He puts the car in park and waits.

The door opens, and Damien drinks her in. Her hair is tied up in a messy knot on top of her head. She's wearing a light blue sweater that looks as soft as a cloud. And her kissable mouth is... well, it's frowning at him. Then she raises a hand and beckons.

Maybe she has luggage? For a trip into town? He kills the engine and opens the door.

"Hi," she says, crossing her arms and stepping back.

"Hi," he echoes. "Is there luggage?"

She meets his gaze, and hers is a guilty one. "No. Um. No luggage. I don't actually need a ride. My car is right there in the garage." She points.

"I'm so confused right now," he admits. "Why am I here?"

Her frown becomes stern. "I'm angry at you. And I heard you're the only Uber driver in this part of Vermont. Please come in."

A startled laugh escapes from his chest. "Okay? Sure. But I have to get someone first."

She gives him a look of pure confusion. "Who?"

But he's already trotting back to the car and pulling the basket-like car seat out off the backseat.

She takes a gasping breath when he rounds the vehicle with Micah, who's passed out in the seat. "Oh my God, you have a *baby*?"

"This is Micah," he says quietly. "My nephew. Zara's second child."

Her eyes tear up for some reason. "He's so beautiful."

"Hey," he whispers. "Are you okay?"

She looks up to meet his gaze and shakes her head. Then she turns to walk inside, and he follows, baby carrier in hand, closing the door against the cold behind himself.

Inside, he finds himself standing in a tidy little kitchen. Nicolette is filling a teapot with water, but her hands are shaky. She abandons it in the sink. "I'm sorry," she says. "I shouldn't have called. It's Thanksgiving. But I'm so..." She sighs, and her shoulders droop. "I'm *angry*."

"I'm getting that," he says, setting the baby down gently, so he doesn't wake. "Why don't you tell me what's wrong?"

She steps away from the stove and kneels down in front of Micah's sleeping form. "It's harder to yell at you now that you brought a sleeping baby out in the cold to drive me somewhere. On a holiday. I feel like a heel."

"He seems pretty okay with it," Damien says. "If you talk fast, I might not even miss Thanksgiving dinner." He reaches down and takes her hand. "Come on, Overland. Let's have this out."

When she rises, she looks sadder than he's ever seen her. The urge to wrap her in a hug is strong. But he leads her by the hand into the living room, where there's a sofa in front of a fireplace.

They sit down, and she bites her lip. "This felt easier when I was summoning you in a rage."

"What's my crime?" he asks simply.

She braces her hands on her knees. "In January, I received an envelope in the mail. In Boston. Photos of my husband hitting on a woman in a bar."

His stomach twists. "Yeah, I might know something about that."

She frowns. "I couldn't tell from the photos where the bar was. And the note only said, *Sorry. You seem like a nice person.* That's it. No return address, no signature. No other details." She gives him an arch look. "So I didn't mention anything to Cam..."

His heart drops. If anything terrible happened to her this year, he'll feel terrible.

"But I'm not an idiot. So I hired a private detective to watch my husband. It took the guy six weeks to catch him going to a hotel with a stranger he picked up in a bar."

He briefly drops his head into his hands. "Fuck."

"Exactly. And I have the photos to prove it. So I hired a lawyer to start on my divorce. I moved out one day while Cam was at work. I left a copy of some of my favorite photos of him on the table." She rolls her eyes.

A surge of pride fills his chest. "You're such a badass, Overland."

She shrugs. "I was shocked, but also not? That doesn't sound sensible. But the minute I saw those photos, I got it. I still didn't know who sent them, but I knew that person went to a lot of trouble. And then it took all year to get divorced." She pins him with a gaze. "Do you know when I figured out who sent me those photos?"

He shakes his head.

"*Today*," she snaps. "You dickhead."

Something is probably wrong with him, but hearing her say "dickhead" actually makes him grin.

"Why are you smiling?" she hisses.

"Because you're so..." He flails his arms. "So *you*. So unbroken by all the shit that gets thrown at you. It was my sister, by the way. She sent the photos."

Her eyes are still angry, but her mouth softens. "Oh."

"Why today, though?"

She rubs her temples. "I found another set of the same photos. I think Zara must have sent one set to Boston and another here."

"*Oh*. Like she was covering all the bases?"

"Right. And Cam must have found the Vermont set before I did. Today I discovered them torn up at the bottom of a shoebox in our closet." She jerks a thumb toward the bedroom door.

"Shit," he says as it dawns on him. "He must have thought he'd gotten away with it."

She lets out a bark of bitter laughter. "Right. Except that man has *never* taken out the trash. Not even once in his life. So he couldn't even destroy the evidence properly. *God*, Damien. I married him based on a crush from when I was fourteen. And I'd still be married to him if it weren't for your sister."

He winces.

"Why didn't you just tell me?"

Why, indeed. "I felt guilty. I wanted you to know the truth, but I didn't feel like I could be the one who wrecked your perfect life."

"My perfect life?" she demands. "Seriously? Did you not hear what I just said? Why didn't you just tell me? I thought we were friends." Her lip quivers.

"Oh honey, we *are*," he says forcefully. And somehow, he's slid across the sofa to pull her into a hug. "I didn't know what to do."

She lets out a sniffle and melts into his chest.

She smells nice, like flowers, his stupid brain offers up. Yeah, real helpful. "See, it was none of my business how your marriage worked. But I was just so fucking mad at him. And I'd already punched him in the face."

She stiffens. Then she pulls away and looks up at him. "Omigod, really? That was *you?*"

He nods. "I was there that night at the Gin Mill, playing pool with Zara. My brother Alec owns that place."

"*Oh*," she says heavily.

"Yeah, I'm there a lot. Sometimes I pick up bartending shifts, but that night I was just hanging out. And there was Cam—picking up that woman in the photos. I was a dick about it. I told his date he was married. But I didn't lay hands on him until he grabbed me by the jacket and cocked a fist."

Her eyes widen. "God, what an idiot he is. Fighting you over a one-night stand?"

"Yeah. Well." He sighs. "I punched him. But I couldn't be the one to tell you."

"I still don't understand why not."

Seriously? He puts his head in his hands. "Isn't it obvious? I didn't want to be the guy who blew up your life, Nicolette. Because I've been so jealous of Cam. I've had it bad for you for fifteen years."

He expects a gasp. Or maybe laughter. But there's nothing. She's silent. Like, really silent. Maybe not even breathing.

He lifts his head to check, and she's just staring at him. "That's not true," she whispers.

"Oh, it is." He chokes back a nervous laugh. "Maybe this hadn't occurred to you, but I don't take most clients Christmas shopping. Or out for pizza. I don't toss my nephew's baby seat into the car just for anyone who wants a ride on Thanksgiving. It's only you, Nicky Nicole."

She gulps. "You never *said* anything."

"Yeah, no kidding. I was the broke guy living in a double-wide. You were the rich girl in the mansion."

Her eyes bulge. "Do I strike you as someone who judges people by how much money they have?"

Hell. "No," he admits. "But it's not just about money. I was the taxi driver with a high school education. And you were the college girl who'd seen the world. I couldn't imagine why you'd be interested in me. Not to mention that we were friends. And I valued that friendship a lot, even if I wasn't very good at showing it."

She blows out a breath. "None of that should have prevented you from telling me the truth."

"You're right, and I'm sorry." He shrugs. "I was all tied up in knots about it. But Zara was there that night too, so I let her decide. And she thought you needed to know."

"She's right." Her eyes fill. "I did need to know."

She looks so sad that Damien pulls her in for another hug. And he's a little bit horrified by the way she starts to cry into his flannel shacket. Because he's not good at this. He's been single for much of the last fifteen years, because it's hard to find love when you're gone for your favorite taxi client.

"I'm...sorry." She sniffles.

"It's okay. This is washable."

She laughs against his chest, and he kisses her on top of the head.

Mmm flowers, his asshole brain says.

He rests his chin on the spot where he's just kissed her and pats her back. Maybe he's not so bad at this. Not really.

Then his phone pings.

"Do you have to get that?" she asks.

He slips it out of his pocket. "It's my sister, telling me she wants to serve dinner. Come on." He takes her hand and stands up. "Come with me. It's Thanksgiving. Have you already eaten turkey?"

"Theoretically," she says, looking weepy. "But I kind of left in the middle of dinner. My dad is pissed off that I divorced Cam. They have a lot of business together."

Damien closes his eyes for a brief second and fantasizes about punching Mr. Overland, a man he's never met. "Your father is putting *business* in front of your mental wellbeing?"

She cringes. "It's what he does best. When I told him Cam was a serial cheater, he said, 'That's just how some men are.'"

"The terrible ones," Damien says gruffly. "Jesus. Come with me, okay? You shouldn't be alone right now, and I have a very loud family. It's like a TV family, but worse."

"Are you sure it's okay if I just show up? On a major holiday?"

"Oh, I'm positive," he says. "Let's go."

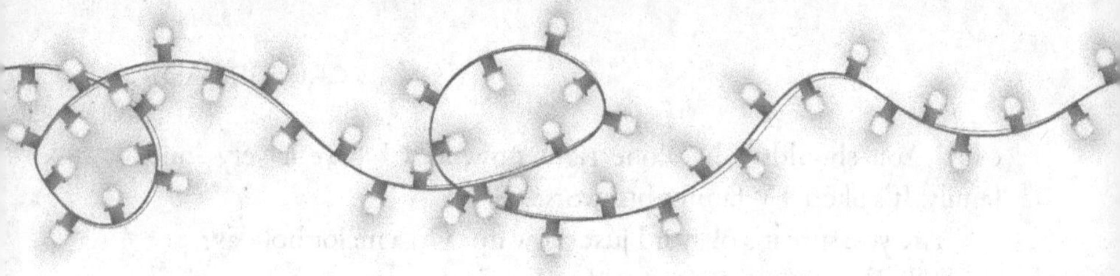

CHAPTER 13
ON THE RADIO: SIMPLE GIFTS

This ought to be really weird, is all Nicolette can think as she rides along to crash Damien's Thanksgiving holiday.

But somehow, it's not. It feels like hitting the reset button on her life. Cam doesn't exist today. Not when she's seated snugly beside Damien as he steers them down another country road.

Sitting here always felt right to her, and today is no different.

The Jeep slows down across from the Busy Bean coffee shop. Damien makes a turn toward the center of Colebury. From the backseat comes a small complaint.

"Oh, buddy," Damien says, reaching into the back without removing his eyes from the road. "We're almost there."

When Nicolette glances over her shoulder, something in her heart gives way. The baby has hair the color of a darkened penny and a firm grip on Damien's finger.

See? She's not alone in thinking that Damien is easy company. Both she and the baby seem to grasp this on a gut level.

His family, though... "Are you sure I won't be imposing?"

He chuckles. "No such thing. My mom is the kind of person who cooks twice as much food as necessary, every time, hoping someone extra turns up to justify her efforts. You'll see."

It's not the food she's really worried about, though. She probably looks like something the cat dragged in. The combination of her messy divorce, her father's anger, and too little sleep has put dark circles beneath her eyes. And she's wearing her most faded jeans with an old wool fisherman's sweater that had belonged to her grandfather.

What will they think?

The Jeep climbs the hill into central Colebury. A moment later, Damien slows to a stop in front of a Tudor home on the town square. "Nice house," she whispers.

"My sister's partner played professional hockey. They do pretty well." He retracts his hand from the back and puts the car in park.

The baby squawks, which seems to put Damien into a higher gear. He hops out of the Jeep and rounds the vehicle to pop open the back door first, clucking at the frustrated baby. He unsnaps him from the carrier and lifts him out. "See?" he says, holding him to his chest. "We're back. No need to shout."

The baby looks up at him with wide brown eyes. Then he rests a trusting cheek against Damien's flannel and curls his little fingers into the fabric.

Now she's jealous of a baby, because she knows how comfortable it is right there on Damien's shoulder. "Let me carry the baby seat," she says, climbing out of the Jeep.

"I got it," he says, easily grasping it in his free hand and hip-checking the door shut. "Let's go have some mashed potatoes."

"Does he eat solid food yet?" she asks.

"I don't even know," he says, giving her a smile over the infant's head. "I was talking about me."

She laughs as he opens the front door into a gracious entryway with views into a comfortable living room. The clink of dishes and the sound of conversation wafts through from a dining room just out of view.

"I'll take your coat," he says. And then, in a louder voice, he calls out to his family. "We're back! I brought a friend."

A sudden silence in the other room makes Nicolette's stomach bottom out. "Maybe I shouldn't..."

In one smooth move, Damien sets down the baby carrier, drops her coat onto a hook and takes her hand. "Guys, this is Nicolette. Let's find one more chair."

He guides her into the dining room, where at least ten people are crowded around a big table. She can feel the flush creep up on her face. They've left an open chair for Damien, but just barely.

She shouldn't have come.

Several people stand up at once, and everyone starts talking. A hot redheaded guy scoops the baby out of Damien's arms. "How's my little man?"

"I'll find another chair," says Zara.

"No, don't," says another tall, good-looking man from the other end of the room. And she recognizes him from the Gin Mill. He must be Alec, the brother who owns the bar. "I'm supposed to be at the Shipleys' in a half hour for their Thanksgiving," he says.

"You double-dipper," chides an older woman who must be Damien's mom.

"Don't hate the player, hate the game," Alec says, picking up his plate and water glass. "You're just jealous. Take my seat, Nicolette." He points at the chair. "It's right next to Damien's. I'll grab you a fresh plate."

She flushes a little deeper, but Damien guides her around the table, unconcerned, and pulls out her chair. So she sits.

"This is most of my family," he says. Then he rattles off a string of names as he gestures around the table. "And this is Nicolette," he says, reaching for the water jug and pouring her a glass. "Be nice to her because you all are a *lot*."

"Hi, Nicolette!" they all say at once.

She laughs nervously. "Hi. Wow. When I was a kid, I always wanted a big family."

"But now she knows better," somebody mumbles.

"Thank you for making space for me," she says, her voice suddenly cracking. "I was having a rough day. I'm recently divorced..." She glances at Zara, who winks. "And Damien wouldn't let me sit home by myself."

"You shouldn't," his mother, Maria, declares. "Someone pass them the turkey platter. I made so much food. Why is nobody having seconds?"

"Because we're still having firsts!" someone yells. "Chill, Mom."

Beside her, Damien gives her a grin while quietly filling two plates with food. And although she hadn't felt hungry a minute ago, Nicolette's stomach rumbles.

"Here," he says, putting a plate in front of her. "Now eat up so my mother has less to complain about."

———

Nicolette spends a couple of hours fending off more food and drink and listening to the Rossi family making bets on various football and hockey games. Damien's mom is warm and funny, and his siblings are, too. Benito's girlfriend is very sweet. There are also two uncles, one of them grumpy, the other one reserved. And in addition to the baby, there's a preschool-aged niece with fiery red hair and an impish smile.

It's the best kind of chaos. Nicolette's favorite part is watching Damien in his natural environment. His role seems to be the quiet sibling. He listens more than he talks. But he's the same Damien she's always known—loose and comfortable. Ready with a smile.

And every time they pass him the baby, she feels a little light-headed. What is it about a strong man holding an infant that's so attractive?

Eventually, though, she starts yawning. It's been a long and stressful day.

Damien notices on the second yawn. "Let me get you home, okay? This family is a lot."

"Take some leftovers!" his mom calls from the next room, where she's doing a jigsaw puzzle with her granddaughter.

"Make her a take-home pack," Zara says, nudging her brother. "I want to talk to Nicolette for a second."

"Zara—" Damien protests.

But Zara is already leading Nicolette toward the entryway. "Can I have a word?"

"Of course," Nicolette says. Because what choice does she have?

They stop in the foyer, and Zara drops her voice. "Look, it was me who sent you those photos."

"He told me," she whispers back.

"You should know how upset he was, though." Zara pins her

with big brown eyes just like her brother's. "Damien is tough, but it takes a *lot* to make him take a swing at somebody. And he didn't want to tell you. He said—and I'll never forget this—'I just want her to be happy. She deserves it.'"

Nicolette makes a low noise of dismay. "It's not his fault I married a tool."

She shrugs. "No kidding. But I just wanted you to know how much he cares about you." Then she hands Nicolette her coat as Damien's footsteps approach.

"What are you two talking about?" he asks, coming into view with a small shopping bag.

"Nicolette was just telling me that I have the cutest children ever. And that you should babysit for me on Saturday night."

Damien snorts. "I *just* babysat for you on Tuesday. And Saturday night is a good taxi night."

"It was worth a shot," she says, holding the door open for both of them. "Nice to see you, Nicolette. Don't be a stranger."

"I won't," she says, and realizes it might even be true. "Thank you for everything tonight. I don't have very many friends in Vermont. And I'm going to be here for a while."

"Come over for hockey night next weekend. Damien—make that happen."

"Will do," he says, leading the way down the steps.

He opens the Jeep's passenger door for her, like a gentleman, and tucks her inside. Then he rounds the car, climbs into the driver's seat, and starts the engine. While it's warming up, he turns to her. "Is it true? You're staying in Vermont for a while?"

"I am," she says, giving him a faint smile. "The head of my literary agency went to Florida for the winter, so I can work from anywhere. And Boston doesn't feel like home to me anymore. So I'm staying at the guesthouse and trying to figure out my next move."

He looks out the window, where the streetlights pool their light onto the dark street, his long fingers tapping the steering wheel. "I know your life is complicated. But if it feels right to you, I'd like to see more of you. Just as friends, if that's what you need most right now."

Warmth fills her chest. It's just hitting her that the upside of having her life implode is seeing Damien without feeling even a scrap of guilt about it.

"Just, well, think about it," he says, misinterpreting her silence. Hastily, he buckles his seatbelt and puts the car in gear.

"That would be great," she hurries to say.

He risks a glance at her. "You don't have to say so to save my feelings, Overland. I know you're going through some things."

"No, I like this idea," she says. "It's almost time to go Christmas shopping again, you realize. I think we might need an outing."

She watches his grin in profile. "I think you might be right."

He pulls up in front of the guesthouse ten minutes later. He puts the Jeep in park but keeps the engine running as he steps out to walk her to the door.

It's not like she can't find her own door, but she doesn't point that out. She's always liked Damien's old-fashioned manners. He waits for her to get the door unlocked before handing her the bag with the leftovers and wishing her a happy Thanksgiving.

"It was," she says, turning to him with sudden shyness. "Thank you for, well, all that you've done."

"Anything for you, Nicky Nicole."

And he really means it. That's the thing about Damien—she knows him. After fifteen years of friendship, no matter how sporadic, she knows the exact way his low voice resonates inside her chest. And the serious expression in his eyes as he gives her one last measuring glance to make sure she's arrived safe and sound at home.

Her heart simmers with emotion. So she drops the bag, opens her arms, and hugs him.

"Aw, sweetheart," he says under his breath. "You're going to be okay."

"I know," she says with emphasis verging on frustration. "I *know*." This hug wasn't supposed to be a play for sympathy. Then again, she's never been good at expressing what she really wants.

What she really wants is for this hug to last forever. Damien's strong arms are holding her tightly, and she rests her head against the flannel of his collar. He has a couple days' growth of whiskers, and the scruff outlines his cheek. She has the sudden urge to test its roughness against her lips.

And, well, this is supposed to be her year for breaking all the rules. So she does it. She stands on her tiptoes and slowly kisses the underside of Damien's jaw.

It's her first moment of flagrantly poor impulse control in over a decade. And, sure, it's a strange place to start—just randomly kissing the nice man's neck.

Although, he seems not to mind. He goes briefly still from surprise, before making a soft, bitten-off noise. Then two warm hands clasp her face, and he looks down into her eyes, his expression serious.

God. I'm such a weirdo, she thinks. *He's going to tell me to knock it off.*

But that's not what happens. Instead, he bends down and places one soft kiss at the corner of her mouth. And then another one. His whiskers tickle her sensitive skin, and every nerve in her body reacts.

Kissing him back isn't really a conscious choice. It's an automatic response—like thunder after lightning. She turns her head by two degrees and presses her lips to his.

He makes another broken sound that gives her chills. And then he swoops right in and firmly aligns their kiss.

It's on. She grabs his flannel with both hands and parts her lips in clear invitation.

Damien tastes her. Thoroughly. And—whoa—he's good at this. *Really* good. Her body crackles like a wood fire as he strokes her tongue with his. He tastes like apple pie and sex.

This is, by far, the single most exciting thing that's happened to her in a long time. So who would blame her for getting a little greedy? She rises on her toes and moves her body closer to his.

For a beautiful moment, she forgets about everything else but this. She forgets about the running Jeep and tricky family holidays and the pile of torn-up photos in a shoebox. She forgets every detail that isn't Damien's mouth and the steady drumbeat of his heart against hers.

He kisses her again and again. She'd happily stay right here in this liminal space, unthinking. But suddenly it ends. Damien pulls back and takes a deep breath. "Okay, wow," he whispers. "This day turned out a lot more exciting than I'd expected."

He smiles, and Nicolette would like to make a pithy comment, but she can't. Not right now. She's too busy remembering to breathe and staring up into Damien's soft brown eyes.

"Look, I'm going to go home now before I forget how," he says. "But let's go out to dinner this week. Just the two of us."

"Like a date?" she asks stupidly. But she really needs to know. Her heart can't take any more uncertainty when it comes to Damien.

"Exactly like that," he says. "If you're up for it."

"Okay, yes," she says, her brain still running at a fraction of its usual capacity. "Um, you pick a night. I'll just be here anyway, reading the slush pile for work and avoiding my family."

He chuckles even though she wasn't trying to be funny. "All right. I'll text you tomorrow?"

"All right," she says. And then she takes a step backward, so she isn't tempted to lunge at him again.

"Good night," he says. "Can't wait to see you again." He leans in and kisses her cheekbone smoothly. "Call me if you need me," he says, just like in the olden days.

After he leaves, she closes the door and listens to the sound of his car receding back down the long drive.

Even when it's silent, though, she stands there, two fingers pressed against the spot on her cheekbone where he kissed her good-bye. Her mind is static, but her body buzzes with desire. She feels like a teenager who just had her first real kiss.

Arguably, she just did. It's suddenly obvious that the handful of people she's kissed before weren't nearly as good at it.

Okay, well, that's exciting. And a little intimidating.

She kicks off her shoes and tosses her jacket onto a hook. Then she pulls out her phone and crosses the room to collapse on the couch.

She makes a call, and Cici answers on the second ring. "God, save me from my cousin's children," she says by way of a greeting. "You okay? Was your dad an asshole during dinner? Do you need bail money?"

The family Thanksgiving meal feels like it happened in another lifetime. "Um, I stormed out," she said. "After the fifth critique of my divorce. I was keeping a count."

"Oh ouch," she says. "Your dad is a piece of work."

That's true, of course, and she's happy to have someone else agree with her about this.

The wild thing, though, is that Cici is willing to discuss this. One weird twist to the end of her marriage was getting Cici back as a close friend.

"Maybe it's counterintuitive," her old prep-school roommate had said during the aftermath. "But you and Cam never made sense to me. And I couldn't take the pressure. I thought one of you would eventually break the other one's heart. But it sucks to be right."

"I guess you had good instincts," Nicolette had said sheepishly.

Now they can speak openly about the divorce. And Cam knows better than to bring it up with his sister, because there was only one cheater in this marriage, and it was Cam.

But none of that matters right this second. "Remember the taxi driver?" she blurts.

"Oh *him*," Cici says with a laugh. "You haven't spoken about him in years. Did you see him?"

"You could say that. I just kissed him."

Cici makes a squeak of excitement. "Omigod, hang on. I have to sneak away." A moment later, Nicolette hears a door slam. "Okay!" her friend says a little breathlessly. "What happened?"

Nicolette tells her the whole wild tale—about the origin of the photos, which Cici has seen, and about summoning Damien to yell at him.

And about Thanksgiving.

And the kiss.

"This is amazing," Cici gushes. "What are you going to wear on your date? Don't forget the good lingerie. Something sexy."

"Slow your roll," Nicolette says with a laugh. "I'm not going to sleep with him."

"Oh, but you are," Cici insists. "You two have so much chemistry you won't want to hold back."

Nicolette squeezes her eyes shut. "That would be a mistake, though. I just got out of a marriage."

"And so what?" her friend demands. "There's not enough passion in your life. There never was."

Nicolette opens her mouth to argue but then closes it again. *That kiss.* "Even so," she says slowly. "It's been a long time since I slept with anyone new. I'm going to have to get used to this idea."

"Do you, though?" Cici asks. "Nobody is more thoughtful than you are, Nic. But maybe this isn't a moment for deep reflection. It's fine to seduce that man just because you both want each other. It doesn't have to be a big deal."

"I think we used to have this same conversation when I was nineteen," she grumbles.

"You trust this guy, right?" Cici asks.

She doesn't even have to think about it. "Of course."

"That means something," her friend says firmly. "When people tell you not to jump into a new relationship, they mean that you shouldn't lunge at the first man you see because you're afraid to be alone."

"Yeah, no. I think being alone might be good for me."

"It could," Cici agrees. "But how many years did you waste making moon eyes at Damien?"

"Oof," Nicolette grunts. "A few." *A lot.*

"That man knows you just got a divorce. He asked you out to dinner. He didn't ask you to set a wedding date."

She chuckles. "Fair."

"So shave your legs and have dinner with the man. Go to bed with him if you feel like it. Don't overthink it."

"But that's what I do best."

"How's that working for you so far?"

"Oof," she says again.

"You really like him," her friend says softly. "When he was in the army, you used to listen to the news about Afghanistan like there'd be a quiz later."

This isn't wrong.

"Trust him. Trust yourself. And wax your hoo-ha."

"Cici!"

They both laugh.

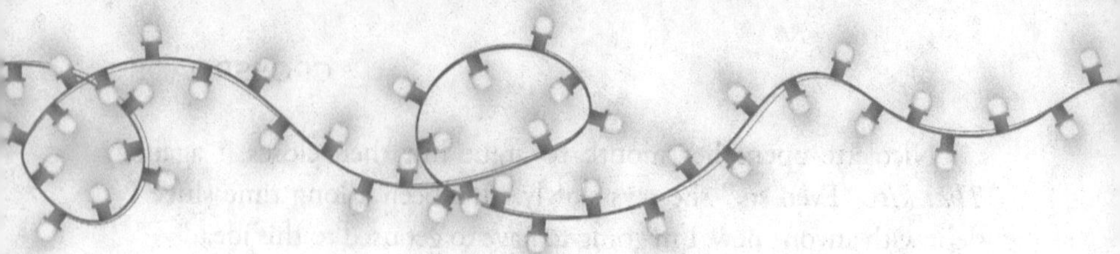

CHAPTER 14
SOUNDTRACK: THE NERVOUS THUMP OF HIS OWN HEART

He makes himself wait until the next morning to text her.

> Hey! I heard my first Christmas carol on the radio, so now I'm thinking about you. I always think of you at Christmas.

> Can I take you out one night this week?

After he hits send, he worries that it's too much enthusiasm. God, it's hard to keep a lid on the way he feels about her.

But she answers only a few minutes later.

> I'd love to. Wednesday?

> Sweet! I'm going to find us a nice restaurant reservation. Any spots to avoid? Likes and dislikes?

> No, I'm easy.

> About food.

> Jeez.

> You pick the spot and tell me where and when.

He cracks up. Then he makes a reservation.

> Okay—I have a plan. Can I pick you up at six? It's a bit of a drive, but I've been wanting to try this place.

> Cool! What's the dress code?

> It's a nice place. But it's still Vermont. So I guess that means jeans, but your nicest ones.

> Vermont dressy. Got it. Dark jeans and a sweater without holes. See you then!

When she emerges from her house on Wednesday night, pausing to lock the door, she's wearing a suede skirt, sleek heeled boots, and a sweater in a shade of blue that somehow looks both warm and expensive as it complements her eyes.

Not that he'd ever admit it, but Damien took a lot of care with his appearance tonight. He's wearing dark-wash jeans and a black merino sweater that Zara bought him when he started art school, with a black wool blazer over it.

Earlier, while admiring his reflection in the mirror, he'd made eye contact with himself and grinned. Yes, he was going all out for this date, almost to the point of being a little ridiculous.

But so what? Sometimes playing it cool isn't the right move.

He gets out of the Jeep and walks around to the passenger door to open it for her. "Madame Overland," he says. "You could have brought along a suitcase with some bricks in it, just to keep me in shape."

Her smile blooms brightly. "Are you ever going to stop teasing me about my luggage?"

"Doesn't seem like it." He gives her a wink as he closes the door for her.

"Why does your car smell like heaven?" she asks after he gets behind the wheel and steers the Jeep toward the road.

"That's my cologne," he says.

"What? No."

He snickers. "It's part of my plan for the evening. Do you happen to know any of the Shipleys?"

She tilts her head. "The cider people?"

"That's them. Griffin makes the cider, but his brother Dylan has a caramel business during the holiday season. I offered to drop off his caramels in Burlington at the Ironwood Hotel if he could get me a reservation at Burly, which is on the same property."

He glances at Nicolette and catches a flicker of something like surprise on her face. "Oh."

"It's a nice place," he says. "And a tough reservation."

"I'm sure," she says. "But Damien, you don't have to take me to the nicest restaurant in Vermont. That seems like a lot of effort."

"Maybe?" He shrugs. "But here's the thing. I've been hearing about this restaurant for a long time. Griffin's wife is a chef, and she raves about it. But I've never been. Every time it comes up, I think *someday I'll go there.* But I never have."

"Okay," she says.

"And Overland? I've often felt the same way about you. I'd think someday maybe the time will be right, and we'll have our moment. But then we never did. I don't know if this is it, or not, but I've got nothing to lose. Let me take you to the nicest restaurant in Vermont tonight, okay? Because we never know how many great moments we're going to get."

She reaches over and squeezes his forearm. "Thank you. I accept. I'm going to google the menu and see what's on it tonight."

"Cool. Just don't read it aloud to me, because I'm hungry already and I'm not into sadomasochism."

She barks out a laugh and covers her mouth. "Noted."

———

As usual, the drive flies by. Anytime it's Nicolette in the passenger seat, that's bound to happen. When they reach the Ironwood Hotel, he lets the valet park the car and mentally kisses another forty bucks goodbye. But he doesn't know if those heels are comfortable and isn't about to make her walk a couple blocks in them.

Before the valet can drive away, Damien pulls a large box out of the back of the Jeep. "This is for you," he tells Nicolette, handing her a small but elegant sampler box of Dylan's caramels. "And the rest of these I have to drop at the concierge desk before we go in to dinner."

A flicker of doubt crosses her face. "Okay, sure." She stashes the sampler box in her bag.

Hmm. Her reaction was a little odd, but he doesn't say anything. He leads her past a pair of double doors that slide silently open for them and enters the lobby. It's sleek, but also warm, with honey-colored wood everywhere, and floral arrangements made from birch branches.

Fancy.

He locates the concierge desk and carries the box in that direction. It's staffed by an attractive woman in a dark green blazer. "Good evening. These caramels are from Dylan Shipley. He said you'd know what to do with them."

"Of course, sir. And welcome, Ms. Overland. I didn't know your family was onsite tonight."

Damien turns to Nicolette in surprise. She'd been trailing behind, almost as if hiding. "Um, no," she says sheepishly. "Just here for dinner."

"Very well," the concierge says smoothly. "Always nice to see you."

"Likewise."

Damien, relieved of the box, takes her hand and leads her toward the restaurant's door, but then pauses before they reach it. "Nic? Something you forgot to tell me?"

She's blushing. "My father built this hotel about five years ago. I'm sorry."

His heart plummets. "Your father...and your ex?"

"No, just my dad." She shakes her head. "He couldn't believe that Burlington didn't have a luxury hotel, so he, um, fixed that. He has a lot of events here, so I've been to this restaurant before. I should have said something, but you were excited about this place."

"Ah." He laughs suddenly. It seems obvious now that there was no way he could take her anywhere she hadn't already been. "Would you rather go somewhere else, though?"

"No," she whispers, putting both her hands on his forearms. "It really *is* the best restaurant in Vermont. But the only times I've ever been here were with my uptight family. Never with you, or anyone who ever gave a crap whether I had a good time."

Oh.

"So let's have a nice meal, and screw the rest of them."

"I like how you think." He leans in to kiss her on the forehead before taking her arm again and leading her into the dining room.

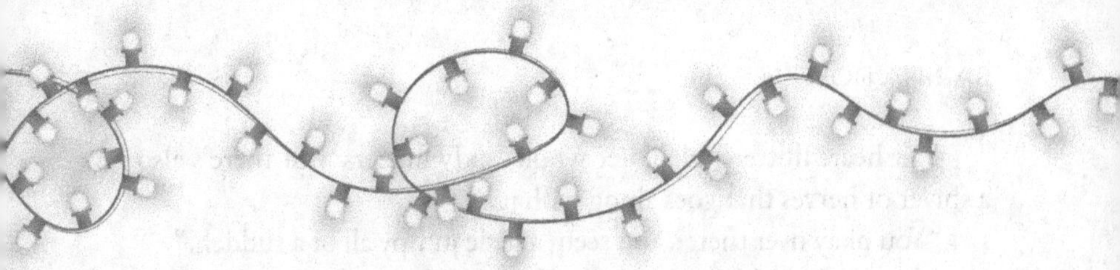

CHAPTER 15
SOUNDTRACK: PIANO MUSIC AND NERVES

"And these are our pâtes de fruits, compliments of the chef," the server says two hours later, placing a tiny silver tray onto the table. "We have cranberry, lingonberry, and plum. Can I bring you anything else at all?"

Damien eyes the little jellied candies with a handsome smirk. This is the third or fourth dish that's appeared *compliments of the chef*. "I don't see how there's anything left in that kitchen that you haven't already brought us, except the check. I won't need to eat again," he declares. "I don't mean tonight. I mean ever."

The server grins. "Very well, sir."

She glides away, and Damien picks up one of the jellied candies and pops it into his mouth. He studies Nicolette with fond eyes. "I have to say that it's been interesting dining with royalty. You're a fun date, Overland."

She feels herself blushing and takes another small sip of wine. She's already had enough, and the bottle is still half full. "Here," she says. "Drink some more of this, because I shouldn't."

He covers her hand with his. "Can't, darling. I'm the driver. It wouldn't be right."

"Oh." She lets out a jittery breath. "Does it get old being the driver? Always the one who has to be responsible?"

"Well, sometimes. But it's a role I chose," he reminds her. "And for you? It's a pleasure."

Her heart flutters. Hell, her whole body flutters. But there's also a shiver of nerves that goes along with it.

"You okay over there? You seem a little jumpy all of a sudden."

It's true. She's had a lovely meal up until now. Damien's enthusiasm for the restaurant was fun. It was his idea to order different things so they could try as many dishes as possible.

They had, and it was all fantastic—maybe even more so because her family wouldn't *dream* of swapping bites across the table.

There are too many people in her life who know how to suck the joy out of everything. Damien is not one of them. Which is why she's suddenly on edge.

"Sweetheart," he says softly. "Everything okay?"

"Yes," she says resolutely. "I'm just gathering my courage for what comes next."

He quirks an eyebrow. "The drive home? I don't think my food coma is actually dangerous." He reaches across the table and takes her hand. "Hit me, Overland. What's bothering you?"

Be honest. This is Damien, after all. He listens better than anyone else. "It's like this—I'm a little nervous because I want you to take me home with you tonight. But I haven't been with anyone new in..." She blows out a breath. "Over ten years."

He strokes her hand. "So another time, then. There's no rush."

That's a nice thing to say, and she knows he means it. But earlier tonight, Damien gave an impassioned little speech about not wasting any more time, because you never know how much you'll have.

She takes another ill-advised sip of wine. It's a 2015 Bordeaux and outrageously good. There's no way she can finish the bottle, and that seems like a crime. "I have an idea," she says suddenly.

The corners of his mouth twitch. "You going to share?"

She raises a hand and gestures to the head of service, who comes shooting over. "Yes, ma'am?"

"Marie? Could you do me a favor and ask the night manager if he has a room open tonight? I don't know if I feel like driving home."

"Of course, Ms. Overland. One moment."

Damien watches her from across the booth. But he doesn't ask what she's doing. He only smiles. "Aren't you going to try the jellied fruit? Or am I the only one who's going to have to roll out of here."

Her heart is thumping, but she takes a candy. The fruity flavor bursts against her tongue.

Marie returns within two minutes, passing Damien the check, and passing Nicolette a key wallet with two cards inside. "Lucky for you, weeknights during stick season are quiet."

"Thank you so much." She checks the room number—702. The top floor, so probably a suite. She drops the wallet into her bag. Then she pushes the wine bottle toward Damien. "Here. Now you don't have to drive back unless you want to. And this wine isn't going to drink itself."

His eyes warm as he considers her. Then he reaches for the bottle and pours himself a glass. "I knew you were a fun date. But you should tell me where you see this going."

Gathering her courage, she reaches across the table and clasps his free hand. "You tell me." She drops her voice. "I shaved my legs, stashed some condoms in my purse, and got a hotel room."

His forehead wrinkles. "I'm not great with contextual cues. Could you be more specific?"

"*Damien.*"

He smiles suddenly. "Just teasing, Overland."

She sips her wine, still holding his hand. They lapse into an anticipatory silence. Until this week, Nicolette has rarely allowed herself to consider this moment, even though she's always been wildly attracted to Damien, from the first time they met.

"What are you thinking about?" he asks in a silky voice.

"The first time we met," she blurts out. "You were wearing a blue-and-white gingham button-down shirt with the sleeves rolled up." She's always secretly admired his forearms. "That day is seared in my memory."

He grins. "You, too? I thought it was just me."

She squeezes his hand. "I was a bit of a wreck, and you were so great. Kind of like right now."

He drags his thumb across her palm, and she feels it everywhere. "You're not a wreck, honey. You weren't then, either. You were just working through some stuff."

"If you say so. I asked you..." She lets out a nervous laugh. "...if you knew how I could become a whole lot more interesting in the next two hours. Kind of have the same question right now."

"Buddy, that's impossible." He lifts her hand and leans forward, kissing her knuckles, and his whiskers tickle her skin. "There's no way you could ever be more interesting than you are right now. I felt the same way fifteen years ago. You're already all the Nicolette that I ever need you to be."

When he lifts his brown eyes to hers, they're full of the same warmth they've always held, plus a new and fascinating splash of heat.

Suddenly she's perfectly ready to go upstairs.

Nicolette has never stayed in the hotel before, so she's never seen room 702. It's an exquisite suite done up in a Nordic style, with lots of blond wood, warm lighting, and pale linens. "Wow," she says.

"Yeah, wow," he says. "At least your father has killer taste. Nice decor."

"Oh, he has people for that." She crosses the room to stand at a floor-to-ceiling window that faces Lake Champlain in the distance. It's been dark for hours, so the view isn't spectacular. But she can pick out the lights of the ferry boat on its way back toward Vermont from New York State.

Damien arrives behind her. She can see his reflection in the glass, and he looks thoughtful. "Nic?"

"Mmm?" She turns around. Since he's standing so close, she's kind of trapped herself between the glass and the solid warmth of him. She inhales a whiff of his cologne, and it makes her heart whir.

"What are you thinking about?" he asks.

A giddy thought bubbles up inside her. "You really want to know?"

"I asked, didn't I?"

Her gaze flickers toward the king-sized bed and its regal white comforter. "I'm wondering how much small talk I have to make before you toss me on that bed."

"Not much, actually." He scoops her up into strong arms, and she lets out a little squeak of surprise. "Gotta say, this is more fun than picking up your luggage."

She laughs into his shirt collar for a second before he sets her down on the end of the bed. "Wait, these boots! I don't want to kick you."

"Yeah, Overland," he says, catching one of her heels in his hand. "The boots were a rookie move." He fiddles with the zipper.

"Told you I was rusty." She pushes his hands out of the way and sheds one boot and then the other.

Damien aims his sport coat at a chair, and the moment her boots hit the floor, he's already easing her onto the bed and covering her body with his.

She sucks in a breath, waiting for his kiss. But it doesn't come. Instead, he pauses, forearms braced on the bed as he looks down at her. "You were wearing a tank top and a pink sweater."

"What?" she gasps, her brain muddled by the proximity of his mouth and the delicious weight of his body against her hips.

"The day we met." He smiles. "I wanted to kiss these freckles." He drags a fingertip across the bridge of her nose. "You're blowing my nineteen-year-old mind right now. Every time I ever saw your name on my schedule was like a gift."

Her breath stutters in her chest. "I didn't know you felt that way."

"I was just a dumb kid, and you intimidated me." His smile is wry.

"Do I still intimidate you?" she asks.

He shakes his head. "Not like that. Sorry for the long wait, but I'm kind of like that wine we drank at dinner—improved with age."

Then, still smiling, he finally pounces. The first kiss steals her breath with its sweetness. He tastes like red wine and good times. His second kiss is hungrier, though. Almost as hungry as she is.

Her hands go straight to the buttons on his shirt. As she gets to work, he groans happily. "Love your hands on me."

"Help me out, then," she demands.

He sits up, straddling her body, his fingers finishing up on the buttons. The muscles in his chest flex as he struggles out of the shirt.

She's been waiting too long for this view—miles of olive skin over a firm chest. A light dusting of hair between his pecs that gathers down the centerline of his abs before disappearing into his jeans.

There's also a big scar cutting a slash down one side of his torso. A literal battle scar. But we all have those, and it doesn't dampen the view. She licks her lips and reaches for his fly.

"You're going to kill me," he rasps. "Can I take this off?" He reaches for her sweater.

"Any time," she says easily. An hour ago, she was nervous about this. And, yeah, this version of Damien—the turned-on, half naked one—might be new to her, but it's still *him*, the guy she's trusted for almost half her life.

That makes it easier when her sweater suddenly whooshes off her body.

And that makes it easier when Damien is suddenly gazing intently at her La Perla lace bra. The see-through one. "Mother of God," he whispers, running a fingertip down the bra's plunging neckline and over the swell of her breast. "You can't even be for real."

She's about to argue when his mouth begins a delicious journey around the edges of the lace. Her body flashes hot, and her nipples harden against the lace.

With a happy grunt, Damien kisses the stiff peaks through the lace. His touch makes her shiver. "Spoiler alert, but I also own the matching panties."

His groan is ravenous. "Show me."

There's another scramble while she sheds her suede skirt and tights.

Damien uses the time wisely, dropping his trousers and toeing off his socks, leaving him in nothing but a pair of black boxer briefs currently strained by a healthy bulge in front.

Nicolette's body temperature goes up another degree as she tosses her clothes aside.

"Just damn," he says, crawling onto the bed again on hands and knees. His gaze is laser hot and making a slow perusal of her body. "I was going to say that I didn't know they made lingerie this hot. But it's probably only this hot on *you*."

She shivers under his gaze. And when he drops his mouth to trace the seam of her panties against her tummy, her muscles clench with anticipation.

"Breathe," he commands.

She gasps for oxygen.

"Good girl," he purrs before nosing his way down onto the lace.

Her skin is a riot of heat and goosebumps as he teases her with his lips, dropping soft kisses over her panties.

It's sweet torture, and he doesn't stop. He spreads her legs and flattens his tongue over the lace until she's writhing and tugging on his hair. "Damien..." she begs.

"What do you need, Nic?"

Everything. She needs everything. But first she needs... "My purse," she gasps.

He chuckles. The he rolls off the bed and retrieves her bag from the floor.

"Sorry," she says, dazed. She unzips the bag and finds the strip of condoms. She's too turned on to speak any further as Damien casually slips off his boxer briefs, leaving nothing but an ambitious, jutting erection.

He moves around the bed, all popping muscles and warm skin, then lowers that warm body down until he's seated behind her. Clever fingers unclip her bra, removing it.

And when his hands slide around her ribcage to cup her breasts? She sighs happily.

Damien kisses the back of her neck. "I feel like a lit fuse," he says against her skin. "Fifteen years I've dreamed about this."

She leans her head back against his chest, looking over her shoulder. "In your dreams, what do we do next?"

He chuckles and buries his face in her neck. "Let's just say it evolved over time. So which version do you want? The scrappy nineteen-year-old fantasy? Or the go-all-night version from when I was twenty-one? Twenty-five? Thirty? Pick a year."

Feeling sparkly inside, she hugs his arms around her body. "All right. I pick *this* year."

"Mmm, good choice," he says, kissing the other side of her neck.

"Year thirty-five is hot and filthy. I'll need you on your hands and knees. Hands on the bed."

He kisses her neck again, and she feels it *everywhere*.

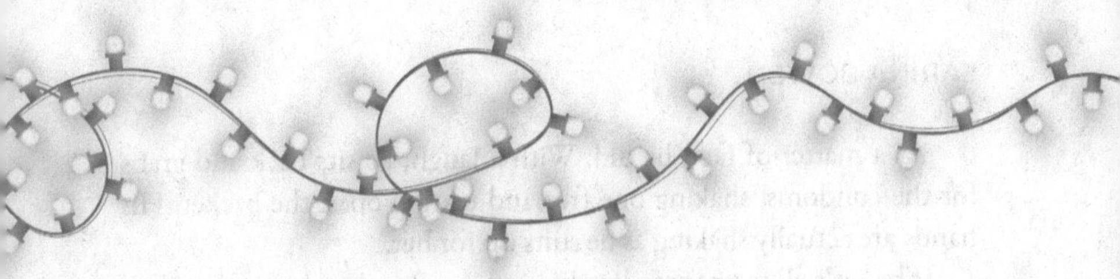

CHAPTER 16
SOUNDTRACK: HEAVY BREATHING

Damien inhales sharply as she drops her sleek body obediently onto all fours.

He really *does* have at least as many fantasies as there are years since he met her. But none of them are half as amazing as the sight of her posing submissively in front of him—her body poised on the bed, waiting. He's never seen anything so sexy.

He runs his hands over her flank, ending with a dirty squeeze of her ass in those outrageous panties. She gasps, her forehead touching the bed.

Oh yeah. He'll never be able to think about lace without getting hard after this. Meanwhile, his hands run wild, skimming over her breasts, teasing her panty line.

He kisses a path down her backbone and onto her lacy ass. He spreads her knees a couple of inches and ducks down between her legs.

She gasps again, her body clenching with delight. When he can't wait any longer, he drags the panties down over her hips. Then he can lean in and lick her properly. With nothing in the way now, the honeyed taste of her slips across his tongue.

She makes a broken noise and buries her face in the comforter.

He spends the next few minutes driving her wild, until she starts to beg. "Please. God. Didn't you give a speech about not wasting time?"

As a matter of fact, he did. With a laugh, he sits back and grabs for the condoms, shaking one free and tearing open the packet. His hands are actually shaking as he suits up for her.

Then it's all too easy to line himself up. But then he catches their reflection in the plate-glass window. "Look, Nicolette," he rasps. "Look how pretty you are."

On the far end of the room, her reflection glances up, catching his reflection in the glass panel.

"Do you see?" he whispers.

She parts her lips and nods.

Still watching her, he kisses the back of her head. And then he finally moves his hips, slowly pushing inside on a groan.

In the reflection, her mouth drops open in a silent moan.

For one more long beat, he holds still, just staring with wonder at the hottest sight he's ever seen. Nothing could have prepared him for this.

But it feels too good to hold out for long. He *has* to grasp her hips. And he has to move his own.

Braced on her hands, Nicolette makes a low sound of appreciation. "*Yes.*"

He bites his lip and finds a rhythm. Like the beat of his heart.

"Damien," she whispers, pushing back against him. "*God.*"

He loses himself in the sounds she's making. The moans and curses. He wishes this could last forever. But if he doesn't change things up, it's all going to come to its inevitable conclusion.

"Nic," he whispers, pulling out. "Roll over and kiss me."

She moans and shivers, pulling him down the moment she rolls.

He joins their bodies again as she runs smooth hands over his shoulders. He sinks into her kiss. Curls his hands in her hair.

"You..." She sighs. "Wow. I need to..." She lets out a keening gasp, and shudders around him.

He moans, because he can't help himself. And then he closes his eyes and lets go, his body chasing after hers.

And catching it for once.

———

They lay curled up together for a long time. His thoughts swirl like mist.

"What are you smiling about?" she asks.

"Um..." He laughs. "Don't take this the wrong way, but I was thinking about an army buddy. Jarvis."

She snorts. "Um...okay?"

"He's the one who told me I should ask you out when I got home. But then..."

"Yeah." She clears her throat. "It wouldn't have worked. Not then."

"Not then," he repeats. "But why do you think I gave you back that lucky marble? I needed some of its magic to rub off on you."

"Took long enough," she says.

"Don't blame me, blame the marble." He sits. "Excuse me a second so I can deal with this condom."

"If you must," she grumbles.

He gets up and heads for the bathroom, which is as big as his bedroom at home. Half the space is taken up by a huge Jacuzzi tub. "Hey, Overland? Whenever I see a hot tub, I take it as a challenge more than a suggestion."

She lifts her face and gazes at him with the blue eyes he's had memorized since she was a teenager. "Turn on the water, then. I'm game."

So he does. And they finish their night lounging in hot water and bubbles, planning their inevitable Christmas shopping trip.

"What are you going to buy the twins?" he asks.

"Hell if I know." She tips her head back against the lip of the tub and smiles at him. "But this year I think I'm going to like Christmas a lot more than usual. It's just a hunch."

He pulls her toward him in the tub. "You know? I think I will, too."

The End

———

www.ingramcontent.com/pod-product-compliance
Lightning Source LLC
Chambersburg PA
CBHW011123190726
48289CB00012B/2886